The Band

A Trilogy

Book 2

'king Rock

Copyright © Cliff Bond 2007
Issue 3   2019

CONTENTS

INTRODUCTION		3
CHAPTER 1	REUNION	6
CHAPTER 2	'KING ROCK	10
CHAPTER 3	BAPTISM	22
CHAPTER 4	FAMILY HOLIDAY	38
CHAPTER 5	NICE PROBLEMS	51
CHAPTER 6	LIFE ON THE OUTSIDE	71
CHAPTER 7	BASS PLAYER	105
CHAPTER 8	HOMECOMING	122
CHAPTER 9	A HAPPY TIME	128
CHAPTER 10	TEA AND CONTENTMENT	138
CHAPTER 11	CONFESSIONS	147
CHAPTER 12	SHOPPING	156
CHAPTER 13	THE WEDDING	171
CHAPTER 14	HONEYMOON	186
CHAPTER 15	GOING SOUTH	210
CHAPTER 16	RETURN	226
CHAPTER 17	SYNERGY.	236
CHAPTER 18	SUMMER HOLIDAY	252
CHAPTER 19	GOOD TIMES – HARD TIMES	260
CHAPTER 20	NEW DIRECTION	276
EPILOGUE		280

INTRODUCTION

I hadn't wanted the assignment; it's as simple as that. I had personal reasons to loath predatory rockers, especially those with modest talent whose 'star' status was based on being in the right place at the right time. It is true that there are some talented originals around but few who justify their later life reinvention as 'rock gods'.

Chris Phillips was an ex-rocker who had been there, done it and failed to make a real mark and I had accepted the commission only because the fee offered was surprisingly generous.

The article I decided would be subtly scathing, would expose the shallowness of rock's roll life and undermine its delusions of self-worth.

It didn't quite work like that; the article was published but gave barely a hint of what had been. Chris and his wife Alison were generous with their information and the more I heard of their story, the more intrigued I became. The result was a biography that threw up many surprises.

The turbulence of their relationship, the highs the lows and the inevitable break up were expected: that Chris both loved and hated his life as a professional was less so.

'The possibility of easy money and public admiration seems to attract a disproportionate number of weirdos,' he told me. 'There are lots of lovely people too but it's an unbalanced profession, it's bound to be, the whole business is about creating fantasies and no-one cares whether the output damages vulnerable people struggling with hard reality.' he continued.

He did tend to continue... and continue before realising that he had lost his audience and offering an apology and a disarming smile.

His wife Alison by contrast remained full of enthusiasm for their profession. When their band and their relationship folded amidst anger, hurt and recrimination she had picked herself up and put together a new band.

It was an act of bravery for a shy girl to take on the task and when her friendship with Chris was renewed she was stronger and to her credit, largely unspoiled.

What was to come would continue to test their relationship.

I was faced with a new problem; my own writing projects were constantly interrupted by the need to earn a crust, did I want to spend more time continuing the story of two ex rockers?

The answer of course was yes. After a bad divorce and a period of misogyny, Alison with her kindness had, if not restored my faith in women at least blunted the edge of my mistrust and I was safely in love with the girl she had once been.

I had ended my anthology of their early times with their reunion unaware that Alison had found the renewed relationship difficult.

'Being together again strained my emotional resources.' She told me.

I asked why and she offered an appealing look of helplessness.

'The break up was so painful that when we met again I was no longer confident in our relationship and was constantly afraid of saying or doing the wrong thing.'

'It was an unhappy experience?'

'Not unhappy, anxious. Chris was kind, we talked like friends and holding hands was comforting but I couldn't relate the situation to our earlier relationship.'

'Did you feel more positive after your first meeting?'

'I felt happier, but when it was time to leave all my uncertainty came back. Chris was holding my hand and said, "It's been good to see you, will you visit again?" I remember the exact words.'

'He kissed my cheek but I couldn't return the kiss. I wanted things to be as they had once been, I couldn't bear the thought that we were just friends.'

She bit her lip and abruptly turned her head away.
I wanted to hug her to make the distress go away.
'Sorry' she said 'I wonder if I'll ever grow up.'

CHAPTER 1   Reunion

The reunion was difficult, love to be controlled, emotion to be contained and so many things to be said that needed a foundation of mutual confidence.

Despite the constraint there was for Alison a renewal of hope, reinforced by the hand that held her own as if she were a child that might wander.

Her companion's recent tragedy and her own fragility remained obstacles to displays of emotion and for much of that first meeting their relationship was that of friendly children, bumping together, apologising, their conversation limited to the superficial neither possessing the confidence to move forward.

When the time for their departure approached, Alison's temporary absence prompted a quiet word from her mother.

'Shall we visit again?'

'Yes, I'd like that. It's been unsettling but it has been good to see Alison again.'

'She seems more relaxed than she has been for a while.'

'Can I ask what the problem was?'

Diane took his arm and moved closer. 'She found the tour exhausting and there were some upsetting incidents, she wouldn't tell me what they were.' She paused. 'At Christmas I heard crying in her room and when I went to sit with her she became hysterical. She kept on asking me "What's was the point, why am I bothering?" The doctor put her on some depressants to calm her and after a week when she was more controlled he put her on some milder medication. He said she was suffering from nervous collapse, but in simple terms she had a breakdown.'

'Poor Al, I didn't know. I should have given her more support.'

'You couldn't have helped at the time, you had your own problem,' she patted his arm, 'she missed you very much and if you are friends again it will help enormously.'

They left soon after six o'clock; Chris holding Alison's hand, reluctant to let go.

'Will you come again? I'm not much company but I would like to see you.'

'Yes, if you want me to.'

'Of course I do.' He kissed her cheek and released her hand.

She nodded and abruptly turned away and ran to the car.

If, afterwards, either had been asked when the turning point in their relationship arrived each may have answered differently. She and her mother had visited on a second time and Chris, returning from a painful visit to Sue's parents, had called at her home. On each occasion, the company of the other had been sufficient.

It was towards the end of May that Chris had asked if she would like to go out for the day and she had said 'Yes' without considering the implications. He had been friendly and mildly affectionate but to wrongly assume a revived relationship would have been unbearable.

She was collected at lunchtime and they had driven in a companionable silence for some time before Chris started to talk. Once he began the anxieties of the previous year flooded out. He began with Sue, the initial difficulties, the happiness then the desolation. It continued with apologies for his awful treatment of her, his partial emergence from the trauma of Sue's death countered by new feelings of guilt.

He stopped the car in a layby and rested his head in his arms. She had never seen him so distressed and felt a rising panic.

After a few moments he took a deep breath. 'Sorry Al, I didn't want to let you go but I had to give Sue all my attention.'

'Yes.' Al said.

'I was jealous when you found someone; I knew it would be hard but I didn't think it would tear me apart.'

'I never found anyone else; Gary seemed to be my way out; a new band, a new beginning, a new…boyfriend. You think it was hard for you? You had a choice, I didn't.'

She could see from his face that he was reliving the time.

'Can you forgive me?'

'Not completely, it changed me. I guessed you had some stupid notion that you were doing it for me but I don't think that you any idea how cruel it was.'

'I'm sorry Al.'

'Sorry doesn't help. I never expected perfection,' she gave a sad smile, 'perhaps I did. I certainly didn't get it but…'

'But what?'

'You were kind and caring; even when you were being cruel you thought you were doing it for me. I love you and don't ever expect me to admit it again!'

Taking a handkerchief from his pocket he blew his nose.

'Is that the same one you had when we first met.'

'Al, you are hopeless.' He wiped his eyes and dragged himself back under control.

They parked on the seafront and walked on the sands, the comfortable feeling returning. They held hands in a small café where they drank tea, giggled together when the pot poured over the table, ate sticky cakes and joined their sticky fingers together; a token of affection which made her cry.

'Let's go to Brean and walk on the hill,' she said, 'like we did before.'

At Brean they climbed the steps, arriving breathless at the top, and walked out to the edge of the rise that looked down on the old fort. Chris took off his coat and laid it down for them to sit on.

'You'll be cold.'

'No. Can I…?'His hand rested on her shoulder and she cuddled up against him.

'We came here five years ago in my old car. Remember?'

'I remember. You said it might not start.'

'I already loved you.'

She put her arm into his. 'I felt the same.'

Chris cuddled her arm and offered a shadow of the smile she remembered.

'We can't change the past but we could try again? I think I kissed you five years ago.' He kissed her cheek.

'Let's go back.'

They walked back holding hands. At the top of the steps he stopped. 'Alison, I'm not ready for a proper relationship. I still care about you and I want to be friends but…oh hell, I don't even know if you're interested, you may have half a dozen guys in tow.'

'Oh yes, all the boys in the area are queuing up to date a crazy unmarried mum.' The facetiousness failed to mask a hint of bitterness.

'I expect they would prefer a lovely girl pop-star.'

'Who is that? Shut up! Don't be clever, I can't take it.'

'I wasn't being clever, it's true.'

She was quiet. 'I'm sorry.' She shook her head. 'Don't say anything until you feel it.' She held his arms. 'Oh Chris,' tears started as a forgotten happiness welled up inside her, 'I'm just as wet as when we first met.'

They returned to her parents' house and parked a short distance from her gate.

'When you said you wanted to be friends, was that all, just friends?'

'I meant,' he thought for a moment 'best friends like we were, more than best friends but,' he shook his head, 'there are some issues, things that I haven't yet sorted.'

'The feelings are still there?'

'I think so.' The tension relaxed. He brushed her cheek. 'Go on, before I make a bigger fool of myself. Will you visit again, next weekend perhaps? Please?'

'I could come up on Wednesday and bring Sarah?'

'That would be perfect.'

CHAPTER 2   'King Rock

Collecting Simon, Chris returned home where, after supper he settled him into bed and told him a bedtime story. A sense of contentment crept over him; the pain of the previous six months balanced by something more positive

'Gen,' Simon had said. Chris stroked his head. He had begun reading the balloon story again when the telephone rang.

'Daddy answer phone. G'dnight Simon, back in a minute.' He hurried to the kitchen and picked up the extension.

A half-recognised voice spoke. 'Chris, mate, how you doing?' There was a pause and the sound of voices in the background. 'Sorry about your wife mate, sad business!'

A shiver ran through him. 'Sorry, I recognise the voice, but I can't fit a face to it.'

'Brucie, 'king Rock.'

'Of course, hi Bruce. Yes, bad business.' That day: the memory of the moment came back with a rush and the pain was as sharp and as futile. He swallowed. 'How's the band?'

'Taking off, sorry you didn't get the first offer. Tell me, how far did you get with practising the songs?'

'I spent the week before I came up for the audition; it was when Sue... when she died, the same day.'

'Yes I heard, bloody rough deal.' There was a pause. 'Listen mate, I've got to push it, have you played any of our stuff since?'

'Some of it, it was hard because of the association but I bought the single and played along with it, sort of laying a ghost. It was a damned good.'

'Did you have any problems; playing it I mean?'

'No. I couldn't make out a couple of the inversions.'

'Right.' There was a muttering. 'If you're still available, you're in.'

For several seconds Chris digested the implications of the statement.

'What happened to Tony?'

'Tosser came off his motorbike, probably stoned. They think he'll be OK but he broke an ankle and some bones in his hands so he's out for months.

'What is your management saying?'

'They will go along with it, but you know the score, nothing is fixed until you sign and maybe not then, I'm asking if you are interested.'

'Yes, of course.'

How long, how many gigs, how much money, a multitude of details crowded his mind. The enormity of the offer began to register. 'When do you need to know?'

'Now, tonight, we've cancelled the next four gigs and you've got ten days to get the set down.'

'Bloody hell! How many in the set?'

'Ten,' a muttering 'no eleven, about six to ten minutes each, but they repeat and there are only three or four different structures. You should already know seven, eight with the single.'

Chris thought for a moment. A degree of excitement began to rise in him.

'Let me have a contact number, I'll let you know first thing in the morning.'

'Tonight, we've no time to be pissed about.'

'OK. Give me an hour to sort things out, half eight at the latest.'

'At the latest, there is a hell of a lot of pressure at this end.' It was a hint of weakness. 'Listen Mate, I'll be straight, Tony's hand is an effin mess. We don't know how long before he can hold a whisky let alone play guitar. You're guaranteed the rest of the tour, but it could be longer. Contact us through your manager.'

'Ok, I'll get back you.'

'You'd better; an hour maximum or forget it. ' Bruce hung up.

Chris sat back in his chair and breathed deeply. Three months of music he could get lost in and he desperately needed the money.

His mind went back to that day; something began to well

up from deep inside and he fought it back. Rising, he climbed the stairs to Simon's room to find his son deeply asleep and untroubled. He tucked the covers around the peaceful form.

Seldom a drinker except for beer the need for something stronger exerted itself. Returning to the lounge he collected the bottle of 'medicinal' brandy and a tumbler and throwing himself into a chair poured a large measure and began to think out his response.

Al? Simon? His mind swayed one way and another with increasing confusion until at a point when there seemed no easy answer, clarity returned. He had to do it, it was the biggest chance he would ever get, "kR were a top band and on an upward roll, it would madness to turn it down.

He had wanted to join before and had given Sue a veto, he would give Al a veto.

But would he? Yes! He would have turned down an offer if Sue had insisted; he could promise Alison knowing that he would comply, maybe with regret but without recrimination.

Reaching for the phone he rang her number.

After a few moments, Alison herself answered. They exchanged a few words of affection.

'Al, something's come up!' The silence told him of her immediate anxiety. 'It doesn't affect what we said today except in a practical way.'

'Oh!' she managed, and he went on to explain the phone call and give her all the details he could.

'That means I won't see you, you will be gone for ages. Is it very important?'

'Yes, it is important. Al, this is difficult for me, I haven't wanted to ask any personal questions; not about boyfriends or other relationships or when you go back on the road with your band; I don't know what your plans are but staying friends is important. If you are really unhappy then I won't do it.'

'Do you mean that?'

'Yes. We've both had a difficult time; we are having a difficult time, and even if I do this stint with 'king Rock' it won't affect my feelings for you.'

'Is it going to be difficult? Is it a lot to learn?'

'Yes and no. I learned a lot of it before but I've only got ten days to get it right'

Al was quiet. 'Will it really be only three months?'

Chris hesitated. 'Three or...I don't know, maybe six, it's until Tony is fit.'

'So it could be a long time?'

'Yes. Would you mind if I was away for six months?'

'It's a decision you have to make,' She was getting upset. 'I don't know! I feel happy again because we are friends.' He heard her take a deep breath. 'That sounds possessive, let me think.'

'You could come with me if you wanted. I'm sorry, that's just stupid.'

'Thank you, I couldn't. If it were the other way around would you stand in my way?'

There was longer pause. Finally, 'I wouldn't make it easy.'

'You are hopeless, why couldn't you say 'No' and help me. Could you say you've got something else in six months and put a limit on it?'

'I could I suppose. Are you saying yes it I limit it?'

'No, you can't do that. I know you have to do it but I will miss you.'

'Thanks Al. It's probably the biggest thing I'll ever do.'

'Do you think so? We were quite big when we went to the States.'

'That was your singing and you and Sue looking good; if it wasn't for the marketing the tour would have lost money, and without your singing we'd never have got it. I mean, three brief TV appearances and two or three records in the top thirty. It's not bad, but it wasn't big time.

'We were good.'

'You were good, we were a good band but not that big.'

'I suppose not.' said Al as if she didn't suppose anything of the sort.

'Chris.' She sounded doubtful again. 'You wont...' she

couldn't bring herself to say it. 'It's one of those bands that attract groupies and they're already known for the drugs.'

'I've just become friends with a girl I care about.'

'That's easy to say. I've been frightened to ask if there was anyone else in case there was.'

'There isn't. You?'

'Me? I told you before, who would be interested in a depressed, jobless unmarried mum?'

'Me especially and every other guy you meet.'

'I told you, don't…' He caught the hitch in her voice.

'Al, are you in tears again?'

'Yes. I'm trying not to make assumptions about us then you say something like that.'

There was a pause while he searched for the right words. 'I thought you knew my feelings for you never changed.'

'I felt…I hoped, I couldn't *know*.'

The conversation returned again to the tentative explorations of people slowly finding affection.

He put the phone down and picking it up immediately dialled his manager giving him an outline of the offer.

Told that the call had been awaited, and 'what kind of arrogant little tit did he think he was to keep him waiting when the biggest deal he was ever likely…'

Chris stopped listening until the conversation returned to practical matters. Finally with a reluctant sounding 'Well done.' he was given the contact number.

Bruce's voice answered with an aggressive 'Yes? Who is it?'

'Chris Phillips. Sorted! Yes please, and I can't wait to get rolling.'

'Right; the only decision, dunno why you bloody needed to think.' The relief was evident.

Other voices could be heard on the end of the line. Bruce's voice came back.

'You remember where we tried out before? Be there 10.30 Monday. 'Music, practice schedules and contracts, your manager had already agreed.'

'The bugger probably checked if I was still under contract before I rang.'

'Yeah.' Bruce wasn't interested in other problems. 'Monday afternoon I want to run through the set and give you some tapes. Oh, and I'll give you a briefing on the contract before you sign.'

'I won't be signing 'till my lawyer has seen it.'

'Your manager has agreed.'

'Come on, I may be soft but I'm not stupid, not with contracts. Give me the basics and if it's OK I'll agree and we can sign later. I'll phone my lawyer in the morning and tell him to deal with it urgently. What else?'

'You are going to need to learn the set and be here for practice with the band on Saturday.'

'You said ten days, that only gives me four days to learn them.'

'And four more to get them right. Look don't piss me about if you can't do it forget it now!'

'I can do it but it is a hell of a lot of work, and there is a difference between playing it and adding something to the band.'

'Just play it with no cock-ups for a start.'

'Don't worry; I'll mark up the lyrics to get it consistent. One other thing, I want to do one of my songs.'

'You're joking. No effin chance.'

'It'll fit the set. Look, I can guess why I'm in and that is OK by me, but I want to contribute. If you don't like it you can veto it but I want the chance.'

'You've got an effin cheek, Synergy was B-list and that's being generous, 'kR are going to the top.'

'I'm reliable and I can play it. You would spend the next three months fighting with the guy you really want and the band would suffer.'

There was silence then laughter. 'OK, I'll listen to it but I'm making no promises and if it is your effin' bubble gum you can stick it up your smart ass.'

'Al says I need to be smart 'cos I don't push hard

enough.'

'Are you back with Smithy?'

'We're friends. Since Sue I haven't really been interested.'

'You should never have let her go. She's top totty.'

Chris gathered that this was some kind of accolade.'

'No women in your life then? Dunno how you survive.'

Chris smiled. 'One maybe, rather special but not in the way you mean.'

'No? I bet she's a looker though.'

'Yes, I guess she is.'

'Right,' Bruce continued, 'that's it, 10:30 sharp see you.'

'I'll be there.' he hung up.

He had a day to reorganise his life and that of his son. He picked up the phone.

The following days passed in the whirl; reviving his company, contract vetting, amending and signing, and the hardest part; making arrangements for Simon. The initial excitement had caused him to forget his responsibility and his affection for the son he was just getting to know. He had considered the possibility of taking him on tour with Alison as a kind of Au- Pair but dismissed the idea as both offensive and impractical.

There were few options; all of Simon's grandparents worked and Diana worked part time. He would go to Alison during the week and, alternately to his own and Sue's parents at weekends.

Her offer had touched him deeply, but had made for a difficult and reproachful meeting with Sue's family. He was sufficiently sensitive to be hurt by veiled suggestions of betrayal and by the shocked silence that followed his admission that his friendship with Alison was renewed.

It was an additional blow; his reviving relationship already tainted with guilt and his sense of disloyalty amplified by murmuring around the village.

Alison had come with her mother and Sarah to collect

Simon. The visit had been brief, Diane leaving with an unconcerned Simon and a desperately brave daughter before emotions got out of hand. Alison had been too wound up even to kiss him had finally clutched at his arm and shouted 'Bye Chris!' as if the parting was terminal.

On their departure he had emptied his mind and shut out the demons.

Carrying a cardboard box with tea making equipment, bread and biscuits he headed for the barn that echoed with memories of earlier practices and there he settled to concentrated practice using the supplied tapes as a starting point.

The tapes were supported by lyric sheets with chord sequences added and cues for vocal harmonies and riffs.

It was the antithesis of soul driven rock but it gave a lifeline until he felt confident. There were no more than four structures and all the songs were covered by three keys though he was initially thrown by some curious key changes.

By the third day he had corrected his charts to match the backing tracks supplied by Bruce and could play the backing and sing the harmonies with some confidence. There was however the pressure of performance in a large venue and some of the riffs had been simplified.

A number of visitors had arrived at various times to interrupt him. Geoff and Marilyn, friends from the adjacent farm had been good to him in the days after Sue's death, their independent visits providing an excuse for a fifteen-minute break, their offer of dinner saving him from a lonely evening in a local pub.

The arrival of the wife of a local worthy had received a more mixed welcome. He had flirted with her mildly at a village function attended with Sue and her visit on a rather flimsy pretext gave mixed signals. She had brought some homemade cakes and offered to make coffee. Returning with the drinks she had put down the tray and approaching him from behind had put her arms around him and kissed his cheek. 'How are you getting on?'

'Not too bad. I'm managing.' He reached behind, ruffling her hair. 'Thanks.' A momentary temptation to turn and kiss her passed.

As the hard work bore fruit he began to relax, though there remained a nagging fear that in performance he would forget where he was in the song.

By Friday he could play the notes and sing the words (with an occasional glance at the lyrics) and he began to work on a little stagecraft. The hall mirror was propped against one wall and he posed and strutted, assessing the sort of movement that fitted the music. On stage it would need to be spontaneous, but the practice gave him a guide to what would work. Just once he had imagined what Dave would say if he could see him and dissolved into laughter.

That evening satisfied with his progress, he packed a bag and the following morning took the train to London.

The next few days allowed no let-up; hard days of practice stretching to fourteen hours; learning to fit with the band, taking notes of movements, equipment, microphone set-up. At other times he practised alone with a small amp and headphones.

The songs were straightforward, but their length had caused him to lose his place resulting in an explosion of profanity from Bruce.

There was also a pressing need for new equipment. In the latter stages of Synergy he had swapped his H&H amplifier for a 50watt Marshall combo. Told that he would require a 100watt head and a 4x12 cab ('Do they come with earplugs?') his assumption that it would solve the volume problem proved false.

'Nah mate,' he was told by the soundman, 'givesa rite sahnd ennit looks good. I do the bal'ncin 'cos it all go'se throo the PeeAy see.

The new band had a sound that required a change from the Strat that he preferred to his Gibson 335.

It was a present brought back from the States by Sue, the

association bringing its own unhappiness. Its rich sound was needed, but it was a guitar that had to be driven, and he needed to adapt to its weight and the different neck profile.

The slender income from his investment in a small flat and the fading sums from records were just sufficient to support the mortgage and provide a meagre weekly sum for Al. The new amp had cleaned him out, and worse, he needed a backup guitar that was similar to the Gibson in feel and sound. A new gibbo was out of the question; even second hand prices were extortionate.

A rapid trawl of the Soho music shops failed to produce anything affordable and it was Alison, searching the second-hand shops of Bristol who found a scruffy sunburst LP junior, its P90 replaced by a humbucker. Dull to look at great to play, in its black polythene bag with a new set of tens it was the best he was going to get. The money was borrowed from his father.

Bruce the singer guitarist with whom Chris had the most contact was a star. He had been around the scene since the mid-sixties, was blessed with voice, talent, determination and equally important the constitution to make use of them.

The drummer known for some reason, as 'Bep' was friendly; often relaxed by the weed and on one occasion shot away on substances about which Chris had no wish to know. Highly respected in trad jazz he had moved to rock when it became apparent that that was where the money would be. Vince, the bass player was hard looking, short tempered and best kept at arm's length. They were supported by a keyboard virtuoso called Greg whose contractual status was different to the other four.

As long as he could hack the music they were indifferent to whom he was, and his transient presence diminished some of the internal rivalries and frictions.

As a band they were moving towards a look that was tough street fashion; their common interest, to forward their own careers by collectively producing a good show.

And the show was good, the first rehearsal demonstrating

to Chris that he was musically outclassed by all except Vince. It was a different world, a tougher, more competitive world. There had been a few free rides at Synergy's level; here there were none and he would need to give 110% just to hang in. That was a reality he had to cope with; if 'kR made it they would be up with the major bands where, unless you were a star on the rise or on the skids you were a dedicated professional supporting a star.

There was one other factor that struck him; 'kR were a 'big' band. At six foot he matched Bruce. Greg and the muscular Vince were an inch or two taller and Bep only a little shorter than the others. He recalled with a smile the tough sneering publicity stills of a band that in life had proved to be seriously pint sized.

The few days before his first concert were ones of intense effort and whilst other members came and went, for him there was no let up.

Never a smoker beyond an occasional cigarette in his student days, he had been offered a spliff at rehearsals that relaxed him and satisfied demands that he lighten up.

He had phoned Alison or his parents daily and had exchanged words with Simon who had called him 'Dadda' which caused serious upset.

By the end of the fourth day he was exhausted, falling asleep in the dressing room to the amusement of Bruce who woke him by gently emptying a fire bucket over him. It was hard; it had to be and he was, sustained only by the indefinable excitement of a band on a roll.

They were rolling and unbelievably he was part of it.

He was reminded of an incident that had occurred near the end of Synergy's three months of practice and poverty.

Sol had magically produced some free tickets to a concert by 'The ....', a band with a reputation for wildness.. Al had made a big effort to look her best, but their bubbling excitement was dampened by the fashionable glitter of much of the audience. Depressed by their shabbiness, demoralised by the stack of fabulous equipment on stage he had turned to a deflating girlfriend and shouted 'Come on; gorgeous, let's boogie.'

The band had been unbelievable; rough, but so exciting that both had been carried away, joining the fans dancing deliriously at the front. He had lived with the knowledge that he would never be that good; now unbelievably he was on the edge.

CHAPTER 3   Baptism

On the morning following the final rehearsal Chris drove from his lodgings to the first of the bands remaining twenty-three gigs. Several were stadium or festival venues, most in large theatres or clubs.

In pop terms it was a big step up. With a tour manager, a stage manager, lighting and soundmen supported by two roadies and a driver, the greater pressure of the gigs was at least partly cancelled by the reduction of the physical burden.

His baptism was to be in a large theatre, and here, sitting in the shared dressing room Chris checked through the order and his input for the show's first half. His guitars were already standing on the open stage and the last act of their stage manager would be to check the equipment. The murmur of an audience assembling reminded him that there were twenty minutes before the off and his stomach began to tighten.

Bruce displayed a superficial casualness but he would expect precision; the nervous tension increased approached panic and he dragged himself back under control.

He gathered up his stage clothes, a white tee shirt, a loose sleeveless red shirt and snug fitting cream jeans worn with white canvas sneakers. Stripping, he was standing naked in front of his mirror, when a tall blonde girl walked in carrying a shirt and some sweat bands. She eyed him up and down, smiled and passed the shirt to Bruce who put an arm around her.

Momentarily surprised he began to laugh, releasing some of the tension and turning away started to dress. Bep passed him a ciggy and he accepted a drag; his head swam and then relaxed.

Al would be present on his first night, and Diane had put in an un-refusable request to join her. In his mind the additional pressure justified his mild indulgence in the weed.

A call came from the doorway. 'Five minutes.'

'When we're effin' ready.' Vince shouted back.

Five minutes passed and he found himself in the wings with the other members.

'Let's give 'em hell.' said Bruce. 'And get it effin right Phillips!'

The warm-up man finished his announcement to a roar and the stage went dark. The excitement terror and adrenaline reached a peak; there was momentarily an awareness of the backstage smell, slightly unpleasant but familiar and comforting. Chris thrust the cotton wool further into his ears; his hands felt clammy and he buffed them on his jeans.

'Go.'

He moved forward picked up the Gibson, checked the controls and took his position on the darkened stage for the biggest gig of his career.

Alison and her mother had been in their seats in the second row for about twenty minutes. Of the two, it was Diane who, in unfamiliar circumstances was most relaxed.

'It is rather exciting. Is this what your gigs were like?'

'Not really, we played mostly clubs and small theatres.'

The atmosphere was heavy and she was nervous for Chris. She glanced at her mother, thankful that she looked good in an audience predominately between 16 and 30.

Turning her eye back to the stage she took in the set up.

The drums and the amplifiers were mic'ed up to a console in the auditorium where the soundman sat reading some notes. He would be controlling the P.A system that drove a vast bass bin and a stack of speakers. She wondered idly if, deafened by years of noise, he would set the volume to suit his own faded hearing rather than that of the audience.

'It's going to be loud mum. Chris said bring some earplugs and he was serious. I've some in my handbag.'

The lights dimmed and the chatter died to a buzz, the curtains drifted shut, the warm up man brilliantly lit by a spot took centre stage and began to give the band a build-up.

She had become too wound up to listen, but heard 'king Rock' and within seconds the curtains were swooping open revealing a darkened stage. A spotlight hit centre stage picking out Bruce, there was a shimmering chord which hung, provoking a roar, a second spotlight, a rapid crescendo from the drums then three more spots in different colours and the band drove into a fast rock number.

For a few bars she was so stunned that she was hardly aware that Chris was part of it, finally taking in his presence, posing in a mix of yellow and white light, foot on monitor.

Diane nudged her.

'I know.' He had kept quiet about the blonde streaks.

The pose was performance, but the stage presence was Chris. She hoped her mother wouldn't notice the tightness of the jeans.

For the second song, the tempo slowed and she was able to watch him more closely than she had since their first encounter at 'The Troubadour'. He was concentrating hard, glancing occasionally at some sheets on a stand, strutting during the guitar passages, tightly focussed at his microphone during his harmonies. She wondered if he was enjoying it or was being driven by the work ethic that had helped to make their performances seem effortless.

The thoughts were swept away as the tempo increased and the band drove into a third song, a fast rock number with passages where bass, guitar and keyboard played semi quavers in harmony over Bruce's chords. It was a virtuoso performance from Vince, and Chris, strained, biting his lip was playing at, no she knew his best, and this was beyond his best. At the end the notes sparkled into the final chord and she saw his relieved grin and took in Bruce's momentary nod.

Bruce acknowledged the applause offered a few words and they were into a fourth and fifth which she recognised as a recent big hit.

Suddenly they were bowing like collapsing dolls and running off stage to a roar from the audience. Fifty minutes had passed and she had been lost in performance.

Diane collapsed back in her seat, a look of excitement on her face. 'That was amazing, Chris was just so good, and the band was wonderful.'

'Let's see if we can get a drink mum. I'm dry.'

'I'm not surprised after all that screaming.'

'I wasn't screaming, once maybe, just cheering...oh come on we'll be at the back of the queue.'

Twenty minutes and two overpriced and none too cool Pepsi's later they returned to their seats.

Their conversation had been limited by the whistling in their ears and, Alison deciding for once to follow the advice given, thrust wax balls in to her ears. Her mother was initially reluctant to do the same. 'It might me my only chance to hear them.' she complained.

'I'm sure you will hear them!'

They did.

After the first number she gave herself up to the performance, the set continuing amid increasing excitement to its conclusion. With the dying of the last chord she joined the rest with shouts of 'More! More!' The band returned for their encore and at its end waved and ran offstage to further chanting.

The chants, continued by a small group from 'kR's burgeoning fan base, subsided and the audience began to disperse.

'Come on Mum lets go and meet them, I've got a backstage pass.'

'Come on!' she repeated. Diane was looking at her.

'Are they good? I mean really good.' I've seen bands on television and I saw you when you were all together, and you were lovely, but I've never been to a concert like this.'

'Oh yes they're good, trust Phillips to fall on his feet.'

They were good; she had found the lighting, the effects and the movement thrilling, the music, heavy and exciting in places, breathtaking. Chris had raised his game, was no longer the competent guitarist in a working band; temporary or not he was now the object of their running joke 'A rock star.' It gave her a moment of fear.

Her mother was speaking again. 'Who was the boy in the yellow shirt, the one who was singing most of the time?'

'That was Bruce. Why?'

'Nothing, he was so, I don't know, so…when you are close its much more exciting.'

'Mum, you aren't turning into a rock fan are you? Anyway you should have been watching Chris.'

'I was, as well.' She paused. 'I didn't realise he was so sexy.'

'Muum! Really!' Mums shouldn't say things like that, but there was a twinkle in Diane's eye. 'He isn't! Come on.'

They made their way through the echoing chatter of the auditorium to the side of the stage where several people were in earnest discussion with a uniformed official. Alison showed her pass and the two were allowed through a doorway to protests from several girls. The official gave Diane a stare.

'Alison,' she said, 'you know what he thought.'

'Yes. The boys used to get a few girl fans chasing after them. Chris had a little gang of them who turned up quite often. Sol used to call them 'Crispy's chorus line'.

'And how about you?'

'Me?'

'Well?'

'Well what? Oh all right, I had a few fans too.'

They had reached the wings, and through the crowd spotted Chris sharing a cigarette with the drummers. He took a drag and passed it back before slumping forward, head in hands.

Alison put two and two together and made an accurate four.

As they approached, her incipient concern gained focus as an attractive blonde walked up to Chris, threw a large towel around his shoulders and holding his head gave him an affectionate kiss. 'Well done Crispy!' she said. 'I think you saved your ass.'

Alison stopped.

He looked up at the girl, 'Thanks love, really appreciated.' and spotting Al waved, rose and walked the few paces towards them wiping his face and arms with the towel. He looked exhausted.

She was hugged then held at arm's length. 'Thanks for coming. You look lovely as always.' and to Diane, 'Your sister looks pretty good too.' He kissed her 'sister' before turning back and hugging her again. 'Missing you.' he whispered loudly.

'Who was the girl?'

'Gayle? She helps out with equipment and clothes, drinks, all sorts of things.' He was high on adrenaline aided by a puff of the drummer's weed.

'It was OK wasn't it?' He put an arm around her and the other around Diane.

'Wonderful and you were very good.' Diane said.

'Thanks. Al, what did you think?'

'It was really good. I'll be worried with all the…'

'Chris!' It was Bruce. 'Great stuff, I knew you were the man. Try to relax more.' He turned his attention to the two women. 'Who's this, where did you find these two? I was worried about your lack of interest in the chicks; now you're set up with two.'

'Just the one,' said Chris. 'This is Al, Alison Smith.'

'Hey, I know you now,' said Bruce. 'Cat's Whiskers and you were propping up a duff guitarist in Synergy. Good to meet you.'

'Good to meet you.' said Al. 'We thought you were great.'

'We are.' He gave her a second hug and looked her in the eye. 'Pity we can't find a place for you in the band.'

She felt a little happier.

'And this is Diane.' said Chris.

'Diane, good to see you!' She too was hugged.

'You were brilliant; Alison says that I have become a fan.'

'We're going to get along.' His second glance lingered for a moment. 'Are you coming to the party?'

'Oh! I don't know; I'd love to but…'

'No buts, I'll collect you in fifteen minutes.' He disappeared towards the dressing rooms leaving a surprised Diane to face a disbelieving daughter.

'I think you've got a date with a rock star.' Chris was laughing.

'Chris!' The daughter was outraged. 'Don't be silly, Mum can't go off with *him,* not at this time of night.'

'Why not?'

'Is there any particular reason why I shouldn't go Alison?'

'No, but...yes. Chris, tell her.'

'Me?' He turned to Diane. 'Well, you might find it a bit odd, and I should warn you that Bruce likes the ladies. I mean it's not a problem, you will be safe with him as long as you make it clear that no means no.'

'Chris! I want a word with you. *In private*!' The last words were emphasised. 'Excuse us mum.'

'For goodness sake that's mum you're talking to! You know what it will be like, drink, drugs probably and mum looks young and he might try to…you know.'

'Come on Al, your mum isn't a silly teenager; she's the most sensible person I know, and one of the nicest. The worst that will happen is he'll show an interest and she will need to put him right.'

'I know, she's sensible, but she's not that old and she doesn't understand people like Bruce.'

Her anxiety registered.

'Sorry, I wasn't thinking clearly. Do you want me to explain the situation? Bruce is a bit of a womaniser, but he isn't nasty or rough and she'll be quite safe as long as she behaves normally. I can warn her to be careful if you want.'

'Will you?'

'Yes, of course, but if she if she wants to go you will have to talk to her.'

'No! Just do your best.'

'One thing, don't go undermining her by saying she is your mum.'

'As IF!' Al's look would have withered a fairly sturdy tree.

Conscious of the irony of the situation Chris put an arm around Diane's shoulder and explained Alison's concern.

'I'm rather flattered that my daughter thinks I might be

propositioned. I would rather like to go, I'm not often asked to a party by a rock star.' She smiled at her joke. 'Do you think he was serious?'

'Certainly he was. You look...' attractive, companionable, sensible? He gave up. 'Really nice.'

He knew a little about Bruce had seen the second glance. Bruce wouldn't push her, but he could be quite persuasive. She had been a very good friend during his blackest period and he didn't want to put her in an awkward situation.

Diane turned to a daughter who was wearing the expression of a disbelieving fourteen-year old.

'It is only a party, he hasn't asked me to run away with him.' She smiled, looked uncomfortably like her daughter and gave Chris a moment of anxiety.

Bruce returned fifteen minutes later. Ready Diane? He took her hand.

'Where is the party?' Alison was finding it hard to accept the sight of her mother in the company of a rock-star.

'At Greg's brother's house. Come on mate you've saved your ass and I can get to know both of your chicks.'

'I wasn't intending to go.'

'I'll bet.' Bruce's smile was wolfish. 'Hoping for a threesome, don't blame you.'

Over Bruce's shoulder Di's eyes widened.

'What's the address?' Chris asked hastily.

Bruce gave him the address and Alison fumbled in her handbag for a small notepad. 'I don't think we will be coming, first gig, feeling a bit shattered.'

Bruce grinned. 'Come on then Di, let's boogie.' He led her out of the theatre to a waiting taxi.

'I cannot believe this. How could you allow mum to go to a party at this time of night.'

'She will be fine.' But what had Dave said three years before? 'Be honest Christopher; don't pretend you haven't noticed that Di's a crack for her age.' Should he have stopped her?

'Al, if you were at the party with Bruce, could I trust you?'
'Of course you could.'
'So is your mum less virtuous than you?'
'Certainly not, don't be silly.'
'Right, that means you are as virtuous as your mum.'
'Pig!'

After a quick change and a clean-up Chris collected his holdall and his guitars and they drove back to the Hotel where he had booked a room for his visitors.

Collecting their keys they took the lift to the second floor. Halfway down the passage outside the room she was sharing with her mother Al stopped, turned and held Chris's arms.

'You were fantastic. You do know that?'

Chris was silent as his mind went back.

'Thanks. It is mostly show, most of the guitar work is fairly easy and there were only a couple of pieces that needed a lot of practice, one is a nightmare.'

'Number three.'

'Yes. I can't actually play it. It's too fast to think it, so I play flat out and hope my hands know it. I can't really explain.'

'When did you start smoking?' The question arrived out of the blue.

'I haven't, Bep gives me a puff on his to relax before and after.'

'Be careful, I couldn't cope if you went off the rails.'

'I won't, it really is just a puff to take the edge off my nervousness.'

'You didn't need it before.'

'There wasn't the same pressure before. Sorry Al, this is something else.'

'I worry about the girls too.' She was still looking at him. 'Can I be your groupie?'

'My groupie?'

'Can we spend the night together?'

The pause was so long that her tension was palpable.

'Al love, it's lovely to be with you but I'm not ready for

our kind of loving relationship. Don't look like that. If you really want we could share a room.'

'Alright.' The tension subsided. 'I need to be with you.'

'Your mother will realise where you are when she gets in.'

She gave the father of her daughter a pitying look.

'Sorry love I'm not in that frame of mind.'

'Mum will be alright, won't she?' he was asked again.

'Of course she will, the only thing in danger is her virtue.'

'Don't be horrid.' Alison's look was unique to circumstances where parents and sex are associated. 'Please don't tease. I'm still uncertain about everything and Mum is so important.'

'I told you Bruce isn't rough and he wouldn't push her. I'd trust my sister with him.'

'You haven't got a sister.'

'True.' A vulgar connection entered his tired mind. 'Mind you,' unwisely it escaped, 'you might have one if Bruce pushed too far, he's a big lad.'

There was a shocked silence.

'You beast,' Al said quietly 'mum thinks the world of you.' There was a hint of tears.'

'Sorry, it was a rotten joke.' He hugged her, a tight helpless bundle, needing comfort, unable to accept it.

'Mum's so supportive and you say something rude like that.'

'I didn't mean it. Sorry, forgive me?'

'Suppose so. Normally things like that wouldn't upset me but I need Mum so much at the moment.' The sniffles stopped and she took a breath. 'I mustn't get upset, I mustn't.' There was a long pause. 'Do you think we could find something to eat in the bar, I noticed that it was still open.'

'I'll run down and see if I can find something. Do you want anything particular? Coffee? Sandwiches?'

'Anything. Chris, do you think Bruce was interested?'

'Listen love, I know what you are worried about. Bruce

might be interested and I know your mum is attractive for her age, but I got the impression that Bruce had picked up on her niceness.' He noticed the frown. 'She will be alright I promise.'

He ran down the stairs and with the mixture of appeal and a small tip persuaded a reluctant barman to seek out some sandwiches and coffee before dashing upstairs for a hot soak in the bath rather than speedy shower. A quarter of an hour later, feeling clean and fresh, the two met companionably in an alcove corner.

Snuggled together they nibbled the cheese rolls that had appeared and poured their coffee. Chris had descended from the high that had followed the curtain and the two conversed quietly, conscious only of each other.

After twenty minutes they left and made their way to Chris' room.

Undressing he slid into bed and Alison, turning off the light slipped in beside him a few moments later. They lay side by side holding hands, moving a little closer together.

Al turned on her side and began to stroke his chest, her bodily movement suggesting increased agitation, her hand beginning to roam further over his body. He was stirred by memories of love that were fragmented by pain and hurt. Unwilling to share her affections he reached across and stroked her hair. With a moan she suddenly rolled over, and lay on top of him. He stroked her back gently, knowing that she was beyond his control.

She was whispering in his ear little disjointed phrases, 'Been too long, sorry darling, so sorry, need you so much.' Her body shook with a kind of bubbling laughter that welled up inside.

Ten minutes passed before she collapsed on him, damp with perspiration, pushing her face into his neck.

Chris lay passively stroking her, a mixture of emotions, confusion, love, guilt and disloyalty running around his mind. He dealt with them as he dealt with all un-resolvable problems, by pushing them away. There remained other issues.

Her relationship with Gary had brought out the worst in him; possessiveness stifled by a stubborn determination to 'do the right thing'. It was followed by an insane jealousy dealt with by slowly and ruthlessly cutting her out of his feelings.

Now she had come back into his life and his emotions were all over the place; moments of love and affection that approached the joy of their first dates, poisoned by images of her with Gary, destructive images that were hard to dismiss.

Alison was already asleep half sprawled on top of him and he eased gently from beneath her and lay with her head partly on his shoulder. Eventually he too fell asleep.

The next time he awoke light was streaming through the half open curtains and he was being shaken. Alison, wearing a pretty dressing gown was standing over him, the face, last seen beautiful and content now looked worried.

The face spoke loudly into his semi-consciousness.

'Mum hasn't come back. What are we going to do?'

It was rather sudden and too much for a mind scarcely awake. When no answer came he was shaken more violently.

'Wake up! What has happened to her? It's your fault you said she would be all right.'

He reached out and held her hand. 'Don't get upset she will be fine.'

'You don't know that, how can you know, anything might have happened.'

Chris struggled to rationalise. 'Let's be logical, what happened the last time we went to a party?'

'What?'

'At the end' Chris persisted 'I had to carry you home because you fell asleep?'

'What about it?'

'Well, I expect it runs in the family…get off; get off I'm not awake. You can be a real sod sometimes.'

'You deserve it. You don't think.'

'No I don't! Go and have your shower Al. I'll make some phone calls. Go on, I promise to have found your Mum by the time you come back. Find me that address.'

'You can't promise.' She picked up her bag, rummaged around and threw the small notebook at him.

'Go on, have your shower.'

When, reluctantly she left the room he picked up the phone and contacting reception gave them the address and number of the house in which Bruce's party had been held.'

A couple of minutes later the phone rang and a receptionist's voice said 'You are through.'

'Hello, is that Des Pullin's place?'

'Who wants to know?'

'Chris Phillips, friend of Bruce.'

'What do you want?' The voice did not sound helpful.'

'I'm trying to get in contact with Di Smith. Is she still there?'

'Who's she?'

Chris described her.

'Oh I know Di, old, nice lady. Why do you want her?'

'Checking she's OK.'

The unknown being at the end of the phone went silent. 'Think she's still asleep, the party went on 'til four. Give me your number; I'll get her to phone you.'

'No that's OK; when she wakes up tell her that Chris will be around to collect her at about ten.'

'Right on.' said the voice and put the phone down.

Chris sat back on the bed. He looked at the bedside clock. Fifteen minutes for a shower, no need to be out of the room until 10:30, half an hour for breakfast. He got out of bed as a pink girlfriend still in her dressing gown slipped back into the room.

'Bad news Al, Bruce arranged for her to be the centrefold in next month's Mayfair. Get off! Get OFF!' His voice cracked as she tickled him. He was pushed back onto the bed.

'Stop it! She's ok.' Al stopped, 'she's getting really good money. No!' he became silly as she found a particularly sensitive spot and rolled over receiving a hard smack on his bottom. 'Ooof. Hey that hurt.'

'It was meant to Phillips, it's not funny. She is alright I presume, even you are not callous enough to make jokes if there was a problem.'

'Yes, of course she is, it went on late and she fell asleep. I'm going to collect her later.'

'I'll come.'

'Better not, she'll be embarrassed at being out all night, I mean she is a married woman.' He turned away.

'She's not just "a married woman" the voice became assertive, 'she's my mum.'

On his way to breakfast Chris borrowed a map from reception and located the road where the party had been held. It was about three miles across town and probably an easy drive on a Sunday morning.

Breakfast completed and suggestions that 'Perhaps I should to come.' firmly rebuffed he drove the three miles to the address where, after a couple of wrong guesses he finally found the correct residence; a large, slightly run down detached house surrounded by a high wall.

The short drive was blocked by several badly parked cars that left him with the option of parking on the street or negotiating the unkempt lawn. Choosing the former he made his way past some ill tended rhododendrons to the front door. His knock arousing no response he pushed it open and made his way into a white painted hallway.

The crispness of the coloured sun shafts through the fanlight was a shock. Since Sue's death his world had been dulled; now, though problems remained his new relationship was bringing moments of real happiness. The thought brought a spasm of guilt that destroyed the momentary good feeling.

'Anyone about.' Receiving no reply he ventured through an open door into a kitchen where he found a solitary figure wearing jeans and a towel drinking coffee.

'Hi! S'cuse me mate I'm looking for Diane.'

The figure looked up. 'You the guy that rang? Hey you're Chris, Tony's stand in.'

'Yes that's me.'
'You did alright last night.'
'Thanks very much.'
'Not as good as Tony but OK.'

Stifling a 'Bloody cheek' Chris accepted that it was probably a compliment.

'Is Diane about?'

'I'll go and see.' He rose reluctantly and made his way upstairs, returning after what seemed an age.

'She's up and running. She said she'll join you in the car.'

'Right. Thanks.'

'No problem. The voice followed him 'You'll never replace Tony, but you were OK.'

'I have replaced him.' Chris thought as he returned to the car.

A short time later Diane made her way down the drive to the car. Chris opened the door and she slid in next to him. 'OK?' he said.

'Fine. Sorry I didn't phone; I intended to but it got late then I fell asleep. I must look a mess; I had to sleep in my clothes, but I did manage to get a shower this morning. I hope you weren't too worried'

'Al was. Good party?'

'Yes, not the sort I am used to, there were some strange people there.'

'There always are one or two.'

She lowered her voice. 'It was rather exciting.'

'Good.' he paused, 'Don't tell me anything that might be embarrassing later.'

His arm was held. 'I know what you mean. There's not much to tell; Bruce is so alive. He danced with me and afterwards we talked for ages, then, when it went quieter some of us played a silly game.'

'Did you?' He knew some of the games and wondered.

She had a decent body; rushing into his bathroom with a poohy Simon he had found her stepping from the shower. She had smiled dismissing his confused apologies.

They drove back in silence and as they approached the hotel he spoke again.

'Di.' he bit his lip. 'We...Al and I, we were a bit worried, I mean Bruce likes girls.'

'Christopher, I think we are friends, and I appreciate your concern, but I don't think an interrogation is called for. I had an enjoyable evening, is that permitted?'

It was a put down.

'OK. I'll be straight, Bruce doesn't normally just chat to women he takes to parties; and Al was worried.'

'Was she?'

'Yes. She worries about her mum.'

Pulling into the car park his arm was gripped.

'Chris, don't say anything to Alison.'

'What's to say?'

'Very little, *certainly* not what you're implying, but it was a party and even mums,' she looked him in the eye, 'are a bit less inhibited at parties. Truly Chris, there was nothing that would embarrass either of you. '

He shrugged.

'Oh goodness, if you must know we kissed and had a bit of a cuddle when we were dancing; and the game was, well it could have been naughty.'

'I can guess what it was.'

'Can you? Well I was lucky on the fifth round.' she pinkened.

'I'm glad to hear it.'

'Don't worry, I was very well behaved so no more questions.' Leaning across she kissed his cheek. 'And stop counting!'

CHAPTER 4   Family Holiday

Wednesday, and the band had moved to its next venue. Chris, alone in his small hotel room was feeling unsettled. The music had shaken his confidence and apart from his requiem for Sue he was dissatisfied with everything he had written.

With a little time on his hands and a feeling for the heavier music he was experimenting with the new style and with the lyrics written during the black period that followed Sue's death.

He had resisted contacting Alison not wishing to lean on her, but he knew that if he left it longer she would feel neglected and he needed to maintain contact with Simon.

He put down the guitar that he had been restringing. He was beginning to enjoy the Gibson but the 'G' had been slightly out of tune at the end of the concert. He had knocked the music stand with the headstock and was unsure whether to blame himself, or complain about slack handling by the crew. Perhaps it would be best to leave well alone, he had the Junior or even the Strat as a fall back.

He sat on the bed and reached for the phone.

Alison was playing with Simon and Sarah in the garden of her parent's home when the phone rang. Picking up Simon, who had been kicking over the piles of bricks that she was building, she headed for the house.

'Telephone.' she said to Sarah who continued to scuff her way down the path on a miniature plastic bus.

Threading her way through the French windows, she picked up the receiver.

'Hello.'

'Hi Al.' said a familiar voice.

'Chris. Thank goodness, is everything alright, how are you?'

'Fine love. Just feeling a bit flat after seeing you at the

weekend.'

'Me too. It was the best weekend since…' she couldn't say since Blackpool, 'for ages, and it was lovely being with you.' '

'Thanks, it was lovely for me too.' He dropped his voice. 'I'm sorry I wasn't much of a lover.'

The phone went quiet.

'I'm sorry I made a fool of myself but I needed to feel wanted.'

'You didn't make a fool of yourself; I haven't got myself sorted yet.' He changed the subject. 'How is your mum, did she enjoy the weekend?'

'She's fine.' there was a change of tone 'I'm worried, she's normally open with me but when I asked what happened at the party she just said it was enjoyable. And,' she continued, 'when I asked about Bruce she said he was "kind, much nicer than she expected" and when I said 'Is that all? She said "Whatever do you mean, it was just a party." And!' before Chris could speak 'she wants to come and see the band again!'

'Great. That means you'll be coming again, soon I hope?'

'If you want me to. I mean, yes of course, but that's different, we're talking about Mum.'

'If she enjoyed the show why wouldn't she want to see us again? Oh by the way, Bruce called her 'a nice lady' and told me to send his love.'

'What do you mean, "Send his love!" Oh my god, you drag Mum backstage, introduce her to rock stars with awful reputations and then let her go to parties with them. No wonder she's gone silly, and goodness knows what Dad must think.'

'Bruce is ok, but 'kind' and 'nice' aren't words I would use. Your mum must have made a good impression if he was on his best behaviour.'

'You're useless!' Alison began to get loud; not unknown when releasing worries or stresses. 'I told you to keep away from drugs and you are already irresponsible.'

'Al darling; shut it!'

'What?'

'Stop it! I know you care, and I don't mind you putting me right sometimes but its non-stop; Saturday, Sunday and now Wednesday.'

Taken aback by the response her voice was quiet. 'I'm worried about mum and I've got no-one to talk to.'

'You're blaming me.'

'Not.' said Al in an even smaller voice.

'You needn't be anxious about your Mum, I told her we had been worried about what might happen at the party and the look she gave me said 'How dare you!' Then she said 'There was nothing either of us would be embarrassed about.'

'Of course she wouldn't do anything embarrassing. It was rude to suggest it, no wonder she was offended.'

'But…' He felt a moment of irritation.

'It's not only Mum; I'm beginning to feel dissatisfied.'

'How do you mean.'

'I was jealous at the weekend, I wanted to stay with you and I want to start work again.'

'The weekend was a bright spot and I would have loved you to stay, but when I feel down, I'm no use to anyone.'

'You are.' Al said quickly. 'Being together is good for me.'

'Thanks love, it's good for me too, and things will come right if you can wait.'

'I am waiting.' Looking over her shoulder to make sure she was alone, she added some affectionate words that stemmed from their most intimate moments.

'Al, there are a couple of things I want to ask. You don't need to answer, but please think about them. The first is that anytime you want to come to the house with Sarah then' he thought for a phrase 'that would be good.'

'And?'

'When this stint finishes, I forgot to say, Tony's going to survive, do you think that we might work together again?'

'As a band?'

'Yes.'

'Oh, yes. That is the best thing you could ask.' She hesitated. 'You do mean it?'

'Yes, of course I mean it. I was afraid you might not want to work with a second-rate guitarist.' The hurt that had resulted from her description could still cause bitterness.

She swallowed. 'When I called you 'second-rate' it meant "I still love you, but I'm very unhappy." I would have given anything to unsay it.'

'I said some cruel things too.' He felt sorry for the moment of anger. 'Let's forget the bad things.'

'Love you Philips and I can't wait to play with the best guitarist I know.' Then, with a happy bubbling return of the old Alison. 'I mean second best,' she giggled nervously, 'Bruce is so good isn't he…sorry, oh Chris I didn't mean it like that!'

The bubble burst.

'I know, Bruce is brilliant and being compared is a compliment, don't get anxious love. Listen, there's not much else to say; give the house some thought.'

'I will. Do you want to speak to Simon? Say "hello daddy" Simon.'

There was silence then a whispered 'say hello.'

'lo dada.'

There followed a minute of one-sided conversation after which the words 'well done treasure' were heard and Al came back on the line.

Hi again!' she said, 'I was going to ask if you read the reviews.'

'No! Bruce said they were OK, but I couldn't face reading them myself.'

'Do you want to hear the important bit about my clever Phillips? It starts with a piece on 'kR then your bit, "… ex Synergy guitarist Chris Phillips, drafted in at short notice to replace the injured Tony Shelton confounded doubters with a more than satisfactory performance. Though lacking Tony's virtuosity his support playing on Bruce's leads showed signs of confrontation which could blossom, into real excitement.

Get well soon Tony."

They exchanged quiet affections and Chris rang off.

Ten days later with five more or less successful shows under his belt, Chris returned to the farm. The next few gigs were mostly in Wales and the South West and he intended to commute to them from home. He had rung Al and to his delight she had asked if she could come and stay.

'You've as much right to be there as I have.' she was told.

He arrived in the early hours of Sunday morning to find her curled up on the settee under a blanket facing the still glowing embers of a fire. The stresses of the previous days melted away and he bent and kissed her.

She woke, looked up and smiled. Surprised by his emotions he knelt and kissed her again.

'Good to see you.'

She stretched then reached up to him. 'Lovely to see you too.'

'Mum's here. I wanted you alone but she wanted to come with the children.'

'That's Ok. How long can you stay?'

She shrugged.

'We're in the Southwest for the next few gigs and I'm hoping to stay for ten days. It might get a bit crowded, I said we'd have open house and some of the band and their friends will be in and out.' He smiled at her pout. 'We could take the children and stay in a hotel.'

'Where are you playing?' Al asked.

'One in the midlands but mostly in the Southwest and Wales plus a couple on the south coast. I thought we might take the children down to the coast for a week. What do you think?'

She reached up and put her arms around his neck. 'Does that mean we are a couple?'

He looked seriously at her. 'Yes, more or less, I love you but…is one and a half ok for now?'

How could they be a couple until he resolved his feelings

about her and Gary? He loved her, but that flaw in his character was still preventing commitment.

'Two halves, I'm not a whole yet.' She took his hand. 'Are we sleeping together or do I go to my room and wait for one of your randy friends to turn up?'

'Don't rush me love, it's only seven months since…'

Alison pouted. 'Are you turning me down again?'

'No…yes, no. I can't explain, I'm not ready for the real 'us', there's too much love and hurt and baggage to sort out. Will you settle for two singles?'

She bit her lip. 'Maybe, with cuddles and a lot of reassurance?'

The following Sunday they drove to the south coast taking the children. Diane's offer to stay on for a couple of days to keep an eye on the house 'in case any of the band turn up' was welcome. In fact, only Bep had taken up Chris's offer, arriving after a Welsh gig with a girl and two friends, making himself at home for two days and disappearing after the Midlands gig.

The economies of touring which had accommodated them in small hotels and guesthouses were forgotten and they were booked into a smart hotel overlooking one of the more remote Dorset beaches.

The income from record sales and airplay together with rent from a small flat bought by their company had carried them through the barren times. Now, speculative forecasts as to his future income permitted a present overdraft.

'I'm a capitalist' he told Al 'and I'm not comfortable with it. People like me work for our living and getting money from investments is…'

'Rather nice' Al interrupted.

'Yes I suppose.' 'It's the old puritan work ethic; money from investment is living off other people's work.'

'Darling you have worked hard and worried about having no money for the last five years, don't start worrying about having money, it pays our mortgages.'

Fit, content and feeling 23 again, happiness was returning despite the absence of sex in her revived relationship.

Should she have made better use of her time with Cats whiskers? Sometimes she wished…but then, whoring didn't suit her and a good relationship wasn't on offer. Surely chastity shouldn't have been the only alternative?

The thought brought amusement. Poor darling hypocritical Chris; so easily deceived by a pretty face, so hurt and censorious when someone he cared about was enjoying life.

The sole clouds in her existence were Chris's descents into unhappiness. There was nothing to be said; she would hold his hand and after a few minutes he would smile and nod his thanks. Sometimes he would pick up Simon and hug him.

Once he had cried and she was unable to cope, patting his arm then hurrying to the kitchen to make tea.

On the first day of their stay the weather had been mixed, the sun occasionally peeping through the overcast but on the following day the weather had brightened and become more settled and after breakfast they made their way to the beach.

Chris, loaded with beach mats and a bag pretended to be a donkey and hee-hawed intermittently much to Sarah's delight.

Al pushed Simon in a pushchair carrying their food and drink in a cool bag slung around her neck.

'We're hardly living up to the image of wild rockers are we?'

'Suits me' he replied, 'I don't think I've the stamina to be one.' He turned with a frown. 'Seriously, there are a lot of pressures that I didn't expect and the shows are exhausting.' Then his mood lightened. 'I'm so glad we are best friends again, it gives me a reason to stick with it.'

They chose a spot on the beach not far from the main entrance and Al at once began to spread suntan cream on all exposed surfaces before laying back in a modest one-piece swimsuit. Chris helped Sarah build sandcastles which required frequent trips to the sea where she paddled, was swung around to splash in the water, screamed and demanded more. Simon ate the sand and knocked over the sandcastles with joyous determination until hit by Sarah with her spade.

'We must get a sun shade,' said Alison suddenly. 'I don't want the children getting burnt. Even with their shirts on they still get sore legs and arms.' She adjusted Simon's sunhat for the twentieth time. 'Have we got enough money?'

'Think so!' Chris dug into the pocket of his shorts. 'Get me an ice lolly, an orange one?'

'I'll see what they have in the shop, coming children?'

'Yes.' said Sarah 'Simon, come.'

Simon tottered to his feet.

'Shoes, Simon.' Chris took his hand. 'Come here, shoes.'

He seized the reluctant bundle and slid the shoes onto a child giving the impression of having his feet tickled.

'Go on mate,' he said setting him down, 'go with Sarah and get an iced cream.' The bundle was already toddling away following the others.

Chris sat back and relaxed leaning on his elbows. Looking around he nodded to a middle-aged woman sitting on a nearby beach mat. She was watching a small child rolling a ball whilst her daughter and son-in-law swam. She smiled back at him.

'Lovely day' he said.

'Yes it is. Are these your children?'

'Yes.'

'They are such a comfort.'

'Yes.'

'Please don't think me offensive' she continued 'but are you Chris Phillips?'

Chris nodded.

'My daughter thought you were. You are a rock musician.' She spoke as if it were something strange.

'I play guitar in a band.'

'Is the girl in the band as well?'

'She used to be, but not at the moment.'

'My daughter thought that she recognised her.' The woman was silent for a moment.

'You lost your wife,' she said.

It was so unexpected that for a moment it failed to register, and then the familiar pain flooded back. He bit his lip.

'Yes.'

'I lost my husband at about the same time.'

'Oh.' He nodded. 'It doesn't really go away.' he said after a pause.

'No. It must be worse for you, she was so young.'

'Yes.' He was suddenly grateful. 'I was on stage last week and saw a girl who looked like her; I just wished it was her. I cried; looked really stupid but I couldn't stop, Bruce gave me a boll...afterwards.'

The woman moved to a mat a little closer.

'Unless they are close, people don't understand. They are kind, but...'

Chris nodded. 'Are you managing?'

'My daughter is very good, she misses her dad, and my son phones a lot; he's working in Scotland' she added by way of explanation. 'It doesn't go away though, I think of him everyday.'

'I think of Sue everyday. It was so unfair, how can I explain that to Alison?'

'Is Alison the girl with you?'

'Yes! She's wonderful; we've always been friends, but when I'm miserable how can I tell her that I'm thinking about Sue?'

'Is she your girlfriend? Sorry, I don't mean to pry.'

'That's OK; it's easier to talk to a stranger. She will be when I've got over the worst; I mean I accept it, but it's only been eight months.' His face clouded and he bit his lip again. 'Thanks for letting me talk.'

'I don't mind. When my husband died I carried on as if he

was still there, right through the funeral and then suddenly it hit me and I couldn't stop crying. Every time someone was kind, I cried. I've made a big effort to keep my tears to myself and now everyone thinks I've got through it.'

'Yes, other people forget quickly, they don't realise how much it affects you.' Chris spoke with feeling. 'It must be the same for everyone.'

They talked on. They talked until interrupted by her daughter and son-in-law returning wet and breathless from the sea. Their conversation brought to a halt; she introduced Chris to her family.

Alison, returning with a huge striped umbrella and a melting ice-lolly joined them and was introduced. The children, without introduction, were soon playing together, inventing games that involved rolling balls into buckets. Simon, given the ball by Sarah, walked away, dropped it, kicked it, fell over it and bawled when Sarah took it away to continue the game.

The sunshade was erected and the children ordered to move into the shade, 'Before you get burned!' The request was ignored until the pretence of deafness could no longer be maintained. Alison's limited patience broke and eventually she rose crossly chased, seized and vigorously dressed each in turn.

Chris, in a floppy hat with a large towel around his shoulders continued chatting and laughing with the adjacent family until at lunchtime he was informed that they needed to seek out a café for lunch and began to pack up.

Goodbyes had been said but a few moments after their departure Chris rose suddenly and hurried after his new friend.

'Thank you so much. It was kind of you to let me talk; can I walk to the car with you?'

She looked surprised 'Yes, if you want.'

'I wanted to say…I don't know how to put this because it's very personal.' He paused. 'I'm not ready for a close relationship even with Alison.' He was frowning and holding her hand. 'What I'm trying to say is that it is good to have someone understanding around.'

She frowned. 'I know what you are saying but I can't even imagine having someone close. Perhaps when you are young…' she broke off, 'it's been good talking to you. I shall have to change my opinion of pop stars.'

'It's been good for me too. 'king Rock is playing in the town tomorrow and I do a song for Sue. If you would like to come and see us I will leave a note at the box office. Mention my name.' He took her arm and kissed her on the cheek. 'Bye, it's been lovely to meet you.'

'Well mum! I've never been kissed by a rock star.'

'He said he isn't a star.'

Their voices drifted away as he returned to the family.

'I saw you Phillips. Sometimes I think you will kiss anything that moves if it's female.'

'She's a nice woman, she lost her husband and she's very unhappy. We talked about losing someone and it was good because we both understand how we feel.' He ruffled her hair. 'I was trying to tell her it is good to have someone like you.'

'Silly.' There was a pause and she turned her head away. 'Don't! Please don't.'

The following evening three people arrived at the box office and were shown to seats at the back of the auditorium. 'Mr Phillips apologises for not meeting you and asked me to give you these.' They were passed a folder containing signed photos of the band and a box of earplugs, which caused them amusement.

Chris Phillips in performance was recognisably the 'boy' on the beach, but only just.

Alison attending the concert with the children was allowed to stand near a rear exit.

Sarah had been frightened by her first visit to a theatre then excited and had cheered when daddy appeared. Within minutes her fingers were firmly pressed into her un-programmed ears and Simon's began to cry.

Alison hovered by the exit with Simon in her arms, her eyes half on Sarah and half on the band. The second song after the interval was introduced by Bruce as 'A number written by our guitarist Chris Phillips featuring Greg Pullin on keyboard.'

There was a cheer and some applause and Al wondered how one of Chris's bright up-tempo songs would fit into the set.

He announced 'This song is called 'Far Country' and is for a young lady I met on the beach' the 'young lady' felt her hand gripped by her daughter.

Alison had never heard of it.

It began simply; Chris sang about a girl who had left him and gone to a far country. Al thought of the past and wondered if it was about her. It was a dark song, no doubt why the band was using it. Bruce was playing a simple rhythm and Chris was supplying little guitar fills. The keyboard was carrying the song, probably the only written part.

She heard 'No goodbyes, no longer there', and with a chill she realised that it was about Sue. With the knowledge, the sound and the blackness of the words fell into place.

When, in the chorus, the bass and the keyboard began rising in semi-tones against the guitars and he sang 'and turn your eyes from stones to pools of love' she began to cry. From his hurt, he had brought together the sound, the words and the structure, and in her still fragile state it was taking her apart.

The chorus wound, for a second time to its conclusion, hung poised and dropped into a major key. Chris sang a reprise with new words and she caught 'a kindness, a blessing and my only one'.

There was a pause at its conclusion, then enthusiastic applause from those who had caught its drift.

Alison, tears running down her cheeks, shouted out 'heartbreaker' then hugged the children to her.

Wiping her eyes, with the band already into its next harder number she knew that it was the best song he would ever write, probably the best performance he would ever give.

The band played to an audience that had largely forgotten the previous song.

The 'young lady' was silent. 'I think I understand.' she whispered to herself.

Chris Story

The tour was a huge success. I had caught the band on an upward roll and found myself part of an enterprise that was beginning to fly. It was Tony's misfortune that having given the initial impetus he was now side-lined and I found myself hoping that the hand would remain damaged for a while.

When the tour ended I was unsure if I would keep my place and pulled the few strings that my manager and I possessed to keep myself in the public eye. The public eye got blackened in a night club scuffle achieving slight credibility for myself, a small fine and a modest amount of publicity. It also provoked a panic stricken phone call from Al and a ticking off from Diane and my father.

Do the genuine articles have parents who remonstrate with them; perhaps it is the lack of such that makes some of them so unpleasant.

Tony's hand was still a mess and I survived to play on the LP from which the next single was to be taken, and 'YeeeHaaa!!' to keep my place for the US tour. It was going to be fantastic, 'kR had already achieved some success in the States and this was going to be their tour. If it were successful the band would move up into the big league.

I was more than excited; I was on a high.

CHAPTER 5   Nice Problems
(Chris' Story)

The rented flat in the Kings Norton area was small and the self-discipline necessary to cover my musical limitations had spilled over into domestic areas, allowing the maintenance of a reasonable level of order and cleanliness.

With three weeks to adapt the set for the US tour, practice with the band and with tapes was paramount. The tour was likely to be heavy going and several of the venues would be huge. As the junior member I was stressed and under pressure; Bruce, carrying the musical organisation and the performance whilst keeping an eye on financial arrangements needed all his tough constitution, and the support of his personal assistant.

Tony had visited at rehearsal spoken to Bruce and exchanged a few not unfriendly words with me. He seemed an OK sort of guy but I guessed he was sounding me out to see if I would try to keep him out permanently. It had crossed my mind, but he was a better musician and when his hand recovered I would be out.

He had made a big effort to get fit, but the damaged ligaments prevented the forefinger and index finger of his left hand from opening fully and limited their movement. Physiotherapy could do no more than encourage the healing process and I saw no reason why it should be too encouraging.

For the time being, there was no way he could be anything but a passenger.

The practice 'studio' was a solidly built Victorian Church hall situated about half a mile from the flat, and we had assembled there on the previous Monday to be given our itinerary, the travel arrangements, and an outline of the music.

My manager had already briefed me on the content, and as

I was now an established 'face' he had negotiated a new deal that gave me a marginally better percentage of the bands earnings. (The suggested income for the operating company was huge though overheads were high and management would take its excessive share.) I wasn't complaining, my share (of Bruce's estimate of the bands income) was a lot of mazuma by my standards.

I had played on the forthcoming LP and would receive an appropriate share of its income. The US version included some different songs and I was included in the back cover photo and the credits. It was also to be issued as a CD.

I returned from the 'studio' with tapes of the revised set and orders to be note perfect.

For practice I used headphones from an old AC fifteen with the tape of the songs plugged into one input and my guitar via the pedals, into the other.

The AC fifteen had been a 'find', battle scarred in the window of a second hand shop, bought for twenty quid a couple of years earlier. Two hours with a saw and a drill and the tattered combo had been reduced to a tidy 'Top' containing just the amp, the rest being consigned to the dustbin.

For ten quid, the guy who set up my guitars, after looking in disbelief and calling me 'bloody vandal', had adapted the speaker output to suit headphones and provided a controllable input for the tape.

After three hours of practice, (OK two hours of practice and an hour drinking coffee) I felt confident that there was nothing to fear from the musical changes.

Retiring to the kitchen I began to fry some onions and diced beef in the pressure cooker.

My mother's instructions 'Make sure you eat properly.' had been accompanied by a set of hand written recipes and I tried with some success to follow her advice.

There had been a fun evening out with band members and their girlfriends, but I was feeling tired and cooking casseroles was a relaxing alternative to junk food.

Cooking for myself in a small rented flat? I was more domesticated than many of my contemporaries. Was this the 'rock'n roll life?' The thought made me smile.

The answer unfortunately was an emphatic 'No! I was faking it.' The smile disappeared.

The vegetables and the stock had gone into the pot and the pressure cooker gently hissed its disapproval of my radio choice. I opened a beer and began to prepare the dumplings, my mind distracted by a predictable sitcom. The doorbell rang.

There was no one likely to call, and entertaining the momentary hope that it might be Al paying a surprise visit I made my way to the door.

The girl wore a beret, and a heavy navy coat. She was carrying a rucksack and, more worryingly, a large suitcase stood beside her.

There were stories of fans that presuming a reciprocal affection arrived at the homes of their hero expecting a welcome; this one looked tired and shabby. Experience advised caution but I retained a certain amount of compassion and envisaged a difficult half-hour sorting her problems and finding accommodation, possibly at my expense.

'Yes?'

'Chris. It's me.'

'Who?' Oh bloody hell, 'Sarah?'

'Yes. Can I speak to you?'

She knows I'm a soft touch; probably working in the area; reckons a sob story will extract a few quid.

I feel ashamed, Sarah is tough but she never had it easy and she looks very tired. We didn't part on good terms so if she has come to see me, she must be desperate.

Thoughts run through my head as concepts rather than words and I hear Dave telling me "Don't be a fool, be a bit street wise!" Getting rid of her will save a lot of problems.

'You had better come in.'

'Thanks Chris.'

She sounds as if means it.

'Let me take your coat.'

I hang the coat on the back of the door and taking her rucksack put it down beside her case.

'Sit down; you look whacked, would you like a coffee?'

She nods. 'Yes please.'

'I'm cooking.' I look at the towel I am holding and wave it at her. 'There are probably some biscuits somewhere.'

There are tears trickling down her cheeks, relief or part of an act? Compassion washes away the cynicism and I go and squat beside her chair.

'Hard time?'

She nods.

I make a decision, Al will skin me but Dave is right, I'm either a fool or a romantic.

'OK I'll do what I can.'

She brushes her face with her hand and nods again. The Sarah I remember was mostly ok, but as I had discovered to my cost, she could be crafty and manipulative; I would need to be careful.

I stand up. 'I'll make the coffee. If you like stew you can join me.'

The coffee is made and taken in. She has already recovered and thanks me in something close to her normal voice. Returning to the kitchen I begin to make extra dumplings aware that the stew will not now last for two nights. A hand grips my sleeve.

'Thanks Chris, you won't regret it.' I am released and she returns to the lounge.

I have no idea what I might regret. Clearly Sarah has.

'Do you like mustard dumplings?' I shout from the kitchen.

'Anything thank-you.'

I add the mustard and stir it in. About fifteen minutes more and they can go into the stew. I return to the lounge and sit down.

'How are you?' She is looking out of the window.

'You guessed when you said 'Hard Time?''

There was a silence whilst I considered what to say. She knows that the soft touch feels a degree of responsibility for her.

'Do you have anywhere to stay?'

'I can find somewhere.'

'That wasn't the question.' I was sharp with her and she looked up. 'If you want, you can have the settee for tonight. You can look for something tomorrow. How did you find me?'

'There was an article about the band and an advert, I contacted your management.'

'You could have phoned.'

'I wanted to see you; you know you have to make use of connections.'

I'll bet. The cynic began to return.

She was weighing up what to say and how best to appeal. I had to tread a delicate line between helping and being used. It was best to start tough and back off.

'Listen Sarah, I'll tell you straight, I'm under real pressure and I've no space for problems so if you mess me about you'll be out before you can say 'bastard'.' I had her attention.

'If you want help and if you are absolutely straight with me... well, we'll see.' She looked on the verge of tears. I didn't know if it was real or tactical but it was unlike the Sarah I remembered.

'It was just chance that I saw the notice and I did come to see you because I thought you might help.' She gave me an angry look. 'My whole life has been 'problems' and lately it's got worse. You've got no idea; you wouldn't last five minutes if we changed places.'

The anger was real; the uncontrolled reaction of someone buffeted by life.

'Didn't you hear what I said? That is exactly what I don't need.' I tried to be a little kinder. 'Just tell me what you want.'

I *was* stressed. With Synergy I had the support of the band which gave me enough slack to cope with upsets and problems, but not now.

She told me. Work drying up, a difficult 'boyfriend', and hints that she could make a good living if she wanted.

Finally, short of money and work she had walked out. That was three months ago, since then it was temporary jobs and social security.

The notice for 'king Rock had mentioned that two backing vocalists were required, and an article had mentioned that Chris Phillips had replaced Tony Sheldon. Broke, she had hitched to Birmingham and walked two miles to find my flat.

It was a sob story, but I had a feeling that the basics were true.

'You want me to put in a word.'

'I know you owe me nothing but I hoped you might give me a chance.'

I thought about the situation. There was no easy answer and it would upset Al.

'I can't give you a chance, I don't have much clout. I can put in a word, maybe get you an audition but that is all.'

'That is all I want. I meant what I said; if I get the job you won't regret it.'

'Huh.' I smiled for the first time. 'I don't know what Al would have to say about that?'

'I mean I can help with things, clothes, ironing, organising; if you're overworked it would help to have someone you could trust when you are on the road. Even without the job I could still be a help to you and it wouldn't cost.'

So that was the hidden agenda.

'Time to add the dumplings.'

We chatted as we ate and as I learned more about her life I began to understand her difficulties. She was right when she said that in her position I wouldn't last five minutes. I had it so easy; a little talent, Al's voice, the right place at the right time, meeting the right people and the support of friends. I had worked damned hard but so did a lot of others. I had paid a price, but also reaped some rewards.

I decided that if I helped it had to be out of kindness. I would try to get her an audition, after that she was on her own, I didn't want anything to foul up my relationship with Al.

Whilst we ate I mulled over her request. She could sing, but she wouldn't get the job on her singing. I could give advice on what was wanted and spend a little time practising; it would give her a chance. Her performance would be good even if her voice was average. The backing vocals were straightforward harmonies with tricky timing.

'You do choreography?'

'Of course that is my business.'

'I've been trying to think of an angle that will give you a chance. If we practice and you get the feel of the songs it will help, but there's strong competition. Maybe if you double as choreographer and arrange the singer's movements you might boost your chances.'

'Would it?' She looked at me. 'Alison never deserved you.'

'She deserved better; I'm grateful that we are still friends.'

'I read about your wife in one of the music papers. I'm sorry.'

Sue's face came to mind, smiling, open and happy. Mine must have shown how I felt.

'I'm getting on top of things but it was hard,' I bit my lip, 'final.' I dragged myself back, 'Could you do the washing up? No, forget it, you look whacked, leave it to me.'

'I'm OK.'

Choosing a suitable song I picked up my acoustic and began to sort out the best way of presenting her. The backing singers had to fill the space between Bruce's vocals and support the harmonies. We would concentrate on the timing, if she got that she would be in with a chance, assuming that it wasn't already fixed.

When she reappeared from the kitchen, I explained the plan and for half an hour we practised. She was quite good, but she was asleep on her feet.

'That's enough, you are getting the idea. I'll talk to Bruce tomorrow, if he agrees to try you, we will practice again.' She managed a nod. 'Go to bed, you can have the bed tonight, I'll take the sofa. The bathroom is in the recess next to the bedroom.'

Sarah picked up her cases and went into the bedroom, returning with a sponge bag. She was in the bathroom for an age and I collected my pyjamas.

When she came out she gave me a nod and crept into the bedroom. I had one of my three-minute showers, cleaned my teeth, changed into my pyjamas and collected a spare blanket.

The sofa was a three-seater and there was a chance of getting a good night. After settling down and getting myself comfortable I switched off the table lamp.

The bedroom door opened and a head looked around it.

'Chris. Come and join me.'

There was no way I was going to join her.

It wasn't morality, mostly emotional hang-ups. Anyway, I had no idea where she had been or who with, I wasn't ready for Al, and I certainly didn't want casual sex with Sarah.

'I don't think so.'

'Chris, I was afraid that you would turn me away and I might end up in a hostel or even on the street. Now I feel drained and I want to be held, to know this is real.'

'A cuddle?'

'Held! I don't do payback; I just want to feel warm.'

Wearing my hypocrisy like a virtue I rose from the sofa, followed her into the bedroom and slipped into bed.

She was like a child, smelling of my scented soap.

'Just a quick hug! Don't get any ideas.'

I snuggled up behind her and cuddled her with my knees tucked up under her bottom. She gave a small contented sigh and two minutes later was fast asleep.

The cuddle made me feel good, but I slid out of bed and padded back to the sofa. Sleep came slowly.

She was still asleep when I left the flat next morning, leaving some money, my spare key and a note telling her to get some dinner and anything she needed.

The morning was spent practising timing and structure with the band. Bruce had kindly sprung it on me that he was busy; that I would take the practice and that he wanted sections of two of the songs perfect when he returned.

It was a formidable challenge. Bep and Greg were no problem, but with Vince it was consent or nothing.

I spent a short while sorting out a structured way of practising which achieved what Bruce wanted without risking life and limb by ordering Vince about. If I had to take a risk, I would, but initially I would try to be subtle.

I explained what Bruce wanted, asked for suggestions as to how it was to be achieved, listened to the answers then had a try out.

It worked, more or less. With breaks for individual practice, we pushed on until one. Only once did I need to correct Vince; it resulted in him calling me an 'effin jumped up wanker who is asking for a fat lip'.

My 'So how do you reckon it?' mollified him to the extent where he said 'Don't get effin clever tea-boy.' and smacked me on the back of the head.

Moving well out of his way and growling 'nuff of that.' left honour satisfied.

I was glad when Bruce got back.

It was after practice had finished that I tackled Bruce about Sarah.

'You shaggin' her?' was his first question.

My 'No.' was not wholly believed.

'If Smithy finds out she'll have your balls off at the neck.' He enjoyed his picture for a moment. 'Is she any good?'

I explained that the singing was no problem and about the dancing. He was interested.

'Bring her in tomorrow, we'll give her a try and maybe I'll see her later. We had nearly forty replies but we are trying out seven, your girl will make eight.' 'You're sure you're not givin her one?'

'I think I'd remember if I was, unlike you, you lecher.'

'You're a soft bastard, you like her.' He said it with a grin, hitting the nail firmly on my thumb. 'OK for you I will try her out.'

'Listen mate, she can hack the singing, and she is a great mover, she knows the business and will be a real asset on stage.'

'I'll see if she can do the business. Bring her tomorrow, mid-day.'

I was dismissed.

She arrived at lunchtime looking neat and attractive, her relief at crossing the first hurdle now replaced by anxiety. Much of my practice time had been taken up coaching her but it was touch and go.

Bruce clearly liked the way she looked and was quite civil as he led her into an adjoining room. The backing vocals, played on a keyboard were on the practice tape.

Bruce played the tape and handed Sarah the words and music. She looked at me.

'Yeah, I know he coached you.' He wound the tape back. 'Let's hear you then.'

She was nervous. It was very important and I was becoming anxious for her; but not for long, she was a Pro and she gave a damned good impression of a being a singer.

The tape was rewound. 'Again.'

This time Bruce sang in the tough aggressive way that was the real sound of 'kR trying to throw her, but she hung on to her line with a gutsiness that more than compensated for her voice.

Bruce was eyeing her.

'Your boyfriend says you can dance. Give me an idea of what you might add to that.'

The tape was played for a third time, whilst Sarah performed some neat steps.

'Is that the best you can manage?'

Sarah modified the routine to something much wilder and sexier.'

'I was allowing for the other girl not being a dancer.'

'Huh! You reckon you've got the job on that five minute performance?'

'That's for you to decide.'

'Too right! Will your boyfriend let you out this evening?'

Sarah said nothing.

'She's a free agent.' I said.

'Come and see me' he wrote down an address, 'here, seven thirty and we will try some more songs.'

I left them to it

She was quiet that evening, ate nothing, took over my shower or an age and came out looking very attractive, the blonde hair in a pony tail that added to her five foot three. 'Good luck.' I said as she was leaving'

'Thanks Chris.' She wouldn't meet my eye.

I knew that she was mentally preparing to prostitute herself whilst appearing excited and happy with the prospect. I was pleased that I had no feelings for her; I didn't need any extra stress worrying about her.

I spent the evening practising a couple of the more difficult passages, took a loving phone call from Al and …damn! damn! went to bed annoyed because I already had a soft spot for a bloody tart.

Unfair. Sarah wasn't a tart; she was a girl who had to fight for everything and was tough enough to sell herself if she had to. CP, pushed out of his moral comfort zone wasn't tough enough to handle it.

She crept home in the early hours and was asleep on the settee in a tumble of blankets when I left the house in the morning. When I returned that evening Sarah was her bright self, greeting me with 'Any news.'

'About what?' I made myself ridiculous doing the offended male thing. 'No none.'

There was no news for a couple of days during which Sarah cooked, washed our clothes and ironed brilliantly. It was quite domestic except there was a barrier between us.

She was worried and I was still annoyed about having

feelings.

After three days Bruce called me into the side room and after a chat, told me the decision.

She knew the moment I entered the flat, standing expectantly in the kitchen doorway.

I took of my jacket and carefully put the Gibson in the cupboard.

'I could really do with a coffee.'

She went in to the kitchen put the kettle on and returned to stand leaning against the doorpost, looking at me with a blank expression on her face. I knew how much rejection would hurt.

'Have you heard about the choice of singers?' Her voice was level and held no expectation.

'Yes.'

'And?'

'You're in.' I let it sink in. 'Welcome to 'king Rock.'

'Thank-you.'

She went into the bedroom and shut the door. I made my own coffee. Through the wall I could hear her crying quietly; I had done the right thing and a good feeling crept over me.

The phone rang and picking it up I found myself speaking to Al; the good feeling evaporated.

'Hello love, nice to hear from you.'

'Hi Chris. I rang at lunchtime and your cleaner answered. She sounded young.'

'Might be, I've never met her.'

I turned the conversation back to the children to re-establish our relationship. The talk turned to more mundane issues and I felt a wave of guilt because my children were being cared for by my girlfriend whilst I enjoyed myself.

I was saying goodbye and blowing kisses down the phone when arms slipped around my waist and a head was rested on my shoulder. Lips pressed against my neck, and with a hasty 'Goodbye love.' I put the phone down.

My 'cleaner' was now nibbling my ear and making me shiver.

Slipping an arm around her I pulled her towards me and

risked a kiss.

'I was glad that it was good news.'

She kissed me, reminding me of an occasion several years before for which I had paid painfully.

'Thank you.' She brushed my cheek. 'You won't regret it.'

'I hope not, I've no room in my life even for pretty dancers.'

'What does that mean?'

'It means I'm not after payback but I'm not indifferent to you.'

'It means you want to screw me but don't like to ask.' She frowned. 'Are you being kind?' There was a long pause. 'Perhaps I can afford to like you a bit.' She gave me a peck on the cheek. 'Thanks again for your help.'

'Don't thank me too soon, 'kR isn't going to be an easy ride.'

'Do you think trying to look good on no money, working my ass off to get a crap job is easy?'

'No. I just meant that playing in a band like Synergy wasn't the fun it seemed and 'kR is a damned site harder. Harder than my last year at college, and I thought that was pretty tough.'

'You went to college?' Sarah looked surprised. 'Where?'

'Bath University.'

'University? My God.' She looked at me in a sad kind of way and shook her head. 'No wonder Sol used to call you 'Jammy Phillips.' You had everything didn't you?'

I didn't know what to say.

'I suppose you've got a degree or something?'

'Yes, I scraped a second.'

She opened her mouth to speak and then frowned and shut it again.

'What's the matter?'

It was an age before the answer came.

'You just make me feel so bloody inferior.'

'Why?' I took her hand. 'You're the most determined girl I have ever met; I may have qualifications but I don't have half your drive and determination.'

She frowned at me, a bit like Al.

'Do you mean that?'

'I promise I mean it.'

'Like an Alison promise?'

'There is only one kind. Anyway this tour could give you opportunities, and if not I'll see if I can help when we get back. Tell you what; I'll introduce you to my manager.'

'It could be a real chance couldn't it. There will be useful people around. Chris,' she said suddenly 'can you teach me things?'

'What things.'

'I don't know?' she said. 'Things, science and books and art. I don't know anything.'

'You know about people,' I said 'and survival. You teach me how to deal with people and I'll teach you a lot of facts about how things work.'

'Deal.' she said. 'Tell me how aeroplanes fly.'

I laughed. 'Now?'

'Yes.'

I explained starting with air being a gas and with many questions worked my way to wings creating lift. She was quick, and picked up the principles easily.

'Is that all it is?' She was quite disappointed.

That night contrary to my expectations she invited me into my bed. I had no feeling of love, but she was attractive and she reawakened a need.

I cuddled her gently, desire and affection slowly filling my emptiness whilst despite her denials; her response suggested that she was paying a debt. I felt a moment of sadness.

'What?' She was looking at me intently to see if I was making a fool of her. 'Don't look at me like that.' She frowned again. 'Just get on with it.'

'You are lovely when you aren't cross, so stop frowning.' I brushed my thumbs across her forehead and kissed the tip of her nose.

'Stop it!' She continued to frown, 'Stop being stupid!' but she relaxed a little.

We lay cuddled together; I had my guilt trip and worried about disease and she gave me a compliment.
'Pig!' she whispered, then, uncertain. 'That was lovely.'
I enjoyed the moment.
The light came on and she sat up, pert breasts and pale skin. She had nice eyes, not as expressive as Al's, but bright.
'Can we have a serious talk?' I nodded a sleepy affirmative.
'I can't afford to give too much.' she began.
'I don't expect ....'
'Shut up for a minute. I've learned not to trust people.' The relaxed face hardened. 'I shouldn't even say that; don't be disappointed if I'm not what you expect.'
'All I expect is for you to be straight with me. Anyway,' I added 'you don't need me now.'
'Do you want me to go?'
How could I explain? 'Listen, it is simple, we are friends who support each other, I support you and you support me. Apart from that, no commitments and no expectations OK?'
'Deal.' She relaxed, smiled and looked much prettier. 'I think we might be a bit more than friends.' She knelt beside me.
I gazed at the slim firm dancers body; a fatuous grin spreading over my face. My hand slid over my eyes and I reached for the light switch. 'I'm worn out.'
She eased across and sat on my stomach. 'Fibber!' she said, and began to tickle me.

I was late for practice the following day and got a bollocking from Bruce followed by 'You lecherous bastard, Smithy will crucify you.'
I had given Sarah some money to get a new outfit promising her that that night we would go out and celebrate.
It was another long hard day, but the band was nearly on top of the music and I was relaxed when we arrived at an

Indian restaurant chosen by Sarah looking attractive in a new yellow dress.

Indian food was not my favourite but it was her night and it certainly did not inhibit her dancing which provoked lustful thoughts when later in a Club she gyrated around me.

Bruce would have described her as a bloody expensive shag, but it was a subject on which he missed the point. The good feelings that came from seeing the dispirited girl of a few days earlier transformed into her sparky optimistic self were well worth the small costs involved.

It had required more effort than she knew to get her an audition; if I discovered she had used me, well too bad; she would lose a friend and I would never have had one.

She had asked Bruce what she would be paid and been told 'Ask your boyfriend.'

I could only guess and made a quick estimate based on limited knowledge.

She gripped my shirt. 'How much, are you lying?'

'No, but it is just a guess, I think that is about what they will be paying'

Her face was that of a younger Sarah overwhelmed by a present. The difference in our circumstance...there but for fortune...I felt guilty and hugged her as if she were a child that I had upset. 'Sarah, it's a guess, I shouldn't have said anything.' I released her.

'Alison calls you a sod doesn't she?'

'Sometimes, I don't think she knows what it means.'

'You are a sod; you just play with people's emotions.'

I was hurt by her bitterness then suddenly it was gone again. 'Don't mean that but you'll never understand.' She punched me then hugged me. 'Chris! You don't think I'm promiscuous do you? I'm not!' she added before I could reply. 'Sometimes circumstances...it isn't easy.'

During our club tours I had seen prostitutes with potential clients; had seen the superficial enthusiasm and the absence of engagement; had become used to the euphemisms that protected their self-respect. My righteous disapproval had dissipated rapidly to a kind of sympathy then a live and let live indifference.

Al, chatting happily to a girl of her own age in a club was shocked when later Dave pointed to her as she left with a client. 'But she's nice, surely she couldn't, not with that fat old man, he's old, surely…oh Chris what should we do.'

Darling Al, she cried when Dave explained.

I knew Sarah was playing it down, but it mattered to her and that was enough. Affection defeated the cynic and I hugged her tighter.

When we got back to the flat she was all over me, uninhibited, vibrant, and even affectionate.

It would need to stop. The band was through the worst, but Sarah's effort was just beginning. Starting the following day she had less than two weeks to be word and timing perfect.

The practice? Sarah walked or rather danced it. She was more used to the discipline than I was, and had the words and the timing right in three days, and the simple dance routines arranged in two more. She had devised some simple natural movements for Bruce and me which introduced a kind of confrontational style to our dual guitar parts. I had a really happy moment as she pushed and shoved Bruce around showing him what to do. 'Crispy!' he bellowed as she gave her orders. 'Keep your effin' tart under control.' Even Vince was laughing.

As the date of departure approached I went to see Alison to say goodbye for three months. I loved her and the situation with Sarah did not affect our relationship. (It would have if she had known).

I was ashamed of the deceit. My self-justification (and I really needed one), was that Sarah would keep me out of mischief. I had already seen enough to know that the opportunity to mess up my life was there.

I was beginning to find my feet again emotionally and there had been a couple of moments when Al and I had come together.

During an evening at the cinema we had held hands and smiled.

I kissed her and said 'I know.' I slipped an arm around her and we cuddled together in a warm intimate bundle. I felt her relax. 'Love you presh.'

Most of my luggage had gone ahead and my journey was by train. The prospect of a long parting was a wrench and my departure at the station difficult with both of us struggling not to cry. The train had reached Reading before I was able to focus on the task ahead.

There were a couple of photographers at the airport, primarily to see Bruce but I managed to ease into some of the photos. I had given up worrying about self- publicity, treating it as fun rather than something to be dreaded.

C.P. had come a long way since his first season. Much of the change was not for the better, but the ability to laugh at myself was still there and a strong conviction that it would all come crashing about my ears kept my feet firmly on the ground most of the time.

I had no illusions about my role. I was a competent stand-in who could play the music and had learned enough about performance to do a pretty good job of faking Tony. When the real thing was fit it would be 'Goodbye Phillips!' if that.

For the moment however, I was part of it, I was going to enjoy it and give it my best shot.

I had staked Sarah, could do nothing else until she was paid. My feelings were ambivalent; she had shown her support but part of me hoped that she would find a new boyfriend now that she was working. She arrived looking like a star, made a beeline for me, dropped her luggage and hugged me.

'Hi Sarah! Good to see you.'

'Good to see you,' she replied. 'What do you think? She twirled, looking neat in a white dress with her blond hair clipped into a ponytail with a white flower.

'I though you didn't want me lusting for you?'

'Didn't say that.' She looked at me. 'We will need to do something about your hair. I'll make enquiries.'

'What's wrong with it?'

'The cut is fine,' she said, 'but the streaks must go.'

'Don't start taking liberties!' I meant it. 'I'm edgy and…'

'And what?'

'Forget it. I don't make scenes in public. Anyway you look great.'

She laughed. 'You are priceless.'

'Don't start any put-downs. Really,' I was serious, 'I'll take a certain amount, but don't push it.'

'I'm here to support you.' She jumped up and down. 'I'm so excited.'

The first week passed in a whirl of interviews coupled with a TV performance where the band mimed to an earlier hit, failed to look tough (except for Vince who couldn't look anything else) and, much to their annoyance played without the backing singers. The week ended with our first major concert.

I knew what to expect though it was twice as big as anything before. Theatres, even big theatres gave a sense of being part of something; this gave a sense of smallness, a cog in a machine. Even the buzz beforehand had a different quality, the harsh metallic chatter of an exhibition rather than anticipatory murmur of theatre. I found that I had to work harder physically to get any sense of reaching the audience and I still had to play the notes.

Sarah had no experience of venues of that size and was nervous. She and her fellow singer had not hit it off; each despising the other though their differences were concealed onstage.

Nervous myself I managed a hug and reassurance before her confidence reasserted itself. The experience had its upside; Sarah learned how to say 'Thanks.' without feeling that she was indebted to her helper.

Her gratitude was inconsistent. 'Don't patronise me! or 'Get lost.' was often heard, but sometimes she managed a reluctant 'Thanks Chris.' accompanied by a sideways look.

We were sharing a room, companionship and occasionally sex.

The sex was infrequent, but one day Al would surely fix me with a hurt look, ask about it, and I would rightly feel like shit.

Too bad, I was in a band that was rocking. Sarah was my shield from the girls, the drugs and some of the pressures. I learned what 'great in bed' meant and about mutual support. It was friendship rather than love but in the circumstances it was exactly what I needed.

The tour was great; bigger than anything I had known, and if they sold out, a couple of the venues would be huge. I was giving 110% until I began to feel tired. Bruce noticed and helped out with some uppers. I had promised Al to avoid any kind of 'substance' but that was before I knew the workload.

It was Sarah who phoned Dave. Where she got his number I don't know, but it carried me through a good time that might have gone bad. I never forgot it.

CHAPTER 6   Life on The Outside

Dave hailed an airport taxi for himself and Alison. 'Can you tell me which hotel would the band 'king Rock' use?'

'Which hotel what?'

'If a major rock band was playing the local stadium which hotel would they use?' Dave repeated the question.

'How would I know? You two groupies?'

'I'm the girlfriend of the guitarist'.

The 'Sure.' that came in response managed at once to be polite agreement and an expression of disbelief.

The taxi dropped them in front of the foyer of a hotel that seemed to cover half a block and Dave collected their luggage whilst the Alison paid the driver.

'Do I know your face?' he asked her.

'I was here with a band called 'Synergy'. We had a record in the charts two years ago.'

'Well how about that! He thought for a moment. 'And you were one of the two chicks?'

'Yes I was!' She answered with emphasis.

They enquired at the desk if the members of 'king Rock' were staying and were informed by the helpful receptionist that she could not disclose that information.

Dave, knowing Alison's inclination to scowl and even stamp her foot when faced with setbacks, took over and explained the situation, asking 'If they gave their names, would it be possible to make enquiries?'

The receptionist smiled at him. 'I'm sure that will be possible'.

She made her way to a small office and returned a few minutes later.

'I understand they are staying at another hotel.' Her tone implied that there had been a mistake.

'Could you guess... ?' Dave changed tack, 'Apart from this one, which other hotel would a major band be likely to choose?'

There were two.

A taxi took them to the nearest hotel; situated about a quarter of a mile away on the other side of the wide highway lined with large, magnificently undistinguished buildings. Excepting the colour and the theme that ran through its decoration, it could have been the same hotel.

A receptionist politely listened to their enquiries and informed them that the band was in residence but was unavailable.

Alison gave Chris' name and her own and asked if they could contact him. 'We are close friends,' she explained, 'and would like to see him as soon as possible.'

'We will do our best' she was told brightly.

They registered and made their way to adjoining rooms on the third floor.

'You realise' said Dave as the lift ascended 'she means you will go on the list with the rest of the tarts who are trying to scrape an acquaintance.'

'But Chris and I are practically married.'

'They don't know that. As far as the hotel is concerned you are just another groupie.' He let it sink in.

For the first time since their reunion Al felt she was on the outside of Chris's life and she didn't like it.

Dave waited for the lower lip to quiver and put an arm around her. Alison brushed at her eyes. 'Sorry.'

'Don't worry precious; we've been lucky to find them so quickly.'

He stopped at the door of her room. 'Go and have a sleep girl. I'll make some more enquiries and I'll see if I can get some tickets for the concert. Maybe we can catch them there.'

They caught them on stage, a stage that backed on to one side of the sports pitch, the other three sides comprising the auditorium. There must, she estimated, be eight thousand people there.

The PA had developed into a wall of speakers on each side of the stage and Chris's rig had doubled in size; a pair of Marshal 4x12s now supported a pair of 100w amps. The 335 was there, but the LP junior was replaced by a second 335 and was supplemented by a new acoustic. She was wondering what kind of set up he was using when the stage went dark.

The buzz of expectation, a delay, then a single chord rang out and a spot picked out Bruce, foot on monitor, he raised a fist, the audience cheered and the drums came crashing in together with a driving rhythm from the bass. The fourth spot, this time yellow, and there was Chris in black and red with a bandanna around his blonde hair. In the three months since Al had seen the band, they had become tighter musically and wilder visually.

'Good lord.' Dave muttered to himself.

If Al noticed, she was already too carried away to care.

After two numbers she turned to Dave 'Isn't it brilliant'.

It was the third song that brought her down to earth. The backing singers appeared for the first time and Al had immediately recognised Sarah. 'Oh my god, Dave, how could he? The beast!!' she said. 'Dave! D'you see, do you see!'

'I see!' Dave shouted back. 'Don't jump to conclusions Al, I'll tell you about it later.'

The concert got wilder but for Alison a mixture of hurt and anger replaced the excitement and when in the last number Chris did a back to back solo with Sarah, mimicking something that he had done with Sue on Television she began to feel sick.

By the time they had exited the stadium, found a taxi and been deposited at the hotel entrance, her spirit had returned and it was a very cross girl that marched to reception and asked if they had contacted the band.

'And what name is that?' the receptionist asked sweetly.

'Alison Smith'

'Just a moment Miss Smith'. She disappeared and returned with a very smartly dressed young man carrying a list.

'Alison Smith? Are you alone?'

'No I'm here with Dave Jones'.

'Would that be Al Smith?'

'Of course it would'.

He motioned to second young man.

'Will you take Miss Smith and her friend to the 'king Rock's suite. Thank you'.

He looked at Al and decided she wasn't a hooker, but if not, why the heavy? Ah well; his mind shifted to a problem of payments.

They were taken to the 10th floor and led to a corridor that ran down one wing. At the head of the corridor stood a large black security man in a dinner jacket. From further down the corridor there was the sound of music and the noise of a party.

'They started early' Dave said in Al's ear.

'It's nearly 12' she snapped.

'Two for 'king Rock' said the young man 'Al Smith and Dave Jones'.

The big man checked his list. 'Ok'.

'Right Phillips,' said Al 'get out of this.' Her face set, she strode down the corridor.

'Hold on a bit.' David gripped her arm.

'Let go, what are you doing.'

'I want to talk to you.' He was pulling her back.

'Let go!' she was getting angry. He dragged her round to face him.

'Al, I want a talk with you. Now!' He saw her eyes blazing at him.

'Come on Al, I don't want to fall out but you are going to listen. I mean it'.

'All right! Let go of me then.' She calmed as fast as she had become fired up. She was breathing deeply.

Dave turned to the bouncer 'Are any of the rooms free?'

The big man smiled 'I think this one at the end. It's open' he added.

Dave pulled Al inside, switched on the light and shut the door.

'Sit down precious'

Al chose a small settee. 'Well? What is it all about?'
He pulled up a chair and sat facing her.
'Friends?'
'Of course we are.'
'Are friends people who give good advice?'
'Just get on with it.'
'What were you going to do just now?'
'I was going to give that sod Phillips a piece of my mind and tell him...'
'And tell him what? That it's all over, he can forget you?'
'We've travelled four thousand miles to give him support because he's under pressure and going a bit wild and your first action is to make it worse.'
'Are you saying I should ignore it?' Al was incredulous. 'Just pretend nothing's happened when he's screwing that vile little Sarah tart.'
'Al, I'm going to tell you something you won't like'.
'What?'
'I sometimes wonder why Chris puts up with you; there are girls beating down doors to get at him, and he sticks to someone who takes him for granted'.
'Me?? I certainly don't, you've got a short memory.'
'You do love. He was always running round after you giving support and you took it for granted'.
'Didn't ask him to.' Her eyes began to fill.
'Al.' Dave moved and sat next to her and put an arm around her shoulders. 'Do you really care about him?'
'Of...' Al said, and stopped. 'I liked him' she said after a few moments, 'when I first saw you both at the folk club. I fell in love when I spoke to him at the 'Hog Roast' and I got hurt for the first time when you said he had a girlfriend. I've been protecting myself against being hurt ever since.'
Dave put a second arm around her and her head rested on his shoulder.
'The only time I've ever felt he was mine I was so happy that I let Sue share a little bit of him.'
'Why?' said Dave
'It's too crazy to tell. I was feeling confident and I wanted

them to be friends but of course being *a man* Chris got it completely wrong. He thought I didn't care; I didn't realise Sue was such a tart. Even then I thought Chris and I would carry on as before. Really Dave, it would sound crazy'.

'We all suffer temptations. If he's having a fling with Sarah do you still want him?'

'No I don't! He's a two faced adulterous sod.'

'Really?'

Al went quiet.

'He is! I don't know; I suppose so. Why, why when I am just getting myself together does he knock me down again? Why?'

'I don't know I can't imagine why he would want anyone but you. Are you sure you want him?'

'Oh don't tease Dave. We are just right for each other and I love him to bits. That's why it hurts so much. Do I really give him a hard time?'

'Sometimes, yes you do'.

'I'll try to grow up a bit.'

Dave released her and stood up. 'Right, I'm going to find out what's going on. You are staying here.'

He turned. 'It was Sarah who phoned me. She said he was struggling and suggested I had better come and bring you with me.' Alison was left to digest the implications of this revelation.

He returned 10 minutes later to find her standing by the window. She turned. 'Where's Chris? Is he all right? Isn't he here?'

'Calm down, he's alright, more or less, and he's here.'

'What's the matter with him?'

'He just got a bit high on something and was sick. They helped him to his room'.

The statement caused immediate panic. Stories of pop artists who had choked on their own vomit came back to her.

'Quick,' she said 'we must go to him.'

'It's Ok' said Dave smiling 'Sarah's with him. And take that expression off your face. Tell me, before that problem at the party, did you get on with her?'

'Sarah? I had to, but I never trusted her with Chris, never.'

'And you assumed you couldn't trust Chris with her?'

'I couldn't.'

'I've been talking to her; she's fond of him, was quite open about it. She said she'd have done anything, but he got her the job in the show out of kindness. The idiot could have had his pick but he chose her. Sorry Al I didn't mean it like that, I meant...'

'I know what you meant. You mean Goldilocks didn't ask for any favours; I'll bet the sod didn't turn them down though.' *'Stop smiling!!'*

'You can understand why she's grateful. One week she's at the arse end of the profession doing strip clubs and the next Chris gets her into a high profile tour out of kindness. As long as the tour lasts she's got two ambitions, to impress and get contacts, and to give him support.'

'Is that true, Dave?'

'I think so, she treats him like a friend and it's mutual, if there is anything else I don't want to know. She's looking after him like you would, protects him from predatory fans, and from what I've seen already it could be worse. At least you know where you are with Sarah; there are some very dodgy females around.'

'Oh fine, thank-you Dave, I'm so pleased that he's faithful to one whore at a time.'

'Don't be coarse Al, it doesn't suit you. Anyway, I seem to remember a girl with an adoring boyfriend who couldn't get enough admiration and praise.'

'I don't believe this, the sod is being unfaithful and I'm in the wrong!'

'I didn't mean that, don't twist things. I meant that a friendship, whatever, with Sarah is better than a different whore every night.'

'Is it? You would be pleased to find out that Judith only has one lover rather than dozens?' Her head dropped and she bit her lip. 'Right! Let's go and see my paragon of hypocrisy?'

The paragon was sitting on the bed and Sarah was drying his face with a towel.

'Alison darling!' he started to get up, 'Sarah is looking after me.'

'I know, unpaid nursemaid and…Dave told me.'

She sat on the bed. 'You're a sod Phillips. Are you all right?'

He took her hand and sank back against the pillows. 'God, I feel rough. Sarah protects me from the worst excesses but it's still tough. I put in a word for her and…' he nodded at Sarah, 'she's been a real support.'

Sarah looked at Alison. 'I was desperate and he helped me. Looking after him,' she smiled at Chris, 'and he needs it, is my way of repaying him.'

'One way.' Al muttered to herself. 'So am I number two again?' There was anger as well as hurt.

'Don't be ridiculous, Sarah knows how things are between us and so should you.' He put an arm around her shoulders. 'Don't be anxious,' he gave her a squeeze. 'Sarah saves me from a lot of the hassle.'

'I expect the Pope will be conferring sainthood on the pair of you. Does the Vatican allow yellow hair?'

She flicked at the blond hair. 'Something else for me to get used to and what's…oh Chris, an earring?'

'Is it over the top?'

'Yes. But I rather fancied you when I saw you on stage; until I knew it was you.'

'Al!' Dave spoke over her shoulder.

'What?'

'*Support.*' He mouthed with a frown. 'Do you think you could take me to the party Sarah my lovely? If there are any fights, I might pick up some customers'.

Sarah seemed reluctant, then with a shake of her head. 'Is that supposed to be Welsh charm? It's only a noisy drunken party like all the others, I can't see the attraction.' She rose and joined him.

As they left Dave was heard to say 'You are the attraction.

Looking really terrific young Sarah.'

'You haven't changed a bit have you?'

The voices faded.

Left alone, Al snuggled closer to Chris.

'Why is Sarah here is she my new rival?'

'She's part of the band and she supports me, she's not a threat to you.'

'You like her, don't you'.

'I've grown to like her; she's one of those sparky characters, full of life, and optimism. She asked me for help and when eventually I said 'Ok' her next words were 'you won't regret it.' She knows people and how to deal with them'.

'Probably had most of them.'

'For christ's sake Al, even if you take her stories with a pinch of salt, she hasn't had an easy time, and she's been a good friend.' Chris frowned. 'This has nothing to do with 'us'. I just want you to be clear that at the moment I need her help.'

'You are a selfish beast; have you any idea what you are doing to me. Any idea at all?'

'The reason she is here and not you, is because with all the randy men around, you would be an additional worry.'

'Affection?' said Al.

'Yes'

'Anything else? Tell me the truth…No don't.' she said quickly.

'All I know is that I am a stand-in with a band that is hot and I can't fake it, I have to let go and *be* the 'Rockstar' that we used to joke about. I love you Alicat…'

'But?'

'I have to be bloody selfish to survive this tour, I need Sarah's support.'

'I don't trust her with my Chris'.

'Listen love, I've never asked you for much, but please stick with it 'till the end of the tour, and try not to give me any extra bloody pressure.'

They sat in silence.

'Why are you sitting here in bed with a party going on' Al asked suddenly.

'Because I'm tired and I try to avoid getting stoned as well. Sarah makes sure I get some sleep.' He tailed off. 'I thought I was pretty fit but I'm finding it tough.'

'Are you enjoying it?'

'It's certainly something. We've got thirty two concerts in eight weeks, then two big ones at the end. I think the next one is the eighteenth, and all I've seen of the USA is a set of identical hotels in identical streets'.

'Are you going to stay?' he asked suddenly.

'Do you want me to stay?'

'Of course I do, but I'm scared I'll lose you to the lifestyle. If you stay you must try to get on with Sarah?'

'You want your girlfriends to get on. We've been here before'.

'Well let's hope you've learned from your mistakes'.

He spoke with a firmness she was unused to 'I mean it Al; we've got a second chance.'

'Shut up Phillips' she interrupted 'I'm not letting you go again. And yes, I can 'get on' with Sarah, it won't be easy but I couldn't go home now.'

He rested his head back on the pillow.

'What a useless life, ninety per cent emotion and ten per cent substance. No more excuses Al, when you have been here for a couple of weeks you'll understand.'

Five minutes later he was asleep.

Al looked at him; hardly changed from the boy of five years before except for a few hard lines around a more determined mouth and the hint of a crease on his forehead. She leaned down and kissed him, and then slipping out of the room she joined the party.

The party seemed somewhat scattered, but the main event was taking place in the rooms at the end of the corridor, and it was towards these that she headed.

Her entrance through an open door confirmed her

assumption but she was unprepared for the size of the room. It filled the whole corner of the building with windows on two sides that gazed over the brightly-lit cityscape.

There were probably thirty or forty people in the room and her first glance took in at least two of the band members and a blonde, recognised from an earlier visit backstage.

An arm went round her shoulder and she was rotated and lifted by a hand under her bottom.

'It's the lovely Alison Smith' said Bruce and kissed her before depositing her back on her feet. She suppressed a feeling of annoyance at the familiarity and even more firmly a recollection that her mother to been to a party with him.

The latter action was immediately undone by the question 'Is the lovely Diane with you?' and the following comment 'Nice lady.' left her red faced and dumb.

'A drink for Smithy.' She was propelled across the room to a kind of bar with an attendant.

'This will sort you.' He half-filled a tumbler with Southern Comfort and passed it to her.

It was a drink she had never tasted. She took a sip, pleasant but quite strong.

'Not like that, a good mouthful, round the mouth and straight down. Go for it'.

She obliged, took a mouthful and swallowed. It seemed as if her mouth, throat and stomach caught fire at the same time. She coughed, choked and reached for a can of lager lying in a bowl of crushed ice. Two large mouthfuls and her throat and mouth came back under control. She drained the can.

'Dance!' said Bruce, and seizing her arm pulled her to an area where a dozen people were dancing in an uninhibited fashion, one of the girls she noticed wore a dress that concealed little.

It had been an exhausting day and the drink the noise and the atmosphere began to affect her.

She could see Dave smooching with Sarah in a corner by the window but couldn't quite work out why it seemed inappropriate. Bruce had disappeared and she found herself dancing with a swarthy young man who was telling her about life on the road.

'Do you fuck?' he said.

'Only with people I like' she replied, feeling that some sort of put down was needed.

'I'm good' he said. 'You'd like me'.

She found the answer coarse and his unconcerned openness scared her.

'Yes, I'd like you to fuck off.' she said, turning away, slightly pleased that she could descend to his level.

'You a dyke? Probably a fukin dyke.' she heard over her shoulder. Her tiredness, the stress of the day, the drink and his comment provoked sudden and unreasoned anger and she spun on the balls of her feet and gave him a straight right, hitting through as Chris had taught her. The man staggered back, a thin smear of blood coming from his nose. He bunched his fists and came towards her. 'Fu...' he managed before Bruce grabbed hold of him.

He was shaking with laughter 'What a girl, did you see that punch'.

'He was going to attack me!'

'Too right, he was going to thump you, what would you expect after you smack him in the mouth. I'll give you some advice Smithy; you start throwing punches you'd better be sure you are going to land the last one. This isn't Cheltenham' he added a little more kindly. He released the swarthy man.

'No hard feeling Jo. Girl doesn't know the rules; give her a break this once ok!'

'If you say so, this time...effing dyke.' The look was threatening. 'Keep outa my face tart.' He made a threatening movement and she recoiled. 'Another time...' He jerked a fist and she stepped back.

Al sat down. She was shaking and her knuckles were bleeding. She felt a hand on her arm and looked up to see Sarah.

'In trouble already?'

Al tried to imagine being at the bottom of the heap, no

Chris, no Dave, on her own like Sarah.

'Sarah' she said 'I feel such a fool. I've just learned another lesson'.

'You were unlucky, most of them are ok. Jo's a pig ignorant prat, but he's a dammed good worker and he knows the business.'

'Oh God, I feel drunk, I can't have been here more than half an hour.'

'Do I need to put both of you to bed?'

Al managed a smile 'Dave will do that, can you ask him to take me to my room.'

As Dave walked back with her she put her arm through his.

'I'm a fool. You were rite...right, I've taken Chris for granted, I take Mum for granted, I lean on you, and t'night I behaved like a school prefect.'

'That was a rough school you attended.'

'Shut up.' Her humour returned and she turned to face him. 'You don trealise the importance of being with people who think the same way s'you until you meet aliens. Family s'easy, then school, then work and people like Sarah who're different but ...what was I saying? Compared with people like Jo she seems like a best friend.'

'You have been talking with Phillips. Be warned beautiful, too much thinking and you will become warped like him.'

'You are hopelesh.' She groaned 'Oh Dave, I'm tiddly. When Sarah talked to me I tried to think what it would be like if she wass his girlfriend and I was so grateful for a job that I helped him and succepted her.'

'You wouldn't'. Dave squeezed her arm. 'That isn't your style, anyway, Chris loves you.'

'What does that mean? Sol wanted t' do it, and others I s'pose, and Gary did do it. You're really good to me, does that mean you want t' do it?'

'I suppose so,' she sensed a slight change, 'you are a special kind of friend and I have feelings for you. Your fling with Gary upset me.'

'Why? D'you care too?' She hugged his arm tightly.

They had reached her room.

'Are you going back to the party?'

'Indeed I am I'm not a hardened rock star like you and Chris.'

'Could you give me a hug without getting too lushful…lustful.' Al asked.

'No?' he replied and put his arms around her.

Sarah slipped into Chris's bedroom and moved towards the shower annex stopping for a moment to look at the figure sprawled untidily over his bed. In her six years of professional dancing she had seen a number of men in similar positions.

She liked him; he wasn't the fool she had once thought. Maybe he didn't have the drive to make it to the top, but he had been kind when she needed kindness and he was straight with her. He was the closest thing to a male friend she'd ever had and she liked the feeling.

Moving over to the bed she began to undress him. He half woke as she pulled the covers from under his body and she stood quietly looking at him until he drifted off to sleep again.

Damn Alison Smith. Maybe not, she had been clear from the beginning that she could not afford affection, yet the last time, a week earlier, she had let go, laughing and crying. Afterwards he had held her gently as if she were precious and gazed at her so lovingly that she had looked away, afraid of an emotion that was stalking her.

Perhaps the Smith woman had arrived at the best time, before she said something stupid like "I love you".

She stripped and slipped into the other bed.

She was still there when Al popped a head around the door next morning. Had she been awake she would have seen a face that went from shock to anger and slowly to something new, certainly not acceptance, possibly resignation.

Al withdrew surprised at her own calmness as she took the

lift back to her floor.

Suppressing her initial temptation to confront had given her time to take stock of the scene. She felt a wave of anger that Sarah had spent the night with her Chris; anger diminished only a little by their separate beds.

Her knock on Dave's door was rewarded with a 'Come in' and she entered to find him on the telephone. He motioned her to sit down. 'Alison' he said. 'No, of course not'. 'Judith' he mouthed at her. 'No, no, tomorrow I expect. No! Al bought the tickets... yes, love you too!' He put the phone down.

'Everything alright?'

'More or less. Judith is missing me.'

'I'm sorry Dave. It was selfish of me to ask you to come but I couldn't have managed on my own.'

She stroked his shoulder affectionately, unconscious of the effect that her vulnerable sexuality had, even on close friends.

'Are you alright?'

'Not really.' Tears began to trickle despite a determination to be strong.

'Tell Uncle Dave.'

She told him. She told him everything, the break up, Gary, the band, her breakdown, finding Chris again, new hope and now a fear that everything was slipping away. She was gathered up hugged and comforted.

'I'm sorry to lean on you.'

'I will tell you a truth which I should not tell.' His face was serious. 'Judith was unhappy about my coming with you; she knows I care about you.' He pulled himself together. 'In the meantime, Phillips is going to get a serious talking too. The Jones' have warned him before about treating their favourite girl badly.'

'I don't deserve you.' Then with a lightening change of mood, 'Are you coming to breakfast'.

'Just need a shower and a shave.' 'Do not worry, I will sort things out.'

He was a long time.

'I'll be in my room' Al shouted over the singing and splashing.

She returned to her room and went to the window looking out over a vast and characterless city-scape feeling again a sense of living on the outside, of not being a part of things. A sense of desolation crept over her.

A knock and it was Chris. She ran to him and as his arms closed around her.

'Good Morning Al presh.'

'Morning Phillips.'

'Sorry about last night. Shattered.' He explained. 'It's fantastic to see you.' The world came back into colour. 'Are you coming to breakfast?'

'I'm waiting for Dave. His shower seems to last until he has sung his entire repertoire of Welsh hymns'.

'Dave's the salt of the earth. You don't understand what real friends are until you're in a situation like this.

'Is it hard?'

Chris thought 'Hard isn't the right word, not when you are part of the band; debilitating is closer. The performing gives you a tremendous high and old Morris is being friendly so the money must be huge. I guess it gives everything many people would want but there is nothing really there, just noise, rush, colour…and sex.'

'It's a bit early to analyse the world'. She knew that when Chris began to analyse he could go on until the entire room was asleep.

'I know.' He smiled at her.

'Sleep well?' she asked.

'Like a log. I thought you had come in with me but it was Sarah…oh sh..! She just tucked me in and slept in the other bed.' He looked concerned, and then his face creased into a grin. 'Some rock star.'

'You are so insensitive! Can't you just be friends?'

'Dave said the same.'

'Well why can't you? It's cruel!'

'We are friends.'

A knock saved him from further explanations and from hearing the resentful 'And what do you think it does to me!'

'That will be Dave, let's go to breakfast'.

He took her hand. 'Are you going to stay? '

'I feel too insecure to leave'.

'No need to feel insecure.' It was her Chris that spoke, his sincerity dispelling some of her doubts.

'Come on, I've got so much to tell you'.

He was still talking when they finished the coffee.

A representative for Gibson had asked if Bruce if he would endorse their guitars. 'I was in the background as part of the band; me, in a publicity shot for a guitar.'

'They only wanted Bruce and the guy laughed when he saw my backup guitar and said if I had any particular ideas as to what I would like, they would do me a custom at cost price.'

'Useless.' Al's muttered, but her mind had wandered only Dave maintaining a degree of interest.

'...so I asked if they could do a standard 335 but wine coloured with a flame front and a white pickguard. Just standard really and...'

Al watched two sober suited businessmen discussing some point of mutual interest on a nearby table. One looked up, met her eyes and smiled. She smiled back.

'...so I still use Sue's 335 and they found one with a flame front, it's not the right colour but the price is the same in dollars as I would pay in pounds in the U.K. Our technician set it up to be similar to...

'Brilliant.' Dave interrupted. 'You must show me before I go back.'

'I was using it last night. Didn't you notice?'

'From where we were sitting,' Dave said, 'you could have been playing a banjo.'

'Didn't you notice the inversions I was playing when I was doing the arpeggios over Bruce's lead?'

'Chris boyo, I could see you had two legs and that was about it. Sorry.'

There was a momentary look of disappointment, and then

the grin returned. 'Dave mate it's so good to talk to someone who listens and can take the piss without point scoring. Anyway,' he leaned back in his chair 'that's enough of me, tell me about you and Judith' He waved to Sarah who was collecting a late breakfast. She came to join them and kissed his cheek.

'Not a lot to tell' Dave was saying. 'Except we are expecting our second'.

Their conversation returned to friends and family and children.

It left Alison missing the children and Sarah feeling discontent.

Dave returned home two days later. Before his departure he had spoken to Alison explaining that he had taken Chris aside after breakfast and had a brief but to the point conversation.

'What did you say?'

'I told him 'Cats whiskers' was reforming and you didn't know how to break it to him.'

'They aren't. Why?'

'The rat needed a shock. I said Gary had been appointed road manager and you were friends again.'

'You didn't?'

'He went white. "Why didn't she tell me?" he said.'

'Like you told her about Sarah? Come on mate. She's had a few dates with an old boyfriend in Bristol, it isn't serious but he's keen on her and she found it difficult to tell *him* she was going back on the road and she knew you wouldn't be happy about it.'

'Too bloody right I'm not happy; Gary was the bastard who was shagging her…damn!' 'What old boyfriend in Bristol?'

'Just an old boyfriend she's dated a few times.' I said. 'She isn't too concerned about Gary. She said "Chris knows that I love him and I'm pretty sure that anything between me and Gary is over."'

'Dave! That's really mean.' Al was delighted.

'He was getting more and more worried, and I mean *really* worried so I went for the kill. "Anyway mate, she's strong enough to cope with you and Sarah, I guess you have to cope with the possibility of her and Gary getting it together."'

'You think it's that easy? God, this is just the kind of pressure I don't need.'

'Then he must have seen the parallels with his situation and he frowned then looked me in the eye.

'Hang on Jones,' he said, 'are you taking the piss?' And I laughed and he glared then said. 'You absolute bastard. God you don't bloody change.'

Then he laughed and hugged me. 'Bloody welsh... thanks Dave mate, I know I'm being a rat, but it isn't as bad as it seems. This band is tough and Sarah is a real help, anything else, and there isn't much is nothing, affection, honestly. Al has always been my true love I promise you, and if she stays she will be my future I promise you that too.'

Dave was seized and hugged.

'Thanks David darling thank-you.' She stood back and smiled. 'How did you know about the old boyfriend?'

'Now do not start making me jealous! If you are going to be nice to other men, be nice to David.'

'There's nothing to be jealous about. A few dates and a few hugs and kisses, nothing else; God Dave, I know I'm supposed to be a saint but I need a life while Phillipest is gallivanting round the world with his tart.'

'I know. I shouldn't tell the pest though.'

'Didn't intend to.'

The tour continued its relentless course and Alison discovered at first hand the pressures that it placed on Chris. The travel, often considerable distances, settling into hotels, maintenance of stage clothes and day clothes, the constant restringing, tuning and packing of instruments all took its toll. Then, at the new venue there was setting-up, balancing the sound and the interviews, always the same questions.

Chris had previously been open when interviewed,

answering truthfully, sometimes saying too much and the change was marked; his answers true but saying little.

She had asked what had happened to the garrulous guitarist from Synergy.

'He's become sensitive to cynicism.' he answered without looking at her.

There was also the pressure of performance. Her first concert in the wings of a huge venue, feeling nervous for him and finding at its end that she was exhausted by the moral support she had given.

Then there were the parties, the availability of highs, easy sex, drugs and strange practices, the darker side of people.

Chris had told it as it was; Sarah seemed like a friend, someone who understood and in her limited way followed the same moral code as herself. Even Bruce and the laid back Bep were normal, approachable compared to some, the cultureless, the rootless and the evil.

She discovered at first-hand how hard the roadies worked. Within two hours of the show finishing, the stage set was broken down and together with the amplification was rolling in the tour truck to be re–erected at the next destination. Over the eight weeks the truck would cover thousands of miles, often travelling on consecutive days to destinations hundreds of miles apart.

Not one to accept bad feeling, she sought out Jo and offered a sincere apology for her behaviour on the first night. To her surprise he accepted the tentative approach with more good nature than she had thought he possessed.

'Just don't try it again.'

'Oh I wouldn't dare Jo. I was very tired and drunk and stupid.' she said, which statement seemed to satisfy him.

'Hey' he said. 'Is it right, they say you were the other chick in the band Synergy?'

'Yes that was me.' She was sure that he wasn't that subtle.

Now that she understood the pressures and could see how cleverly Sarah had eased into his life she felt able to discuss her anxieties with Chris.

'Never expect me to 'understand' how you feel about another woman.' She told him. 'I'll try to be tolerant up to a point since you seem to need her.' She hesitated and added 'I don't hate her and in some ways we get on ok, but I don't trust her.'

'Angry?'

'Yes.'

'Angry enough to teach me a lesson when someone tells you that you are beautiful and your talents are being wasted?'

'Maybe. Probably not.'

Chris shrugged and a rush of thought ran around her head. He's struggling; too tired to fight; if he let her go she would cease to exist. One angry word or action and her whole life would change.

'No!' She continued hastily. 'No, of course not darling.' She flung her arms around him and clung to him. 'I love you but I feel hurt and I can't help being angry.'

'I would feel the same. I'm sorry.' They hugged and he kissed her with more passion than he had shown since their reunion.

It was left at that.

Two crises arose for Alison during the final three weeks of the tour, the first of her own making.

A very pretty actress had attended a post gig party where, flanked by a manager and a minder she had spoken to the members of the band making a huge impression on Chris.

Alison in pretty Marks and Spencer's underwear and her best black evening dress felt shabby and when told for the third time 'She really is gorgeous.' had scooped up iced water from a bowl and emptied it down the front of his trousers. This had caused a shout of laughter from Bruce who was nearby and in a flash she had dropped an ice cube down the neck of his shirt. 'You're just as bad!'

'Mistake Smithy!' was all he said. He was good-humoured as he cornered her but there was no escape. The top of her dress was pulled out and his tumbler of iced whisky was emptied down the front flooding through her cleavage into her pants.

The chill and the stinging provoked a scream and rushing to the nearest exit she dived into the corridor to find Chris removing his trousers. She rapidly removed her briefs.

Her escape was momentary, seized from behind, her dress was lifted to her hips and she was carried scarlet faced and kicking around the room before being deposited in the bowl of iced water.

Dripping and burning with more than humiliation she exited the room for a second time to the sound of laughter. Chris was still in the corridor wearing underpants and one shoe.

'I was attacked, why didn't you help?'

'Taking ice cubes out of my pants.'

Dripping together they made their way back to their room where Alison began to laugh. 'It's not funny.' Chris wasn't pleased.

Al was helpless 'I hope no one wants any ice in their drinks.' she stuttered.

The second and more significant incident occurred as the tour neared its end.

Sacha, the second of the backing singers had been concealing a throat infection, struggling on until her failings were noticed. She had been in tears at the thought of being replaced and it was Bruce who suggested Al could stand in. 'Six songs and some dancing; can you do it?' he said.

She took the suggestion with a calmness that masked a rising excitement saying she was really grateful for the opportunity.

'I've listened lots of times and I think I know it.'

Her first action was to reassure Sacha that the arrangement was temporary; her second to assure Chris that she hadn't slept with the management as Sacha had suggested.

For the rest of the morning she worked out her part for the songs. It seemed quite easy, straightforward harmonies on the choruses, a few difficult timings, and some simple dance routines. That afternoon she practised with Sarah and on the following morning with Chris playing acoustic guitar.

She was feeling good and was excited at the prospect of appearing on stage; in a support role it was true, but on a very large stage.

How large came home to her at that afternoon's setting-up.

She had joined the band several times, watching from the wings or from the back of the auditorium.

It was when she joined Sarah at her microphone that the size of the stage and the auditorium hit her.

Chris was far away below and to her left and apart from Sarah her nearest contact was Bep five metres to her right on a raised podium. She adjusted her microphone. 'Remember! Jack will set the volume, just listen to the monitor and sing with me.'

Chris had disappeared and Bruce called for their attention. He started to play Chris's part and, as the drums joined in began to sing with the drive that she had learned to recognise.

She missed her entry. Bruce stopped, glared, shouted an obscenity and started again. Her entry was note and timing perfect but she fluffed the second chorus. Told to remove her finger from 'that tight ass' and concentrate, the pressure began build but her third effort completed the whole passage and it was a relief when Bruce called Chris to take over and run through the rest of the songs.

Some of Bruce's manner had rubbed off; Chris' 'requests' were orders to be obeyed; discussions were confined to the technical experts.

In the nine months since her last gig she had lost her edge, had become an observer. After an hour of concentration she had regained her focus; she was there to do a job, not to enjoy the show. The enjoyment came when she could do the show backwards.

She was content as she rode back to the hotel with Chris, Sarah and one of the electricians with four hours before she was on stage again. The first was spent with Chris and Sarah running over the part again, after which the three of them curled up together on the double bed. It was something of a relief to note that with an arm around each of them Chris was asleep in minutes. Cuddling comfortably against him her own tiredness took over and minutes later she too dropped off.

She awoke to find Chris shaking her. 'Come on sleepy head, time for a quick snack.

She raised a tousled head, was kissed affectionately and, swinging her legs from the bed walked with him to the hotel restaurant.

Chris appetite appeared unaffected by nerves as he attacked a tuna salad. 'I hope none of the fans sees me,' he confided as he emptied a second cup of coffee, 'my image would be seriously dented.'

It raised a small smile. He smiled back.

Sarah, who was quite slight, managed a coffee and a bowl of mixed fruit, but Alison found her stomach closed. She had suffered nerves before, but never, except before her first big concert, to this extent.

Sarah was speaking to her '...I said, you are so lucky; they are filming tonight's concert.' This good news added another dimension to her rising terror.

She had to get on top of her nerves, she had to concentrate. It was impossible; the size of the stage was a deterrent, her lack of preparedness a worry. She must focus on her strengths. She could sing 'Great voice Smithy.' Bruce had said. She knew the words and the music, had them on a stand beside her, it was her entries, the timing and the difficulty of concentration. A knot formed in her stomach.

'Nervous?' Chris asked.

'Yes.' she said it quietly and saw him frown. He reached for her hand.

'You can do it; in the last run through you were better than Sacha.'

She was silent.

'If you lose it, fake it until you pick it up again.'
'Bruce will notice.'
'Yes'.
'He'll be horrible to me afterwards.'
'He'll roast you. You won't be the first, I cocked up a passage in one of the songs and I thought he was going to flatten me right in the middle of the show. Perhaps you shouldn't have agreed to do it.'

'Don't be silly, there are people who would kill for the chance and I had it handed on a plate. I need to do it but I am scared to death.'

'There's nothing I can say. You can do it bloody well and I'm confident that you will.'

'But?'

'But nothing. I might break a string, cut a finger, an amp might fail, worrying doesn't help but you can't avoid it.

Listen,' he took her hand, 'if you need to, count the bars and read the words. Rock'n roll it ain't but you'll sound good.'

The comment raised another smile.

She forced herself to shower, to pack the stage outfits, to run through some of the music, feeling sick with her stomach now a tight knot. She wanted to turn to Chris for comfort but knew that he was preparing himself mentally. Fifteen minutes before the car was scheduled to arrive, she broke down. It began with tears, then sobs.

'Al? Pull yourself together darling.'

'I can't.'

'Yes you can, you must!' He was edgy and abrupt.

'I can't!' she screamed and stood up and stamped her foot, 'I can't!' and for the first time since she was four, she wet herself. The final humiliation brought on stamping screaming hysterics.

Shocked for a moment Chris took her arm. 'Bathroom!' She was immovable.

What would Bruce do? Slap her face? Anger began to rise and in desperation he pushed her onto the bed and smacked her bottom hard enough to shock her out of the hysterics.

'Bathroom! Now!' he pulled her off the bed and propelled her in.

'Clean up! Change, I'll clean up in here. Now!' he growled again. Al, shocked at his anger, was at last silent.

'You make me look a bloody fool and you'll be sorry. Now clean yourself up, you're disgusting.'

He had never before been harsh with her. 'I...' she began, and gave up. She shut the bathroom door and began to clean herself. Five minutes later she exited clean and presentable with the red mark on her bottom tingling. An unsmiling Chris and a worried Sarah were waiting for her.

'Ready? Clothes? Music?'

'I need to go to my room for a moment.'

He picked up his spare guitar and gave her a hard look. 'Ok. Let's go'.

Chris hadn't spoken a word to her. She had gone through some breathing exercises in the wings and now Sarah slipped an arm round her waist. 'We'll be fine.' she said.

The band finished their second number to a roar of applause and she went on stage to a world of noise and light, a subdued pink spotlight hit her and as the band started she glanced at Sarah and began to move in time. The world shrank to her words and her movements and at the critical moment she started to sing; by halfway through the song she was less than terrified, by its end she knew she could do it; she was a singer with a band.

As they exited the stage at the end of the first half she turned a delighted face to Sarah. 'Thank you' she hugged her. 'Thank you, it all came back.'

Bruce, following behind smacked her bottom and she yelled.

'Well done, girlie.' He moved on to his dressing room. Al stood for a moment rubbing her bottom as Chris passed, ignoring her except for a nod.

Apart from a gruff 'Well done' he remained silent after

the second (wonderful) half was finished. The permitted autographs were signed and they made a rowdy exit in the hired car. He was silent until they arrived in the room they were sharing.

'Are you going to speak?' Al began.

She was held and pushed onto the bed.

'Get off.' What are you doing? He began to reach under her skirt.

'Don't you dare.' She was annoyed by his assumption and pushed him away. Behave yourself!'

He was lying on her, breathing heavily and began to move away.

'No!' she held him against her.

She had enjoyed it, at least, after an initial resentment at being taken for granted. She confronted a fear that had been with her since she was 17 when an automatic reaction had prevented a frightening situation from becoming damaging. In a loving situation her desires would often overcome her reluctance.

'Why? You're always so considerate with me.'

Chris reached for some paper towels and dabbed a scratched shoulder.

Pushing her arms away he rolled on to his back.

She curled against him. 'I've had a lot of learning to do today. My nerve went, then you frightened me, I've never seen you so angry.'

He remained silent. It had been an awful day, on edge and worried about her, losing his temper then smacking her bottom. She had performed wonderfully, just as he knew she could, and then he had wanted her so much that he practically forced her, the sick feeling returned.

She was kissing his shoulder.

'Chris,' she said, 'I love you, but that's not our way.'

He turned and stroked her arm. 'I know. Sorry, I can just cope with the situation most of the time, but when you threw a wobbler I had to be hard.' 'Please forgive me?'

'Of course I forgive you I love you, but we've always been equal partners and you shouldn't just assume its ok. I don't want it to be like that.'

'It isn't like that, tonight was…oh hell, I promise it won't happen again.' His face softened. 'You sang wonderfully tonight, you know that.'

He rested on an elbow and looked at her. 'Highs too high, and lows too low; this apology for a 'Rock Star' was being sick in the loo ten minutes before the start; it isn't the first time. The crazy thing is that it's all quite awful but I'll really miss it when it ends.'

Alison performed with Sarah on three more occasions and stepped down with reluctance. The adrenaline of performing at that level, of being part of the team was a drug that was addictive; she understood Chris's absolute dedication to the performance despite an ambivalent attitude to the scene.

The tour ended with a massive concert, the largest of the tour; Alison stood in the wings wishing that she had fought to keep her place in the band, hating not being a part of it.

End of the Tour:
The week following the final concert was cathartic for both of them.

Alison had seen enough of the tour to recognise the stress and during her brief involvement had enjoyed the adulation and the highs that performance at that level could bring. The end of tour party was a large and more formal event than the rather sordid affairs during the tour.

Determined to look her best she had shopped with Sarah for clothes, settling for a backless yellow dress some lacy tops and a gorgeous printed silk wrap shirt. Despite her efforts both Sarah and Chris were still outshining her.

Perhaps Sarah with her need to look stylish on no money had a justification for her well groomed look but how had Chris metamorphosed from the scrubbed but scruffy boy into her almost glamorous partner. By observing and practising, the way he does everything else. The thought told her so much about him. He would never 'make it' because he didn't have the God given talent and drive that is needed but what had her mother said 'Chris is adaptable and very focussed.'

On her final day the two hired a car and drove north stopping eventually on a low cliff that overlooked an area of the shore.

During the drive they had talked together, mostly concerning their situation and their relationships.

'I don't dislike Sarah,' Alison told him, 'but she cannot be part of our life.'

'She isn't part of *our* life,' he replied, 'she *was* a necessary part of my life with the band. It would have been a problem for me if you had been difficult.'

'It was a problem for me; it might have been worse but that didn't make it easier. We got on because we had to; I suppose we had enough in common to understand each other but, that 'brave little girl struggling' act is just an act.'

'Not all of it. She accepts 'use and be used' because that's what she knows but she is vulnerable to kindness and appreciation like the rest of us.

'Maybe. For the first two weeks after you got her the job she was waiting for the catch.'

'What sort of catch?'

'She expected...' Al's voice dropped to a whisper.

'How do you know that?'

'We've been thrown together and we talk. She asked me how I got on in the business and I said "luck, some talent and my best friend". She told me not to waste you because if I didn't want you she could make both of you stars.'

'That sounds like a compliment and I'm not used to them. Well not from people who know me. I read a book where a character said that women were like Jews, they've been reviled for so many centuries that you can't be complete friends with them; they are always holding something back.'

'Isn't everyone like that?'

'Maybe.' He paused. 'There are some thing I need to say, things I've been holding back because they were too painful.'

She waited.

'I've always loved you. When I let you go, pushed you away in that hotel…God Al, it was so hard.'

'What do you think it was like for me? At least you had Sue.' Her face hardened. 'You were everything to me, I was learning to live with a part of you and then you took that away.'

Chris remained silent. Then he reached over and took her hand.

'Why do you stay with me? I know I don't deserve you.'

'Can't let you go, it's not obsession or clinging,' she shrugged, 'and it certainly isn't a lingering belief that you are wonderful. I don't know, we just fit, you are right for me and I love you for the good bits. Anyway, even the horrible bits are mostly a "stupid man" thing.'

'Have I hurt you a lot?'

'No. Little things that are soon forgotten but only two mattered. When you got married and then the awful ten minutes in a hotel room when you broke my heart…yes you did. I felt suicidal.'

'I'm so sorry Al.'

She pushed his hand away. 'No! I wanted to die. I was in hell when you got married but compared to that day accepting your marriage was easy.' She went very still and quiet. Then with a rush she came back. 'But all the rest was wonderful Phillips.'

'Why did you let me marry Sue? I knew that refusing to marry me was about protecting your freedom. You were angry but you didn't argue or try to stop me marrying her. I thought you really didn't care, then when it was too late you said it was a mistake and I had misunderstood you.' He looked into her eyes.

'Don't tell me if it's too painful.'

'The whole story?'

And she told him. Her friendship with Sue, their closeness as a threesome, her desire to make Sue feel part of the gang because she was anxious about her situation.

Then the discovery that she has a selfish beast for a

boyfriend who knew perfectly well that 'friendly' didn't mean bed friendly. His phone call, Sue is pregnant, she getting really angry and hysterical, her mother bringing her to her senses and telling her to ring back to stop him.

When she had finished he looked distraught. Exiting the car he shut the door and leaned against it with his back to her staring over the sea. Then she saw the deep sigh and after a moment he then turned back to the car.

'When you phoned me it was to say that you had made a mistake and you wanted to discuss it?'

She nodded.

'And you said nothing?' He was shaken. 'Oh Christ, Al darling you bloody idiot. I can't believe it, how could you?'

'I don't know, it seemed too late, you had asked her to marry you. How could you go back to her five minutes later and say "Sorry I didn't mean it." Even an insensitive sod like you wouldn't do that.'

'You're the best girl I've ever known, but I wouldn't expect such kindness even from you.'

'Kindness? You must be joking. I was shocked and very very angry; it was just a moment of stupidity.'

He shook his head and dabbed at his eyes.'

'Is that the handkerchief you had when we first met?'

'Silly sod. Come on, let's walk.' Her hand was taken and they followed a path down to the near deserted beach and walked together at the edge of the surf. They had covered a half a mile in silence when he turned suddenly to her. 'Love you Alicat.'

'Love you too. Always have; always!'

'Alison Smith, will you marry me?'

For two seconds the question failed to register; it took two more before she could respond. Chris found himself entangled with a younger Alison, the girl from the folk club. 'Yes' and in case it wasn't clear 'YES! Darling Philipet, Yes! Yes!'

'You can think about it if you like.'

'Beast! You never change.' She threw herself on him and pushed him farther into the surf. Up to their knees in water he reached into his pocket.

'Something for you.' He gave her a little box.

Taking it she turned away and walked back onto the wet sand. Opening the box she took out the ring, biting her lip, silent, scared of the happiness that seemed to be welling up inside. When a hand touched her arm she turned and buried her face in his shoulder.

'Horrible beast, you...heartbreaker.'

Taking the ring from her hand he slipped it on her finger. 'I've waited three and a half years to do that. I never thought it would happen. I know it's only a token but it makes everything complete. I couldn't ask until I knew you were going to accept Bruce's offer.'

'You knew?'

'Of course. I'm not quite the fool you and Sarah think. Vince has been poached and Bruce asked if I would take over the Bass for six months because I have played most of it at rehearsals and my face is known as part of the band. I said yes on Vince's terms.'

'Did he agree?'

'No, but Morris will negotiate a deal. To be honest I didn't really care. If the LP does the business, the money is going to be...oh to hell with money.'

'Oh' said Al.

'Shall we go home, take the children to Wales, Pembroke perhaps; we can discuss the future on holiday.'

'I'd like that.'

'Are you happy?'

'I don't know. I feel tearful and silly and happy and content. I think I'm so happy that there isn't room for sensible things.'

'I know. Oh god Al, I'm crying too.'

She flew back to a cold Britain leaving Chris with his manager to complete some business and add the final touches to some recording work. A year previous both had been part of yesterday within his small empire of performers, now, as part of the 'king Rock organisation, both were valuable assets.

In one way her departure was a relief. She had always enjoyed attention and had come alive at several of the after show parties, attracting interest from the band and crew. It wasn't a big problem, she stayed close and never gave him cause for anxiety, but one party at the finish of the tour was wild. There was a larger than unusual proportion of the weird and woolly and several big personalities. Al had made an effort and her 'nice girl' look was appealing.

Out of his depth Chris found it hard to both let go and have fun and maintain a link with his girlfriend. Al, becoming giggly after a glass of champagne had soon joined the dancers and he found himself listening to a girl who'se conversation was rapid, extensive and exclusive to acting. He saw Al pause in her dancing take a drag on her partner's cigarette, spot him then rush over grab him and drag him out to dance.

'Enjoying yourself soulmate?'

'Yes, don't let me drink anymore or I'll succumb to the charm that starlet who was talking to me.'

The green eyes focussed. 'Starlet? More like an anagram.'

'What?'

'Les Tart.' She giggled. 'This is amazing; some people are so free and open.'

'It's like a children's party, free but only because the grown-up have created a safe space.' 'Are you going to become one of them?

'Silly philliposopher! I just find it so liberating perhaps a bit scary because there are no rules.'

'Not really scary, the big personalities are a bit overwhelming.'

'Mmm. I might not want to escape if I was pursued.'

'Shall we leave?'

'No, it's fun but promise to rescue me if someone gets heavy. I'll trip and hurt my ankle and you can pick me up.'

She was a bit disappointed that no one was interested.

A second parting was made with a subdued Sarah.

'Getting you on the tour was a good move. Your first words were "You won't regret it." and you were right.'

'Thanks.'

''I've a small present for you, to say thank you.'

He produced a small gold locket.

'This is in case anything goes wrong. My phone number and Dave's are inside. The locket will raise a few dollars, and if you need more I will try and help out.'

'You probably won't, need it 'Old Morris' is a good manager, he'll see you alright.'

'Thanks for giving me a chance.'

'I just put in a word, I didn't do anything special.'

'You didn't make any demands either, that was why I was able to repay you a little.'

'It was appreciated. Why are you leaving?'

'My opportunity arrived. Jack Cavill asked me to marry him.'

'What?'

'He's just got rid of the previous Mrs Cavill and I convinced him I was just the partner he needed.'

'Is that Jack Cavill of Cavill and Neilsen; they are pretty big in country. This is a bit sudden isn't it we only met him a fortnight ago. '

'Americans don't mess around. As soon as I met him I knew he was a winner and it was a case of catching him while he was reeling. It's going to be Cavill and Lewis now.'

'Who's Lewis?'

'It's my new stage name.'

'Can I give some advice Miss Lewis?'

'You generally do.'

'Know what you want and follow the rules that work.'

'You told me before. "Get your life right with God" you said.'

'Did I? Same thing really but it sounds a bit pompous.'

'It was; we had just had sex.' He was hugged. 'Oh Chris, you are so funny, I'll really miss you'

CHAPTER 7 Bass Player
(Chris Story)

Do bass players have a special talent or are they ex-guitarists who can just hack it? Listening to Graham Maby confirmed that I fell into the latter category.

Who cares; the time spent understudying Sol was reaping rewards, I was 'kR's bassist and grateful to Bruce for giving me the opportunity.

Grateful? The word was an understatement, 'king Rock was becoming big and C P, once described by his biggest fan as 'an amateur' was part of it.

The previous tour was a huge success by the standards of Synergy, the next would go mega, or so we were told.

Despite reservations about the music and its direction, I would have been crazy to turn down the offer and if I could hang in and ride the politics, I was going to be in with the big boys.

There was also Al. She was a good girl, but there was no way I could trust her on her own with either Bruce or Tony. Both had shown an interest and she showed her less attractive side by revelling in the attention. To be fair, whenever she behaved badly she would be contrite and affectionate.

'Sorry about flirting,' she once whispered, 'it's only a bit of fun and I am being awfully good.'

'What do you mean?'

She stroked my arm. 'Engaged to my Chrissie, interest from two rock stars, the probability of fans at the stage door in a week or two, and my knickers might as well be glued on.' She giggled at her own analogy.

'You said you wanted to make a new start; you asked me not spoil our engagement with sex.'

'I said.' She looked at me morosely. 'Perhaps I did, but I am human; it's two months since *you* showed interest, six if you don't count being taken advantage of, and I haven't had a blonde to keep me happy.'

I had no kind of argument. 'Al, if it is too hard for you…'

'It isn't too hard.' 'It isn't ever hard.' she added under her breath making an un-Al-like joke. 'I could find someone if I wanted; why shouldn't I have my freedom, you've had yours?' She pouted. 'You wouldn't know.'

'I probably would.'

'You wouldn't, how could you? It's time I started to have some fun.'

'I can't stop you; you can do anything you want.'

'I can't, you would be jealous and get cross; you would probably break off our engagement.'

'Not probably, definately. I still might, I don't know what you got up to with Andy when I was away.'

She looked up sharply and blushed.

'Nothing. Nothing like you anyway.'

'Hell Al, what do you want, I mean really want?'

She didn't answer for a while. 'Everything I suppose. You and me mostly, but you know how it is, you can't help being curious.'

My worries must have shown.

She gave me a hug. 'Don't be anxious darling. Some people are always looking for new sensations, hoping for something different or better but I'm not one of them. I would hate to be part of the cattle market, you can trust me.'

I could, but never completely. She was human and not always in control of her emotions.

Tony had not fully recovered and I reckoned that I could have played marginally better, but he was brilliant for a man with only three fingers under full control.

He had something that I never would, he was Tony Shelton, I had been Chris Phillips some of the time, but the rest of the time I was CP playing at being Tony.

Al called it testosterone, and once I caught her looking at him the way she sometimes looked at me. She saw me, blushed, put out her tongue then came over and whispered 'Sorry! You fancy other women.' Then she rubbed noses.

'I fancy you best.'

'I know.'

I was out of my league, but I was there and the music was great, better than before.

Tony and Bruce struck sparks off one another in a way that I had sometimes managed and I worked with Bep and Greg to create a solid foundation that enhanced the sound.

There was one piece I had to fake; a virtuoso performance from Vince that I could only just manage on the guitar. To compensate, I was experimenting, changing or holding notes to add tension and sometimes playing different patterns with accidentals that sent shivers through me.

These earned me a bollocking from Bruce until I forced him to listen. He generally agreed with a 'Yeah OK but watch it!'

I was also part of the front line and singing some of the backing, Al was there and 'kR was on a roll.

There had been a two-week layoff after the states which, apart from a brief holiday in Dave's father's cottage, had been spent with the children and families. Then there had been a month of recording, contracts and rehearsals.

We began the new tour in Denmark for some obscure reason, returning to the UK for ten concerts via a stint in Holland and Belgium. After a brief respite during which we rehearsed some new songs, we would return to Europe for a tour that took in several countries. It was incomprehensible to me but presumably someone knew what it was all about.

My manager watched the money; I watched him watching it and kept my ear to the ground. The organisation of the tours, the publicity and the equipment I left to the management team.

I couldn't do 'hard' so the posters tended to show a tough looking Bruce, Tony saying 'come and get it' Bep wondering what day it was, Greg looking benevolent and Chris Phillips looking suspicious (Al said I looked as if I was going to sneeze.) Threatening to put her over my knee received the response 'Don't sneeze on my bum.' followed by shrieks of laughter.

She loved the situation and there was a closeness returning that reminded me of our first tour. It was her way of establishing me as the man in her life; a kind of 'you are wasting your time but please don't stop wasting it' to Tony and Bruce.

There were also girls; some attractive, some nice, some professional, the moral, the amoral and the immoral. They appeared in ones and twos and in small groups, sometimes they appeared with boyfriends attached.

I learned to make judgements, to sort the fans from those on the make and once or twice to step in to protect the very young or the vulnerable from emotional upset.

Saddled with a tacit agreement to be virtuous until marriage, I was generally kind, and friendly, but one girl hit the Phillips weak spot.

She and her friend had been brought to our hotel by some of the crew 'to meet the band.' I had been on the terrace with a coffee, had looked up, caught her eye and smiled. She smiled back and, together with her friend was reluctantly introduced.

She was called Linda and as we talked, something clicked. You can never be sure, but I decided that Linda was a decent girl.

We had been chatting inconsequentially for a pleasant half hour when I was told shyly that she liked me. It was rapidly corrected to 'I mean you are the one in the band I like. You come over as fun but sensible. Are you really like that?'

I told it like it was. 'Linda, we get a lot of fans backstage and some of the guys make use of the situation; I try…..to show respect, I don't know if that's sensible or stupid.'

'Is that true?' She put her head on one side questioningly. 'I suppose it could be.' She blushed slightly. 'Sorry. I'm feeling a bit nervous.'

'That's ok, you don't know me; it would be silly to believe what I say.' I took her hand. 'Your problem Linda, is that you are the first fan who could change my mind.' I don't know if she believed me but it was true.

Later passing through the bar area I saw Alison curled up in an armchair talking in an animated fashion to two admirers. I waved. 'Linda needs a taxi.' She looked at me, looked at Linda and appeared to understand.

We passed through to the foyer where I ordered a taxi. A few minutes later Al joined us sharing our conversation until the taxi arrived. After Linda had left (I was allowed a chaste kiss.) Al spoke: 'I hope you didn't.'

'It wasn't easy.'

'I could see, Sue and her sister rolled into one.'

'You are very understand, she ticked almost all the Phillips boxes.'

'Which ones weren't ticked?'

'She wasn't you.'

I guess I make the whole enterprise sound like schoolboy fun. It wasn't, it needed stamina and resilience; we had to keep our ears open and sometimes be firm to get our own way. It meant arguments, taking the flak and giving it; if you aren't seen to contribute, you are disposable. Without accepting that side of things I would have been the support player that no one remembers.

It was harder for Al, more easily replaced and pursued by Tony. 'He is fun and he makes me laugh' she told me. 'If you weren't here,' she admitted, 'I would find it hard to resist him but I think his interest is because I'm not available.' she gave one of her giggles.

Back in the UK we completed our short tour, took a break after which we would return for a week of rehearsals before the second stage of the European tour.

A Party
The management informed us that a launch party would be held at a London hotel prior to the second part of the tour. We would both attend as members of the band.

We were excited because we were told that there would be a number of celebrities there including an MP, some top rockers, a film star and a number of people that I had never heard of but were apparently highly thought of within the art/ pop world.

We decided to stay in the hotel on the evening of the gathering despite the cost, which horrified me.

The cost had risen because Al had asked her mum to come and Diane had done so much for us that I couldn't refuse.

I like Di, she was supportive during my difficult time but I rather hoped Tony would persuade her not to come. It's not that she is an embarrassment, on the contrary she's rather attractive and I feel protective towards her because she's Al's mum.

I was nervous and took a lot of trouble with my appearance settling for a black suit with a green silk shirt that I thought went very well with the blonde hair. I was giving the hair a final tweak when a voice behind me said; 'I wouldn't cross any roads if I were you, the traffic won't stop.'

I turned slowly thinking of a suitable reply and was stopped in my tracks. Al looked wonderful. The chestnut hair was layered at the sides with ends curled forward and the sparkly ear-rings seemed to light up her face, but it was the white halter neck dress that demanded a second glance; it fitted everywhere.

'Go on then.'

'Nothing to say except,' she raised an eyebrow. 'you look fantastic.'

'Thanks Chrissie, looking good yourself. I am OK then?'

'Glam and lovely with it.'

'Thanks darling. Just a second, she dived into the bathroom.'

There was a knock and I went to the door.

Wow!

The black dress is simple and neat but I am distracted by the amount of firm bosom on display. My nice, rather attractive mother-in-law to be looks dishy.

'Hi Di. Looking great.'

'Thank-you.'

'Hi mum. Ohh.'

Al is less impressed by the cleavage. She recovers. 'Let's go then!'

A few people were known to us, our agent, a couple of members of other bands and their girlfriends and, of course, the management and entourage of 'king Rock.

We waved to a writer and his wife we had once met at a party. I had found him highly intelligent and needed to concentrate hard just to keep up with his very quick mind. Even then I had felt depressingly dim until his equally sharp wife had said as they left 'Peter enjoyed talking to you. He was amused by your comment about the sons of Adam having to cook their meat.'

I couldn't remember saying it, but it was a relief to know that I had said something sensible.

We had been there for fifteen minutes when Bruce found us.

'Diane! Great to see you again, how are you.'

I can't believe it; Bruce is being polite.

'Hello Bruce,' she kisses his cheek, 'I'm fine. How are you, are things getting easier?'

'Yeah, they're improving. You were right about that situation and I wanted to ask you about something else.' He put an arm round her shoulder, 'Glad you're her.'

They moved away.

I am open-mouthed, I mean, Bruce isn't a bad bloke, but 'Hi chick, nice tits.' is the sort of opener you would expect, not 'How are you?'

We began to circulate, chatting with people we knew and with people who knew us. We were very much together which pleased me because Al's good reputation is a bit like virginity, an asset some guys want to take. I was collecting some drinks at the bar when a voice said 'Alison, darling, you're looking wonderful.' and turning I saw Paul, a singer who I liked less as I knew him better, take her arm.

He acknowledged my presence saying 'Chris good to see you, I mustn't let you hog our lovely Alison all night.' then led her away. Looking over her shoulder she mouthed 'sorry'. As they departed I heard him say 'Are you still with that deadbeat?' I stiffened, but I had heard that his career was on the skids and let it go. Anyway, it was too early to start a fight and I didn't want to be the first.

I caught Al saying 'Hardly a deadbeat, darling, "king Rock' have had two big hits and a very successful LP in the last six months. But tell me about YOU.'

She isn't normally bitchy. I love that girl.

Since the hotel was 'home' I felt I could drink a little more than usual and as the evening passed, began to enjoy myself. There was a brief moment of calm during which some short speeches were made and the band gathered for photographs, after which I found myself sitting with the blonde girlfriend of the photographer.

I was never very good with women who had attitude or agendas and I liked Gayle because she was straightforward. We were snuggled together on a settee when a head came between us and said 'Behave yourself, Phillips.'

'This young lady is with that bloke over there.' I said waving vaguely to the photographer. He waved back.

'Is she? I can't imagine why she's sitting with you then.' she said then squealed as hands slid round the front and squeezed her breasts.

'Hey enough of that!'

Paul's face appeared over the back of the settee. 'She loves it.' the face informed me.

I pulled the face down by its collar, my fist informing its jaw that I wasn't pleased. It crumpled behind the settee.

'Sorry.' I said to Bruce who was passing.

'Any more of that and you'll be chucked out' he said.

Then over his shoulder, 'I own those hands, don't damage them.'

A fist hit the side of my head and I fell sideways, its elbow struck Gayle in the face and with a scream she fell in the opposite direction. Stunned by the blow I momentarily lost interest in the situation.

'You bastard!' I heard the photographer shout as he threw himself at Paul.

'You okay, love?' I slurred when the shock of the blow had died away and my senses began to recover.

'Yes.' She rose unsteadily. 'He just missed my eye.'

I reached across and stroked her head very gently with my thumb. 'Thank goodness! I'd hate to be responsible for a pretty girl having a black eye.'

'A bruise on the forehead is OK?'

She was definitely not pleased and my standing had slumped to zero. 'Should I give Rich a hand?'

'No he can look after himself.' 'Men!' she added; the piercing eyes boded ill, but the shake of her head merely reduced me to a loved but irritating son.

'Come on *charmer* time for an exit.' Alison who had moved well clear took my arm and I stood up. We eased away from the fracas behind the settee.

I slipped an arm around her as we headed for the next room. Al bit my ear and kissed it whispering 'Thank you for showing I'm worth protecting.'

'Never did like the creep, just needed the opportunity.'

Al smiled. 'Don't be silly, Paul is a lamb compared to some.'

I heard something smash in the next room and some shouting. I saw Bruce heading back into the room with a glint in his eye. As he passed I shouted, 'Be careful Brucie, your hands are my living.'

'Phuk off Phillips' he mouthed at me.

Al and I started to dance and took no more notice of the proceedings. After a minute it went quiet and the party regained its noisy swirling.

Al put her lips to my ear and spoke 'I forgot to say,' she became excited, 'I think I saw one of the Stones.'

'Which one?'

'One of the guitarists. He smiled at me and I went all funny.'

'Is that an ambition achieved?'

'Yes, in a way.' She was bright and silly like a schoolgirl.

I gave her a hug. Over her shoulder I could see Di dancing with the MP. He was holding her too close, whispering in her ear and fondling her bottom.

We cuddled together and shuffled; Di was forgotten until at around two Al extracted her from Bruce and led her up to our rooms, talkative, and giggly.

'Nice evening?' I asked.

'Yes. Very flattering to have men showing an interest at my age, Edward just wouldn't believe I was 41,' she laughed, 'and I don't think Bruce would be so friendly if he knew I had a granddaughter.' The lift stopped and she fell against me; a strap fell down and momentarily a shapely bosom was revealed. She quickly replaced the strap, realised I had looked and put her tongue out.

I had no doubts why Bruce was friendly.

It makes me uneasy. 'Mother in laws to be' shouldn't have nice breasts.

Final Rehearsal (Alison's story.)

Her permanent role as a singer had brought about a softening of Bruce's attitude towards her. He remained unforgiving with mistakes, but her success with some clever harmonies had led to an upfront duet on a new song. Not really a duet, that was hardly Bruce's style, responses to his lyrics would be more accurate.

There was a kind of chemistry when she sang with him though it was more to do with professional respect than affection. The tour had opened her eyes to the possibilities and she appreciated the open interest.

Bruce was shouting at her again, she was daydreaming. 'Get over here Smithy. I could see what you were thinking about.' She reddened. 'And I was right.' 'I'll start with the last line of the verse, and then you come in.'

They ran through it and she began to put some movement in. They ran through it a second and third time. She had got the feel of the song and was getting the movement consistent.

'Okay. I need a word about our vocal set-up so keep your mind focussed on the singing. His wolfish smile was mechanical but she reddened again.

Sitting on an amplifier she ran through the song in her mind. She could see Bruce making a point to the soundman. After a late night and an early start she felt tired and her mind drifted. Leaning back against the wall she took in the high windows above the cream painted walls on the other side of the old church hall. To her right was the much-used kitchen with its blank serving hatches, the source of endless cups of tea and coffee. To her left was the stage where the soundman was setting one of the big mixers for the PA. A faint rhythm could be heard, emanating from one of the rooms behind the stage where someone was quietly practising. Her eyes shut and she made the most of the break.

There was a shout and looking up she saw that something was wrong; the soundman was struggling with Bruce who crumpled to the floor. The man looked frantic.

'What is it?'

'He's collapsed. He just fell on me.'

'Al hurried to where Bruce was lying in a heap, a chill creeping over her.

'Help me turn him over.' She was becoming frantic too, the soundman was little older than she was. Together they turned him over. His eyes were open. Where was everyone?

She had attended a first aid course in the Guides and tentatively she felt for a pulse; nothing, but she was never good at it. Think! Think! The kiss of life, pressing the chest. Straightening him out she tilted his head and getting out her handkerchief spat on it and wiped his face.

'Phone an ambulance! Fetch someone, idiot!' she shouted at the soundman. 'Go on, do it!'

He ran off and she was alone with what? She started to work alternately pushing down his chest and breathing into his mouth.

After what seemed an age, the soundman returned…and just stood there.

'Have you phoned for an ambulance?' She was screaming at him.

'Yes, and Gerry has run for the doctor. There's a surgery not far away, down the road.'

She felt a hand on her shoulder and Chris' voice whisper 'Oh Christ!' then, artificial, controlled, 'Do you want me to take over. I don't know if I can, let me try.'

'No! No!'

He knelt beside her and put his fingertips over Bruce's eyes trying to close them. She saw that his hands were shaking.

She was getting tired when the doctor arrived, called out in the middle of his surgery. With a nod he took over, and suddenly she felt sick. Rising to her feet she ran to the lavatory to retch endlessly in the sink. The need to wash was overwhelming, the need to scrub clean, to get rid of the smell and the taste.

When she emerged Chris was waiting to take and hold her hand, to lead her to the kitchen, miraculously produce a small flask of brandy and pour a measure into a paper cup.

'I didn't know what to do! I should have done something else. What should I have done?'

'No-one knew what to do. I felt sick and it was a struggle just to be there. You were brilliant.'

'He's dead isn't he?'

Chris paused.

'Isn't he?'

'Yes I think so; I don't think you had a chance.'

'Oh God!' Her stomach heaved again, the muscles strained painfully and she was sick over her jeans and shoes, caught between revulsion and a kind of panic. Chris dampened some paper towels and began to clean her up.

An ambulance arrived and by the time it was heard to leave

he had cleaned the worst of the mess away, leaving damp patches on her clothes and on the floor.

She went to the sink and washed her face, gargling with water in paper cups and talking incessantly.

'I'll see if I can catch the doctor. Wait here.'

'No.'

'I'll be two minutes.'

'No, stay.'

'What?' He put an arm around her shoulder.

'Don't!' She flapped and wriggled away from his arm.

'Come with me then.' He took her hand firmly and she relaxed slightly.

They found the doctor about to leave and Chris introduced himself.

'How is he?'

The doctor looked at him. 'Are you close friends?'

'Yes, I'm one of the band.'

'I don't believe there is much chance of saving him.' He turned to Al. You did very well, young lady, and you gave him every chance. Not many people are prepared for an emergency when it arrives.'

Al looked distressed, gripped Chris's hand more firmly and turned her face away.

'Can I have a cigarette?' she asked. The sound engineer, white faced, produced a packet and with shaking hands, she lit one. Chris looked at her, saying nothing.

'Sorry, Cats Whiskers, I've given up, but just now I need something.

He nodded and she was grateful for his instant understanding. During the year of pressure and chastity with her band she had discovered cigarettes, three of which together with the single drink permitted each evening became her pleasure and relaxation. At the end of the tour she had given up. She had missed them at first, but now her new life compensated for the loss.

'Come on Al, we'll go to the hospital and give our names, and we'd better phone Tony at the hotel and get him to contact Bep.'

'I don't know if I want to go. Will we have to see him, identify him?'

'I've no idea. Do you want me to go on my own?'

'No.'

'Ok, let's go then.' He hesitated for a moment. 'Wait here; there is something that I must do.' He dashed away ignoring her protest.

His mission took him to the room behind the stage where their personal equipment was kept. Letting himself in he locked the door behind him and extracted a briefcase belonging to Bruce from beneath his guitar cases. The equipment standing waiting to be used gave him a moment of horror.

Opening the case he searched through files and papers until he found what he was looking for, a small album of Polaroid photos.

Flicking through he found and extracted a photo of Sarah, before riffing through the remainder. He stopped again and extracted two larger photos placing them in his pocket. The album and the case were replaced and he hurried back to Al.

'Where did you go?'

'I had to collect something.'

Since finding one another nearly a year earlier they had not been lovers except for a moment when Alison's need to re-establish herself had overwhelmed her. That night, traumatised by the day's event she had asked to share his room and had curled up beside him, her head on his lap.

'Leave a light on please? I'm sorry but I don't want to be on my own.'

She had talked on and suddenly burst into tears.

'Poor Bruce, I was a bit afraid of him. I can't believe Mum liked him; she did you know; she said he worked so hard and had to deal with a lot of problems.'

Chris listened, his own thoughts triggered by her words. Slowly she quietened and he drifted off into sleep, only to be startled into wakefulness by a scream. Alison was in the throes of a nightmare, eyes wide open.

'Al, precious, it's Chris, its okay.' He repeated it sitting up holding her hand. At the third repeat she began to register his presence and slowly became calmer.

'Hold me.'

'His eyes were open,' her voice was rising, 'he was looking at me all the time. When I was putting the pressure on his chest, I didn't want to breathe into him...his eyes.' The distress was coming back.

'I know, I closed them, I didn't even want to do that. Let's get up, why don't you ring your mum? I know its past midnight but we haven't told her. I'll ring up then you can have a talk.'

'No! Leave it until morning. I'm okay with you.'

'I'd better ring; it would be rotten for her to hear it on the radio.'

He got up and went to the phone, dialling the number. After an age, a sleepy voice asked 'Who is it?'

'It's Chris.'

'What's wrong?' The voice took on an urgent note.

'It's OK, Alison is fine, were both fine.'

'Why are you phoning me in the middle of the night? Something must be wrong.'

'Say hello, Al.'

'Hello, Mum.'

'It is some bad news. It's Bruce,' he let it sink it. 'He had a heart attack or a stroke or something.'

'Oh no! How is he?'

'It's bad,' He took a deep breath and let the words sink in, 'he didn't recover, he died in hospital.'

There was a silence.

'I'm sorry, Di. I know you liked him.'

'Yes, I did. Poor dear boy.'

'Al was wonderful, just wonderful. She was there when it happened and she spent fifteen minutes trying to save him.'

The silence was unsettling.

'Di?'

'Thank you for telling me Chris. He was so alive.' She

was crying quietly. 'I'm so sorry.'

'I'm sorry too.'

The phone went dead.

'What is it?' Al asked.

'She's upset.' The implications of Bruce's death had been overshadowed by Al's more immediate need. 'We must go home tomorrow.'

He sat on the bed. 'Lie down and put your head on my lap.' She did so and let him cradle her. He felt better holding her.

'I'm all right really. I've never had an experience like that; I've never seen anyone die.'

She began to talk again repeating concerns. Chris was asleep before she fell silent.

It was when they collected their equipment that Al remembered his previous visit to the storeroom.

'What was it about?' she asked.

'Bruce had a fetish,' he told her, 'he liked to photograph his conquests.' He showed her the photo of Sarah.

'That's disgusting! She's showing everything.' She pushed the photo away.

'That was part of the price for joining KR.' he said. 'What was yours?' he added unkindly.

'There wasn't one!'

'No? Sarah had to fight for everything she wanted.'

She frowned then bit her lip 'I'm sorry, that was thoughtless.'

Chris' Story

The rest of the tour was cancelled. A session bass player was drafted in, but after an intense few days during which Tony sang Bruce and played Tony and I played a version of Bruce and sang Tony/ Chris Phillips we knew that it wouldn't be the same. It was damned good, good enough to continue but it just wasn't...something, neither 'kR, nor sufficiently different. Maybe Vince would have given it that extra edge but as it was, legal and contractual problems intervened.

I wasn't too unhappy. The band itself was ok, there was a need to fight your corner, to ride the insults and the wind ups, but we were a team. It was the management that added to the pressure; the deceits and false faces, the need to look out for the knife in the back. Synergy was a cushy number by comparison.

There was also a more fundamental problem; music had moved on. I had cut my teeth on Dylan before being enticed away by The Stones and had grown up with prog rock. By the time Synergy was touring or keeping seaside visitors happy, punk had already exploded on the scene. Al had taken it on board and dragged me to a couple of shows, treating me like an old man who needed educating.

In a way she was right. I could see my future in music; it was melodic rock, fun and sometimes exciting, but musically…I was yesterday.

CHAPTER 8   Homecoming

A subdued Diane brought the children with her to the farm. She was hugged by her daughter and by Chris who offered whispered sympathy for the loss of a friend. Bruce's attention, he suspected meant more to Diane than she could admit even to herself.

The affection lavished on Simon and Sarah, now a proper little girl of four was more extended. 'My little treasure will soon be at school,' Diane told them, 'her reading is good already'

'I can read 'Through the Rainbow' I'll read it to you? Simon likes it too!'

It struck Chris forcibly that his daughter whom he had seen irregularly, and his son, of whom he had seen only a little more, were nervous with him and more comfortable with 'Nanny'.

That was it, he made a decision, he didn't want to be in a new band, and he didn't want the big time with its pressure and compromises. He wasn't sure that he would be wanted in the band that would rise phoenix like from ashes of 'king Rock. There was no sentiment. Bruce would be decently buried and the publicity would kick-start a new 'king Rock.

His new band would include Alison and some professionals. For the first time in two and a half years he felt content, everything was coming together, the children, the house, the prospect of a band and marriage, not for itself but as a symbol of their togetherness.

The day after their return Alison had gone to the village with the children. In the small Post Office she bought milk, bread and some essentials for lunch together with several newspapers. It had been Sarah who shouted 'there's mummy', pointing at a small picture on the front page of a tabloid.

In the corner of the front page below the main story, was a

small picture of Bruce and herself with a caption saying 'Singer's frantic effort to save star.' Inside was publicity picture of Bruce with his arm around her shoulder. The story described the two as intimate friends who were working together and detailed her efforts to save her friend and mentor when he collapsed. She was quoted as saying she would miss him dreadfully and that he was a major influence on her life. Taken separately there was some truth in all the statements but collectively it made them sound like lovers. Sarah was reading it slowly. 'What is f-r-e-iy-nn-d mean?' she asked phonetically.

'It means friend darling.'

'You were friends?'

Was she? 'We worked together.'

'What's d-iy-e-d. It says 'diy-ed' by the picture.'

'Your reading is very good for someone of four and a half.'

Al picked up and folded the paper.

'Granny says I'm a progy.'

'A prodigy! You are a clever girl, soon you'll be able to read better than me; well better than daddy.'

It wasn't supposed to be a special morning. Al opened her eyes to sunlight streaming through the curtains; a slightly open window brought into the room a drift of air heavy with the scent of fields. Warm and relaxed, her quiet was broken only by the slight noises of Chris and the children breakfasting downstairs.

She was to be married in two months, and the formalisation of her relationship gave a sense of contentment. No, she thought, more than that; it was commitment before God. Her Sunday school classes had been forgotten except as part of her development, but her subsequent experiences had brought back their rightness. She was beginning to recognise that the rules were more than rules, they were social truths understood for four thousand years and she had been forced to re-evaluate her belief that she could choose her own path and have it all.

Her mind drifted back to that Saturday in Wales, could it be nearly six years, when the world was as near to heaven as it could be. There was a knock and whispers.

'Come in.'

The door opened slowly and Sarah came in with a little tray. Chris's voice was saying 'Careful my love. That's right.'

She sat up.

'I've brought breakfast.' Sarah was excited.

She took the tray, the smell of the buttered toast evoking another happy time.

'Come and sit with me darling.'

Sarah ran round the bed and climbed in to be cuddled. Chris placed a cup on her bedside table 'For my girl' he said, mouthed a kiss and left the room.

Sarah snuggled in closer taking for granted the total security of her mother's bed, an invulnerable father and infinite life. It became a special morning.

Content expanded into happiness and became joy; she knew it was the beginning of a happy time. Not hope, not wish, she knew. For over a year she had been climbing out of the black pit into the light and now the pit was gone. Chris still had 'his funny five minutes' when his face would cloud but they were becoming fewer.

She felt happy nibbling toast, drinking tea, hugging and talking about dolls to her chatterbox of a daughter.

Downstairs in the kitchen Chris was amusing Simon by pretending to burn himself on the parts of the kitchen that might be hot. He sat down drying his hands where after the last pretend burn he had put them under the cold tap.

'It's funny if daddy does it' he said smiling, 'but it hurts. It's nasty if Simon does it.'

He gave him a beaker of orange juice to go with the cereal he was playing with. Leaving the kitchen momentarily he went to the foot of the stairs and shouted.

'Do you want a cooked breakfast?'

'What is there?' came the reply.

'Lots of eggs and bacon, and we can share a sausage and a tomato, and I can have fried bread.'

'What about me.'

'You've already had toast.'

'I'll have fried bread as well if you are, and I think there is a courgette.'

'I said breakfast. Okay and more tea?'

'Yes please, and eggy bread for Sarah'

Chris returned to the kitchen to find Simon stirring a spoon of orange juice into his cereal.

'Is that nice?' he asked.

Simon continued to stir.

He set to work to demonstrate that cooking was not his greatest talent. Not that the result was unpleasant and Alison, who was not much better, was delighted with an egg only slightly crispy at the edges, the perfect sausage and the overdone bacon hiding beneath a collapsed tomato. It took Sarah, trying out a new word (learned from her mother) to confirm the situation. 'Disgussing' she said.

Chris sat on the bed, balancing his breakfast tray carefully on his lap. 'Okay?'

'Lovely. It's nice if someone else does the cooking.'

'I meant everything?'

'Yes. I'm glad Sarah is going to have a proper mummy and daddy. It was a long time before mum told me about me.'

'She told you?' Chris sounded surprised. 'I thought…'

'She told me when I was seven.' Al looked up sharply. 'What do you mean, what has Mum said?'

'Sorry, Di told me that you came to her when you were one.'

'That wasn't what you meant. What did she say to you?'

The reply was casual. 'She told me about you being adopted.'

'No it wasn't, you always knew that, I told you when we met. Oh my God it something else. Tell me!' she took his hand. 'What did she say?'

'Either you know or you don't, I'm saying nothing.'

'It's something awful isn't it?'

'Stop it Al!'

'Don't get angry.'

'I wasn't. I teased Di once when she stayed and she went red and told me something.'

'I will ask her now!' and getting out of bed she went downstairs. Sarah clattered around the bed in Mummy's shoes and Simon made tents with the eiderdown.

Chris picked at the breakfast.

After an age Al returned.

'She's going to write to me and she's furious with you.'

'Thanks' he rose looking cross 'you can be a fu... a real pain, you just don't care what damage you do as long as it suits you.'

'Don't spoil the day.' She caught his arm.

'Me? I made a slip of the tongue, you've spoilt it.'

'I'm sorry, I didn't think, don't go.'

'You never think. You've spoiled the day for the children you've made me cross and you've upset your mum.' He marched to the door and turned. 'Anything else you want to foul up before you get dressed!'

Alison sat miserably on the bed, the contentment of early morning gone. A tear of self-pity explored the corner of her eye. She rubbed the tear away and slid her feet onto the floor.

It was two days later that the letter arrived. She had pretended unconcern until Sarah had run into the kitchen bringing the post. She had seen the thick envelope with her mother's writing and a nervous thrill had run through her.

She kissed Sarah, thanked her for fetching the post and made herself a coffee. While the kettle boiled she glanced at the rest of the letters. There were seven for Chris, eight others for her, and a couple of circulars.

She made the coffee and took it to the lounge. Settling into an armchair she opened the envelope with unusual care, took out the letter and began to read. Half an hour later, having read it twice she was drained.

Sarah rushing in shouting excitedly was told roughly to 'Go away!' Only when she had found Daddy, been picked up and hugged did she cry, saying 'Mummy shouted at me.'

The letter had shaken her. As Chris had hinted, it was 'good' but it had changed everything. Her mother was now another woman with feelings, desires and weaknesses. She was less that special person, mum.

Chris came in and bent to kiss her asking if she was 'Okay'.

She nodded. So many feelings were disturbed, some bringing happiness that had yet to blossom and hung as a promise below her heart, others disturbing and upsetting, her unshakeable rock shaken.

'I'm amazed she never told you, she's so sensible and open with you. Still, I suppose you can see why?'

Yes she could see why, but it was so silly.

Twenty-five years earlier things were different enough to matter. With mum unmarried and her father working away on a long-term contract discretion was justified. The 'visit' to her aunt, the subsequent marriage and then the discreet 'adoption'. The modest subterfuge was understandable at the time; that she had never subsequently been told was utterly incomprehensible.

It must have been difficult for her dad because his pretty girlfriend had several admirers. She would write and tell him how much she loved him.

Mum really was her mum. The thought brought a flow of something that bubbled into her. She laughed a small and secret laugh that externalised a feeling with no name, so pure even love stood in its shadow.

'Sarah, come to mummy darling.'

Sarah sat on her lap and she hugged her tingling with happiness.

'Chris.' She motioned to him and he came and sat on the arm of her chair. Looking at him, she shook her head.

Not wishing to intrude an emotion that was so personal, he nodded and found that his ability to love had returned.

CHAPTER 9   A Happy Time

It had been agreed that before the wedding Alison would spend most of her time at home with her mother and father. Since her reunion with Chris much of her confidence and happiness had returned and although she had spent time with him in their farmhouse they had not been lovers.

She understood Chris' grief, accepted his reluctance to commit before he was ready but their 'new beginning' was frustrating for a 'rock chick' who in the period with her own band had not been short of offers.

It didn't matter. She was looking forward to marriage as a token of her commitment and as a way of pulling together a life that had become fragmented.

There was also the question of the children; she loved Sarah treated Simon as her own and wanted the stability of a real family after the period when her life had seemed to be on hold.

There remained a difficulty with Sue's parents but bridges had been built. She would never be accepted, but the shared attention of his grandmothers and her own mother had created a situation where she was not resented.

The stability she desired was returning and she was renewing her relationship with old friends, especially Margaret who had been good to her during the black period a year earlier and towards whom she felt a particular kindness.

Whilst shopping locally she had met Heather, little changed from her youth club days and over a coffee each had discovering that the other was to be married. It provided a common interest and Heather, part of a group that remained friends asked if she would like to join them when they next went out on the town.

Alison's delight at being included and her eager 'when?' was unexpected.

'Next Friday?' was greeted with 'Super, what time and

where?' and it was brought home strongly to Heather that she was talking to an older Alison Smith from the club, not Ali the local 'rock' celebrity.

'We usually meet at seven thirty at my house. I'll let Jane and Pauline know you are coming.' Then with a perception beyond her normal thinking she added, 'You won't be too glamorous will you? Only, we wouldn't want to feel...'

'Glamorous? Me?' Al replied looking moderately glamorous. 'Of course I won't, I look forward to it.' She hesitated before venturing an explanation.

'When you are part of the business you need to look your best and be a bit larger than life but that is a different me,' she smiled at the two men on the next table, 'I'm the same Alison and its lovely to be with old friends. Chris says I need to be liked because I am an only child.'

'By the way,' she spoke to Heather who was still reeling from the sudden change of direction. 'Who is the lucky man? Is it anyone I know?'

'Yes, I think you went out with him several times.'

'Not the dreaded Randle? Once was enough. Oh!' she clapped a hand over her mouth.

'Andy Potter. We went out for a while before he went to university. When he finished his degree we met and started to date again.'

'Of course I remember Andy, he was nice. If Chris hadn't come into my life then we might have stayed friends; life is so much chance isn't it. Give him my best wishes when you next see him.'

'He has mentioned you once or twice; I think he was a bit upset when you broke up with him.'

'Yes. I was sorry too, but I had met someone special.'

At seven thirty exactly Alison made her arrival at Heather's house in Chris's new car. His scruples 'cold in winter' and 'foreign' had dissolved when confronted with her delighted 'just perfect'.

She had deliberately dressed down, but tall and slim in tailored jeans and a brightly printed T-shirt she managed to turn heads as she stepped from the car.

At the door she greeted Heather with 'I'm so excited. This is the first time I've been out with the girls for ages.' The hug and kiss were accepted by Heather, greeted with surprise by her mother and avoided by her father. An elder brother who had collected another of 'the girls' was pleased to receive the treatment in his stead.

'Jane!' She had never liked Jane. 'Lovely to see you.'

Jane, an admirer of Andy had never liked Alison.

With the arrival of the fourth 'girl' Pauline, minor conflicts of the past were forgotten. Two years older than the others, she had been one of the club leaders and retained a degree of authority that she exercised gently and without thought. Alison, who from the age of fourteen had regarded her as an adult, was surprised to find she was smaller and prettier than she remembered.

Habits remain, and a peck on the check reflected Pauline's status. Alison, who had been introduced to a minor royal, thrown ice down the trousers of a rock star and survived a serious attempt at seduction by a politician, missed the incongruity.

'We usually travel by bus' she was told in a tone that meant 'we will travel by bus.'

'Super, I'll fetch my coat.'

Leaving the house, she raised the hood, locked the car, and clutching her silk jacket ran to join the others at the bus stop.

'We go to 'The Llandogger' and then on to a disco.' She was told.

'Super.' said Al, so genuinely delighted that even Jane's antipathy was diminished.

The bus carried them to the centre of Bristol in no more than ten minutes. It was an important ten minutes in that it re-established 'Al' as Alison Smith in the minds of her companions; rather smart, but definitely one of the girls.

Their short walk to the chosen public house found her

chatting inconsequentially to Heather and experiencing a growing happiness that had been dampened slightly by her initial reception. Seven years had passed and she was not the seventeen-year-old innocent who had last mixed with these friends. Much of that vulnerable girl was still there but there was a confidence and a toughness that she could not have guessed at, and experiences that ranged from ecstasy to the depths of despair.

There were also embarrassing experiences mostly shared with Chris that caused her to squirm but none of which she was ashamed. Gary had been a need, support at a time when she needed to punish Chris. She was content that her actions in the challenging and occasionally wild situations in which she had found herself had been moral.

The sound of Jazz could be heard emanating from the 'Old Duke' as they passed and Alison hesitated in front of a poster stating that 'The Blue Notes' were playing.

'Shall we try in here,' she ventured, 'there's a live band.'

'No. We go to the Llandogger.'

'Lovely.'

Their entry into the lounge brought interested looks from a group of businessmen standing around the bar.

Alison's 'Excuse me, boys.' accompanied by a smile cleared sufficient space for her to request an orange and lemonade before turning to her friends with 'Please let me, it's so nice of you to take me out.'

This brought Heather to the bar with orders whilst the others settled themselves at a table in the corner. As she waited for the drinks, one of the men at the bar confronted her with the question that sometimes disturbed her evening.

'Excuse me, but are you Ali Smith?'

Summing up the situation as one having the potential to spoil her burgeoning friendships, she made use of her imaginary sister.

'We are not very alike and I don't see much of her these days.'

This added statement she had found distanced her from

the source of interest.

'Sorry to bother you.' the man said.

'It's no bother, it's nice sometimes.' She picked up the tray of drinks.

'By the way,' the man smiled, 'don't tell her, but you are much better looking.'

'Thank you.' She returned his smile. 'I might.'

They joined the others carrying the drinks.

'Alison's treat' Heather explained.

'We normally buy our own' Pauline informed her.

'Just a thank you for letting me join you.'

She turned to Heather and their talk turned to their forthcoming marriages. As their conversation progressed she sensed that her friend was anxious about something. Finally she gave in to curiosity. 'You are sure you want to get married? I'm sorry if that sounds rude but you seem worried about something.'

'Oh yes, quite sure.'

'But?'

Heather looked at her, then making sure that Pauline and Jane were engaged in their own conversation;

'I think Andy still has a thing for you.'

'Of course he hasn't!' She thought for a moment 'Its years ago.'

'He said he might just pop into the club later to see us; he meant to see you.'

Alison frowned to conceal her embarrassment.

'I wouldn't have thought Andy would be so silly. Mind you,' she added, 'Chris is intelligent but he doesn't understand women at all. Well,' she continued, 'we will need to deal with it. If Andy does turn up tonight I think he will be disappointed with the Alison he meets.'

'It may be nothing, but it's a worry.'

'Of course it is. I had a few dates with Andy but they were quite innocent; I liked him and I expect he liked the person I was. I'm sure he doesn't…wouldn't like the person I am now. I need to put him right.'

Heather was looking at her. 'I don't see what you can do.'

'When I marry Chris I want it to be perfect. I'd hate to think he was still hurting after Sue.'

'Sue?'

'His wife, his first wife. It was a mess, but he loved her and she died and he was so unhappy. She was my best friend too and I lost them both. I was having a hard time with my band and I was in hell.'

Heather was staring at her seeing her distress.

'Anyway!' she dragged herself back. 'It's Andy we've got to deal with. I remember Bruce saying that if he didn't fancy a girl he told her that he had syphilis but was having treatment. He said it usually worked.'

'That's horrible' Heather replied.

She noticed that Jane was half listening to the conversation.

'I wasn't going to say that.' said Al. 'It mustn't be serious, something minor so he can show generous sympathy whilst secretly pleased to avoid someone flawed. I could say I'm incontinent or my front teeth are false. I think the false teeth; he'll never be able to look at me again when I'm smiling.'

She broke into peals of laughter.

'Do you think it would work?' Heather asked.

'I don't know, but I think Andy was one of those boys who would find even a minor flaw off-putting. We'll see.' She broke into laugher again.

Pauline who suffered from intermittent bouts of cystitis was less amused.

Jane who had been a little bored by an interminable story about Pauline's cats began to like Alison.

It was as Heather had predicted. Successfully detaching Jane and herself from a group of boys, she returned from the floor of the disco to find a young man sitting at their table.

'Andy, how lovely to see you.' He was good looking, a bit like Chris.

'Alison.' He rose feeling shy when confronted by the slightly wild young woman in place of the girl he saw in his mind's eye. Wild or not, she was a stunner.

He was kissed. 'Andy.' She had a momentary recollection of standing outside of the Youth Club, kissing him, darkness, a total certainty of place, the world ordered and protected. She pulled herself back. 'You are going to marry Heather; I'm so pleased, she is very lucky. Chris and I are being married at about the same time...' The words flowed on and the tiny nag in his heart returned.

At eighteen he had been late joining the youth club and on his first evening had been attracted to the neat girl with the chestnut hair and an anxious expression. Enquiries amongst some of the lads elicited that she had dated a lot of boys.

'Ask Pete' he was told. He knew Pete Randle from school and his enquires were met with 'Smithy? Easy meat, you'll be alright there', but Pete was a known bullshitter.

He had talked to her and begun to like her. The following week he had asked her out and been told 'No!' abruptly.

She had relented and touched his arm saying 'Sorry I didn't mean to sound rude, it's difficult at the moment, in a few weeks perhaps.'

Asking if there was a problem he was again told 'No!'

She had gone quiet, then said 'I think I can tell you.' and the story had come out. Her pregnant friend, finding out about boys, all very innocent and then, only a few weeks earlier she had been attacked. She had escaped but been very frightened.

Looking up into his eyes with a candour that touched him she had said 'I need things to be special.' She had smiled and her eyes had sparkled. 'Perhaps you ought to ask someone else.' The first signs of the vulnerable sexuality were emerging and he had completely fallen for her.

'I'll wait if that's ok.'

A few weeks later she had agreed to a date and he had taken to the local cinema. At her home, remembering her nervousness he had kissed her gently and she had responded with a hug and a happy smile. By their third date, confident that she would be shown respect they had kissed, cuddled and enjoyed some gentle exploration. In his mind he could see her face relaxed and lovely. He remembered their final affectionate hug as he left her at her gate with an arrangement to meet at the weekend. On the Saturday she was subtly changed, friendly but distant. It was exam time and for several weeks their meetings had been brief and unsatisfactory. Finally she admitted that she had met and dated someone else. She had been kind, even contrite, but he had been dreadfully hurt.

'Come and dance? Can I take him Heather'? She wrinkled her nose at Heather and taking his hand had pulled him onto the floor where her display overwhelmed him. When the music slowed she had fallen on his shoulder, vibrant life and expensive perfume. 'So lovely to dance with a friend,' she began, 'it can sometimes be so difficult.'
She had enjoyed their modest dates, had been clear a year earlier that they were friends, nothing more. A new strategy was needed.

After the group separated he had remained with Heather outside her house.
   'What did you think of Alison?' he was asked. 'She's fun isn't she?'
   'Yes, she's super. Don't get the wrong idea,' he added, 'she is attractive but in a way I feel sorry for her.'
   'Why?'
   'Don't say anything to the others because she told me in confidence. Do you know what she had to do to get into 'king Rock?''
   'No, what?'
   He told her.
   'What, with the singer?' a shocked Heather had asked.
   'She had to do it to join the band. She was worried about losing her boyfriend and needed to be with him.'
   'She seems so nice.' said Heather.
   'She is nice,' he had answered generously, 'but she told me openly that sometimes you need to make compromises.'

He had been hurt again when she told him how she had been used, a little repelled by the implications. Heather was almost as good-looking and she didn't have a murky past. He almost felt sorry for Alison's husband to be.

Heather was quiet. She appreciated what had happened and that it appeared to have worked. Some of Alison's boisterousness had rubbed off and she threw herself at her fiancé and hugged him.

'Love you Andy Pandy.'

'Love you too Bushy' he replied.

The following day Diane received an early phone call that necessitated fetching her daughter from her bed; rarely an early bird it was a drowsy, tousled girl with her dressing gown over her shoulders that took the phone from her patient mother.

Her 'Yes?' was met with 'Alison, you are wonderful.' from a still delighted Heather. 'It was just as you said, he still likes you but it's a different sort of liking, as if he is being generous.'

'Good, I'm glad.' Alison's immediate aim was to return to bed where she could graciously receive the toast and marmite with the cup of tea that was promised by the aroma from the kitchen.

'Is it true?' the voice requested.

'Is what true?' Alison was getting irritated. The comfortable feeling of expectation was being stolen moment by moment.

'What you told Andy?'

'Does it matter, it achieved the purpose, or so you are telling me.' She was fully awake now and the prospect of a relaxing lie in was gone. Relenting, her stance softened. 'No, of course it isn't; there are situations when you make concessions but I was told by someone wise that compromise can be a slippery slope so I've always behaved sensibly.'

'I wanted to say thank you. It may not have mattered really, but it was a worry.'

'That's great then, and I had a super evening.'

'It was nice to have you with us, and you must come again, to tea, you could bring your Chris.'

'I will. It really is nice to have friends who are friends. I'll ring you soon, bye.'

'Bye Al.'

CHAPTER 10   Tea And Contentment
(Chris' Story)

Writing these notes it sounds as if life consisted of endless parties, fun and excitement interspersed with the thrill of performance. It was emphatically not. Ok, there was an exciting element but the rewards were balanced by the grind of practice, the arguments, the pressure and the travel that took up much of the band's time.

A few incidents stick in the mind. One, a breakdown in the rain on a deserted road in Norfolk, the second a potentially catastrophic accident on the motorway when a loony cut straight across in front of us to avoid missing his exit turning.

We clipped his rear corner with a huge bang and swerved towards the motorway bridge supports before coming to a halt. The loony ended up with a rear wheel jammed on the Armco and locked himself in the car when approached by three fairly annoyed musicians. We expressed our disapproval and returning to the car, set to work to lever the bodywork off the tyre and change the wheel. We were ready to go when the police arrived, their enquiries delaying us for another hour.

Al, travelling with Terry in the van passed without noticing.

The accommodation was equally unmemorable; most of it was adequate, but we had our share of lukewarm baths, smelly, grubby lavatories, poor food and dodgy beds.

As for our real life, it was the same as anyone else; maintenance, painting and decorating, shopping, cooking, washing up and work. Enjoyable, tedious and depressing at different times, rarely glamorous.

The tour with 'kR had provided comfortable accommodation and decent food, but the travel, rehearsal and argument remained the same and the added pressures required cat-napping to stave off exhaustion. By the end of the tour I was resorting to other methods, but enough of that.

I was never a high flyer. At my peak, I was a minor celebrity, part of a band that was becoming known and was going to be big. When that stint came to its abrupt and tragic end I knew that 'fame' such as it was over and was more anxious about where and how I was going to earn my next penny.

Al, who had taken to calling me 'Jammy Phillips' and sometimes in private 'Golden Phillocks' pointed out that my previous investment in a small flat provided some income. 'Anyway,' she added, 'you told me that 'king Rock will pay off the mortgage, and if the LP sells well we could buy a second flat.

The point she missed was that I was uncomfortable living off investments, my class didn't have investments. I won't pretend that I minded having the money but it made me feel like a parasite which I suppose I was.

Fortunately, Al has a lovely way with her and when, in the village pub one evening with a couple of friends I had innocently said 'Whose round is it?' she had called me a 'miserly young git'.

It was hurtful, but she never realised that her remarks were wounding so I shut up, paid up and promised to fritter my assets on fast cars and loose women.

She responded that the fast car should be my first acquisition because I had no chance of pulling any decent women in my old Ford. This sent her off into laughter that prevented me from saying 'I pulled you.'

We were to be married in eight weeks and the flash of an idea came to me. If she agreed, I had our short and long term futures mapped out (almost), and I would put something back into life.

'Ok,' I said, 'tomorrow we look for a car.'

'Really?'

'Sometimes I get a glimpse of myself when you have a little pop at me.'

She looked at me and frowned.

'I wasn't "having a pop at you". Honestly I wasn't.'

She turned to Marilyn, Geoff's wife, with a little hitch in her voice.

'The car doesn't matter; he cares; that's why I love him.'

She looked at me then kissed me and made me feel funny. Sitting back she gripped the front of my shirt with a wicked look in her eyes.

'No second-hand Skodas mind.'

We bought a car next day; a nearly new silver BMW convertible. I think I bought it because Sarah went quiet when she was overwhelmed, and when I said 'Do you like it love?' she nodded and looked at the seat. I sat in the back next to her and held her hand and said 'I like it too, shall we buy it?' The little face looked up and nodded. 'Yes?' She nodded again. 'OK then we'll buy it.' She threw herself at me and gave me a hug and a moment of immense happiness.

I kept the Ford, I had a feeling that the BMW might disappear when Al went home.

Sure enough, when she returned to her parents the car went with her. In the weeks before the wedding she was spending only a day or two at the farm so I didn't expect to be driving it for a while. She did offer to take the Ford, but Sarah was so proud of the new car that I wanted her to enjoy it. We had avoided spoiling the children except (belatedly) with our time and her happiness at the unexpected treat had touched me.

Al rang a few days later saying that she had had a night out with the girls and had a lovely time. She sounded really bright and asked me how I was enjoying myself. I said I had written a song, serviced the mower and had a lunchtime meal with Simon in our local pub.

I didn't mention being chatted up by two girls who pretended to take an interest in Simon. She still assumed that I chased every girl I met, and although there were opportunities, I avoided them. Only once, when my defences were at rock bottom did temptation strike and that in a situation that could have been disastrous.

Al was talking again. We had been asked to tea by one of her new friends and she wanted to go.

'Why me too?' I asked ungrammatically.

'The family are curious to see if you've got two heads' she replied.

I went.

I had grown into a situation where appearance mattered and into the routine of taking care of myself. I used Al's hairdresser who coloured my hair and gave it a similar cut that just fell into place. A contrived 'rough look' had been expected on stage with 'kR, supported by a well-groomed casual appearance off stage. Ashamed by my vanity, I compromised by writing a note on the bathroom mirror which said "God sees what you are, not what you pretend to be." (So had Vince.)

It became a habit to read it, smugly, after admiring a well shaven face in the mirror, but the reminder allowed me to laugh at myself. With 'king Rock it had been hard to stay level-headed and it was taking time to come down to earth.

Told to 'be smart', I showered and changed out of the scruffies worn to mow the orchard and it was a well groomed Chris Phillips who drove Simon to the local for a lunchtime half and a ploughman's before setting off.

Exiting from the Ford at Al's house with the shirt hanging outside the trousers and no jacket did not enhance the image. Nor, as I lifted him from his seat was Simon's neatness helped by a bit of coleslaw stuck to his ear.

Al greeted me with a peck and a squeeze, reserving a special cuddle for Simon and the question 'Has daddy been behaving himself?'

Simon, who didn't know what she meant, said 'Yes.' Unfortunately she followed it with 'Has daddy been talking to ladies?' to which he also said 'Yes.'

She looked at me over her shoulder. 'Out of the mouths…come on in darling, another of your fans hasn't seen you for a while.' I hoped she meant her mother, or Sarah. She put Simon down and as I went in through the door she gave me a hug 'I had the same problem when I went out with the girls. Fans?' she added inquiringly.

'I expect so; I don't think girls are normally interested in men with children.'

'I don't know,' she said looking into my face. 'I rather fancy you.' she added with a happy smile.

We drove the half-mile to Heather's house during which I accepted that our 'five minutes of fame' was over. When we were part of 'Synergy' I would have walked, now I felt the need to make an entrance. It was a bad moment because I knew that I would never top what had recently happened.

On our arrival we were met by a couple of girls who shyly asked for autographs and I wondered during a morose walk up the path if they would be the last. By the time we reached the door I remembered how much we had enjoyed being minor local faces and felt relief. There was no possibility of contentment if I started chasing adoration, no amount could be enough.

Heather met us at the door. Al kissed her and I did likewise saying 'Are all your friends good looking?' She had a nice face, was trim and seemed pleasant. (Stop making instant judgements Phillips!)

Heather gave me an encouraging smile and introduced me to her mother who went scarlet when I kissed her. Embarrassment was saved by the wonderful smell of rock cakes coming from the kitchen; they were my favourites and I asked for her recipe. I was told that they were just ordinary rock cakes with a little cinnamon and a drop of lemon in the dough, nothing special.

Heather then introduced us to her fiancé who was called Andy. I shook hands but when Al kissed him he backed off.

We were taken into their front room to meet the family; a married brother his wife and a little boy about Simon's age, a younger brother, a youngish aunt and her husband.

'Where's your father?' Heather's mother asked. She was

saved from needing an answer by his entrance from the garden. We were introduced to each of the family in turn and the moment I had shaken her father's hand I knew he wouldn't like me. I had met the problem before and didn't take offence; people generally had their reasons.

Heather's father was a good solid citizen; his reluctant handshake and dismissive glance told me that men with dyed hair and flash clothes were either gays, pimps, actors or paedophiles, all of which were despised with an unprejudiced lack of selectivity.

I made an effort to talk to him finding that he was a skilled fitter with a local company. He was one of those unsung engineers who do all the dirty work to keep the country running and are invisible to the talkers the squawkers and those with no grasp of how things get done. There were doers and wafflers and I formed the opinion that Heather's father was a doer; that said he didn't like me.

I turned my attention to his sister in law who after a few minutes conversation asked me if we were going to sing.

'I'd love to' I said 'but professionals have a sort of rule that we don't, anyway I haven't got a guitar with me.'

'Of course we'll sing if you want.' Alison spoke over my shoulder, and to me 'Don't be a spoilsport Phillips, this is just family.' She smiled winningly and for a moment I thought Heather's father might be won over.

'I haven't got a guitar,' I said.

'Heather's brother has one,' said her aunt.

'There!' Al had me cornered; she was in a happy mood and it was spilling over. I was the centre of attention.

'Ok, if you are sure?' There were nods of assent. 'Let's see this guitar.'

The guitar was fetched and proved to have a good action and a mediocre sound. I put it into tune and Al reached across and took it from me.

'I'll play...can I?' She looked at me. 'Heaven in Your Eyes?' I could see the heaven in her eyes. She strummed a few chords, played an intro and let go.

They were quite unprepared for the quality of her voice and her professionalism. She was good on stage, but in the confines of a front room, she was magic. When I joined in with harmonies something clicked as it sometimes did, and we became one.

At the end of the second verse she burst into tears muttering 'Sorry, sorry everyone, lovely family, so kind, it makes me feel so happy.' Heather's mother bless her, went and dabbed her eyes with a tissue saying, 'Well now, fancy getting upset, come on my love, let's dry those eyes.'

I explained that Al often cried when she was happy, but after a nose blow and a couple of sniffs she interrupted me.

'Let's start again. We will do Soul Friend' she announced, handing me the guitar.

'Thanks Al.' The song had a tricky guitar part that I often got wrong.

I played Dave's introductory chords and Al came in with her Ooh's. I joined her in the harmonies and the middle eight, at the end of which she leaned back and pointed to me with mischievous look on her face as I went into the solo and got it wrong. Al gave a little whoop and tried to look innocent so I rather neatly changed key, which caused her to sing near the top of her range. We finished it to a round of applause and Al simply preened as if there were 10 thousand rather than 10 people listening.

I noticed that she had made another conquest. Andy's expression had changed from doubt to adoration.

'Oh my dear,' Heather's mother was first to speak, 'wasn't that lovely.' There were murmurs of assent.

'Well,' she added, 'to think that little Alison could sing so beautifully.' If it were possible I think Al was even more delighted. I put the guitar down and was asked immediately by Heather's aunt 'Do you earn a lot of money playing in a band?'

'We only get paid if we are working, and we aren't working at the moment.' I told her.

Al's voice cut through the chatter. 'You were averaging

six hundred a show in the USA darling.' She followed it with one of her delighted laughs.

'Al!' It was a warning; I don't like to talk about money because it makes me feel guilty.

'And he's going to make much more from marketing and the LP, aren't you?' She poked me in the ribs and saw the frown. 'Oh dear, he's in a strop now?' She was quite unconcerned.

'Al! You're hopeless.' My crossness went as quickly as it arrived. 'Wait till I get you home.'

'Promises.'

I felt that we were becoming a bit silly and turned to Heather's mother. 'I really would like the recipe for your rock cakes; if it isn't secret, could I write it down.'

'A secret? They are only rock cakes. I can find the recipe and you can copy it.'

'Thank-you. And just out of interest,' I told the room, 'if I make any money my manager takes forty per cent.' Alison was talking to Andy and pretended not to hear. He was gazing at her affectionately and I saw her smile and shake her head then squeeze his hand.

Andy? Where had I...ahh yes, of course. The next time Kate was mentioned...

As we drove back to her house, I turned and looked at her and she glanced at me before turning her attention back to the road.

'Thanks for asking me Al, it was nice.'

'It was, wasn't it?'

'You looked wonderful and when you sang I wanted to cry too. Were you happy?'

'Oh yes, I love being with a family and feeling safe.'

'We will be a family soon. I mean the four of us and our parents and cousins and everyone.'

'I know!' There was a slight hitch in her voice. At that time, that was all there was to be said.

After five years of discovering, of developing, of incredible highs and appalling lows, life could have felt flat, but I was feeling fitter and more relaxed than I had for a long while and Al was happier than I could remember.

She had largely recovered from the trauma of Bruce's death though unsurprisingly she still suffered nightmares and on a couple of occasions had frightened Sarah by babbling. The incident had occurred a little over two months before and already, the vibrant circus that was 'king Rock was beginning to fade.

The band as such had died with Bruce and though in our short acquaintance I had begun to like Tony (except where Al was concerned) I could see where he was going and the darker side of heavy metal was not where I wanted to be.

I had just managed to hang in with 'king Rock because the music was good and the wild side was partly showmanship. It had attracted some unpleasant people, of whom one was evil in my understanding of the word. Razor sharp in his own narrow world he manipulated drugs, girls and money with a callous nastiness that made me angry.

I had intended to tackle him, but Sarah told me with a very concerned look to 'Leave it! Don't get involved.'

Tired and under pressure I did so, ashamed that despite my moral concern, my inaction was letting down his future victims. He disappeared towards the end of the tour and I was pleased when told that he had been knifed and seriously injured.

I was glad to be out of it, the music was great, but as well as attracting the skilled, the talented, the camp followers and the fascinating if barmy inhabitants of the sub-existence of a band on tour, the money also attracted the ugly underbelly of life.

Without Sarah I would have been in trouble.

CHAPTER 11 Confessions.

'Can we go somewhere quiet?' Al asked as we drove away. 'I'd like to talk.'

At that time the countryside began just south of the river and we took the road into Long Ashton before taking a left turn into a country lane. After about half a mile we pulled onto a grassy verge and parked. Nothing more had been said but after a few moments she turned and reached for my hand.

'When we first met, what did you like about me?'

'Can't remember. You were cheeky and full of life and there was something about you that was very attractive. I just fell for you.'

'Is that all? You were supposed to say my beauty and my virtue.'

'I'll give you the good looks; I'm not sure about the virtue. On our second meeting you implied you doing it with Andy. Would that be the Andy you were all over twenty minutes ago?'

'Shut up, didn't, wasn't, as you well remember from our first time.'

I smiled. 'You might have been in a serious relationship. If we hadn't met, you probably would have been in Andy's bed instead of mine.'

'That's a horrible thing to say. You were in bed with Katie.'

'I knew you'd say that, anyway, that's exactly what I mean. I was lucky to find someone who wasn't promiscuous and who was honest.'

'Supposing I had been promiscuous and devious.'

'I guess I would have been your transient number three, and you would have settled for number seven, big Dick from Knowle and moved into your council…get off… flat with the mixed race baby from…get off!.. loveable number six or…stop it!'

'Pig! I hate it when you are clever-clever.'

'I fell for the girl you are what you are and you liked me,

that's what makes us Us.'

'Soulmates?'

I nodded.

'I want our wedding to be a new start with no secrets. Today has been so lovely I thought it was a good time to clear the air, I need to be sure of where we are.'

Then out of the blue came a most unexpected question. 'Was Bruce mum's lover?' She winced as she said it and glanced sideways.

'What? Why?'

'It's something I need to know.'

I was surprised that Al would consider the possibility. As far as I knew, the relationship was no more than a slightly intimate friendship, but that wouldn't satisfy Al.

'Ask her!'

'Don't be silly, we aren't that close. Please, it isn't curiosity, in a way I don't want to know.'

'They met several times, and he came to our house when she was there.'

'I know they met.' Al crumpled a little. 'I've been afraid that…poor mums.' She paused. 'Do you think she loved him?'

'Al, stop it! Di liked him. I think there was affection and she was a bit flirtatious, but that's all. You are saying things that could cause trouble.'

'Did Bruce say anything; I mean did he say if they were close.' She went quiet and I left her to her thoughts. People like the idea of confessions but seldom the realty.

She looked up. 'Sorry, I need to talk to someone.'

'Bruce spoke to me once, nothing deep, but she must have made an impression.'

'What? What did he say?'

'He said "Diane is one nice lady." Then he became confidential, the only time I can remember and said "She's not after anything, she listens and understands and if I ask a question she gives advice that makes sense. Can you believe that? I thought women were just for shagging.' Believe me,

Al, from Bruce that was about as deep as things got.'

'He said what? Oh my God, did he mean…?'

'No he didn't. I don't want to hear any more of this. You've got an idea in your head and you're putting the worst interpretation on everything.' I tried to be realistic. 'Your mum's good looking otherwise Bruce wouldn't have noticed her, but there were attractive <u>young</u> girls available, what Bruce was missing was someone who listened and cared.'

'I suppose so. If there was something it would be your fault!'

'What do you mean?' I was stung

'You let her go to a party with him. Pimp!' She added.

'Hey, that's enough.'

'Sorry, I didn't mean it. I'm not getting at you but the thought of mum being 'flirtatious' is unsettling.'

We sat in silence then she slipped an arm around me.

'Confessions. Tell me all please.'

'There isn't an all. I've made a bit of money and if the LP buys a second flat we will have enough income to maintain our home. If I get a job we will be ok financially. Anyway that is planning, not confession.'

'Women!' She came straight to the point.

I hesitated. Except for Sue, which was a crazy episode, Al had always been unforgiving and retribution had been swift and painful.

'You were close to Sarah?'

'Yes.'

'Beast!' I felt her stiffen. 'Lovers?' There was a long Pause.

'No.' I hesitated then reluctantly admitted what she knew. 'Yes. Not love, affection and circumstances. I'm not making excuses; you know what it was like. I wasn't ready for a serious relationship even with you. There were girls around after the show and some were available. Sarah was a sort of safe option and an infrequent one. She was there because she made my life easier, looking after clothes, stopping my drinking too much, things like that.'

Al had gone quiet again. I knew how I would feel; knew I was hurting her.

'I'm sorry darling, without her I could have become a serial lecher.'

'Why? You had me.' She said in a small voice. 'You liked her, didn't you?'

'Appreciated, she wasn't easy to like.'

'You're a horrible shit!'

She added some more abuse but quietly, then slapped my face gently with a look that said 'I'm not going to cry.' 'Cruel insensitive beast!' She slapped me again a lot harder and I held her wrist to prevent further blows. 'What else you sod? You seem to think that being cruel is something to smile about.'

'You insisted in this confession.'

'Stop prevaricating.' I was told. 'What else?'

'You warned me against drugs.' Her face was a picture. 'It wasn't that easy. The occasional puff on Bep's ciggy was no problem, well sometimes it was a couple of puffs but nothing much.' How could I explain? 'There was a lot of stuff around, mostly the weed, but hard stuff too. I'm pretty fit but the show was draining and the parties and the travel was exhausting. I started to get very tired.'

'I was fine when we went to the States and I kept going for the first few weeks on adrenaline. About half way through the tour I knew that I couldn't get through the next show so Bruce got me some uppers. It was brilliant, not in itself, I felt drained next day, but suddenly I knew I could get through the show.'

Al was looking at me with a mixture of concern and horror.

'And?'

'And nothing. Towards the end of the tour I needed a little more support but after the last show I cut back then stopped. Felt like death for a while.'

'I thought you were ratty because it was all over.'

'When I had my first decent night's sleep I decided that I would ask you to marry me. I haven't wanted anything since.'

'You were using it when I was singing?'

'Yes.'

'You were good. I shouldn't say that.'

'I didn't make me any better, but it did give me the energy to keep going. How about you?'

Her disapproving frown suggested that confessions should be one sided. Then she looked away.

'No! Sol was using the weed quite often and…oh alright!' she looked up, 'once or twice I might have, but never my own, only a drag on his (I smirked) and I was smoking with Cats Whiskers, only two or three a day. I needed some comfort.' she began to justify herself. 'My soulmate had married my best friend and I didn't intend to become a whore!' She dared me to suggest otherwise.

'Men?'

She gave me a funny look. 'No. Sol and I used to do it sometimes but that doesn't count, it wasn't emotional, just need.'

A knife twisted just under my heart. She was looking concerned. 'Honestly it didn't mean anything; I need pleasure sometimes like anyone else.'

The knife twisted again; 'Miss Perfect' looked pleased.

'That wasn't true but I wanted you to know what it feels like.'

I didn't need reminding what it felt like.

'So,' my voice was shaky 'no men.'

'No. I had a few dates, but if they were expecting anything they were disappointed.'

'No sex then?'

When she didn't answer I felt another twinge of jealousy.

'No, not really.' She frowned and bit her lip.

'Honestly, you don't need to say anything.' That wasn't true; I would be knotted up until I knew.

'I was…assaulted!'

She began to speak quickly.

'It was at one of the clubs. Quite a nice friendly one and the bar manager said he knew restaurant that opened late and would I like to come out after the show and have a meal. I hardly ever socialised except with the band but we finished early so I agreed. It was enjoyable and afterwards we went back to the club to pick up my guitar from the dressing room.'

I could see she was reliving it, when I reached for her hand she pulled away.

'When we were inside he put an arm around me and started to kiss me.

I kissed him and said 'Thank you for a nice evening but I don't get close to people.'

He became like an animal; I struggled at first but he was quite big and strong and I was helpless; it was frightening; something nice turned into violation. It's all sorts of violation, choice taken away, and your clothes pulled, then ugly words, 'you're all effin whores', so hurtful because I wasn't, I wasn't.'

She was angry and I didn't want to hear, was too weak to share her distress.

'He made me kneel down in front of him, I thought he was going to kill me but he ... it was humiliating, I hated him.'

'Then he pushed me down on the floor; I struggled because I thought he was going to rape me, and then suddenly he fell over.

Terry had hit him. He was with a friend, they heard our voices when we went back to my dressing room but it wasn't until later when he heard me crying out that he realised something was wrong.'

She shivered. 'Terry was so good to me, take me home now.' she said in the same breath. 'I can't drive.'

I just sat there. I had overcome my jealousy of Gary, but this was different, it threw my emotions into turmoil. Al was fastidious, her action, if I understood correctly, in a violent situation would have been appalling.

She had started to speak again, the urgency and hurt returning.

'It made me feel dirty. It was just after Sue died and I felt

I was being punished.'

'I'm glad you didn't tell me before. I don't know how I feel.'

'It frightened me, took away all my confidence when I was trying to perform. Terry understood and he shared it with me.'

'Chris,' she was looking at the floor, she was struggling 'it would have been worse if Terry hadn't been there.' She was staring at me and some of my confusion must have shown. 'Oh my God, you can't handle it, you despise me.'

'No! Don't be silly.' I spoke quickly, 'I'm feeling angry. Did he hurt you much?'

'No,' she was quiet, 'not much, not physically, but I was helpless and being helpless is terrifying.'

'My poor darling.'

She took my hand and squeezed it.

I thought about it for a few minutes. No one was going to get away with hurting my Al. The guy was going to be paid back double, but that could wait.

'Can I hug you?'

'Please, just gently.'

She leaned across me and I held her gently. She lay silently whilst I sorted my gut reactions from my immaturity, my feelings from her needs.

'I'm sorry I'm not very supportive, I'm useless when the subject is sex and other men.'

'Apart from Gary, who was your fault, there weren't any 'other men.' Not like you, you unfaithful beast.' She turned away.

'Why?'

'Because I don't do casual and there were no other choices. Anyway I loved you.'

'But I was married. You knew I still loved you but I had made the break.'

She went quiet and I waited. She dropped her head into her hands and muttered something.

'What did you say, I couldn't hear?'

'Knew Sue…whisper…'

'Sorry love you are speaking too quietly.'

'Knew Sue was going to die.' She whispered.

It made no sense. 'What does that mean?'

She told me slowly. The dream, a previous incident and her fear. It made no sense.

'I couldn't say anything; you would have thought I was mad.'

She wouldn't make up something like that. It was ridiculous but she had acted as if it were true, kept it to herself when she must have been in hell.

I held her away and looked at her; something beyond words passed between us.

'Al darling I don't know what to say.'

She gave a sad smile and leaned against me. It was five minutes before I spoke, five minutes of whirling thoughts and confusion.

All this time and …you were saving yourself for me?'

Her face changed slowly, very slowly, then her eyes began to crinkle. Suddenly she began to giggle then laugh quite helplessly. 'Oh dear,' she said, 'sorry.' attempting and failing to stifle further giggles. Eventually she recovered, coughed and tried, but failed to look contrite.

'Oh darling I'm sorry,' she said, 'it was the "Saved yourself for me."' she giggled again. 'Poor old fashioned Phillips,' she managed between snorts, 'no one is that stupid, not even me. It's about my self-respect; loving you helped and I never found anyone to replace you but that was all.'

She composed her mouth into a slightly offensive smirk. 'Saved myself? That's like something out of Dickens. And take that hurt look off your face or I'll tell the girls. They won't believe it.'

The trauma of five minutes earlier was overlaid with the humour of the moment.

'So what are we going to do?' she said. There was still a hint of suppressed amusement in her voice.

'Survive. I have a few plans for the future.'

'What?'

'I'll let you know when they are sorted, but 'kR is finished and I'm unemployed.'

'Do you wish you were still part of it?

'I don't know, it was hard and I couldn't handle a lot of the people it attracted.'

'You could darling, in your own way. Sarah said that the crew liked you. They had a nick-name for you; they called you "Tea-boy".'

'That was Vince; he despised me because I was faking it. It was a bloody cheek coming from a Hells Angel who couldn't ride a motorbike,' I managed a smile, 'not that I would have said so.'

'I wondered if you enjoyed it or whether you were driven!' Al was looking at me again. 'Did you?'

'Initially I thought it would be like 'Synergy' only bigger, I didn't know that the money made it a totally different game. I don't want to go on about Sarah but if you had seen her face when she was told roughly what a gig would be worth.'

'I'm surprised she was wearing enough for you to look at her face.' Al had recovered and there was a hint of resentfulness in her tone.

'Believe me Al, Sarah kept them on. She was vulnerable and couldn't afford to give much away; I think…'

'I know,' Al broke in, 'you think she liked you. She was a fibber and a manipulator and I don't think she liked or trusted anybody, but she told me that you were 'someone she almost trusted'. I suppose it means that you can't be all bad Phillips.'

My arm was patted. 'Take me home please, I've a lot of things to come to terms with and my feelings are all over the place.' Then suddenly. 'Why did you make me say all this? It's too much all at once!!'

I felt helpless as I always did when her emotions were fluctuating.

CHAPTER 12 Shopping

Margaret was delighted when asked if she would be a bridesmaid. Of the good friends made at college only one had as yet decided on marriage, and she had chosen elsewhere.

She was happy that her school friend remained a best friend, a little sorry for her when Alison candidly admitted that few of the many friends made on the road were close, female or suitable. Her renewed friendships with Heather and Jane from the club and those with Marilyn, Anne and Vickie from their village were too recent.

Margaret recalled the shock of their meeting eighteen months earlier when a phone call from Alison's mother prompted an overdue visit.

Her friend had been sitting in the corner of their lounge looking thin and tired; a picture made worse by her efforts to look smart.

She had talked with her, disturbed by the effort that her friend was making to appear normal.

When she left they hugged and Alison asked her to visit again. She did so several times in the weeks that followed, noticing small changes for the better.

Diane phoned to thank her for the visits and one evening had brought Alison to Portishead. She walked with her on the short promenade and Alison had begun to talk about the day Chris told her of the offer to turn professional.

'It was just here.' she pointed out the spot.

'I was cross because he didn't want to tell me.' Then she began to cry and Margaret had not known what to do.

A few weeks later Diane phoned to say that she had taken Alison to see Chris. 'I think it has helped her,' she was told excitedly, 'she came and helped me with the washing up and talked about the farm.'

It was a couple of months later that Allen showed her a small item in the paper which said "Local guitarist, Chris

Phillips, whose band Synergy has achieved chart success is to replace the injured Tony Shelton in 'king Rock."

She wondered how it would affect her friend.

When the band came to Bristol she went with Allen to see them and been taken aback by the noise and the energy, finding herself alienated from the wild and arrogant guitarist that she once fancied.

She and Al were very close; friends who told each other everything, sharing teenage worries and knowledge of life. She was annoyed when, after meeting Chris, Alison was suddenly, not a stranger, but someone that she had to share.

Until then both had casual boyfriends with whom relationships were explored and tentative sexual contact made. Suddenly Alison, her best friend, was in love, totally. She had found the special one that she talked about and Margaret felt cheated.

Her father was calling.

'Your friend is here.' My word, it's true what they say about people in the music business.

Margaret went to the door to find her father already there.

'Nice motor!'

Alison waved, shut the car door and ran up the path.

Margaret gained an impression that the unhappy girl of her last meeting was now a confident and glamorous version of the girl she knew at school.

She took in the expensive hair, the dark glasses, the perfectly fitting casual T-shirt with its diagonal legend 'king Rock Chick, the tailored jeans.

Before she could feel envious, Alison was hugging her.

'Maggie, Maggie, it's so lovely to see you. You look wonderful.'

She was hugged again and overwhelmed by her friend's unfeigned pleasure.

Welcomed into the house the affection was spread with remembered squeals of delight.

'And this is your little brother?' The little brother held out a hand.

'Nice to…' he managed before Al hugged him and kissed

his cheek.

'Would you both like a cup of tea before you go out?' she was asked.

'Lovely. It's so good to see you all again; I was in a state when I last came. You have no idea how much your kindness helped me.'

'Come and sit down and tell us what has been happening.'

Al curled up in the corner of the settee and blossomed in the comfort of friends. She told them about Chris and 'king Rock, about her trip to the US and about her time with the band culminating in Bruce's death.

'We read in the papers that you tried to save his life. They,' Margaret's mother lowered her voice, 'they implied you were close friends.'

'Not really, he was OK, but I didn't particularly like him.'

She looked up. 'He was a fantastic performer and really good at getting the band to work, but he was rather predatory.'

Margaret's mother looked a little shocked.

'It was alright, you expect some interest and Chris looked after me.'

'That's terrible.' Margaret's mother turned to her husband. 'Isn't it awful that a young girl can't feel safe?'

Her husband shrugged. As a young soldier in Italy during the war he had seen sights that made him angry.

'Bruce was ok really; I didn't feel unsafe, just pressured.' Al repeated. 'Mum met him, she went to a party with him and they became friends, I mean nothing serious, just friends obviously.' She reddened a little. 'Perhaps I shouldn't have said that.'

'Your mother went ..? Margaret's mother looked even more shocked, or perhaps envious. 'Well I never.'

Alison is a dear girl, she thought, but she has led an awful life. Pregnancy, affairs, travel and now we find her mother is consorting with rock musicians, well I would never have thought it. It's probably just as well that Margaret's lost touch with her. She softened; maybe not, for all her faults Alison was loveable.

'I'm glad things are coming right for you.'

'They have.' Al smiled, her happiness infectious. 'I'm so happy.'

She turned the smile on Margaret's brother who unwillingly capitulated.

Half an hour had passed and Margaret was suggesting that it was time to go.

Alison dragged herself reluctantly away from that safe cocoon of family, of being with people you could trust. She kissed them in turn.

'So good looking.' she said to Margaret's brother. 'If only I was seventeen.'

'Is this new?' Margaret asked as they walked to the car.

'It's new to us. I told Chris he should buy a decent car, fit for the member of a top band. Sarah loves it, she feels like a queen when I take her out, especially with the roof down.'

She waved goodbye blew kisses to the family and they set off for Bath.

By the time they were passing through Bristol they were two school friends again and Margaret was relating the time at university and her meeting with Allan.

'I thought he was shy but when I got to know him I realised he was just laid back. From that moment we go on really well.'

'Tell me' she said suddenly. 'Was Chris really your special one? You've had some difficult times with him.'

'I think so. I can't pretend that I never fancied anyone else, but not enough to spoil us. That sounds silly because I have met some very attractive, men and if Chris hadn't been with me I could easily have become' she touched her T-shirt 'a real rock chick.'

'It's a bit rude, isn't it' Margaret ventured.

'Why?'

'Well, I mean its obvious isn't, the 'king bit.'

'Oh!' Al blushed, 'And I keep telling 'Phillips' he is naive. You get so used to it you never gave it a thought. Oh my God, I'll have to cover up.' And pulling into the kerb, she reached for a linen jacket on the back seat.

Margaret wondered if she realised that she looked like an expensive tart.

The discussion moved on to her time in the US.

'Why did you go there? '

'Chris needed me. I didn't know what a crazy bunch they were when they let go and with that and the stress of the gigs Chris was going a bit wild. He had this girl Sarah with him; he got her a job in the show.'

'Oh Al! How awful! How could you put up with that?'

'I didn't know about it at the time. It wasn't for long and though she was hard at least she protected him from the other girls and there were some really dreadful ones, believe me.'

'I can't imagine Chris needed to be protected.'

'Temptation, pressures and the stress of performance. Once the tour is rolling you are carried along and there is this huge responsibility to do a good show. There is no back-up so Chris was under a lot of strain. I only really understood when I was asked to do the backing for some of the shows.'

Maggie glanced at her sensing a change in her voice.

'It's hard to explain. You are in the wings and there is a huge audience, like a football crowd and there is noise and the band goes on and there is a roar. Then we go on and you can feel it, you can really feel a kind of tension. Chris is down on my left and the drummer on my right, two beats and a great ringing chord that sends a shiver through you, and then you are part of it, you can hear yourself...' she glanced across 'and you feel so alive. At the end of the tour Bruce asked me to stay with the band. If Chris had been dropped, don't ever say this, I might have joined anyway.'

'Maybe not.' She shook her head. 'I don't know.'

Maggie stared at her. For a moment she had seen the animal inside.

Bath, with Poultney Park on the left and they took a sudden left, so sudden that the blare of horns followed them up the hill. At the top she took an equally sharp right, hurtled into a two-car space leaving an empty bay between the BMW and the car behind.

Chris would have told her to move back and park tidily.

'I think I'm alright here.' She looked around. 'Everyone else is parked so it must be OK. Phillips gets a bit funny about parking tickets though I don't see why. I mean I'm parking on roads that I pay for, why should I be stopped by people whose wages I pay?'

'I think the idea is that you don't park in dangerous places.'

'I don't, I want to know why they charge me to park in safe places. Help me with the hood.'

With instruction from her friend, Margaret pulled her side of the hood to the windscreen where it was firmly clamped.

'Great! Let's go.' Al locked the doors and the pair set off towards the town.

Their slow progress through the shops proved successful. The outfit coming together when they returned to the first shop visited. Margaret's support was appreciated and she could not fault her friends final choice, which if a little odd, suited to her situation.

A four year old child and a rollercoaster lifestyle, she was hardly the virgin bride to which lip service was still paid, but the lacy white high necked dress and the little white hat with a wisp of veil and a feather were wedding without pretence.

It required no prevarication when asked if the outfit suited.

'You look fabulous Al.'

'Thanks Mags.' A glance in the mirror, 'I do don't I?'

Her own outfit, a fitted cream dress with a little jacket and an elegant hat suited her equally well.

'Lovely Mags,' she was told. 'Alan for one won't notice me, and a word of advice, keep away from Tony if he comes, he's very attractive.'

'As if I would? I am engaged you know.'

'Seriously, I know how persuasive he is and I have had some practice avoiding seducers.'

'I'm not stupid Al.'

'I know you aren't Mags, but you don't know Tony; two glasses of champagne and twenty minutes of charm,' she lowered her voice to a whisper, 'and you could find yourself looking at the ceiling with your pants around one ankle wondering why Alan's face seems different.'

'Al!! Don't be so rude.'

Alison burst into giggles. 'I'm so happy.' She raised her arms threw back her head and performed an elegant spin in front of the mirror to the amusement of the assistant.

'I'll have it. Can you send it to me at this address; I would hate to spoil it by carrying it with me.' She turned back to her friend. 'Do you think stockings? I've never worn them,' she giggled, 'I've no idea whether Chris would like them or find them horribly old-fashioned.'

'I wouldn't know, I mean about Chris.' Margaret's voice dropped to a whisper, 'Alan likes them. Why not try.'

'I think I will. White will match. Lacy or plain? It is so good of you to come with me, Phillips is quite good with style but he gets bored, and Mum would have me looking like a Christmas Fairy. Let's get changed then I will need to find shoes and a bag and I suppose some gloves. I'm not a glove person, but it seems right with this dress, it must be the short sleeves.'

Margaret's mind wandered; her answers owing more to politeness than interest.

So assertive; her friend always had her own mind but her actions had required preparation to overcome shyness. She recalled their first visit to a club, their promise to be good and to be outside at an early hour for collection.

At seventeen it was a new experience and standing at the periphery of the dancers clutching their bags, they felt dowdy wearing clothes that were part fashion and part school.

Suddenly Alison grabbed her hand. 'Let's go Mags.' and she was dragged onto the floor. They danced together in a cramped corner and for the first time she had noticed the determination on her friends face. They were joined by a group of boys and Alison came alive, partly as a result of the interest shown, partly because she had overcome a new challenge.

The shoes and a nonsensical pair of lace gloves duly bought, the pair retired to a small café for lunch. During their passage through the City's shops, Margaret had become used to the occasional turning of heads. It wasn't unusual, pretty girls attracted looks, but once at least Alison was recognised and only their rapid change of direction had avoided a meeting. Now, static in a café corner table with their coffees, waiting for the arrival of a non-glamorous lasagne and a plaice and chips, it was apparent that the occupants of one table recognised her companion and were in discussion as to their next move. The situation made her feel uncomfortable.

The two men approached slowly and she sensed trouble, their manner did not suggest they were fans. The first put his hands on the table and leaned towards her companion.
'You Alison Smith?'
Al looked up. 'I might be. Why?'
He turned to his companion 'I bloody knew it.'
People were looking.
'You're bloody boyfriend took my girlfriend away, that's why.'
He was working up anger and Margaret began to panic.
'What do you mean? How is he supposed to have taken her away?'
'She went to the Bristol gig and when she came back she was crazy about him, been back stage, met him and got chatted up, Chris bloody Phillips.'
  Alison made a quick guess; Damn Tony; but an explanation wouldn't help, would make things worse for the angry boyfriend. She stood up. 'Who would you prefer your girlfriend or me?' When he failed to answer. 'Well? Which?'
'What's that got to do with it?'
Margaret saw one of the waitresses run out of the door. Alison stood her ground. 'Everything. Chris and I are a couple and I make sure he doesn't chase other girls.'

'You callin' me a liar.'

'I'm saying you've made a mistake! Now go away.'

'You're rubbish, like him.'

Margaret saw that Alison was white faced but she stood her ground. With a huge wave of relief she saw the waitress pass the window with a policeman in tow. The people at the adjoining tables were staring at them.

'The police are here?'

The policeman's arrival brought about calm. Alison's antagonist became silent. Enquiries were made. 'It was nothing; he made a mistake; if you could just make sure he leaves.'

It took several minutes before enquiries were completed and the two young men were shepherded out into the street. Alison, still standing addressed the nearest tables. 'I'm so sorry for the upset, people are usually kind.' She sat down again and Margaret saw that she was shaking. She reached out and held a hand that gripped hers.

'Oh, Al, that was awful, he was really angry.'

'Why?' Her friend was muttering through the tears. 'Why, whenever I'm happy does something spoil it'? We were having a lovely day.'

'I don't know, perhaps you expect too much.'

'What do you mean, what do you know about what I expect?' The face through the streaked make-up was now annoyed. With little experience of fluctuating emotions Margaret was silenced.

'What do you know, with a cosy family, a nice start at university and a steady job? You've no idea what I've been through.'

Stung, Margaret reacted. 'Most of it was your choice, or so you tell me.' She saw that she had hit too hard. Shock showed through the streaked make-up pinching out the sensitivity.

'Mags, I thought…' the sniffs began again.

'I'm sorry, Al. You were so brave just now.'

'Yes. I often need to be brave and I'm not so I go up and

down like a lift.' She gave a half smile at her simile and reached in her bag for a tissue. The face, despite the streaked make-up, was already calmer.

'Sorry, Mags. You must think I am awful. Flashy clothes and cars and loud and deceitful' she paused, 'and immoral. Can I explain?'

'There's no need.'

'I'd like to. Friends are important; it's because I'm an only child; a lot of me is to do with being an only child; I need friends and family and I don't have very many. The business is a good place for making lots of friends who have forgotten you the next day. I don't think I have made more than a dozen real friends in the last five years and that includes the blonde cow. Most of me' she began again 'is the girl you remember from school but I realise that I seem different to other people. I get loud and I can be a bit of a show-off.'

'Yes.' Margaret thought.

'It isn't really me,' she continued 'but you need to develop those characteristics to perform.' Maggie was fixed with a look. 'Try to remember what I was like at school.'

She thought.

'Well?'

'Quite shy and sensitive but determined and fun.'

'All that is still there but if I am performing I have to be strong because some venues are hard. When you were in your first year at university I was in a bar waiting to perform and this man, who looked like a gangster, came up and offered me a drink. He thought I was a prostitute and asked if I did…things.'

'What things?'

Al leaned over and whispered. 'There, it's made you blush. I was terrified; I didn't really understand what he was suggesting. The barmaid whispered afterwards 'He's alright luv, but best not to get involved'. After that I had to go on and sing with people whistling and shouting for me to take my clothes off. I was eighteen and, well we didn't know much did we?'

'No. I wasn't judging you, but you've changed and I don't know you as well as I did.'

A smile was returning. 'Thanks Mags, I'm no good at explaining. It is about being two people, a performer and the real me.'

The manager of the café approached them with their lunch, a lunch that somehow had lost its charm.

'I am very sorry about the incident young ladies. We do occasionally get nuisance but it is thankfully rare.'

'I am sorry too,' Alison said. 'He wasn't cross with me, he had a grudge against someone I know and you never know how to deal with these things.'

The manager gave her an appreciative look. 'I thought you dealt with it very calmly and very well.'

'Thank you,' she offered an appreciative smile. 'I didn't feel calm, but I did my best.'

'Thank you. Enjoy your meal.' He backed away as if taking his leave of royalty colliding gently with a waitress as he did so.

'I don't really feel hungry' Margaret informed her companion. 'My stomach has knotted up.'

'That's nerves. I felt like that at the time but now it's over I feel quite elated. Anyway I've eaten some awful food in the last few years and this looks quite nice.'

She attacked her fish leaving Margaret to pick at her lasagne.

'Do you think they will come back or lie in wait for us?'

'I shouldn't think so. He was angry with someone who had spoiled his relationship. It was Tony of course; he told the girl he was Chris Phillips.' Al returned to her attack on her fish. 'I was serious about keeping away from him.'

As predicted, their afternoon grew more relaxed. By the time they returned to the car the sky had clouded and the breeze rustled a few fallen leaves but the threatened rain had failed to appear. Al loaded her purchases into the boot and was opening her door when Margaret heard a loud 'damn!' She looked up to see her somewhat deflated friend waving a piece of paper.

'A ticket! 'Why?' There are no signs. Phillips will have a fit.'

'I think the yellow dashes on the kerb and oh!' Margaret pointed at an 'ING' emerging from beneath the rear of the car.

'What a stupid place to put it. They are mean minded people who steal money to spend on ways of stealing more money.'

'Will Chris be really cross?'

'Not really, but he'll give me that that 'stupid woman' look and wind me up. I expect Sue had a miserable time, she was an awful driver. Oh dear!'

Al got into the car and opened the passenger door for Margaret to join her.

'Oh,' she said again, 'poor Sue.' and her eyes clouded.

'Sorry,' she sniffed, 'she was like the sister I always wanted. We were different but we got on well right from the start even though I was worried that Chris might be involved with her. He wasn't, not then, but Sue was pretty and I was pregnant and I couldn't know for certain.'

'It was a wonderful year until I fouled it up. You can't imagine how good it was to have a girlfriend in a situation like that. It was like having you with me.' Al sniffed and smiled. 'We were close friends, we did everything together, shared a bed quite often, not in a naughty way,' she added quickly, 'but we did share Chris once, I mean not literally, I must have been mad.'

Margaret wondered if she was hearing what she was hearing.

'I can't believe I was so silly, I was mad, but life was wonderful.' Alison started the engine and affecting a sudden U-turn, started back towards Bristol.

'I was with a girlfriend who shared and understood the problems of being in a band. I had got my figure back and when Sue and I went out together, we were practically fighting the boys off. I had everything and was enjoying it. Did you notice how often I said I.'

'Not particularly.' Margaret found herself back in the conversation.

''I' sums up the situation. Then I had a dream in which my best friend died; it was so real it had to be true: It was like today, everything was good and it was spoiled. Sue adored Chris and she was going to die so I told Chris that he must be kind to her.'

'You shared him?'

'No. I meant just that, be kind, and be friendly.'

'But that is ridiculous.'

'Yes, that is what mum said but it was too late; the sod took advantage and interpreted 'friendship' as 'sex.' Then just because I told him he didn't own me, he thought I didn't love him. When Sue became pregnant he felt he ought to marry her and everything, everything went totally wrong.'

'Oh, Alison, that's awful. I never knew what happened.'

'God,' her breathing shook 'it was such a small misjudgement, I feel sick thinking about it; in two minutes of conversation my life went from heaven to hell. That was bad enough, but later Chris shut me out so that I could get on with my life. I knew he didn't want to but that made it worse. I died a little inside, Chris is as loving as he can be, but it can never be the same. Never!'

Her distress was so absolute that Margaret reached over and held her arm. Increasing amazement at the confessions swamped by affection for her school friend. She found her emotions fluctuating with Alison's mood and was glad that emotions did not rule her life. Al was talking again.

'Sorry again, Mags,' she spoke more quietly. 'There have only been two really bad things in my life so I don't talk about them often but I get upset when I do. Thank you for being here and listening.'

Margaret leaned over and put an arm around her. 'You always were a darling.' She dropped back into her seat, surprised at her own behaviour. Her hand was taken and held creating a bond between them.

'Was it always hard being my best friend?'

'No. Sometime you shock me but my feelings aren't so

different to yours and in the same circumstances I probably wouldn't behave as well as you. I found it hard at University for the first few months. Lots of work, finding people you like, moving on from the boy at school,' Alison winced, 'then finding someone you like and, well, I'm not perfect. I was lucky finding Alan in the second year, he was quiet and I didn't take to him immediately but when I got to know him he was lovely',

'Did you tell him about previous lovers?'

'Did I what? No, we never talked abo...' Margaret was pleased to be saved from answering as her friend continued.

'Men are silly about things like that. Sarah told me there are only two things you need to know about men; they have a one-track mind and they never 'understand' about other men. It's true, even Chris who was unfaithful to me and told me to get on with my life was insanely jealous when I found a boyfriend and *he was married,*' she added with emphasis.

I asked him, before, well just after our first time, and he said "It's about being sure your children are yours, but when we make love it's so intimate, so absolute I could never feel the same if you were doing it with someone else.'

'Did he really say that? That's sweet.'

'Yes. It was so romantic.'

Did you? I mean tell Chris about other boyfriends?'

'He was my first.'

'I meant, like now you are back together.'

'He knew about Gary, he was there. I did it to get at him and ...well I needed someone.'

'I meant later, when you were on your own, with your band.'

Alison was silent. 'Nobody.'

'Surely...'

'No. I can't do casual, well I could but I don't, not my nature I suppose and the only options were casual or nothing so it had to be nothing.'

'Really?'

'Honestly Mags. Without someone caring and loving, the next easiest option for me was no-one.'

When she was dropped outside her house Alison spoke.
   'It was a good day wasn't it?'
   'Yes, a lovely day.'
   'Still best friends?'
   'Of course we are best friends. I hope we always will be.'
   She saw Alison's face light up. 'See you very soon.'

CHAPTER 13   The Wedding

The day of the wedding was going to be perfect. The drawing together of the loose ends of life and the formalising of a relationship that had meant so much for so long was like the climax of a long sigh. Alison woke registering in her mind that today was going to be a wonderful day and that there would be no regrets.

A conversation with Chris a month earlier during one of her visits established that both were certain. Dear Chris, even at that eleventh hour he had asked her to think about it. 'I've no job, I don't want to carry on with 'king Rock even if am asked, and though I've some plans, I'm not sure where I am going next.'

'You're not having second thoughts?' she said.

'God, No!'

'In that case nothing will stop me.'

Opening her eyes provided what was to be the only disappointment of the day. The light peeping through the curtains was grey. As she watched the shaft brightened slightly before dimming again. She rose quietly and eased her way to the window through a clutter of underwear and discarded blankets.

Parting the curtains revealed a light grey sky with small patches of blue. These were seized upon to be the receivers of the bubbling happiness that threatened to explode into laughter; silly laughter that had no meaning beyond the calcium waves that flickered through her like shadows from some fifth dimension.

Suddenly she felt an immense need to share the moment. Margaret, after a disturbed night on the camp bed next to her was sound asleep and slipping on a dressing gown she quietly opened the door and crossed to her daughter's room.

Sarah was also fast asleep. The late night that she determinedly enjoyed until slumping into an un-wakeable sleep, had taken its toll.

The sight of her sleeping daughter brought new happiness. Illegitimacy was no longer a stigma but earlier ideas of freedom had received sufficient blows for her to consider that having both mother and father was if not essential, highly desirable.

A moment of disturbing emotion overwhelmed her causing her to kneel by her daughter's bed and pray. It was a prayer without words in which her feelings gave thanks to a benevolent power. Words would have tied her emotions in knots. The tragedies could not be recalled with thanks, only as part of the strange thread of events that had brought her to this waypoint of life. Chris, so close and supportive, could never understand what her emotions really were. That she was emotional yes, but never the strange other being that worked on a plane of feeling that was almost external to herself.

Just once he came close. 'Your co-spatial aura is having a bad day!' He was holding her hand following a brief flare up. Then he had said 'I've only met your other you a couple of times.'

'When?' she asked.

His answer had shaken her.

Rising to her feet she kissed her daughter and made her way downstairs to the kitchen. As the kettle boiled she heard a quiet creaking of the stairs and after a few moments Diana appeared in the doorway.

'Morning mum. Just making tea.'

'Thank you darling.' Diana sat on the stool next to the small freezer that also served as a work surface.

'Is everything alright?'

'Yes, of course, I woke early and it just felt good to be up. Anyway, it's nearly eight, not that early, I'm surprised it's only you and me. Margaret was dead to the world and even Sarah was asleep. He asked her you know.'

'Who dear?' Diana was confused by the change of tack.

'The Blonde. She won't come, of course, but he said it

was only fair, so I said "well she can sit on your side with Katie and all the others".'

'What others?' asked her mother, 'and who is Katie.'

'Never mind.' Al could not restrain a pout as she recalled Chris's uncharacteristic retort that perhaps she'd like to ask Gary and all the others from her Cats Whiskers tour. She was stung by the unfairness and it had taken a second 'Sorry Al' before she muttered 'Weren't any others' and the subject was dropped.

'Sarah, you met her, she was one of the dancers in our first season and was a backing singer with 'king Rock. Phillips got her a part in the show.'

'Oh, I know, the nice little girl with fair hair.'

Alison's disdain at the description was confined to the expression on her face.

She saw her mother's face cloud.

'Sorry mum. I know you liked him.'

Diana looked up. 'What do you know?'

Alison crossed the kitchen and knelt down with her arm around her mother.

'Bruce liked you too. He said you were the nicest most sensible person he knew.'

'What else did he say?' Diana was whispering.

Al looked up into her face. 'Bruce talked to me often, it wasn't always welcome but he didn't know you were my mum and I didn't tell him. You've shown understanding when I didn't deserve it and I took it for granted. I think I understand how you felt about Bruce.'

Her mother looked shocked, then she looked away.

After a long, long moment 'I liked him, he was so alive and so different from anyone I knew.' she said.

'Oh mum.' She hugged her mother. 'Bruce used most people but he respected you.'

She stood up. There was nothing else to say. Only feelings to be controlled organised or suppressed. She poured the tea and began to talk about the coming day.

As the morning progressed her spirits rose and the happiness of early morning returned. The bouquets arrived together with the buttonholes. Phillip arrived with his wife to be and was greeted enthusiastically by his tousled cousin still wearing a dressing gown over woolly tights, and a tee shirt.

The rota for the bathroom allowed her the final bath and during her luxuriant soaking, Margaret had been attended by the hairdresser. 'Trust me' Alison told her a few days earlier 'he does mine and he's wonderful.'

'He does Chris's too' she added 'believe me Phillips has turned into a peacock over the last couple of years.' Margaret looked at her friend's beautifully layered bob that seemed to organise itself and consented.

It was a worried looking face that came round the bathroom door. 'What do you think?' the face asked. Alison looked at her. The mop of curls had been subtly changed and narrowed, bringing out the bright eyes, the attractive smile and the slope of the cheekbones.

'Brilliant isn't he. Looking great Mags.'

'Are you sure?'

'Absolutely. Honestly, you look good! What's the time Mags?' she shouted at the closing door.

'Nearly 11.' came the reply.

She lay back in the hot water and drifted.

Her mother knocked. 'The hairdresser is waiting for you; he's finished with me and Margaret.'

'Let's see mum.'

A head came round the door as if reluctant to enter. 'I'm not sure…'

'Brill mum. Keep close to Dad or Chris might marry you.'

'I don't think so.'

Alison stretched and reluctantly rose from the bath, a farewell to a last private event in her home.

Towelling herself, she ran through the coming events, hair, nails, eyes, perhaps a little make-up. Glancing in the mirror she perused the reflected face. Not pretty exactly but enough men who mattered had been attracted for her to be confident of her looks.

It wasn't, she thought, the Bruces or the Tonys of the

world who gave you confidence, they were mainly interested in sex. It was people like Dave's father, like her hard-bitten manager who patted her arm and advised her; 'Take care of yourself on the road luv, you will attract some wrong people.' And there was Terry; darling Terry who had kept her sane during her 'Cats Whiskers' year with his unbiased compliments, gentle put downs and protection. It worked both ways; her friendship and uncritical listening had seen him through more than one black moment.

She began to dress carefully.

'The cars are here!' Margaret called from the window and Alison, taking her father's offered hand rose from the piano stool and in an impulsive gesture, threw her arms around him. 'Thanks, dad, for everything, support and doubts, it all helped.'

'I'm glad things have turned out well. It must seem strange that we should still worry about you, but you have given us a lot of worry.'

'I know. I'm sorry dad.' She paused. 'You and mum have been a rock for me, all my stability. I can never pay it back, but it has always been appreciated.'

'That is why we never minded,' he replied, 'we always believed it was worth it.'

Her mother entered with Sarah.

'We are going, darling.' she said unnecessarily. 'You look lovely.'

Then turning to her husband she brushed his collar with her glove. 'Very handsome, I'll see you at the church.' She kissed his cheek and turned back to her daughter. 'Perfect.'

She took in the short sleeved cream silk dress with the Chinese collar, the embroidery and the pearl decorations, the little cream hat with its feather and veil. It was perfect, elegant, almost traditional 'Lovely darling.'

Margaret was calling her; she turned and taking Sarah's hand led her to the taxi.

A few minutes later Alison contentedly took her father's

arm and exited the front door. The neighbours waiting for her at the gate had been joined by a small group of local fans who whistled and waved. She smiled and waved back. Her father was muttering.

'What is it?' She blew a kiss to the cameras.

'I'm not used to this.'

He helped her into the car and got in beside her.

She squeezed his arm.

'It's the best bit, dad!'

Dave, looking rather paler than usual, was sitting next to Chris at the front of the church.

'Ok mate?'

'Better than you. Never could hold as much but I recover more quickly.'

Cliff had rescued him.

The band members of Synergy together with Tony and Bep from 'king Rock and a couple of friends from the village were determined that he would get legless. He had danced with a plump girl in a disco and was being photographed kissing her when her friend recognised Tony and all hell had broken loose.

They had made a rapid exit and gone on to a strip club where he remembered being on stage with Dave taking his trousers off at which point an inconsiderate management suggested they leave, their manner implying that the alternative would be unpleasant.

It must have been about then that Cliff bundled him into a taxi and took him home. But who had blackened his testicles with shoe polish and when? It had required a cloth and white spirit to remove the worst, followed by detergent and hot water. By the time Dave and Sol appeared, the one in a state of shock and the other fragile, he was clean and his headache was gone.

He refrained from asking why Sol who was booked into a hotel with his wife had spent the night on his parent's sofa.

The church was quite full with family, band members, and

friends from the business, the youth club and the village. He felt relaxed and shutting his eyes for a moment murmured a prayer of thanksgiving. Turning he smiled at Simon sitting on his mother's lap and at two teenage cousins who were children when last seen.

'Hi Beck, hi Jo' he whispered, giving a little wave. They giggled, smiled and waved back. 'Hi Uncle Chris' one whispered. 'Cousin' her father corrected her.

'See you at the reception.'

He turned back to Dave.

'Got the ring?'

'Yes, I've still got it.' Dave's headache was improved but sarcasm seemed the appropriate option.

They sat silently whilst subdued conversation, mostly whispers, with occasional greetings filled the background.

It was five past one when the buzz ended. The organ striking the first chords of Mendelssohn's march brought them to their feet. He heard a collective 'Ooh' from the back of the church and the whisper of comment as she approached until with no more than a rustle she was beside him.

He glanced across catching her look, eyes bright and sparkling, and a fleeting smile before she turned back to the priest and the service began. They made their vows to one another; Chris in a firm voice and Alison with a contented one.

'Do you Christopher, Li…' he had been dreading the moment. There was a snort from his right and open laughter from Tony's direction. A moment later there was a sniff on his left and the love of his life began to quiver. He adopted a serious face and continued with his vows.

At the end of the service, with the register signed, they processed down the aisle to have their photos taken under grey skies broken by patches of blue and moments of sunshine. Arm in arm they faced the official photographer and the press camera that had joined him.

'Kiss the bride then.'

They faced one another

'Love you Alicat.'

'Love you L…ovely husband.'

She threw her arms around his neck and stifled her laughter with a kiss.

There was a reception at lunchtime when speeches were made.

Dave and Alison's father, after a shaky start, had both been rather good. His own speech was impossible; the truth would have been too painful and he funked it. 'He had known Alison for six years. After Sue's tragic death they had met again and fallen in love. She had helped him to find the happiness than he felt could never return.' It was like describing a football match by stating the result.

There was to be a party for many other friends in the evening and then they would leave on the honeymoon. He had wanted to take the children on a 'start as we mean to continue basis', but Alison had dug her heels in saying it would be a nonsense. She wanted a proper honeymoon, with her husband, *her* only honeymoon. She had been near to tears before he realised how much it meant to her, had apologised and promised a romantic holiday together.

'I needed to start showing commitment to the children. I didn't think about us.'

The evening was a different kind of event. The reception had been a chance to catch up with families and close friends. Even their manager had been invited, had more surprisingly arrived and been greeted affectionately, if respectfully, by Alison. It had been a closed event that had still run to over a hundred people.

The only recognisable star was Tony from 'king Rock who, in a dark red suit, cream shirt and shades, looked the part. He also was the part and Chris felt a moment of concern when he saw him chatting to and subsequently being photographed with his two hero-worshipping cousins. Jo was just sixteen and Beck fourteen? Perhaps a word with

Auntie Liz, yes? no? Oh well, it can't do any harm.

He greeted people he had not seen for a while, spoke to cousins and aunts, causing Auntie Liz to frown when he commented that she was looking good. And so she was. How old? Early forties? Good looks marred by a habit of severity.

He recalled an incident when as a teenager he had been staying for the weekend. She had brought him morning tea, and when placing the cup beside him her dressing gown had fallen open and a breast was exposed. He had gazed with curiosity and she had been cross.

Catching her eye, he realised that she knew what he was thinking.

How could he now deliver his warning about Tony; oh well, like everything that was difficult, go for it.

'Auntie Liz, could I have a word.' It proved easier than expected.

Happiness was settling on the day. Sue was not forgotten, how could she be with Simon holding his hand, but she was external, another life.

When his path and Al's crossed they touched for a moment, the world was how it should be; the attractive girl with the blue-green eyes transformed into something lovelier trailing happiness like fairy dust.

He had spoken to Dave about his strange sad happiness and had been told a story.

'It was a children's party in the Church Hall, you know the kind, silly games and sandwiches. Our little girl was only crawling, but we took her because Judith helps with the Sunday school. There was this little waif about five years old with her brother and sister. The other two were playing games but she stayed with her mother and I was told she was not very strong and might not have a long life. The game involved passing a balloon, so simple and she joined in. Tentatively at first, then she began to smile and finally she was excited. It brought a lump to my throat and there were tears running down my cheeks. Would you believe that? I felt silly, dabbed my eyes and pretended to blow my nose. I wasn't the only one.'

'I feel the same about Al.' he added, 'you know happiness after her bad time, sorry boyo. She was so brave.' A tear explored the corner of his eye.

Chris put an arm round his shoulders. 'We're a soft pair of buggers.'

The band providing the entertainment was a little like Synergy; competent and professional, but playing covers and lacking the edge and the dynamism that Synergy had developed.

When they took their break, Chris approached the singer. 'Doing great mate, wanted to thank you now 'cos we may not be here at the end.' The conversation drifted to band equipment, guitars and amps, valves versus transistors, then on to life at a higher level. ''kR? Hard work mate, much tougher than Synergy and more travel. It nearly broke me.'

'Your missus wants to do a song.'

It was half expected and it was difficult; guitarists don't like loaning their equipment 'Could we borrow...' he asked.

'Sure Mr Phillips, she already asked and I said no problem but could we have a photo with you and your wife.'

'Of course...and its Chris. Shall I call Tony and Bep?'

'Yeah, that would be great, a photo with big stars, fantastic.'

"Big stars?" In a family environment the words had more resonance but what did they mean? Tony was a star maybe; a good guitarist classically trained who had gravitated to a band that had caught the wave. Certainly he had more musical talent but counted in months, he himself had contributed more to the band. The analysis became pointless and he called his new wife.

'Are we going to sing now?' She was excited and gave the guitarist from the band a winning smile.

'Yes. Get Tony and Bep over and ask Arwen to take some photos.'

'He's already taken a whole film of me. He said I was the

most beautiful bride he had ever seen because happiness shone from every photo. Aren't the Welsh just lovely?'

'Some of them.'

'Arwen is *very* special so don't even think anything unkind. I'll tell you why one day.'

'More secrets? Chris smiled. 'Good secrets I hope. Go on, I'll set up.'

Chris selected the most suitable guitar, a curiously curvy Aria with strat-like controls, setting it and its amplifier to give the most acoustic like sound possible. The band gathered round and the photos were taken.

Chris handed the Aria to Alison and picked up the bass.

'Look to me.' he said, and she looked up sharply. It was a song that she had played with Cats Whiskers.

'Yes, I know it.'

Chris made an announcement and she began to play. After two bars the bass joined her. She sang like an angel and when he added Sol's harmonies, she gave him a look that was part happiness, part uncertainty. But it was a good feeling, like returning home.

Later that evening, he cornered his busy wife and suggested that it was time to change.

'Oh dear, there's never enough time, I just want this to go on forever. Must we go?'

He explained that they had to travel some distance and needed to get away within an hour.

'I'm so enjoying it.'

'Me too, I should have delayed the booking and stayed the night here.'

She was torn between her departure on honeymoon and her lovely evening. Sometimes having a little spare cash helped, and a solution came to him.

'Just a thought love, but when we get back, why don't we have an all day party for everyone. Most people here live less than an hour away. We can hire a marquee and you will have time to catch up. We could call it a 'Midsummer get together' and all the families could come. We could put the marquee on the side lawn and...'

'Oh yes, that would be lovely.' She jumped to her feet ran to the stage and waiting till the band were between songs, spoke to the singer.

He passed her the microphone and she announced a special midsummer party for 'everyone that I haven't spent enough time with. Invitations to everybody.'

She blew kisses and foolishly announced that they would be leaving very soon.

It was two minutes later whilst talking to his grandfather that Dave interrupted and apologising to the aged relative seized him in an arm lock.

His struggles were wasted, seized on the other side and by the legs by a gang of savages ('I'll get you bastards') he was bundled into an annexe and held down, his trousers and pants were removed and the (still sore) testicles were re-blackened. The flash of a camera and his 'friends' left the room howling with laughter, taking the trousers and pants with them. The annexe was a tiny reception room with a low table and some chairs. There were no loose covers or magazines and all his clothes were in the car except for those intended for the journey which were in an upstairs bedroom. A dash to the bedroom seemed his best hope; his shirt was square cut and offered no concealment.

He cursed Dave, confidant that this was his doing. He was his best mate and he accepted that the Welsh have a funny sense of humour which often involves humiliating their mates. Turning off the lights, he opened the door and peeped out.

There were one or two people visible in the foyer but he could see part way up the staircase opposite the double doors. There were no guarantees, it would be a quick look and go for it.

He listened carefully, glanced around, and dashed across the corridor then crept towards the stairs past the double doors to the reception room, opened at the critical moment by a grinning Dave and Sol. There was the flash of a camera (Friends???) and he dashed past the open doors and up the stairs followed by wolf whistles then down the corridor to the room that contained his bag of casuals. Hurling himself into the semi darkness of the room he was confronted by two bodies on the bed.

He had encountered it during the 'kR tours, but things like that didn't happen at family gatherings; they just didn't.

There was a squeak and a muffled voice said 'eff' off!'

The voice was Tony's; the question was who was he humping. He didn't want to know. It would sound hilarious when repeated but was hard to deal with in his current state.

Grabbing his bag of clothes he made a rapid exit.

Safe in the lavatory across the corridor he locked the door. The first task was to remove the worse of the blacking and he set to work with a flannel soap and hot water. It was a slow process and his recent shock continued to occupy his mind. Who was it? There were a dozen or more young women as well as a sprinkling of teenies and several older women who would meet Tony's criteria of 'shaftable'. Creeping from the refuge clean, tidy and dressed ready to leave, he thrust the thought from his mind and made his way back to the reception.

'Very smart young Christopher.' Dave greeted him while Sol thrust a pair of underpants into his top pocket and a pair of trousers into his carrier bag.

'Evil sods.'

Dave was delighted with his description. 'We do our best boyo.'

Al, still in her wedding dress, was talking to Chris' father and his two young cousins. Relief settled and he made by way towards her. She smiled on his approach.

'What have you been up to? I saw you running past the doors and what these two thought' she motioned to two grinning cousins 'I can't imagine.'

What they thought was written on their giggling faces.

'And your mother was disgusted.'

'Good God, did everyone see?'

'Dave shouted 'Look at this! Disgraceful! Everybody

looked and you ran past. We all thought you were doing it for a dare.'

'They stole my trousers and blacked…' The presence of his cousins silenced the protests.

'Listen Al, it's time to go, really! You've got 10 minutes to change and I can rush around and say goodbye.'

She gave him a smile and made a quick dash around the room, waving, smiling and kissing before reluctantly disappearing upstairs with her mother.

Chris kissed his cousins, spoke to his father and together they made their way upstairs stopping briefly at reception for keys. Ten minutes later they returned; Chris feeling more comfortable in a leather jacket with underpants now protecting his cream jeans.

He made the rounds and a few minutes later Al returned in jeans and T-shirt with her bomber jacket over her shoulder. Kissing his parents again he gave Sarah and Simon a last hug and with a 'See you soon my loves.' collected his new wife.

'Ready?'

'Ready'

'Come on then.'

Clutching a couple of soft bags they made their way out to the car park and the BMW.

'Is everything is loaded?'

'Mum said it was.'

'Not this one,' Chris stopped. 'that one.'

He led her three spaces away to where a red XJS convertible was parked.

He was missing the excitement of 'kR, and needed a substitute. It had been concealed in Cliff's garage until today.

'Leather jacket on the seat, hat and scarf in the glove box, case in the boot, mine on back seat. Anything else?'

She went quiet like Sarah, then gave her father and mother a last kiss and got in.

Chris gave Cliff a wave and offered a friendly two fingers to Dave.

'See you mate.'

'Good luck young Christopher, and to you my lovely.'

'Thanks for everything Dave, it's been great.'

They pulled away in a shower of confetti and as they passed he noticed the condom on the BMW's exhaust pipe, and the trail of cans underneath.

Both were quiet; Alison wrapped in her thoughts and Chris getting used to the new car. As they reached the edge of the city heading south, he spoke for the first time.

'Everything ok?'

She gripped his arm. 'I'm so happy. No, better than that' she snuggled up against him and spoke quietly 'happy and warm and content. Where are we going? I think it's about time I knew, I may have the wrong clothes.'

'No you have the right clothes and everything else you need.'

'So where are we going?'

'France, maybe as far as Italy. OK?' 'I've booked a few days in Paris then we travel to just outside St Tropez for ten days, in between will be pot luck.'

She took it in. 'Thanks Phillips.'

'It doesn't get any better, I think this is it.'

'I would be just as happy staying at a youth hostel in Dorset. Really I would.'

They drove on, arriving in Portsmouth with forty minutes to spare, and once on the ferry collected their bags and made their way to the tiny two-berth cabin.

He shut the door and they stood facing each other.

Al looked around then shook her head.

'Is this the honeymoon suite then?'

'This is it.'

'Give me a kiss.' She began to laugh quietly and hugging one another they slipped onto the narrow bed.

'Cuddle me for a little while then we can go on deck when we leave harbour.'

It would have been about then that Dave and Sol discovered that their cases contained newspaper, confetti and women's underwear.

CHAPTER 14 Honeymoon
(Chris' Story)

The loud speaker announcement that we would shortly be leaving harbour dragged us back from our warm bundle of togetherness, and stopping only for shoes, a sweater and a final kiss, we left the cabin and walked down the carpeted steel tunnel to the deck.

Feelings were as full as they had been when we had walked together on Snowdon only an irrational fear of losing her taking the edge off my contentment. Our entrance onto a wet deck caused my grip on her hand to tighten.

'What?'

'It's nothing.' It had to be nothing, life had to be lived and grief's mastered. I brushed the back of my hand against fluffy hem of her cardigan. It was a comfort.

'There is something isn't there?' She turned 'Are you are afraid it will all disappear?'

I nodded. 'Now always disappears, life's just a succession of moments.'

'Don't say that' she shivered, 'I don't like that! It makes me feel helpless; life running past, never allowing me to just be.'

Her tension communicated itself, I understood and had that same feeling of impermanence and momentarily absolute loneliness.

'Rub tummy.'

It was a silly expression that meant she wanted comfort. I slid my arms around her and gently massaged her diaphragm.

The lights of Portsmouth and Southsea with its now deserted fairground were fading and the ferry began to take on a noticeable heave.

We remained by the rail until the lights became pinpoints, the scene marred only by the ugly orange glow reflected from the clouds. It was time to settle in.

'Coming back to the cabin?'

'I'd like to stay a little, just to think and take everything in. You go.'

'Right! See you in a minute.'

I pulled open the heavy door and looked back at her resting on the rail gazing into the blackness.

A moment of hesitation, a fear that if I turned she would be gone; I shook off the feeling and entered the bright security of the restaurant area where I could see a gaggle of drinkers topping up their alcohol level, taking the crispness out of life.

Carried home from my stag night, (was it only last night?) I was in no position to feel morally superior.

I unlocked the door of the cabin and, left it on the latch, cleaned my teeth and tottered to the bunk, shedding clothes as I walked.

The expression 'life is a succession of moments' ran around my head. Could I and my Universe be the manifestation of elementals existing momentarily in phase? Maybe the spaces between my moments of existence contain other Universes out of phase filling the space/time between my own. I was considering the possibility of death being a phase shift when the brain lost interest and I drifted off to sleep.

The ship was rolling slightly and occasionally there was a shuddering vibration as the diesels hit a resonance point.

'Well!' Al's voice penetrated my consciousness and she sighed. 'I'm supposed to be on honeymoon, and my stud,' she made it sound like mud 'falls asleep in circumstances that would wake the dead. I bet Mick Jagger wouldn't fall asleep on me.'

'He told me it was the only time he lost interest…get off! Don't do that!'

'Move over!' She removed her cardigan, jeans and t-shirt. It was a tribute to her figure that I hadn't noticed she was bra-less. 'He told me… huh! I think I saw one of the Stones at a party, *you* never even got that close.'

'Lights,' I reminded her. She flicked the switch, squeezed in beside me and we lay looking at one another with the bunk light shining down on us.

We made love in the truest sense. The sexual element became something more, something transcendental as the anxiety and the hurt of the previous years was shared and released.

She stroked my forehead with her thumb. 'Don't be anxious darling. We really are 'Us' again.' I looked into her face, content and beautiful. I wanted to hold the moment but she eased from the bed and slipped into the washroom.

'What are you doing?' The spell was broken.

'Never you mind; getting clean, you could do the same.'

It spoiled our closeness and Al was fastidious enough.

I followed her, pulling the sheet down so that the bed got cold.

Snuggled together again she leaned over and tickled my face with the ends of her hair, then rubbed noses. 'I'm ready for you next time.'

We lay silently for a few minutes during which I had a huge wave of sadness and said a prayer to bless Sue.

'Chris?' A long pause.

'What?'

'Was that better than Sarah?'

How insensitive can you get? 'Al! What sort of question is that and now of all times?'

'Don't get cross, I only asked.' Her expression was mischievous but there was a hint of resentment.

'Sarah gave me support during a difficult time with 'kR, she kept me half-moral, if there is such a thing.'

'There isn't.'

'Well she stopped me becoming immoral. It was never the same as 'Us'.'

'Suppose.' There was a pause. 'I bet she did disgusting things.'

'Well if you think you're missing out, you can do the same.'

'What things?' She rolled on me and we cuddled. 'What

things?'

I whispered in her ear.

'Huh! No chance.' She frowned.

Curled up together we drifted, comfortable, loving. I was almost asleep when Al stirred.

'Ugh! That's horrid! She didn't do that, did she?'

I pretended to be asleep.

The next morning we were woken by a gong from the Tannoy which informed us that breakfast was being served.

Al, up before me, was washing at the sink, naked to the waist.

I sat up and whistled.

'Don't look!'

'Why not?'

She had just finished shaving under her arms and was concealing a small razor.

'Don't have to give up all my privacy.'

'Sorry.'

'You will be.' She aimed a jet of deodorant spray at me.

'Al, you idiot, you've just varnished the inside of my lungs.' She can be thoughtless as well as insensitive. 'It could ruin my voice!'

'What voice is that?' She was reaching into her bag for a towel and I pulled her pants down....causing her to fall forward and bump her head on the cabin wall.

By the end of a breakfast of coffee and croissants we were speaking again and our relationship was almost back to normal. Half an hour later, seated in the car with the bow doors open and the morning sun shining on to the dockside scene, the incident was forgotten.

I passed a 'Good morning' with the driver of the heavily loaded estate car just ahead of us and we talked for a few minutes about holidays. He was spending a fortnight camping with his family near the Dordogne.

'It's a beautiful spot; river, history, super little mediaeval towns. Nice car.' He said referring to the Jag.

'Yes. Not very practical but Al likes it.'

His wife joined us.

'Are you Chris Phillips?'

I made a quick judgement. 'Yes.'

'My sister took me to a 'king Rock concert, she thought you were terrific and was very upset when you died, I mean, not you, the other one.'

'It was a terrible shock, Bruce was the soul of the band and we were flying. Still,' I dragged myself away from the subject, 'good things happen too, Alison and I married yesterday.'

'Was she the girl who tried to save him? My sister was a fan of 'kR and she followed the story. Oh, I am sorry, I'm sure you don't want to talk about it.'

'That's Ok.'

'Could I have an autograph for my sister?' Her husband gave a wry smile.

'Yes, of course.' I reached under the seat for the map inside which were a dozen publicity photos. I selected and signed one that showed me sharing a microphone with Al.

'Best wishes to…?'

'Lynda.'

Engines were starting at the front of the queue.

'Nice to have met you, enjoy your holiday.'

I got into the car as Al rushed out of the door onto the car deck and leapt in to join me.

Two small girls in the back of the estate car knelt on the seat and waved to us.

We waved back.

We were still waving intermittently when, just after the Pont de Tanquerville we headed for Paris.

Following them had given me a chance to get a feel for driving on the continent and to get used to French traffic lights and road signs. I was grateful.

After about 30 kilometres I pulled off the road at a picnic area and suggested to Al that she had better take over and get used to driving on the right.

'Gentle on the throttle love.' We leapt out of the picnic area like a Grand Prix car leaving the line. I also suggested that she changed up as we approached sixty in second.

'I know!!'

She changed directly into top after tentatively exploring third.

We arrived in Paris late on Sunday morning and at the peripherique took the anti-clockwise carriageway. After a nightmarish fifteen minutes, during which were overtaken by everything, we turned into the city at the Porte du Lyon and headed for our small hotel near the Gare Montparnasse.

At reception, we held a brief conversation in stumbling French, registered and were told that for a modest daily sum the car could be parked securely in an area below the adjoining building. The modest sum was paid and we were taken to our room; clean, comfortable, as pretty and as dull as modern hotel room can be.

By the time I had investigated the shower and toilet facilities Al had changed into a skirt and a skimpy striped sun top.

'What do you think?' She slipped a red beret onto her head, pulled it to one side and posed like a french maid in an am-dram production.

'Wow! Can you carry it off?

She slipped a loose blouse on over the top and buttoned it up. 'You didn't think I was serious about the beret did you?'

''Money, passports to reception, keys, bag.' She grabbed my arm and snuggled against me. I wondered if I would rather stay in the hotel.

'Later.' She said.

How did she know? Was I so obvious?

We left the room clinging to one another, giggling, silly, loving and silly.

Almost all of the happiness was being together; the car, Paris and the holiday were just a bonus. We descended the stairs to the reception area collected a parking-disc and parked the car.

My 'Where then?' as we walked to the metro station at Montparnasse was answered by 'Everywhere.' Al was already in love with Paris. 'Isn't it lovely, just like the films.'

It was noisy and smelt of drains and food, but the street was wide and there was a life about it. With the car safely parked I was feeling free again.

The situation gave me a Jesus moment when I realised why having nothing but skills and ability gives freedom... if...if you are young and healthy.

'Damn,' I muttered.

'What's the matter?'

'Nothing. I had a moment of real happiness and spoiled it.'

'Poor darling I must teach you to be happy.'

I glanced at her, love washed and tingled through me; it was as if we had just met. She caught my glance, stopped and reached for my hand. 'Hold the moment.'

We stood holding hands for an age then she shook her head.

'Come on,' I was pulled after her, 'and stop making me cry.'

We entered the station and bought a pack of tickets each. After poring over the map of the metro and agreeing where we would meet if we got lost we found the appropriate platform and waited for the train.

The excitement of being there and exploring overcame me; our first ride on the metro, emerging at Chatelet, the first real sight of the river, the Pont Neuf. Our chatter quickened, hand in hand becoming arms around waists.

Paris was beautiful; sordid no doubt, as full of unhappiness and happiness as everywhere else, but it had something that London lacked. Space maybe, style possibly; London had those in a different way, but London was a city used and possessed by absent or faceless people who had a miserly reluctance to provide any quality of life for or even acknowledge, its natives.

Paris seemed to belong to its people; perhaps that was the good legacy of revolution.

Notre Dame, its dark crowded interior relieved by coloured sun shafts from the high windows. It was a church where for a thousand years music had been sung. Choral music flowed around its vast pillars and captured me.

The crowds faded into the fabric. The music offered harmonies that were unknown, harmonies that wove with a sweetness and a magic that affected me. It was music beyond music; science beyond science, another existence; it made me hungry for unknowns that I couldn't express, it uplifted but left me unsatisfied.

Life had given me more than I deserved but had distanced me from the eternal. I forgot Al, forgot time and space and self.

She was holding my hand again.

'Are you alright, you seemed lost. Was it the music?'

I nodded.

'I didn't know that you had another you.'

We sat hand in hand until the music finished then leaving the great Church, wandered along the riverbank saying little, taking in the ambience.

It was hot and on a corner shaded by it awning a café beckoned.

'Drink?'

'Good idea.'

We crossed the road, and took refuge.'

'I think we just sit and wait until someone asks for our order.'

We sat and were ignored. The arrival of the smiling proprietor coincided with my decision to sit there all afternoon if necessary.

'M'sieu?'

I looked at my watch. 'Une biere, demi-litre; et pour vous Al?'

'The same.' Her French is as good or bad as mine but she has a lower threshold of humiliation.

Our waiter disappeared.

'I'm "tu". Perhaps you keep that for Katie?'

The waiter returned with our drinks and the 'billet'. I picked it up, paid and added what I thought was about right, but he hovered. I looked him in the eye and realised that 'oui' did not necessary mean 'what do you want?'

He was half smiling.

'M'sieur Phips?'

Synergy weren't big enough, it had to be 'kR, but 'kR never played France.

'Oui.'

'Mon fils' he switched to English, 'recognise you.' He gestured towards the bar where a lad of about seventeen acknowledged my look. 'Is it good if he speak to you.'

'Yes, of course.' I waved him over.

He made a shy arrival so I stood up and shook his hand.

'Chris Phillips, bonjour. C'est ma femme Alison.' He took her offered hand and kissed it. Ali smiled delightedly and began to take interest. He spoke good English and I struggled in French.

He had seen the filmed concert on TV and recognised 'La Belle Alison' from her brief appearance.

We spent a happy hour in the Café being introduced to other members of the family, exiting with 'Au Revoir. C'etait une plaisir.'

'He didn't understand a word you said.' Ali informed me as we walked away. 'And I even know that 'champignon' is mushroom not companion.'

'She really can hit the nail on the thumb, 'Wives are supposed to be supportive.'

'Sorry,' she said, 'I think that not everything you said was fully understood. Better luck next time.'

I aimed a smack at her bottom.

'Ee's a brute.' she said to a passer-by in her Eliza Doolittle voice.

The Eiffel Tower is a must. Huh!

I mentioned that I am not a good sailor but I can put up

with some discomfort and if necessary I take a tablet. I don't believe there is a pill for vertigo. I was fine when the lift deposited us at the first stage, not happy but confident enough to walk to the outer rail and lean on it. Ali was running about with her camera saying 'ooh' and 'look'! I remained leaning on the rail, in control and admiring the sunlit city.

'Let's see the other side.'

She seized my arm and for a moment my knees belonged to someone else. I allowed myself to be led around the outer terrace, walking carefully to the opposite side where we stopped to view the river, the buildings, the sheer integrity of the whole scene. The 'Oohs' and 'Looks' had ceased and her arm was around my waist.

'Take a photo of me.' She passed me the camera.

'Ok, lean on the rail, no, change places, I can get the sun on your face.' I shuffled around her and lined her up with part of the City and the structure of the tower in the background.

'Come on! Let's go to the top.'

I followed her to the lift and we joined the queue. After a wait of about fifteen minutes we were on our way, rising through the narrowing lattice until we reached the upper platform. Ali stepped from the lift with a 'Wow, isn't this great.'

My mouth agreed with a certain amount of determination from my brain, but my knees had developed a will of their own.

'Come on.'

I snatched away from the encouraging hand.

'What is it?'

'Not too good at heights.' I muttered. I think my knees laughed at the understatement; certainly they quivered.

'its okay' she said, it's quite safe.'

'I know.' My knees disagreed. 'I'll follow you.' I managed.

To her credit my best friend looked concerned. 'Oh

darling, you have gone grey. I didn't know you didn't like heights. You don't mind aeroplanes.'

'Different.' I managed, 'Go on love and I'll try to get over it.'

She smiled and skipped on to the terrace, an action that turned me to jelly.

Alone, I shuffled stiff legged but rubber knee'd to a side wall and, after taking stock of the situation, climbed the steps to the inner terrace, moved to the windows and carefully looked out at the spectacular view.

Someone brushed against me and my fibia dissolved; I gripped the edge of the window. A few more minutes and I was able to shuffle around the terrace, an appreciation of the fabulous view displacing the terror. A mad confidence crept over me. 'I can do it.'

Descending the steps I slowly, casually, headed for an exit to the outer terrace knowing that if I stopped I would freeze. Through the door, into the light, on to the terrace, four steps. I put my hands on the rail, my grip compresses the wood. Please, please don't let anyone bump against me. I adopt a kind of frozen nonchalance and after an age am able to look around.

Ali, in her 'Rock Chick' T-shirt has acquired two admirers and is being photographed with them. They move in my direction chatting, one of them is pointing out places of interest. By the time they reach me I am in control…just.

Ali cries, 'Well done Chris,' and to her two companions, 'He doesn't like heights.'

They are American students on a tour of Europe and after they have shaken hands, an activity that stretched my resources, I am told that they saw 'Synergy' in Baltimore.

'Good band. You were brilliant.' I begin to like these guys.

'Don't encourage him.' Ali tells them, and to me, 'They know a café with music and we are going there this evening.'

'Ok. Give me five minutes to take in the scenery, I'm damned if I'm going to waste all the terror that it has cost.'

'I'll meet you at the lift' she tells her new friends.

'You'd better take a photo to prove I was here.'

I rest an arm on the rail and smile, a sense of leaning back into nothingness hits me and I feel dizzy. The shutter clicks and Alison, taking my hand leads me around the terrace pointing out places of interest. Eventually we head for the lift; Ali puts an arm around me, 'You still look a bit grey but…' she kisses me and whispers, 'I think you'll live.'

Our two American friends were waiting and during our descent, with my spirits rising, their conversation showed them to be polite, intelligent and amusing, and I wondered yet again why Hollywood presents young Americans either as either sex-obsessed morons or violent super-heros.

Nice guys, but I didn't want to spend the rest of the day with them, and when we were back on terra firma decided that assertiveness was needed.

'Listen guys, it has been nice meeting you, but we have a few places still to see. Would you mind, we had better be going.'

'They've promised to show us Paris then take us to a café with music.'

'The café will still be there this evening. If we get directions we can meet later.'

Al looked annoyed but said nothing as the name of the café and its address in Montmartre was given.

With handshakes we parted.

'We'll be there at eight thirty.' Al's words left no doubt.

'Meanie.' she said as we walked away.

'I'm not wasting Paris and you on other people.'

'They might ask us to sing.'

I should have guessed. Her life was stable and she was keen to perform again. I had some ideas of my own, but at the moment was saving them.

'Not if they have ever heard you,' I said, getting my own back.

'Double meanie.'

'How many times have you knocked my singing.'

'That's different' she said, 'you can't sing.'

'Oh? And how big was the biggest audience when you fronted a song.'

'Double meanie with knobs on.' *(She can be so infantile.)*

She was pouting. sarcastic

'Give me a kiss.'

'Don't deserve one.' She pecked at me.

'A proper one; and stop being childish.'

Her look would have melted glass, then, while the crowd meandered around us, she offered a proper kiss that lasted for two minutes.

Making up was nice.

We walked to the metro, climbing the steps to the platform, and after a few minutes were humming our way towards Concorde where we exited, finding ourselves at the end of the Champs Elysee.

I had visited once before as a fourteen-year-old when everything had been fascinating but superficial and my confidence was based on ignorance. It was a more cynical CP who finally capitulated and conceded that Paris was a lovely city. It was impossible to resist, especially when accompanied by a girl whose 'joi de vivre' (what a great expression) made her beautiful. Always attractive, happiness added a sparkle and in a city filled with lovely women, she was turning the occasional head.

So we strolled up the avenue hand in hand, stopping at a pavement café. When the waiter arrived Al said 'Pernod s'il vous plait, et pour vous Chris?' I offered the conspiratorial wink of a best friend and she wrinkled her nose and smiled.

We sat watching people stream by; some busy, some looking, some on show. Once a passing couple caught my eye and I was tempted to smile, enjoy recognition. Moments later they were gone, forgotten as the endless pattern of colours drifted past, part of, but isolated from us. The noise (and the smell) of the traffic faded; the ever present rush punctuated by the buzz of scooters and the occasional horn became remote.

Now and again I would look at Alison, and she would

smile, seeming, in my romantic haze, to become the girl I had met at 'The Troubadour'.

Reluctantly we rose from the protected status of observer and joined the race, arriving at the Arc and descending the subway to pay our dutiful visit.

Our return to the hotel gave us a chance to shower and change following our exhausting day of 'relaxation' as we soaked up the feel of the city. It also offered a chance to give in to that mix of love and lust that had been stalking us all day.

We left the hotel early, intending to eat in Montmartre prior to finding 'La Fenetre.' Al suggested that we try a side street pointing out a small restaurant which even early in the evening had several customers. It was a rule of thumb that if the locals ate there it was safe.

Once we were settled at a table in the corner, a smiling waitress approached, completing over her shoulder a conversation with someone in the kitchen.

'Bonsoir.' she set about providing us with menus.

'Bonsoir.'

'Engleesh?'

'Oui. En vacances.'

'Ah,' she informed the other customers.

She was about Al's age, tightly brushed, professional. We would be her best friends for three minutes.

'You stay in Montmartre?'

'Non, pres de Montparnasse. Ce soir nous visitons une café qui s'appelle La Fenetre.'

She said something that seemed to doubt its existence, then 'You play music?'

'Oui.'

She looked a little surprised, which gave me a twinge of anxiety. With a smile and a shrug she left us.

'What did she say.'

'You heard everything. When I said we played music she looked a bit surprised.'

Al inspected the menu. 'Perhaps she didn't understand your subtle use of language.'

I pretended to ignore her, but saw the corner of her mouth twitch.

'What is steak tartare?' She asked.

'I don't know.'

'Well, if it's steak it must be okay. It wouldn't be horse, would it?'

'I don't know.'

'For someone who knows everything, why is it whenever I ask for useful information, you never know.'

'I'm going to have Cous-cous.'

'What is it?'

'I don't…I think its Arab.'

'You don't know do you? It might be horrible.'

'Listen love, if it's on the menu it follows that people eat it so it must be edible.'

'It might be like tripe or chitterling, people eat that. Ugh.' She gave an expressive shudder. 'I think I'll stick to the steak with frites.'

'Okay, I'll take a chance with the boiled camel hump.' This provoked a giggle. ' Honestly Al, I'm happy to eat anything.'

We teased one another for a few minutes until the waitress returned for our order. I ordered our choices and requested a carafe of house red. There were a couple of other tables with a carafe of red so I guessed we were safe.

It was after about fifteen minutes of friendly conversation that our meals arrived.

My vegetables and wet sawdust looked reasonably appetising, Al's blob of uncooked pink mince and bowl of chips, less so. The green eyes opened wider and she looked at me. I smirked, and felt sorry for being mean. Only a little bit sorry; I didn't mind her little digs, but they could get wearing.

'All right?'

'Fine,' she said, 'it's always nice to know you are with

someone who will eat anything.'

'What does that mean?'

'It means, darling Chrissie, that I think I prefer the look of yours and since you said, you don't mind what you eat…'

'I didn't say that.'

'and you love me.' she added. 'Could we swap?'

This was a new tactic.

'Go on,' I said, 'and don't you dare pinch any of my chips.'

She pinched a few of her own and changed plates, leaving me with the pleasant task of working my way through a blob of cold shredded beef. At least, I hoped it was beef.

It was fine, but the wine was awful and after a mouthful I shook my head and waved to the waitress. Now I had the food, I could take a chance.

'Le vin. C'est un peu … tarte.' I said and made a face. Al smirked into her cous-cous and muttered *'Don't call the waitress a little tart.'*

She shouted across the café to the man at the bar something that began 'L'anglais…' and gave me a French look. Several diners looked up. The carafe was whisked away and a couple of minutes later returned with a clean glass. I was offered a taste, it was better, well different or lighter or something.

'C'est meilleur,' I said, hoping it meant 'better'.

She nodded and left us.

'Wow!' said my companion. 'I can remember a Chris Phillips who wouldn't have complained about short measures in a pub.'

'I guess 'king Rock raised my humiliation threshold.'

Before the evening was over that statement was going to be tested.

I quite enjoyed the 'Steak Tartare', it was more interesting than the Cous-cous that Al had in exchange. I was feeling rather pleased with myself when, after a coffee, we left the restaurant and headed for 'La Fenetre.'

It proved to be not a café, but a kind of bar with 'La

Musette' on a sign, over the door and next to it a narrow alley with a small sign saying 'Club Fenetre'. We arrived at 8.30 precisely and were greeted outside by our American friends.

We exchanged greetings and Al was kissed in the French manner; a couple of people pushed past us and headed down the alley. It was dark and I was wondering if we were being too trusting when a group of students greeted our friends and entered the alley.

We followed them to the side door and entered.

'We have paid.'

'Thank you. Aren't they darlings.' Al offered her most devastating smile. 'Chris will get the drinks.'

Our entry to the club revealed a much larger room than expected, a high beamed ceiling with concealed lighting supplementing the coloured lights and reflected shapes arranged around the small stage. The décor gave a focus to the stage and it could be seen that the reflected light represented the glass of a window; the black background creating the frame and its shadows. Candles flickered in holders surrounded by three sided coloured shades, each of which replicated the window motif.

We were led to a table near the stage and introduced to its two occupants.

Once settled I asked the difficult question. 'So am I right in guessing that you lads are Manny Quin?'

The stage supported a drum kit and several guitars, to its right was a piano and double bass. On the drums was the logo, Manny Quin. Concluded that the name connected Manfred Man and The Mighty Quin, I dismissed it as awful.

'Good guess mate!' the drummer was Australian. 'That is our name for this place.' He laughed.

'Tell me, did you pick us up? That's not a complaint, I'm just curious.'

'Do you want to tell him…?'

'I guess, there's nothing sinister about it. Synergy had a couple of hits and the two chicks were pin ups. Some of the guys at college at that time had posters and we recognised Miss Smith' he nodded at Al, 'when we saw her at the tower. It was like a teen dream coming alive, though Kevin preferred the other girl. What was her name Kev?'

Kevin had returned with the drinks.

'Who was the chick in Synergy you were into?'

'Sexy Susie.'

It shook me. 'Listen guys, I'd better give you a potted history before you get in too deep.'

Al bless her, was reaching for my hand.

'Let me tell them?'

The offered hand was squeezed, 'Go on then.'

She explained the situation, giving the bare outline, avoiding details. There was a silence at the end.

'You couldn't know, but it's still difficult for me.' I was rewarded with a nod and blank faces.

'So tell me about your band, how long have you been together?'

The change of subject proved welcome and over the next fifteen minutes the relaxed situation returned. The three Americans were college friends who had come to Europe for fun, with a hope of earning a little money. The drummer had been found at one of their early gigs; an itinerant Aussi trying his luck in Europe with his locally bought kit filling the back of a 2CV.

'When are you on?' I asked.

'About now! Then the jazz trio takes over, and then at 10.30 we do a second spot.' Paul paused. 'I wonder...'

'Yes we will.' Al surprised him. 'You were going to ask us?'

His choice was now limited.

'Would you? We just wondered if you would come up and say something; we do a couple of your songs, they're simple and kinda easy to play and...shit.'

'Which ones?'

'*Soul Friend, and Look to me.*'

'I think Al would like to sing; if she does could I borrow your guitar and sit in? I'd like to set the sound before we go on and explain what we would want from you.'

'Chris! They haven't actually asked us to play.'

'It would be great to have you join us; we know that you don't ask pros.'

'Perhaps that's why no one has ever asked us.' I laughed. 'We would love to join you; it's the best offer we've had since 'king Rock folded.'

'kR?' The drummer frowned. 'I thought you were Synergy.' 'I was in 'kR, I replaced Tony Shelton when he was injured and stayed until they folded. Al joined us in the States as a backing vocalist.'

There was a moment of awed silence.

'Paul and I went to your Baltimore gig and it was wild. I recognise you now, you were the other guitarist.' Kevin ended rather lamely. 'Hell, we didn't know you were that big.'

Big? Certainly 'kR were on the up, but it didn't seem like 'big' from where I was; just a lot of people, a lot of pressure and a lot of work. I changed the subject.

'Listen, Al's right, it was good of you to ask us along, and we don't want to muscle in on your gig.'

'We hoped you might join us but we didn't connect you with 'kR.'

'We're between bands so guesting with you is great, but we will need to set ourselves up, we would hate to be the low spot in your set.'

'Don't be a fusspot sillyphillips.' Al giggled at the little twist of words in her head and muttered 'Phillipot' before giggling again.

She is meticulous about her own performance, warming up her voice and practising phrasing and technique, but she was never very interested in technology, strumming happily on her acoustic or on my spare Strat provided it was pre-set. I took a lot of trouble because lacking a special talent I had to make the best of what was available.

Apart from a great deal of practice which gave me the space to perform, I worked at the details, looking after my hands and my nails, being careful with the setup of the guitars, amplifiers, pedals and microphones. Together these added the 10% that made us better than bands that took less trouble. Bruce, for all his wildness, was even more obsessive. It was something on which we agreed absolutely and one of the details that got me into 'kR.

'Fuss or not,' I was firm, 'it is important otherwise we'll make a hash of it, 'and,' I added, 'no more wine for you until we have performed.'

Al didn't quite know how to take it and the members of Manny Quin looked embarrassed.

Paul looked at his watch. 'We are on.'

'Sure, I understand. Good luck, and go for it!'

They were good like a lot of US bands, precise, good harmonies, and competent guitar work. You could take them anywhere and they would put on a good show, but they didn't have an Al or a Bruce to lift them to the next level, and I said so in slightly kinder terms when they came off stage.

Al clapped furiously and stood up when they joined us. 'Super! You were wonderful.' She gave each of them a hug displaying genuine affection.

'They were good!' she turned to me for confirmation.

'Brill, great performance lads. Don't take Alison away from me or I could end up singing in subways. Let me get another bottle.' I stood up. 'None for you until we've sung.' I ruffled her hair and she viciously pinched the back of my thigh.

The jazz group, as might be expected in a club where they take jazz seriously, were brilliant. The pianist and the bass player were good, but the drummer was a revelation. I had never heard such subtle, varied, neat supporting playing. Not only did he provide a solid basic rhythm but pointed it up with sparkling fills constantly varying in emphasis. I knew nothing about the technicalities of drumming but I knew 'brilliant' when I heard it.

Leaning over to Al I whispered that with him in the band Cats Whiskers would have gone stratospheric. She turned on me telling me abruptly that the remark showed that 'I had no idea how much Terry had done for her.'

I had belittled her in front of her admirers and she was getting her own back. She also explained the Manny Quin joke, which I had got wrong. 'Mannequin? In the window, fenetre, get it?' She tossed her head; yes, she actually tossed her head.

In the interval Paul took me on to the stage, where I adjusted the small PA to what I hoped would make us sound good and tried his Gretch. It felt awkward, but played well. The band introduced us. 'We have in the audience two well-known rock stars, Chris Phillips of 'king Rock. and Alison Smith of 'Ali et les Chats'.

'Not really stars.' I thought and so, from the sporadic clapping, did the audience.

We stood up, waved to the sole table that recognised us, walked to the stage and shook hands with Paul.

Moving to the microphone I managed 'Bonsoir! Je m'appelle Chris Phillips et la belle femme ici est Al Smith. (Despite Al undermining my confidence.) Ce soir nous …' I ran out of words. 'Le premier chanson est *Soul Friend.*' I was reminded of our first Welsh gig and hoped that I hadn't said anything too stupid.

I glanced at Kevin, then at the drummer, and nodded. He struck into a replica of Terry's intro and with a glance at Al I chimed out the opening chords.

Al performed. She more than sang, she sang with soul flowing out of her. When Kevin and I joined her in the harmonies, there was a little crack in her voice.

Sol's bass line thudded away on my left and together with the rest of the sound it almost overwhelmed me. It wasn't Synergy, but it was pure, pure joy.

It wouldn't have mattered if the audience had been indifferent, but on the final note, cameras flashed and we received what for a cynical Parisian audience passed for warm applause.

We took a couple of bows and before we left the stage and returned to our table Al kissed the band members.

'You were wonderful,' I told her.

'You were pretty good too.' she replied. 'No, you were terrific.' She kissed me. 'Professional.'

I frowned. 'Sure?'

She nodded.

I sat close and put an arm around her while we listened to the rest of the set. They played 'Look to me,' one of our B sides as a tribute to us and came off looking pleased to more ecstatic clapping from Al and much thanks and praise from me.

It was one of those super evenings; my own enjoyment amplified by Al's infectious happiness. Paul told me quietly that he had never seen chemistry in action. 'She's great isn't she?'

I nodded and whispered 'She can be bloody hard work, but she is worth it.'

We caught the metro back to Montparnasse and walked from there to the hotel hand in hand talking quietly, two people in love. Everything that was said had an intimacy of its own, as if we had just discovered it for the first time. Al was saying how kind it was of the boys in the band to let us play and I remarked that it was strange to hear another band play '*Look to me*'.

'Apart from Cats Whiskers, I don't think anyone else has played it.'

Al stopped. 'How did you know we played it? She was suddenly tense. 'How?'

I went a bit red.

'I came to see you once.' I felt uncomfortable saying it.

'You came to see us?' Her eyes opened wide and her breath quivered. 'You came to see Cat's Whiskers?' She was gripped by an emotion that I couldn't work out. 'Where?'

'Cheltenham.'

She stood quite still. 'You came to see us?' she said again,

'Why didn't you speak to me. Why?'

'Couldn't handle it. I knew that if I spoke it would open up old wounds. I missed you.'

She stared at me, but she was somewhere else; in Cheltenham, two years earlier I think.

'You were near to me and I didn't know.' She spoke to herself, close to tears. 'You Pig! That is so hurtful, even now. Surely you could have said hello.'

I gripped her hand. I was afraid she would run away.

'It was cruel.'

'It was a difficult situation, I did what seemed best.'

'Best for you.' She threw the words back at me. 'Didn't you wonder how I might feel?'

'Of course I did. I wanted to come up and hug you but my emotions were all over the place and I know you...' I left the sentence unfinished recalling the turmoil of that evening.

'What do you know?'

'You might have been unkind to get back at me, or done that 'What are you doing here?' thing. You looked as if you weren't enjoying the evening.'

'I was enjoying it,' she contradicted, 'it was everything.'

She withdrew her hand, and I could see tears.

Back in the hotel we got undressed in silence and after a spell in the bathroom I got into bed and lay down. She slipped in beside me and reached for my hand.

'I'm sorry I got upset, you couldn't have known how I was feeling at the time. If you had spoken, praised me or been kind it would have helped me so much.' She went quiet, 'I might have pretended I didn't care but probably I would have thrown myself at you and hugged you.'

She gave a sad little laugh that evoked memories of that evening for me.

'I wouldn't have let you leave, I would have clung to you and made a scene. It would have been awful.'

My mind considered the possible scenarios. They were all too painful to contemplate and I pushed them away appalled by the thought of tiny decisions affecting life and death.

'Poor darling.' She too had seen the possibilities and

understood them. 'You couldn't have known how I felt. Anyway…'

'What?'

'We are on our honeymoon.' She snuggled up closer.

CHAPTER 15   Going South

(Alison's Story.)

Two days later, leaving behind beautiful Paris we headed south.

During our short visit I had fallen in love with the city, with performing, and with the boys in the band who had been so complimentary that I felt like a star.

I was also in love with my new husband; so happy with life that I had started to tease him. The teasing had begun early in our relationship; it was a reaction against his self-assurance at a time when I felt very insecure. After the 'bad' time when our friendship was renewed he told me that he had been struggling too and was often hurt by my comments. I promised that in future I would confine my put-downs to when he deserved it.

I knew it was a flaw in my character just as my actions in 'La Fenetre' had shown another flaw; a happy girl on her honeymoon flirting with two members of a band.

I thought for a few moments on the repetitive nature of soap operas where the characters constantly make the same mistakes and 'hope' the outcome will be different. I suppose if they learnt the 'right' way, there wouldn't be a story. I shook my head. I was beginning to analyse things like the dreaded Philliposopher. Leaning across the car I kissed him.

'Love you Phillips; sorry if I don't always appreciate you.'

'What?'

We were travelling at about 80 mph down the Autoroute du Soleil. There was precious little soleil.

'Appreciate you. You were wonderful last night and I should tell you.'

'When we played or when we got back to the hotel?'

'Both. Especially at the club; Paul was seriously chatting...admiring me and it would have been disappointing if you hadn't shown you loved me.'

'You deserved the admiration; I knew that you had developed but no idea how far.'

'Really.'

'Seriously. There was an upside to your 'year of penance.'

I put my arm around his shoulders. 'Thanks, it was for you.'

He smiled across at me, a boyish grin beneath a set of expensive sunglasses, the ridiculous gorgeous blonde hair and the back to front baseball cap. I reached for the camera and took a photo. It sits on the table in the bedroom with its legend 'The original dead-head.'

I was wearing a white bowls caps with my sunglasses and a little red neckerchief. My father had once said that I could wear a tea cosy on my head and make it look chic. Dads say things like that.

'Like it?'

Chris meant the car.

'Great!'

We had left Paris about two and a half hours earlier and were about a hundred and sixty miles south. The car was quick and comfortable, but with the hood down it was noisy and even with the windows raised I had to sink down in my seat to avoid the worst of the draught. I enjoyed the looks when we pulled in for petrol or food, but the more practical side of me would have swapped the power and style for a saloon with air-conditioning.

It was a time of living. As we progressed south we simply enjoyed the scenery and the picnic areas and the differences. I was learning to love the simple things after a period when I felt the need to be loved by the world.

The gigs in the US and Europe with 'king Rock were so exciting that when they ended I was afraid I would become discontent. It was a relief to find that family and friends, normal life was what I really enjoyed; it was the foundation on which my life would be based.

I wanted to sing again and other ambitions floated at the

edge of my thoughts. Renewing my education and starting a business were two. The best thing was that I wanted the obtainable.

Paris was a ray of brilliant light at the end of the dark tunnel I travelled after my tour with Cats Whiskers. My 'good time' with my own band had been hard and exhausting leaving me frustrated and unhappy. I had gained the 'independence' I sought but the price had been high.

I didn't do drugs and with love unavailable, a couple of brandies and a few cigarettes after the show had been my sole pleasure.
I never drank much but one evening after a miserable show I lost count and got smashed.

The following day, judging my mood Terry took me aside and said 'Al treasure, I can't have my best girl becoming alcoholic.'

I told him I could look after myself but he said 'No darling, you may not think so but you are still an innocent, and someone must look after you.' He was quite serious and after some bluster I was soft enough to say 'Okay I promise; one brandy, two if you buy the second.'

Sue's death came as a terrible shock. I managed to finish our commitments, but when I went home to the normality of my parents and the pressure came off, the whole horrible mess seemed to explode.

It was a small thing that triggered it off. Mum had taken Sarah to see Chris several times and I asked her how he was.

'He's very unhappy' she said, 'he misses Sue and the poor silly darling feels guilty about everything.' 'He always asks after you' she added.

I broke down the following day.

Mum became anxious and called the doctor. He gave me some pills which helped a bit but I felt as if I was in a black pit with no way out and when I was alone it seemed as if nothing mattered or made any difference and I might as well be dead.

Sarah was my lifeline, she was a small bundle of life,

loving and dependent and with Mum's help I managed to get through Christmas in a state of blankness as if it went past me. I thought of Chris on Christmas day and how miserable he must be and that set me off again.

In the New Year Margaret and a girl from the church came to see me. I appreciated their visits and felt a little better but I couldn't drag myself back to a state that meant anything; life was just grey. Then one-day mum went up to the farm with Sarah and rang to see if I was okay. She brought Chris to the phone and as soon as I heard his voice I broke down and began to cry. He put the phone down but Mum must have asked him to talk to me again. He said something that brought back memories and that he hoped we might be friends. It helped more than I realised at the time.

It several weeks later that mum asked me if I would like to go with her when she next took Sarah. I thought about it for two days, terrified that he would be polite but cold, not the person I knew.

When we arrived I couldn't get out of the car and sent Mum in with Sarah. She came out after a few minutes and waved me to come in. I tried to look confident as I went to the door but I was terrified.

He was waiting at the door and we shook hands; I looked into his eyes and was shaken to see the sadness. We went into the kitchen still holding hands and I went totally emotional and threw myself at him. He said it was good to see his best friend again.

It was like a weight lifting, and from that moment I began to improve. In small ways at first, then, after our first day out, it seemed that the world was good again. It wasn't just finding my best friend, it was healing the rift, putting things right.

It was good to be friends again but there remained a shadow over our relationship.

Chris is possessive; he tries to be cool about things but my relationship with Gary had hurt him badly and his only way of dealing with it was to shut me out of his life.

I was afraid to mention the subject but eventually I tentatively asked if it was forgotten and he said 'Can't forget, I know it's stupid and unsophisticated, but the situation was very painful.'

I panicked and said 'We can still be friends can't we?'

He frowned and said 'When we met again I was afraid you would have changed.'

'Changed, how?'

'You know, lovers, becoming more knowing, less the person I loved.'

'I told you…'

'I knew things would be ok when we met again; you were sad and anxious but I you were the same person. I had to grow up and deal with my jealousies because I still loved you.'

Chris is my special one because despite all his faults there is this magic between us.

OK I admit it he can be a bit dishy sometimes.

We had rented a mobile home on a site in a pine forest close to the beach. With the money that was coming in, it could have been a hotel in Nice or St Tropez but I thought it was wonderful.

My first glimpse of the Med as we descended from the hills was breathtaking. It had to be, an open car at forty-five miles per hour, brilliant sun and wow, blue and green, really really blue and green.

We booked into the site at the reception building where a girl of about eighteen ignored Chris's French and spoke determinedly in English. Chris, who has learned to be a sod, carried on speaking in simple French, pretending he did not understand.

A couple of years previously he would have listened politely but 'kR had toughened him. When he had got his way and she had spoken to him in child-like French he turned on the charm saying it was necessary that he practice her beautiful language, especially with a beautiful girl. He then took off his shades, reached into his bag and gave her a signed photo of himself taken from the wings at one of the US concerts looking absolutely 'The Rock Star'.

'Pour vous.' he said, and with a 'merci belle m'mselle' made an exit. The poor girl was open-mouthed. Outside I called him a 'slimy git'.

'I'm getting better at it aren't I?' he said with his smile crinkling his eyes behind the shades.

Beaches and Colour
We had been lovers for five years but I could still remember our first time; my first time. Like most experiences it wasn't what I expected, but what had I expected? Purity? Something transcendental?

Perhaps that was what I received, a coming together of two souls and a physical lust that tied me to Chris. I was lucky to find my special one when I did, would have given so much worship to my first lover that I could have wasted the best of myself on someone worthless before I found my soulmate.

It's impossible to explain, just being together almost orgasmic with the lovemaking as an exquisite extra…wow.'

After the first time our lovemaking was irregular and I worried that I was a disappointment to him. Later Chris told me that he wanted me all the time but he was afraid it would spoil things. He was a silly old fashioned darling.

Gary was altogether different, leaving me in no doubt that I was wanted. Unfortunately for him his activity was limited to my occasional needs though …never mind.

That was all in the past, I was on my honeymoon with my first and only love, and it had all come together. With his emotions and feelings let off the hook he was love and sex with a vengeance; all over me, sometimes embarrassingly so and I would tell him to behave himself though he knew that I didn't mean it.

We managed some sightseeing, and spent a lot of time on the beach, heavily creamed and in my case under a sunshade because my skin is quite fair and the dreaded freckles can appear if I am not careful.

I became accustomed to the nudity, by the end of the first week was prepared to go topless and for the last couple of days, provided we were reasonably isolated, enjoyed the strange sense of freedom that comes from being naked in a safe environment. I felt relaxed enough to tease him saying 'I only married you because I thought you were a blonde.'

We were lying in the shade of an umbrella at the end of a beach where an outcrop of rocks ran for a short distance into the sea.

The reply was a long time coming and I supposed he was thinking of a suitable response. I was wrong.

'I've been trying to think…'

'Difficult in this heat.' I responded.

He ignored the remark '…to think who 'kR resembled. Bruce came out of the Rock'n R&B scene and Tony believe it or not was a classical cellist.'

I thought of Tony and wondered what made him attractive to women. Chris had been quite jealous and asked me why women couldn't see through him, getting annoyed when I said 'The same reason they can't see through you.'

He was continuing. 'I reckon if you mixed Supertramp with 'Men at work' you would be close.'

He wasn't getting away with that. 'More,' I said, 'like a mixture of 'Bread' and 'Marmalade' then cut the crusts off. Don't be silly!' I recognised the look.

'It's the sea for you missus.'

I was on my feet and heading for the point where the rocks joined the sea. A glance over my shoulder showed him on his feet following. The sand was dragging my feet and I dashed into the sea and out toward the end of the rocks. Another quick glance to see him plunging through the shallows behind me and I was around the end, splashing towards the adjoining beach, the excitement almost sexual. I look over my shoulder; there is no sign of him.

The family near the water's edge are staring at me. Apart from a young girl who is topless they are wearing swimwear. Farther down the beach is another topless girl but most people are covered. A young man standing at the water's edge smiles.

For an awful moment I thought I was going to faint, then I turned and splashed back. Could that be laughter? French laughter? The few seconds were an age when the world seemed to be staring and laughing.

Around the rocks, the water dragging at my knees and there is the rat lying unconcerned on the beach mat. I could see the smirk and could almost hear horrible Dave Jones hooting with laughter when the story was told. There was a plastic cup floating at the water's edge.

'Nice run?' he said before I threw the cup of water over him.

I sat on my beach mat feeling utterly humiliated, and throwing the towel over my head I started to cry.

After a few seconds a wet hand passes me my bikini bottoms and I put them on. The rat now wearing shorts, places our holdall between me and the rocks and sitting down wraps the towel then his arms around me.

Sensitive rat.

Our stay in the south took on a life of its own. The pine trees laying their carpet of sharp needles on the paths to the beach; the sun dappling the sand around our mobile home with shadows. The hot days, French bread and bottled water on blinding beaches; warm cafes and cold beer in garlic laced food smelling streets: The expensive evening restaurants with a smart clientele on promenades at Cannes or Nice. It was enveloping but unreal, like being in a play where the only workers were background staff, behind the scenes. I loved it but had not felt part of it until the end of our first week.

We had returned to Cannes, to a restaurant that served good food at preposterous prices but allowed us to sit on the raised terrace overlooking the promenade and the sea.

We were so into one another that we might as well have sat on the sea wall eating sandwiches and saving money but I wasn't complaining.

Chris's miserly habits (sorry darling) came from our first

year in the business, a year of poverty when he inked cardboard to fill the holes in his shoes, darned his clothes and held the band together. It was a time when we all ate the cheapest food and struggled to find the money to survive. Now, he was beginning to reap the rewards of 'kR and our finances allowed him to be generous.

We had finished eating, conversation had slowed and we were holding hands and gazing out over the sea when a waiter arrived with a note that he passed to me. Chris tipped him as I read the note. "The occupants of table 7 would be honoured if Mlle Alison would join them."

The waiter motioned towards the table where a smartly dressed man was standing. He seemed familiar.

Rising, I acknowledged the note and he motioned us to join him and his two friends. Chris raised his eyebrows in answer to my look and rose, taking my hand and leading me towards a face that was becoming more familiar.

The owner of the face stood, took my hand and kissed me on both cheeks.

'Alison.' He was French but his English was good. 'It is a pleasure to see you again, but you do not remember me.' He gave the impression of great disappointment.

'Yes,' it was coming, 'Jean, Jean Bernard; we met when you visited Mr Morris in London.'

'It is of course,' he said, 'easier for a man to remember a beautiful woman.'

I like this man.

'Let me introduce my husband Chris. I am Mrs Phillips now.'

They shook hands.

'Jean was connected with the distribution of 'Cats whiskers' material in France.' I explained. Chris was looking a little grumpy.

'Alison, she is as you say 'the cats whiskers', I am sure you agree.'

'Yes indeed, but no longer one of the Cats.'

'A great shame when they were no more. But let me introduce you to my friends. Please sit down.'

We were introduced to a young man and a girl of about my age. Chris began to show a little interest.

I discovered in the course of our conversation that 'Cats Whiskers' had some success in France. The blend of jazz and rock fronted by 'a beautiful m'mselle' (he said it so nicely) had more appeal on the continent which explained why our royalties had been larger than would be expected from our miserable showing in the UK charts.

I knew of course that 'Ali et les Chats' had had some success, I did not know that at the time of my breakdown, a tour of France and the Low Countries was proposed.

I began to enjoy myself recalling that Jean was amusing, flirtatious and rather dishy. Here in France, the environment, his charm and their superior wine began to work its magic. I had almost forgotten that I was on my honeymoon when a voice said 'Mais non?' very loudly.

'Jean!' The young girl interrupted us. 'Sa mari, c'est Chrees Pheeleep.'

'Oui, je connais.'

'Chrees Pheeleep.' she repeated her eyes opening wide. 'King Rock.'

Her mouth was slightly open and she gave my husband a look that said 'Here or in private?'

'He is a big star.' she tells Jean who begins to take an interest.

You sod Phillips; every time I start to gain attention you have to top it.

He is shaking his head and making deprecatory noises, but he is reaching into his bag for a publicity photo. The girl is holding his arm and looking excited.

'Alain photo.'

She is posing with his arm around her and people are looking. He is a bit of a dish and after the flash he looks at me and winks. He didn't interrupt my half-hour with Jean and it is the longest we have been apart for the whole holiday.

Jean is talking to me again.

'King Rock?' It is a question. 'The name is familiar?'

'A rock band, they were becoming big. I was singing with them.' I added.

'Indeed. When you say 'big' what is that?'

'They toured the USA, thirty concerts, up to fifteen thousand people, and their LP it is suggested will sell a million or more.'

I had impressed him. The million was pure speculation, though it was a possibility.

'What kind of band did you say?'

I try to think of a description but there isn't one, they were 'kR. Phillips is smiling and I put my tongue out; and stretch a point, 'Like the Rolling Stones.'

'No way,' I hear Chris mutter, 'but thanks for the compliment.' He passes the publicity photo to the girl who gazes at it and then at him. 'I sign it to 'La Belle Nicki' from Chris?' The girl nods with an expression that says 'Anything!'

The conversation returns to 'Cat's Whiskers' but I notice the girl is all over Chris. Thankfully he isn't all over her but he has an arm around her and is being charming. No doubt he will have another adoring fan by the end of the evening, possibly two; he is sharing his attention with the young man.

Jean is talking. 'Your husband seems to have made a conquest of my daughter.'

I am amazed and say so. He only looks a little over thirty. 'Nearer forty,' he replies. 'Nicki is nearly sixteen.' I save the information for later.

He begs me to sing at a party to be given on the Friday. He will arrange a professional trio and ensure that they have my music. There will be people there that would like to meet me. In the business! He adds.

What can I say?

'I would love to sing. Thank you so much for the invitation.'

I explain to Chris and he nods agreement. Jean passes me the address neatly written on the back of his business card. I arrange for a rehearsal with the trio before the party starts.

I stood up. Fifteen-year-old Nicki is now sitting on my husband's lap. 'We must go.'

'But of course, I look forward to Friday.'

I am kissed in a way that makes me feel funny. 'Chris,' (Put that juvenile down, Phillips!) 'are you ready to go?'

On the drive back I ask him about Nicki.

'Very attractive and pretty hot, not really my type.' he replies. 'She would have scared me a few years ago.'

'Do you know how old she is?'

'Seventeen, Eighteen?'

I tell him.

'Whoops!'

'Yes, best avoided darling.'

He looks at me and we laugh.

'As if I could fancy anyone else with you around?'

I think he means it.

On the morning of the party Chris washed the car with the help of the two middle-aged men in the adjoining mobile home. They had arrived a day after us and we had joined them for an evening meal in the camp bar on a couple of evenings. The wives were nice, but I was happier laughing with Chris and their husbands. Discovering we were entertainers they asked jokingly if we could give them a song and were rather taken aback when we said OK and ran into *Only One* with our best two-part harmonies. They clapped when we stopped and we were delighted.

We had no idea what to expect at a party in France so the situation made us both nervous. We had one decent outfit each, Chris a white jacket and black trousers and I my black back less. I was in agonies as to what I should wear, 'I'll look a fool if everyone is in jeans,' I told him. I had some black trousers and he suggested that I bought a fancy top to go with them. I found a white sparkling evening top that looked good; I could take the dress and change for the song if need be.

The house on the outskirts of a small village was quite large and modern with a terrace that had a wonderful view down the valley and a glimpse of the sea away to the left. It was simple, beautiful and at the same time; sparse, with drapes and flowers giving splashes of brightness.

From the moment of our arrival Jean was attentive, extracting me from Chris and taking me to meet my band, a middle-aged trio. My heart sank until we began to rehearse; like the trio at La Fenetre they were brilliant. Jean had even provided a microphone and a tiny PA that was perfectly adequate for the situation.

I suspected that his intentions went beyond having me sing at his party but since I was doing him the favour I gently gave out the signals that he was wasting his time. I learned what 'suave' meant as he subtly shifted his attention introducing me to several of his guests.

The party began to warm up and I saw Phillips, now jacketless, was one of the first to dance with the juvenile when the trio began to play. Why is it that my husband has attracted a small group of underdressed underage, oversexed teenagers whilst my sole good looking young admirer has been displaced by a group of men old enough to be my father?

That isn't to say that they weren't attractive. One of my circle who spoke good English with a wonderful accent, was a bit of a dish. Tall and slim with dark hair going slightly grey and piercing blue eyes he gave me the shivers. Almost imperceptibly the others melted away until I found myself in a corner of the terrace sharing a wicker armchair with him. I was so at ease that I knew he must be a successful seducer.

Jean came out to gather me. 'Alison cherie will you come now and treat us to your singing? Excuse me, Lucien, Mlle Alison will sing for us.'

'But yes,' he replied in English, 'I will join you.' He took my hand and led me into the large central hallway. There were about sixty people, some of them elegantly dressed.

'I would like to change.'

Chris appeared with a teeny on each arm. 'Would you like a hand? Excuse me, girls. Alison is going to sing.'

'Juliette has Chrees' records.' Nicki informs me. 'Later we dance with King Rock to King Rock.'

'Yes?' She turns an appealing face to "Chrees."

'Mais oui. Later, my loves, 'C'est un plaisir dancer avec les plus belles jeunes.'

The girls laughed and giggled and I wondered what he had said wrong.

Chris collected my dress, carefully draped and wrapped in tissue, and brought it with my shoes to the bedroom in which I was to change.

'Nervous?'

'A bit. I'll be OK with you nearby.'

'I'll be at the front. Don't worry.'

We went downstairs where I was met by Jean and led to the piano. It was only a gathering of friends in a modest house, but it was the south of France and I felt as if I was in a film.

I took a few deep breaths as he introduced me and went to the microphone.

'Merci, So kind.'

I nodded to the keyboard player and he played an intro and I began to sing. It was so easy that I didn't want to stop; the trio, my ridiculous trio was wonderful. I sang three songs, was warmly applauded, asked to do an encore and was fawned upon by everyone.

Phillips kissed me saying 'Fantastic, you don't need me.'

'I do.' I looked at his face and experienced another moment of happiness before I was swept away amongst congratulation and conversation. My husband and his juvenille harem returned to an adjoining room where, no doubt they "dance with king rock to king rock". Huh!

Later, the trio began to play and I found that I was with my admirer again.

'Dance?' he asked.

'Love to.'

It was an experience. How, in a room full of dancers, even in subdued lighting, he managed to explore a wide-eyed singer was a mystery. I was simply aware that as we shuffled around the floor, whilst talking amusingly he was turning me on. The backless dress helped, but it was magic.

I didn't even know how to protest without sounding like a country mouse. Why, I thought, didn't I meet you when Cat's Whiskers were rolling? I could have forgotten Phillips.

'Come!' he said quietly shepherding me towards the patio. I knew what he meant and where things were heading, but the charm, the gentle grip and the propulsion were almost irresistible.

Almost, and I was on my honeymoon. Tripping over my heel I sprawled full length on the floor, hurting my ankle.

I heard some cries and Lucien helped me to my feet. He knew it was tactical despite my smile as I limped to the side of the room.

Phillips appeared like magic.

'What happened?' He looked ready for a fight.

'I tripped. Lucien and I were dancing.' He had disappeared, together with my possible future as a French recording artist.

'I think you had better take me home.' I hobbled with an arm on his shoulder. 'We must see Jean and thank him.'

We found him talking to or being talked to by Lucien. I thanked him, then Lucien, giving him a kiss and whispering. 'Very tempting, but too late.'

He smiled. 'Jamais.' he murmured in my ear.

Chris drives more slowly when he's had a drink and we had plenty of time to talk on our return.

Are you OK?'

'Fine,' I said.

'What about the ankle?'

'Tactical.'

He understood.

'How about the teeny-boppers?'

'Knowledge without wisdom; lovely but scary. Tony would have been in.'

'Yes. He has it. I mean you've got it darling, but not to the same degree, and you don't make use of it...often.'

'It must come with the job, I didn't have it when we met.'

'I thought you did. So you didn't lust at all this evening?'

'There was a blond girl with huge eyes; she was actually seventeen and only looked about eighteen. She would have been my number one.' 'How about you?'

'I was sounded out as to my future musical plans, explored in the course of a fifteen minute dance, propositioned and sorry darling, slightly tempted by a middle aged seducer. It sounds awful but he was charming.

'Can you imagine saying that to your father?' It was an unexpected reply.

I thought for a moment. 'No. I'm becoming coarse? Sorry.'

'You aren't coarse, but our standards have changed.'

'Only a little I hope.' I changed the subject. I enjoyed the evening, it was a good party.'

'It was and your singing was great and so sophisticated.'

'Thank you. No naughties for you then?'

'Certainly not, that ended when I got engaged.'

I looked at him.

'Well just a little kiss and cuddle, very modest, but she was irresistible.'

'Pervert.'

CHAPTER 16 Return

(Alison's Story)

The next morning we loaded the car and while Chris went to the reception building to return the key and collect our passports, I wandered alone down to the sea and sat on the beach gazing at the horizon.

It was going to be another beautiful day. There were few people around at that relatively early hour and I relaxed and soaked in the feel of the south for the last time. I must have been there for twenty minutes when Chris sat beside me. He looked fit and tanned and I knew how far the tan extended.

'Come on love. Time to hit the road, it's going to be eight hours.'

'We will come back with the children?'

He took my hand and pulled me up.

'It wouldn't be the same, perhaps we will come on our own in a year or two.'

'Sometimes I want 'now' to last forever. Not forever, long enough to feel stable and unchanging.'

He put his arms around me and kissed me for a long time. The sun warmed us, the sea splashed quietly, the sounds of man and nature hummed, became remote. Time stopped, my inner self experienced eternity.

'I feel the same.' His voice dragged me from my other place. 'We are so lucky.'

We walked back to the car, and with a last glance back at the beach reluctantly opened the doors and got in. Chris leaned across to kiss my cheek then started the engine and we bumped our way past the entrance to the campsite waving to the English couples we had met.

Taking the main road we followed it for a mile or so before turning off towards Grimaud, finally reaching the M7 and heading towards Aix en Provence. It was a silent pair who began the journey north.

My head was still full of our holiday, with a small part of me looking forward to seeing the children and the family. Chris, I know, was slowly relaxing as he did before concerts and bless him, he would treat a six or seven hundred-mile journey as something to be organised, like a performance.

We were three hours into the journey; three hours of intermittent conversation and affectionate handholding. Chris was driving quite quickly and once we had reached the autoroute the speed had risen to around 85 and anything more than shouted comment had become difficult. Since our journey to the south we had avoided fast driving and I had begun to like, if not love, our pose-mobile. Now, as I tied my white cap more firmly on my head, I was tempted to risk upsets by offering my real opinion of convertibles at high speed.

Lyon was behind us when we pulled into a service area for fuel then parked some distance from the café. Chris got out of the car and trotted around to my side.

'What's this?'

He opened the door. 'I want to admire those legs as they exit.'

The legs exited and were duly appreciated.

'I would have thought you had seen enough.'

He smiled, but there was something wrong, no, not wrong, something I couldn't fathom in the way he took my hand and walked me across the car park. We ordered coffee and rolls with little pots of jam and butter and made our way to a table with four seats by the window. Once settled, I looked him in the eye and he took a deep breath.

'Yes! There is something.'

I began to feel nervous. 'Go on.'

'I thought it was sensible to wait until now before I told you but it's giving me some bad vibes.'

What was it? Were we broke? Had he got Sarah pregnant? It was unlikely and I had a worry of my own on a subject not unrelated.

He began to explain.

'I had this idea for a sort of surprise and it seemed exciting, not that it isn't. I meant to tell you when we were packing yesterday, but...'

'Oh, get on with it.' He was always deliberate when about to explain, it was something I hated.

'Just explain, tell me!'

He told me.

It was wonderful, unexpected, and crazy except that it was perfectly sensible.

A week after 'king Rock had folded Chris had placed in advert in several local papers saying that Synergy was reforming and that a bass player and a drummer were needed. From the replies he had chosen half a dozen for auditions and had quickly found a bass player.

'He's a bit like Sol, keyboards and vocals really, but he can play bass well enough and we worked well as a comedy duo, he's very funny in a dry sort of way. He's a semi-pro and he wants to get his union ticket.'

Chris rambled on, précising about six hours of audition while the coffee grew cold. His biggest decision had concerned a couple of black guys who had arrived together.

'They were both good; the drummer could manage the musical culture jump and play folk, rock and bubble-gum but the bass guy stamped his own sound on the music. I was tempted to try the different sound but we simply didn't have time, so I funked it. I phoned the drummer later asking if they came as a pair or would he be interested on his own?'

'And?'

'Yes please! We have a band but I never found a singer guitarist. Do you know of one?'

We fenced for a bit before I stood up, leaned across the table, grabbed his shirt front and in a rattle of cups and plates gave him a passionate one.'

'There is something else.' he said as we sat smiling at one another.

There would be.

'We start Saturday fortnight.'

I sat down, a little more heavily. It would be Tuesday

before we were settled at home. Chris was laughing at me; the kind of loose happy laughter that I remembered but was heard less often since Sue's death; this was a return of that bubbly good feeling that was part of Synergy.

'Tell me the rest.'

'Well, I worked out a set, a couple of sets, mostly 'Synergy', a bit of 'kR and some 'Cats Whiskers' and got the boys up for a weekend. We had a great time, Gary fitted well and I knew it was going to work.'

'Gary??'

'The black guy, sorry that's his name.'

'Provocation.' I muttered.

'I was worried there might be a problem with his different musical background, different ideas, different approach, but he coped really well and the music works a treat. You'll like him; he did the jazzy Cats Whiskers numbers brilliantly. Anyway when I was convinced it would work...'

Chris, when explaining things, can send mum to sleep and she thinks the sun shines out of his bottom.

'...I got on to old Morris.'

'Old Morris? I remember it was 'Mr Morris' and then only if you were holding my hand.'

'Shut up Al. I asked if there was any chance of some work if Synergy was reformed and he said... well I won't tell you what he said, but despite that he phoned a week later and said that he had got us a cancellation. D'you remember the Judie B band?'

'Yes. They weren't as good as us and she was a cow.'

'Apparently her guitarist,' Chris gave me an unnecessary look 'found that he was sharing her with the rhythm section and a virulent S.T.D. As a consequence the band is now water under the bridge.'

Chris's eyes creased up and he began to laugh out loud. 'In their case there was little water under the bridge, and none down the loo.'

He continued to laugh at his own pathetic joke in the way that men do when talking about bottoms or anything sexual. 'You could say' and of course he did 'that Judie B banned passing water.' and then he was off again.

He drank his cold coffee still chuckling to himself.

'That coffee was cold!' he informed me. I raised an eyebrow. 'Would you like another?'

'No thank you, but if you are getting one for yourself, buy a bottle of water for the journey.'

'Right.'

He stood up and went to the serving area. I knew what he was thinking but he had failed to come up with anything rude by the time he returned.

'Come on love. I can do without another coffee; I'll tell you the rest on the journey.'

He slipped an arm around me and I felt that affection again. Everything he had done was for me, it was everything I wanted and as usual it was taken for granted. I put an arm around him and squeezed his bottom as we left the cafe.

'You really are my hero'.

Then he looked at me with that look that just made me melt. 'Daft cow, I love you.'

'Me and no udder?'

'Al you made a joke!'

Our drive to Paris gave us time to talk about the summer season. The children would be with us and the work would be fun again. It felt like a happy ending to an increasingly good period in our lives, except that it wasn't an ending.

The summer would be hard work, probably a little sordid and would undoubtedly include difficult and embarrassing moments. The other side of the coin was that we would be together as a family, meet new people and get that thrill of performance. I gave a little shiver; apart from our impromptu set at the Musette, and the sophisticated soiree, my last performance had been with Bruce. I was reminded of that awful day and something inside me heaved. I opened the window and spat.

'What is the matter' Chris was shouting.

'Nothing, a fly or something.' I picked up the water and washed my mouth, spitting again; it was one of the foul brands that tasted of dirt.

'Sorry, I needed to wash my mouth.'

We stopped just short of Paris and found a bar-tabac with accommodation. We had had a cloudy day in Paris and for two days in the south, a hot wind had made life uncomfortable, otherwise the weather had been wonderful. Now, as we drove northwards the weather clouded and it looked as if it might rain.

We sat for our last evening under one of the umbrellas in a little courtyard, relaxed and comfortable in one another's company. The skies were now grey but there was no anti-climax as we talked about our coming musical venture. I felt a new excitement tinged with nervousness.

The next day we drove to Le Havre over roads shiny with overnight rain enclosed in the gloomy womb of a convertible with the hood raised.

Standing on deck as the ferry left the port with a chilly wind whirling under grey skies, Chris turned to me. 'One upset, one surprise and a lot of love. Kiss?'

'It was perfect.' I kissed him.

It was one o'clock before we cleared the ferry, the customs and the port, and another fifteen minutes before we found a public telephone and contacted our parents.

The children were in bed and asleep and we agreed that it was too late to collect them that night. It was another two and half-hours before we could reach the farm so we decided to go to a hotel.

Chris, who is normally straight forward, can be quite devious sometimes and phoned a taxi firm saying he needed to find a hotel. He was given a name and was obviously asked where he wanted to be picked up. 'I just wanted the name of a hotel.' He put his fingers in his ears and made a face. 'Let's get out of here quick.'

We paid for our cheek. It was a mediocre hotel, clean enough, but the look the receptionist gave led me to suspect that it was used by men who had made casual pick-ups. Chris had the same vibes.

'Come along then…sorry, what was your name?'

'Daisy' I said, 'Oh Mr Phillips, it is so exciting being with a rock star.'

When we got into bed Chris cuddled me and we lay in that creaky bed snuggled together.

'Listen.'

'What?'

'Ssh.'

From the next room I heard a faint rhythmic creaking.

'What are you doing?' Chris had rolled on me.

'Come on, keep time!' He began to bounce in time with the creaks from the next room. Just bounce; I was wearing a cotton nightie and Chris had pyjama trousers on.

'Don't be silly.' He was getting giggly.

'Come on, they are beating us. No noise otherwise we can't keep time.'

'No, it's silly. Stop it!'

'If we can get a resonant frequency the whole building could come down.' He was laughing and bouncing at the same time.

Creak, creak. A faint 'Oh' from the next room and I became angry; it was cruel.

'I think the floor is going.' There were tears running down Chris's cheeks.

I was helpless and becoming hysterical I began to push him off, lashing out, tangled in the bedclothes with something crushing me. I felt trapped with the world collapsing around me.

In blind panic I smacked the side of his head, hissing 'Stop, stop it!

'What is it?' He was aware.

'Get off. Get off!!'

As he moved I threw off the covers, ran to the window, and throwing it open, put my head out.

Hands gripped my waist.

'What is it?'

'Go back to bed, its ok.'

Five minutes later I got in beside him and held hands.

'I hate being trapped; it's something that I dread, like you and heights, and it was cruel to mimic people making love. It's everything to them, like it is to us.'

Chris said nothing.

'It was horrid to make fun of people.

He was still silent. 'I didn't realise how crude I had become. Bloody 'kR.' He was ashamed.

'I just meant…'

'Alright! I've got the point.' Silence.

'You're right. Sorry presh, I was disgusting.'

We met them next morning at breakfast. They were younger than we were; he medium height and slim and she the same height and even slimmer, nice looking, almost elegant. I smiled and said 'Good morning' as we seated ourselves, rather late, at the next table.

'The breakfast looks nice.'

'Yes, it is fine.'

'We are just here for the night, and we got in rather late.'

It was sufficient to start the conversation.

Chris, still ashamed of himself was subdued and polite.

They were on their honeymoon and had been married the previous day. I felt happy for them and ashamed of Chris. She was twenty and a secretary and he was twenty-five and an engine room artificer whatever that was. They were going by coach to Paris for a week and on their return his ship was leaving for two months on exercises.

'That is why we put the wedding forward.'

Our breakfast arrived but the conversation did not stop. She was so easy to talk to and we hit it off immediately, just as I had with Sue. It is strange how some people are on the same wavelength.

I told her that we were on our way home from our honeymoon and I was looking forward to seeing our children. I said it unthinkingly and only when she looked a little surprised did the incongruity strike me. I explained briefly. When the time came for them to leave, I felt as if I was losing a friend.

'Nice couple' Chris said as we headed back to our room. 'He is responsible for the auxiliary power on one of the frigates. It must be exciting to be in a position of responsibility on a ship.'

'Oh yes!' I was thinking about people passing through our lives, most of them quite ordinary, then by chance, someone on the same plane; probably a similar background, the same education, the same outlook. It was a shared cultural background that made us instant companions.

I was stupid enough to ask Chris's opinion and he thought about it until I felt like kicking him and then said

'It's about national culture I suppose. Some cultures are about hard work and reliability and common goals and they deliver, others are laid back and don't deliver or are fragmented so that the poor can be exploited.'

I got the picture just before I felt like screaming and he must have recognised the look. 'When the culture is fragmented a wealthy elite controls a repressive government; you can't have democracy without a reasonable amount of common ground.'

I kept silent in case he expanded on it but what he had said stuck in my mind. I assumed good countries simply existed and the thought that if people change their way of life the country doesn't exist anymore was upsetting.

Now that he hasn't got Dave to argue with, "The Dreaded Philliposophy" gets aimed at me. I don't mind, his grumbles about the world are rare enough to be tolerated and he's pretty well balanced most of the time. So he should be.

We arrived at Chris's parent's house just before mid-day after a leisurely drive in the rain. I could see two excited faces at the window. We got out almost simultaneously, Chris locking the door and racing me to the gate.

We were laughing and bumping together as the front door opened and Sarah came running out with Simon trailing behind. I held my arms open and she just flew at me and was swept up and hugged. Chris did the same with Simon, his 'Missed you mate!' a cover up for his emotions. As he joined me I experienced a wonderful, wonderful sensation of being family, the four of us hugged together.

'I missed you my darlings, we had a lovely time but I missed you.'

'I cried when you went' Sarah informed me.

'Did you darling? That is so sweet.' I wanted to cry myself. 'Come on, let's go and see Granny and Grandad.'

'Grandad said that only Simon and I can call him Grandad, everyone else must call him Frank because that is his name.'

'I must remember.'

We greeted Chris's parents with hugs and kisses. They had always been an older generation when Chris and I were first together and unlike mum, who had hit it off with Chris from the first; it had been very much a parents and girlfriend relationship. After Sue they had not known how to react to me and it was only in the last six months that we had become friends.

They had prepared lunch, just a salad, which was perfect and we chatted excitedly about the holiday and distributed presents to the children and bottles to the family.

I was anxious to see my family and poor Chris had the daunting task of visiting Sue's parents. They had given him a difficult time when he had broken the news of our impending marriage. 'Not nasty' he had told me, 'but it is a no-win situation.' He was tight lipped. I suspected it had been harder than he would ever admit but there was nothing I could do except stay out of it.

CHAPTER 17 Synergy.

The family returned home to their house in the Cotswolds; the phrase was curtained in the back of Alison's mind as she drove the luggage filled BMW down the lane and into the drive.

The Jaguar had been returned to its owner, loaned for a modest sum and a set of publicity photos. The admission that it was not their own had come as a relief. Chris pleased to drop the pretence and Alison unhappy with the car. 'Too everything for me.'

'Wait until you see the alternative before you dismiss the Jag.'

The alternative was visible in the yard behind the house as she drove on to the hard standing in front of the garage; a second-hand Transit van.

'We can be like 'The Brotherhood'.

'Who are they?'

'A trio. We met them in Watford; good band, but they hadn't had our luck and were travelling and living in a big camper van. No space, almost literally living on top of one another and trying to stay smart and sound good. I promised myself that if I were ever in a position to hire a warm up band I would get in touch. I've still got their agent's card.

'It wasn't an all-girl band, by any chance?'

'No, it wasn't, and cut the sarcasm otherwise you'll be looking for a new band yourself. Come on, Sarah love, I think mummy's going to sit making faces at the steering wheel all day.'

'Mummy's got a nice face.'

'She has, hasn't she? Let's go to the house and see if we can find where she keeps it.'

With that, laughing and swinging her around, he made for the front door. The letters 'ess oh dee' followed him down the path.

'What's es o de?' asked Sarah.

'Ask Mum.'

'What's s..o..d?' Sarah shouted back at the car.

'What daddy is.' she replied.

Chris opened the windows and the doors put the kettle on and, by the time Alison had unloaded the car he was playing football with the children.

'Do you need a hand?' He shouted.

'Now? No, your timing is perfect.' So much happiness after the emptiness: a sea change; even the small irritations were fun and he needed to relax after his visit to Sue's parents.

She had asked him how the visit had gone.

'Ok. They try to be normal but it wasn't the easiest of visits. Some good bits, they get on fine with mum and they loved having Simon for a week but Liz, who is normally easy going, was quite sharp with me.'

'It is getting better, for all of us; except when I think about it. If only...it was so unnecessary.' He repeated for the hundredth time, and for the hundredth time she felt helpless.

A day was allowed for reorganising the house and their lives. It was quite insufficient. Anne from the village had paid a weekly visit and provided cleaning but the garden and their small orchard had a neglected look; the grass overgrown and littered with twigs and branches from the last gale. They also had to deal with the pile of correspondence stacked on the hallstand and a second pile in the kitchen.

A mountain of washing, lunch and a studio inspection out of the way, it was late afternoon before they settled down to answer the correspondence. Urgent notes from their management were answered over the telephone: fan mail (Alison ignored the large pile for her husband) was set to one side and cheques written to cover outstanding bills. Chris had begun to read a letter from his accountant concerning an unexpectedly large cheque made out to the Alisband company when Alison emitted a whoop.

He looked up. 'Something interesting?'

She was still reading. 'Yes! Just a minute; when are we

playing? I mean, when do we finish at the Holiday Camp?'

'Early September. Why?'

'I've got a part in a film.'

'What? A film about your band or something?'

'No, a proper film. I was talking to someone at a 'kR party and he said he might be able to use me.'

'Oh, you mean as a singer.'

'No, as an actress.'

'But you aren't an actress; great singer but not an actress.'

'Who says I'm not? You always put me down.'

'I don't, but acting is a profession and actors have a special talents and lots of training and experience and techniques and even then half of them can't get employment.'

She thought for a moment. 'Well, anyway, I've got a part in a film.

'Let me see.'

'No!'

'It just seems strange that someone should want you in a film when there are hundreds of actresses and models ready to drop their pants to get a part.'

'Don't be coarse, and before you ask, *don't you dare ask*!'

'I wasn't going to.'

She passed him the letter.

He read it slowly. 'That's really inconvenient. Do you want to do it?'

'Yes, of course I do. It's exciting, like when you joined 'king Rock.' She twinkled at him.

'Clever clogs. OK but find out a bit more about it. It might be some low budget rubbish where the cast take their kit off and a celebrity bush enables them to sell it.'

'You're so cynical. I told you before, don't be crude, the children might be listening.'

'Sorry. I wouldn't want Sarah opening a magazine and seeing her mother naked.'

'Just Simon. Oh! I didn't mean that, it was just a reaction.' She cuddled him. 'Really sorry.'

'OK, I guess I was getting over the top.'

'Give me a kiss.'

'Mmm.' He kissed me. 'One of the pleasures of marriage. I hope it isn't spoiled by all the work we have to do. We've nothing for tea, the boys are coming tomorrow; we need to feed them, and we must clear the spare bedrooms and discuss the set. You will be playing guitar and you have a lot to practise The boys know it but you have a few things to learn.'

'I know most of it; is there something you haven't told me?'

His mischievous grin was met with a frown.

'We need about thirty songs because the 'In concert', and the 'entertainment' sets are different. Most of them are covers or Synergy or Cats Whiskers songs but three were re-arranged for Sue so you need to be aware of the changes. The rest are 'kR songs; you know them but you will need to put in some work on them.'

'What! So who am I, top rock guitarist Bruce Kay or Chris Phillips my devious husband?'

'Say it again.'

'You know what I said.'

'You are me.'

'Chris, I'm flattered, but there is no way that I can play what you play.'

'I can't sing and play like Bruce either so we cheat. I sing Bruce and play a simple version of his guitar part and Paddy sings me.'

'And I?'

'You sing backing and play an easy version of my rhythm part and sustained chords instead of arpeggios during the solos; it will sound good, believe me.'

She looked doubtful.

'I made a tape for the boys come and listen.'

He took her to the other room, searched out a tape and inserted it in the hi-fi.

Al noticed the light streaming in on to the dusty surfaces; a cobweb seemed to dominate the corner of the window.

'Now listen, it's not 'kR but it....'

It wasn't 'kR, but she could hear Chris guitar playing the

simple rhythm that she would play, and his voice, not Bruce but not bad. Over it she could hear simple riffs that were Bruce with the soul missing made exciting by her sustained chords. She felt a shiver of excitement; in a small venue it would blow them away. She forgot the cobweb.

'Who's a clever Phillips,' she muttered half to herself.

'You know most of the songs but you will need to learn the guitar on the 'kR ones and Sue's part on several others.'

Al's protest was silenced. Any that Sue could play, she could play.

'Did you bring Sue into it to wrong-foot me?'

'Don't be silly. Heaven forbid I start manipulating you or anyone else.'

'But you…' she stifled an automatic response. 'Can I use my acoustic? I could use the Ricky, but I never really got on with it'

'No.' He frowned, and rising, left the room. When he returned he was carrying a guitar case which he placed on a chair, standing for a second to look at it.

'You can use this one if it suits you.'

She knew what it was. 'Oh Chris, are you sure?'

'Yes. No point in wasting it.'

Al opened the case and as expected, was confronted with Sue's Telecaster. A lovely guitar, maple necked and finished in translucent cream with a strat neck pickup in a tortoiseshell scratch plate. She was reluctant to pick it up.

'It's been there since our last concert; probably needs a re-string.'

She turned to see that he was struggling with his feelings and was moved to hug him. 'It's alright darling, let it go, it's me, I loved her too.' She was gripped, then the tension went and he cried into her shoulder.

'Poor darling.' Her bad time had come to an end with their reunion; his never could entirely.

'Thanks.' He was gruff and embarrassed. 'Sorry.'

'Never be sorry for showing your feelings, not with me.'

'Thanks, it was a release. Try it, it will lay another ghost.'

She picked it up, clipped on the wide cream strap and

slipped it over her shoulders. Strumming a couple of experimental chords told her that it was a guitar felt 'right', better than Chris's strat, easier than his Gibsons. If it sounded good it was a great guitar.

'Good?'

Unable to speak she nodded and leaning across, kissed his cheek.

It was a hectic week; over thirty songs including five from 'kR were recycled between the sets to provide a different flavour for each. In addition there were several children's songs and a couple of waltzes.

After a lot of bad tempered practice, she could just manage the guitar part on four of the 'kR songs and began to see why Chris had been so ambivalent about king Rock.

During these sessions she began to appreciate his kindness; Sue's Telecaster was a dream to play, ringing the changes from country leads to acoustic rhythms and warm crunchy chords. He could have locked it away but 'Meant to be used' he said, 'and anyway, you would hardly get that sound from the old EKO.'

She remained silent.

Their first set at the holiday camp would include candyfloss songs, children's songs and comedy 'business' from their first season. Towards the end there would be dance numbers and a twist during which the two would be expected to dance with the children and probably their parents. It was going to be lovely, even the embarrassing moments could be laughed about later.

The 'In Concert' set for the theatre would last for an hour and would include the most musical of their numbers to showcase individual talents.

She would need, she guessed about six outfits. It was easy for the boys; a change of shirts and a white jacket or T-shirts and jeans but she had to match them and look girly.

There was a fine line between looking girly and looking tarty.

The boys arrived on the Sunday. Gary was the first with his kit in the back of a small van. He was introduced to Alison and the children and taken to the kitchen for lunch with the family.

Earlier visits in Al's absence had made him at home in the house but he was initially awkward with Alison herself. 'Seen you on T.Vee, strange to be sitting with the real woman.'

The children, after a slight initial alarm, gave him the seal of approval; Simon only after a head to head discussion of the lunchtime sandwiches, Gary's consumption of a half-eaten sandwich offered by Simon sealing their friendship, though Chris assured him that his action was beyond the call of duty.

'I would baulk at eating anything of Simon's.'

He picks his nose,' Sarah informed the gathering.

'We don't want to know that'

'Well, he does.'

'Sorry, Gary,' Al said 'very uncivilised children. it was brave to eat Simon's sandwich.'

'I've eaten worse.' he replied with good humour.'

Paddy appeared soon after lunch and with Gary went to the barn to set up.

'What do you think of them?' Chris asked?

'They seem OK but you can't tell until they are under pressure. At least they didn't show any obvious problems or give the impression of being on their best behaviour. Why do you ask?'

'Nothing. I think the same but you will see the problem this afternoon when we practise. They know the songs more, or less. If they hadn't practised after the first session they would have been out by the end of the second. I told them what I expected and that if they didn't deliver then it would be 'Goodbye.''

That afternoon Al experienced her first performance with the new band. It was great to be singing; it was great to be doing her songs and she knew after an hour that it was going to work despite the flaws, and there were several. Her guitar was needed on all but two ballads with Paddy on keyboard and Chris on bass. She didn't like using a guitar, it inhibited her singing and her performing but without it the sound would be lacking.

On keyboard Paddy was good and his singing was an asset but his bass playing was mediocre.

Gary's problem was much simpler; his drumming was excellent but the kit was worn out. 'He will need to do something about it,' Chris said during their conversation after the practice. 'We have a saucepan lid that sounds better than one of those cymbals. I'll speak to him and see what we can do. The tom-toms and the hi-hat are OK but he needs a really good snare, a ride and a new skin on the bass. Sol's the man. Do you know where we can reach him?'

Al looked away. 'No. We didn't part on very good terms.'

'Why was that? Oh, don't tell me, I can guess.'

'There was no animosity just…anyway,' she continued, 'I wouldn't want to ask favours. I would ask Terry, but I think his band is in the Europe.'

So it was left to Chris to explain to a drummer that his equipment was crap, a chore carried out with tact and a promise of some financial support for the required equipment.

But he remained unhappy and on the second day of practice stopped playing with a loud 'It's no damned good!' He glared at them for a moment in the embarrassed silence. 'Sorry, Paddy, we need Pat.'

'What does that mean?'

'It means we need you on keyboard and singing or the sound is weak.'

'Right. Do you want me to ring him?'

'Give it a try.' He hesitated. 'It means less money, we'll take a hit too but we will all be about 5% worse off.'

'Perhaps,' said Al, 'someone would like to tell me what

this is about.'

'Pat, the bass player from Paddy's old band.' Chris explained. 'He practised with us a few times, but I said we probably wouldn't need him. What do you think Pad, will he be interested or will he tell me where to shove my guitar?'

'I reckon he'll be here before the kettle has boiled.'

Chris relaxed. 'Ok, give him a call.'

It took two hours to locate him and another hour and a half before he appeared. During this period Alison grumbled incessantly about 'finding clean sheets, room not aired, should have warned me.' until she was wrestled onto the bed by an exasperated husband and tickled until she promised to stop complaining.

Her shrieks were loud enough to be heard in the village. 'What must the boys think? They knew where your hands were, I can't possibly face them.'

He carried her down over his shoulder half way between delight and annoyance.

'Had to beat some sense into her.' He put her down.

'If you do that again, you will be looking for a new singer! Don't you dare do that again!'

As the first week ran into the second she began to relax, discovering the joy of being a rock guitarist; Playing with Chris she had, on a couple of occasions felt a rush as they began to generate excitement even at rehearsal.

Chris, of course, had to find something to worry about and had asked her if she thought the sound was big enough.

'When we two are playing in the rock set, we will blow them away. It is a terrific sound for a live five-piece.'

He was unsure.

'Honestly,' she told him. The sound is far bigger than Cats' Whiskers and we had a keyboard and two guitars sometimes.' He was looking tired and she was and protecting him from further self-generated work. The sound was good and she was finding her modest overdriven guitar solos a turn on.

They were ready – well, as ready as they would ever be. The

van was packed with their equipment and people were beginning to arrive. Their parents, Gary, his wife and little girl, Pat, his girlfriend and his brother, Paddy with his wife and their two boys, Dave and Judith, Margaret and Alan, Heather and Andy; all would be joining them later for a party.

It wasn't the big party for the family that she had hoped for, that had been postponed, but with friends and half a dozen children expected, Alison was at her bubbling best. Helped by Marilyn everything was under control and the lunch for thirty people would be ready.

She had insisted that Chris take the day off; a lie in, breakfast in bed and 'Nothing!' to be done that morning. He had complied and slept until after nine, sitting up for breakfast and falling asleep again for another hour.

When he arrived in the kitchen at eleven, she had said, 'Feeling better?'

'Yes,' he had said with a frown. 'I hadn't noticed I was getting tired.'

'I must look after you better. You work too hard.'

Dave arrived with Judith and the children just before lunch bringing with him his parents. Alison, delighted, found herself slapping Chris and saying 'You didn't tell me.'

'Dave said 'Would it be OK' and I said fine.

'Oh! How lovely.' The kiss for Judith and Dave was followed by a loving hug for Dave's father. She took his arm.

'Come and see the farm. Can I take him away?' she asked his wife.

'It would be difficult to stop him.'

'Thank you. Come on.'

As they passed the window her happy face was looking up at him. 'You said it would come right.' They passed out of earshot.

'What was all that about?' Chris asked Dave.

'Dad has always had a soft spot for Alison and when things were difficult she used to phone him and he would cheer her up and offer advice.'

'I didn't know. I'm glad she had someone, I was no use.'

'Hey, now Boyo, enough of that, this is a happy occasion.'

'Yes, I know. It's something I have to live with.'

'Don't be daft.' Dave gripped his arm firmly. 'It's something you need to put behind you otherwise you both have to live with it. Isn't it?'

Chris frowned. 'I know, when I feel miserable I make her feel the same. Thanks mate. Simon! Stop that! Go and find Sarah. She's playing races on the lawn with the other children.

Simon put down the china cup which he was banging on the table and headed for the door.

'We will have to get gates to the drive. He's becoming too adventurous.'

Chris followed him out of the door, spotted Al sitting on their bench deep in conversation with Dave's father, waved and pointed to Simon. She nodded.

'The lunch is ready,' Marilyn informed him as he returned. 'Is everyone ready?'

'Everyone is here. Is Geoff coming?'

'Too busy, but he said thanks for the invite.'

'Right then, if we give it a couple of minutes. Plates hot? Rice hot?'

'Plates warm. It is a buffet.'

'OK, I'll run round and collect people and they can help themselves.'

'Hi, Di. Sorry I haven't spoken. You're looking good.'

Wearing a loose yellow dress she was looking very good. 'Hello Tony, sorry I haven't spoken, I've got to call everyone for lunch. It's just a buffet, chilli and rice, some quiche and salads and some puddings, cheesecake and things. Help yourself, I'll see you later.'

He busied himself calling the gathering together for lunch waving to Al as he approached.

She rose. 'Here's my other half; that's the truth, isn't it?'

'Hi Arwen, Al whisked you away so fast I hardly had time to speak. How are you?'

'Very well for seeing my favourite girl looking so happy.'

He gave his favourite girl a squeeze.

'I'm just an old romantic. I am sure it is unwise to admire girl pop stars.'

'I think you are safe with this one. She's not bad as they go.' He took her free hand and the three made for the door. 'Just about the best really.'

Al who loved praise was driven to say 'Don't be silly.'

The crowd had departed, leaving just the band and the children sitting together in the large lounge. The evening sun filtered through the curtains onto Simon cradled in Chris's arm, fast asleep.

Sarah, feeling very grown up, sat safely between her mother and Pat as the band held their final conference.

She was developing some of her father's habits and as he spoke outlining the arrangements and his expectations, her mother was astonished to see a frowning daughter aping his hand movements as a point was emphasised. Chris noticed too and with more understanding than Al would have expected, nodded approvingly. Her astonishment increased as Sarah performed an appreciative preen which was a replica of her own.

They reached their new home by mid-afternoon the following day and were directed by security to the offices of the entertainment manager. Their welcome was more effusive and warmer than expected from that busy man, who himself took them on a tour of the theatrical facilities before passing them to an assistant. Given an itinerary they were shown to their accommodation, a chalet for the family and another for the rest of the band.

'I hope you guys are compatible, open house ended at the farm.'

'We'll manage.' Paddy nudged Gary. 'We have the common ground of being oppressed minorities in a foreign land.'

'Knock it off mate, I used to get enough of that crap from Dave, bloody Welsh invader. Forever winding me up about oppressed people and 'the yoke of the English,' and he's my best mate.'

'Ah!' said Paddy; 'You wouldn't understand what it is like to have your country taken over.'

'Certainly do, my country is being invaded by every Tom Dai and Gary from the Emerald Isles to the Solomon isles. In a hundred years the English will be writing mournful ballads about the good old days…if there are any of them left.'

'Chris!' his wife became assertive, 'Shut up! You are turning a joke into a lecture.'

'Now I have heard everything,' said Paddy, 'a second generation English Welshman complaining about oppression.'

'Certainly rarer than an Irishman asking for a fat lip.'

'Chris. Shut up!'

'Yes Al. Sorry Pad.'

'I don't mean shut up, just don't go on and on.'

'Right. Sorry Pad.'

'Do you wish you had brought the wife and family Gary?' Pat asked.

'There are compensations.'

Whether the compensations resulted from bringing or not bringing was left unsaid.

They carried their cases, their five guitars and the children into the new home.

'It's a bit small' was followed by a horrified 'Where is the bathroom.'

Chris opened the door to a room the size of a large cupboard, which contained a lavatory a sink.' I think this is it.'

'But where is the bath.'

'I think the shower block is in the middle of the group of chalets.'

'You mean I have to walk thirty metres to get a shower?'

'You don't have to be naked. Mummy is going to walk to the shower with nothing on.' He spoke to Sarah.

'Don't be stupid Chris. You never said it was going to be

squalid. I can cope with being cooped up like a battery hen but now I find I'm going to have to stink because there is nowhere to wash.' She was getting worked up. 'You are hopeless, one moment we are living in five star hotels and touring the world, the next you get a rotten little deal staying in a dump like this.'

'Thanks. You piss me off too, or you would if you did anything for anyone but yourself.'

'What do you mean?'

'You've got a bloody cheek.' He was suddenly angry.

'A couple tatty tours with a good band, then you have a breakdown and send your mother to soften me up so that you could come back and lean on me.'

'Oh that's mean, I didn't. We've always been…'

Yeah I know. 'Close'. Close when you fu....need something. I've worked my balls off to create something as a wedding present and you spit on it.'

He was shaking with fury and Sarah looked frightened.

'I should have stuck with the blonde she knew what 'hard' really was 'and' he threw open the door and turned back 'she was a bloody good f… not a tight arse.' He walked out slamming the door.

Al stared after him then slumped on the bed with tears starting.

Sarah clutching Simon's hand crawled onto the bed next to her mother and began to cry.

Her face in the pillow Al sobbed her heart out, stung by the unprecedented violence of his response.

As the tears faded anger at the injustice replaced the hurt. She sat up sniffing and cuddling the children.

It was so mean. How could he suggest that she had wheedled her way back into his life when all she had wanted was to help?

'Daddy is being horrible.'

'Daddy was too tired to play.' said Sarah.

It took a moment to sink in. 'Of course he is, that is why he blew up. While I was buying dresses he was putting a band together. The tiredness had shown on their honeymoon when, after a long day he had suddenly lost his usual bounce, crept to bed and gone instantly to sleep. Their return had been continuous effort for both of them.

Thoughtless and selfish sometimes she was also fair-minded; 'Even so,' she thought 'there was no need to be so unkind.'

She slipped her feet to the floor and dabbed her eyes.

'Come on darlings lets go and find Daddy.'

'Don't want to.' Sarah said 'Daddy is mean.'

'Daddy is very tired and you were a clever girl to tell me.'

She found him hunched over a coffee cup in the restaurant and putting her hands on his shoulders rested her head against his.

His hand rose and reaching back he stroked her hair.

'Sorry, shouldn't lose my temper, especially in front of the children.'

'You don't have a temper and our clever little girl told me you were tired. You are tired aren't you?' she continued without waiting for the answer. 'I know I'm insensitive sometimes and ungrateful. Dave told me, and Mum, and Margaret, and Gary lost his temper with me three times in the few weeks we were together.'

'I'm glad your sensitivity is returning.' His voice was steely, the anger just below the surface.

'Darling.' She kissed his neck. 'I am ridiculous, I must think before I speak.'

The hand stroked her hair again. 'And I have to get over my tiredness and stop overreacting when you are just being you.'

'That doesn't make me sound very nice. This is supposed to be a holiday as well as work, we can lie-in in the morning and play with the children. It is only four gigs a week.'

'We do have to move the kit once a week and I'm involved in other events. Judging the talent competition and the 'Miss lovely legs' and I have to play in the 'Camp All Stars' football team.

'With your hair?' 'I've done it again, putting you down

without even thinking about it.' She changed the subject. 'Do I have any duties?'

'We all have. You have some poolside duties for a swimming competition, some judging activities for the children and, sorry love 'Mr Muscles.'

'Love you Phillipet. Don't intend to hurt or be ungrateful.'

'OK.'

'People who care even if it doesn't seem like it.'

'Sarah!' she turned 'Come over here.'

The children returned from their first fascinating encounter with a one armed bandit and its dedicated acolyte.

'The man put money in the machine and more came out.'

'Usually you put money in and nothing comes out.' her mother explained. It was as well to get the consequences of gambling clear at an early age.'

'He got lots of money.' said Sarah.

CHAPTER 18   Summer Holiday

They were booked for three shows a week at the camp, a mid week 'Synergy In Concert' spot at a local theatre and, to Chris' annoyance they were expected to provide backing for the comedian's songs.

The shows at the camp required two different sets, one a repeat of their 'in concert' show with more dance numbers, the other, an entertainment evening where the music was supplemented with comedy and dancing for the children and adults.

For the first time in her career Alison had taken an interest in setting up the sound. In the past she had been content to leave it to the experts and was surprised to discover that it was technically so simple but in practice so difficult to achieve a balanced sound that suited the acoustics of the venue. It had taken an age but she enjoyed the satisfaction of understanding some of the tricks. Afterwards the band had assembled for a sound-check when she and Chris could try a few of their dual guitar riffs.

Several staff or entertainers had gathered at the back and a small knot of youngsters bulged through one of the side doors, staff or early arrivals. Chris had relaxed and after a brief discussion with her had said 'OK lets go for it and see if the practice has paid off. We will start with the second 'kR straight through no breaks. Ok Pad?'

'Sure. Ready?'

They went for it. She found that by the end she was on a high. She understood her husband's ambivalence about 'kR, loving it, hating it; being part of that guitar sound at volume and sharing it was a turn on.

She saw a couple of girls at the back punching the air in time. Two of the boys by the side entrance had moved towards the stage watching her as she caught the moment, a mum in old jeans and a baggy T-shirt with her hair in bunches.

There was a stutter of applause as they finished and she

could feel the buzz hearing Pat's whistle and 'hey man that was something' from Gary. She smiled at her admirers, could have done nothing else, her face locked in a state of delight.

They were good. Not 'kR, but far better than their previous bands. She had come together with Chris and the two had pulled the boys along. They were 'Synergy' again.

The young comic, the credibility of whose worldly-wise patter was diminished only by his age, introduced their first performance on the Saturday.

His introduction brought Al into a spotlight, her opening staccato rhythm pointed up by the timed echo. It brought applause cheers and whistles from an audience determined to enjoy their holiday.

Their first set was a history of Synergy and Cats Whiskers, picking out their chart successes and their changing style. 'Once upon a time,' Paddy narrated, 'there was a schoolgirl called Alison who wanted to play folk music. It was just a dream, then one day she met a guitarist called Chris and…'

The musical volume increased and they ran into their first minor hit.

Chris was relaxed; excepting 'kR, the new band was better than any he had played in. He had known it could happen but there had been insufficient preparation time and he was nervous about failure.

The pressure had caused anxious moments and one all out row with Paddy. Al had built bridges explaining to their resentful keyboard player that there was no second best to professionalism and that Chris pushed himself and expected everyone else to do the same.

'Truly Pad, if I wasn't good enough he would replace me. He'd be sorry.' she added and dissolved into laughter.

It had broken the ice and brought them together again. Chris's apologies for losing his temper had been sincere but he was unbending in his demands that they 'Get it right!'

He had acquired some of Bruce's mannerisms and Al could still be surprised by the confident assertiveness that 'kR had given him.

The sound was good and it benefited from the idiosyncrasies of the band members without which it would have lacked the life that was stirring even in their first concert.

Al's hitch in her voice, Pats bass with its minute delay on the first note of a phrase, Gary's double beat all added to the experience that made live music so much more exciting than a recording. It was why TV's manufactured stars could be so dull and it's miming dancers so un-engaging.

As their story unwound, the songs became more sophisticated. The end of the first half saw them bow from the stage leaving Paddy alone. 'That wasn't the end, "king Rock' was still to come. The stage went dark.

Alison made her way to the darkened side aisle stopping occasionally to catch a comment from the crowd. She had settled for 'great sound' and 'more entertaining than I expected' ignored 'not a folk group' and 'too bloody loud' when she struck gold.

'Dad thinks she's lovely, don't you dad.'

'I didn't quite say that.' The voice was not displeased.

'She was in the pool this morning playing with her children, at least I suppose they're hers, and Dad couldn't take his eyes off her.'

'Don't exaggerate, I enjoyed seeing them having fun.'

Al was all ears.

'You called her a pretty little thing when you recognised her.'

'Well, she is. Actually I said 'She a good looking girl.''

'Hardly little and she looks a bit tarty when you see her on stage.'

This was less welcome.

'That's the make up.'

'She was full of life this morning, Dad wasn't the only one watching her.' a third voice joined in.

'One of those women that men go silly about.'

'Nonsense; she's was an ordinary girl having fun with her

children, tonight she's singing with her band and she's good.'

Al enjoyed the moment then slipped through the arch into the main auditorium.

'Hello, I just caught a few words. That is so kind of you.'

Her fan was about her father's age and looked startled.

She bent forward and offered an expression that had melted less vulnerable hearts.

'It is lovely when people like us; otherwise we feel that it's hard work for nothing.'

Her fan found his voice. 'We were saying that we thought you were very good. We saw you on Television a couple of years ago but now you seem different.'

'There were two girls then,' his wife chipped in, 'one of them was very pretty.'

'She still is' said her fan, earning an appreciative smile.

'The other girl was Sue. She was married to Chris the guitarist and she died in an accident.' How simple it sounded. 'We all had an awful time.'

They were strangers and she was blurting out private matters.

'I'm sorry; I'm terribly talkative when I'm happy.'

'Would you like a drink, are you staying for a minute?'

'Thank-you, a grapefruit and lemonade would be lovely. You don't mind? We generally split during the interval to relax and unwind because Chris can be a bit of a taskmaster.'

One of the daughters was given money and made her way reluctantly to the bar.

By the time she returned Al was holding court. She was thanked for the drink and settled down to listen as Al amused her fan and his family with a detailed account of an incident that had happened to her and Sarah in the US. She had just completed her narrative when the 'Taskmaster' found her and chivvied her back to the stage.

'Lovely to meet you.' She kissed her fan and fled.

'Well, who would have thought it!'

'Dads in love.' giggled his younger daughter.

'Shut up!' He settled to watch the second half, his mind

full of the girl. 'Maybe, if I was twenty years younger,' he thought 'and not saddled with you lot.'

The second spot kicked in with some jazz-rock from her Cats Whiskers period. She had overcome the sense of time wasted; had shed her tears for a time that was good but unfulfilled. Now she could enjoy what could have been.

The set moved towards the 'kR finale and its memories; focussed and alive she revelled in the good feeling, leaving the stage clutching her Telecaster like a friend.

Chris was congratulating the band.

'Well done boys, great for a first performance; brill Gary.' He looked at her, smiled like the boy at the Troubadour and shook his head again.

She put her guitar in its case and turned to see that Chris had been called away and was talking to the entertainment manager. He frowned, argued then shrugged and turned away.

'Sorry guys after all that work we have to cut 'Requiem.' Too morose, entertainment and fun is our aim. Al sorry love 'Right Hand Man' is out too.'

'Why?'

'He said he doesn't like the innuendo; it's too rude for a family show.'

'What innuendo. What is rude about it?'

'Aah, well,' he hesitated, 'you remember Sol and Dave used to pull your leg.'

'They were always pulling my leg.'

'I know.' He ducked his head then looked at her out of the corner of his eye. She didn't like the smirk. 'We were messing about and Dave said something and Sol added a bit and half an hour later we had a song. Dave bet me a quid that you wouldn't realise that it was filthy and he was right.' 'Sorry love I sort of forgot about it; it works perfectly well as a straight love song it is only when Solomans or Jones get their minds working that it becomes rude.'

He hugged her 'You were great tonight.'

'You were great too, so I will let you get away with it.'

She kissed his neck then bit it. 'Almost.'
'That hurt.'
'It was intended to. Now tell me what the song is about.'

'I'm not going to be cross because I know you are tired.'
She wasn't too cross next morning, but a muttered 'Letting me sing that for years.' was heard at breakfast accompanied by reproachful looks.

At lunch she sat up from her salad.
'Oh my God. I remember Sol and Dave doing those actions with their hands, on stage behind my back. I didn't know why the audience was laughing; I thought they were just having fun. That's really foul!' She was scarlet.

'Just wait till I see that Jones. I would tell Arwen but he thinks I don't know about things like that. Well I don't, obviously.' she added after a pause.

'That was really mean. Did you forget?'

'It was just a joke, honestly. After you sang it I felt ashamed so I convinced myself that it was a straight song.'

'Truly?'

'Yes.'

'You had better be nice to me to make up for it.'

'I always am. OK especially nice.'

'And stop taking an interest in that red-headed dancer.'

'I'm not.'

'Huh!' she added. 'Some hope; I guess they can spot a soft touch at a mile. It must be the training.'

'I think its hard experience.'

'Perhaps you're right. Kiss?'

Tuesday was intended to give the audience an entertaining evening. A few jokes, some business and comedy routines. The 'middle of the road' set was supplemented with a few waltzes and foxtrots and Paddy with Al's help provided some old favourites.

Her tongue in cheek insistence that this part of the set was shared had resulted in the erstwhile member of a wild rock band hamming his way through 'The Last Waltz' his fixed smile saved only by the twinkle in his eye. The smirking of the rest of the band and the open giggles from Al were seemingly accepted philosophically.

It was at the end of their second performance that, when announcing their last waltz Chris had added 'Our female vocalist loves to waltz, and if there were any un-attached men who would like to dance, yes you sir over there, really, she would love to.'

His female vocalist passed him with a smile and cast doubt on his parentage.'

The tiredness was still there, the first couple of weeks required much adjustment and adaptation to their lifestyle and the 'kR experience had taught Chris to give and to push the others to give 110%. In performance it was the difference that gave them the buzz. Now they were to lose Al for over a week.

She was nervous and excited. The scripts had arrived before leaving home and she had made a dash to London to see their agent and to talk briefly to the producer. She had about forty lines and would appear in a number of scenes. Beyond that she knew little except the basic plot.

She had rehearsed her lines with Paddy. 'Sorry, darling, I would feel anxious working with you because you would make comments; sensible ones but it would put me off.'

'Perhaps I would. I'm a bit worried about the whole thing and I don't want to get ratty and spoil it for you.'

'I'm sorry about giving you extra work, but don't be worried about me.' She leaned over and whispered, 'If I could keep my pants on when I was alone for a year I don't think I'll have any trouble now.'

'Do your best; I know what you mean but there are all sorts of scenarios where you could be eased into it.'

'Like what?'

'I don't know! If nudity is part of the plot you could look stupid if you refuse. Coercion isn't just about bullying.'

'I'm not stupid darling?'

'Go on, then, spend the entire fim naked.'

'Is that permission? Don't be silly.'

She jumped to her feet, raced for the door and dived through it with her husband in hot pursuit. Her screams attracted attention as she dodged in and out of the bushes making for the ladies. She was quick on her feet and Chris was hampered by being barefoot.

She hurtled into the shower block and as Chris came to a halt popped her head around the door.

'Truce? Are you all right?'

He was looking pale.

'Yes, sure, I got up a bit suddenly.'

'Are you sure?' She exited her refuge and came over to him.

'Fine love. Just a bit tired, the extra work has been wearing.' His colour was coming back.

She left them on the following Sunday, kissing the children and hugging her husband.

'Love you.'

'Love you too. Take care.'

They had parted with affection.

The offer had been talked through and Alison, recognising the difficulties had said she would turn the part down if it was too disruptive.

Chris had offered to turn down 'kR if she had asked but he would have regretted it. He couldn't ask.

He had felt tired when they arrived, but four weeks on, with plenty of sleep and relaxation the tiredness had been forgotten. Now the extra rehearsals and a new song had swept away the energy that he had regained and the hard work was just beginning.

CHAPTER 19   Good Times – Hard Times

(Alison's Story)

Chris was good about the filming. He was faced with extra work but made an effort to be supportive. It helped me a lot because if he had been difficult and I reacted, a non-situation might have become a situation.

I was looking forward to my first taste of acting since school and had booked into a small hotel full of nervous excitement. Early next morning I took a Taxi to 'the church hall??' that was the base for the location filming. There I was introduced to the director who greeted me like an old friend before passing me on to his assistant.

My first impression was that the crew was very small. The assistant introduced to me an actress that I recognised from TV. She was kind and friendly greeting me as an equal though she must have known that I was a novice. In conversation before my first scene she gave me some tips about performance, explaining about the different length of shots saying she expected that most of *this* film would be in medium shot.

'Try and act as if it were a real situation, but remember the camera is watching. I pretend it is someone I am trying to attract.' she added.

She also told me about adapting the size of my acting for the length of the shot. 'You have nice eyes, use them in the close up.'

I had had some drama training as a teenager but knew little about screen acting and though my voice coach had helped my singing she had offered nothing regarding the delivery of dialogue.

The niceties of expression and gesture seemed to be important and my new friend's tips began to sap what confidence I had gained. My anxiety must have shown because she said 'Lets walk, I can see you're getting worried.'

She took my hand and since it was half an hour before we were needed in make–up we went for a walk and she let me talk out my concerns. I felt that I had found a friend and when we got back I gave her a hug and said 'Thank you so much for your help.'

The filming turned out to be small time, with two cameras, one on wheeled base and the other on a trolley that ran on rails. Two vans stood in the background and a large trailer served as a makeup and dressing area.

I had three scenes, all of which took place in or around a back street café.

My role was that of a girl motorcyclist, and I was wearing jeans and a 'kR t-shirt with my leather motorcycle jacket. The jacket was Chris' present to me to show his support but when I first tried it with the jeans and boots he frowned.

'No good?' I asked him.

'Too good?'

From his subsequent actions I think he liked it.

In the first scene, I had to exit from the café where several local lads in biker's gear were standing by some shiny motorcycles. As I passed the boys I had to say 'Bye guys, see you again sometime.' and they had to nod and say nothing. I continued walking towards a large motorcycle with the camera on the trolley backing away from me. I then sat on the bike and put on my helmet and goggles.

I had a chat with the motorcycle boys while the crew were setting up. They knew who I was and were really friendly, so to fill the time I went into the café with them and had a coffee. We talked about Synergy and 'kR.

The makeup girl found me and spent several minutes repairing me. I was then given instructions by the director and went into my first scene. It was a doddle; we ran through it several times from different directions and on the second take my 'line' came out as if I was talking to old friends, and I strolled to the bike showing off to the boys. The director waited until I had the gloves on, shouted 'Cut', and 'Thank-you Al, excellent.' and that was it.

The second scene was delayed briefly until the 'star' arrived attached to a girl with more hair than clothes.

We were introduced and I instantly disliked him. He exuded a coarse sexiness and thought he was God's Gift. I had met several like him and guessed that underneath the veneer there was very little substance, which generally meant 'Spiteful if crossed'.

The first shot was of him running down the road towards me. He then said 'Where are you heading darling?' about three times and then 'I'm heading north too, I need to get to Scotland to meet an uncle of mine and a ride with you will be great.'

The cameras were reset and he ran a few paces and stopped in front of me, holding me up. The camera facing me moved in and after an age of resetting and stops and starts I said 'I'm heading north, do you want a ride?' (Personally I thought 'do you want a lift' would have sounded better). I then had to say 'OK, I guess you can come with me.' and he said 'That's the best offer I've had today darlin.'

There were several more lines where I said it could get cold on a bike even in summer, and he invited me back to his hotel where he would pick up some clothes.

It doesn't sound very much, but we did it a dozen times, initially with the camera on him then on me.

The last scene was where he got on to the bike. One of the lads had showed me where the starter button was, and I had to put on my helmet, start the engine then turn and shout 'Let's go then, hold on tight.' and as he got on he said 'Sure will darling.' On the second take he pushed his hands up my jacket and grabbed my boosies. I squealed and elbowed him so we had to do it again. When we got off the bike, he laughed and said 'Nice tits' and walked away.

'Excellent Al.' the director said. 'Thank-you, great!'

I thought filming could take days and require dozens of repeats and even script changes to get it absolutely correct. We had seen TV professionals in action and although clearly the crew knew what they were doing there was a kind of hurriedness about everything.

I had one other short scene with no dialogue, after which I was told 'That will be all for today darling.' My doubts began to grow.

I was still cross about 'the star' and went back to the café to join the lads.

'Bloody creep.' one of them said. ' D'you want us to give him a kicking?'

I had a feeling they meant it and said 'Thanks, better not.'

The day began to improve, and that evening my actress friend invited me out to a restaurant and back to her flat afterwards even asking if I would like to stay because it was late.

I had early start with several scenes the following day and my hotel was only a short taxi ride away so I thanked her and went home.

I was up early next morning to film a scene which required me to walk from a parked motorcycle into a public library, then a second scene when I exited carrying a large book. We then moved across the street and the cameras were set up again to film 'God's Gift' stepping from the bike and shepherding me into the foyer of a hotel. He then put on a leather jacket and we were filmed exiting the hotel carrying bags, getting on the bike and leaving.

One of the lads had been co-opted to actually ride the bike and I rather hoped he would dump our star onto the tarmac.

The second camera and some lights were set up in a corridor inside the hotel and there was a brief scene where we walked down the corridor to a door that he opened saying 'I'm expecting a call from my uncle and I need to take a shower.'

I said, 'I'm in no hurry.' and he said, 'Good, I expect we can find something to do while we're waiting.'

I had to look up with a smile and say 'I can think of something,' kiss him and enter the room looking as if I was ready for naughties.

The bedroom scene was shot six weeks later when we did

the studio scenes. I was filmed leaving the shower wrapped in a towel and then had to melt into his arms and be eased onto the bed. We had to do it three times because on the second take he whisked my towel away.

By then I knew what to expect and was suitably covered under the towel.

A scene was then shot of him changing into leathers with me in the background sitting on the bed pulling on my boots. There was quite a lot of dialogue in which I asked questions and he explained the plot. It was spoiled because the writers never missed a chance to include innuendo. It was like a 'Carry On' except that it wasn't funny.

When the hotel scenes were completed I caught the train to Glasgow and from there took a taxi to the coast near Ayr where we were booked into a small hotel. The rest of the crew, and the 'Star' together with two young actresses arrived late the following day.

The cheapness of the whole set-up was demonstrated by the fact that I was sharing a room with my actress friend. I didn't mind, because she was easy to get on with and helpful, but she was one of those rather physical people who are a bit over friendly, and having your bottom patted when you come out of the shower is a bit much.

During the next two days I appeared in a number of related scenes and in three of them I had a lot of dialogue and was involved in the action. I seemed to have more dialogue than I first thought.

My character was supposedly a spiky, 'been there, seen it, done it biker,' and in one of the villages, in the role of 'transport' I had quite a long scene. We then all moved to the beach where several other scenes were to be shot.

One of these represented my arrival with my passenger in Scotland, and at the edge of a deserted beach we had to dismount from a motorcycle that even to my non-expert eye was unlike the one on which we had begun our journey.

The beach scenes included one where 'the leer' was

supposed to reward (they had to be joking) a grateful motorcycle girl by having sex again, and as the script had hinted I was supposed to get my kit off.

I explained that I didn't do nudity, but after some discussion I was persuaded to compromise.

I would be seen unzipping and removing my leather jacket then starting to remove my t-shirt in close up. Subsequently the dark-haired actress would stand in and be filmed from the rear removing her/my jeans. Later, when they did the rest of the beach and swimming scenes she would be seen getting bounced in longshot.

There was a free and easy atmosphere, and I felt comfortable with my compromise and although 'The Star?' seemed keen to display his equipment it wasn't getting anywhere near me.

I had another couple of days of work in Scotland then, after we had finished our stint at the holiday camp two more in a studio and one to complete my dubbing.

Was it worth it? Yes, it was really interesting, but the time passed too quickly and I never really felt part of it. Suddenly found myself on the train heading back to our holiday camp and the real work.

Return to work.

Chris knew that Al's filming was an opportunity that she could not miss. She had made her decision and he wanted her to enjoy it, but producing a decent show as a four-piece had proved difficult; the extra energy that he and Paddy had input, failing to compensate for the weakened sound.

He also needed to make an effort to 'be there' for the children; Sarah had become hysterical when discovering that Mummy would be gone for a week and needed much love and attention.

By the Sunday he was feeling exhausted, remaining in bed whilst Gary took the children to the pool. He had appreciated Gary's offer to join Paddy in judging the 'Miss Lovely Legs' competition, taking on a task he found slightly demeaning.

By Tuesday afternoon he had recovered sufficiently to collect Alison at the station. She had greeted him with affection before the constraint set in, their conversation desultory and confined to practicalities.

The lack of communion took away the resources he had husbanded over the preceding days.

It was Al who broke the silence.

'This can't go on.' She said suddenly. 'You can't make me feel guilty about everything I do.'

'I'm not trying to make you feel guilty; it's about whether you want to be part of this band.' He was instantly angry.

'Not if you are going to shout at me every time something doesn't suit you.'

'Right! Bugger you then. You can start your own shitty little outfit, if you can find someone to manage you. Perhaps if you waggle your arse in the right direction Tony will take you on as a singing whore in his new band.'

'Perhaps I'll ask him. I enjoyed the freedom to speak to people without getting the Third Degree.'

'Well there was never much doubt about that. As soon as you are feeling good its "Bugger off Chris, I've got my own life to lead as long as I can lean on you when it all goes to rats".'

'That's mean and it isn't true. You've always been my only one.'

'Yes! The only one who's stupid enough to prop you up.'

She went very quiet. 'I had an exciting time, I was looking forward to and telling you about it, now it's all spoilt.'

'Well I had a ..'king' hard time and I was feeling like shit before I collected you. Now I feel worse.'

It was a few minutes before Al spoke again.

'I'm sorry darling, not about the filming, but about giving you extra work.' She leaned over and took his arm. 'I know it was selfish but I'll make it up to you if possible. I'm not trying to get round you, you know me better than that.' She leaned across and kissed him. 'Best friends? Please.'

'Too tired to care. Ok, thanks.'

Al had the character to settle for that. He had tried to be

generous and he looked worn out. She had had an enjoyable time; the sense of freedom only partly spoiled by the pressures. Explaining the beach scene was going to be difficult and would require a situation of affection and trust.

She stroked his arm. 'Thank-you. You are my precious and I will make it up to you.'

'Thanks. Let's leave it.'

He collapsed after the Wednesday show.

Returning from the washroom she found Paddy kneeling over the crumpled form but failed to take in the situation.

'What is it?'

'Paddy looked up. 'He just slid off the chair. Gary is ringing for an Ambulance and the S.M. has called the camp doctor.'

It was then that the situation resolved itself in a rising wave of panic. Her self-control slipped and she began to shout 'No!' sitting on the floor and pulling his hand towards her. She waved it back and forth. 'Chris, stop it. Stop it!'

It was nonsense.

Gary returned 'I've called the ambulance. It will be about fifteen minutes, but the doc should be here soon.'

'He's still breathing.' Paddy spoke.

What did he mean? Al's thoughts were incoherent. What else would he be doing?

'It's pretty shallow.'

'Can you do the kiss of life?'

'No.'

'Nor me.'

Knowledge came in a rush; it was the same, it was Chris. She began to scream.

'Oh God that's bloody helpful.' Gary held her shoulders and shook her then, receiving no response gently slapped her face. She began to fight him.

Other people were arriving, the S.M with the doctor.

Gary was holding her tightly. 'Calm down Al, calm down. The doctor's here, it will be alright, he will be fine.'

The doctor was speaking to her 'Are you his wife?' He

was looking into eyes that were frightened but clear and bright. 'Tell me,' he lowered his voice, 'in confidence. Is he using any substances?'

'No!' She hesitated. 'In the US, we... he did a little on tour, only bennys, not hard stuff, but he stopped as soon as the tour finished. It wasn't recreational; he needed it to keep going.'

'You are sure? It could make a difference.'

'Absolutely...I think so. What is the matter with him?'

'Has he been getting tired, I mean very tired.'

'Yes. He said that on the US tour he couldn't have kept going without the support.'

'Right.' He bent over his patient.

Chris' eyes flicked open, vacant and blank and she experienced another moment of terror remembering Bruce's face.

His white coat had been folded into a crumpled pad under his head and the still blonded hair tangled over it in damp skeins.

She forced herself to look at the rest of him terrified that soiling might reveal what she dreaded.

'His breathing is a little better.' The doctor spoke again.

Chris' eyes flicked open for a second time and remained open. He gave a slight grunt and immediately she was clutching his arm, a hand on his forehead.

'Chris darling it's Al.'

'Don't crowd him'

She sat back brushing dust from his sleeve noting little splashes of her tears on the grubby floor.

Her mind was praying silently to a neglected God, one who had heard her in the depths of depression and given her friends, love and Chris. 'Please let him live. It isn't serious, it can't be.'

He moved slightly and she reached for his hand hearing him breathing. The contrast between the small motions of the face, pale under the tan, and the awful nothingness that had been Bruce gave her comfort.

It seemed hours before she was gently moved to one side

and the recumbent form was lifted onto a stretcher that had arrived unseen.

She clung to his hand as he was carried to the ambulance oblivious of the several entertainers and campers who were watching the proceedings; her other hand held tightly to Gary's.

'The children! Gary go with Pad and relieve Caren she'll be wondering what has happened.'

'I'll go with Chris if you like.'

'No! Don't be stupid!'

Gary turned; surprised. It was the first time the mask had slipped, the passion revealed. 'OK love I'm on my way.'

'Thanks.'

As they drove the eight anxious miles to the local hospital she crouched beside him, leaning forward every few seconds to check his breathing. The paramedic in attendance gave her an encouraging smile, but she could only nod stony-faced back at him. Chris was sleeping but the memory of Bruce was too recent.

A nurse was speaking to her and she forced her mind to wonder why. Her awareness of the situation returned in a rush as she came fully awake.

'Mrs Phillips.'

Panic. 'Yes! What is it?'

'Mr Phillips is awake and would like to see you. He is tired so don't excite him.'

Led to a ward she found her husband propped on pillows half asleep but with a little more colour; her heart was bubbling, overflowing with relief. Something told her that other people should never matter so much, should never be able to cause so much fear and pain.'

'Would you like a cup of tea?'

'Please that would be lovely.' She turned a grateful smile onto the nurse, a smile that was familiar; relief, gratitude and unspoken prayer.

'Oh darling how could you frighten me so much? Don't

ever frighten me like that again.'

The tired eyes focussed on her. 'Didn't intend to; don't know what happened. I sat down feeling totally whacked then everything went grey and that was it, I still feel drained. Are you alright?'

'Yes. When I first saw you lying there I was terrified but after a minute you moved and it wasn't so bad.'

'Are you ok now?'

'Tired. No not tired, drained. Can I hug you for a bit?'

She sat on the bed facing him and released her pent up feelings with a hug that exhausted him and an outpouring of tears.

'Just hold my hand love. I'm all right but I need to rest. Wait until the doc has seen me, then you had better get back to the children. I don't know if I will be able to play the next gig, you had better…'

'Stop talking, you will make yourself worse.' She reached into her bag for a tissue and dabbed at the tears and mascara. 'Leave everything to me. Shhh.'

She sat with him until he was asleep, then taking the tea and biscuits returned to the waiting room where she drank the tea and sat collecting her thoughts. Still wearing her stage clothes the makeup from the night before, she was thankful for Chris white jacket somewhat the worse for wear, comforting around her shoulders.

Her mind drifted.

She woke to find the same nurse, neat and comforting in her blue uniform speaking to her in a waiting room that was becoming more crowded.

The doctor had completed his rounds and would have liked to speak personally but a crisis had arisen and he was unavailable. She, the ward sister was to say that there was no immediate cause for concern and that the initial tests had shown no obvious problems. He was very tired and would be kept in for further checks.

'Would you like to see him? He is awake.'

He was awake. 'Hello again darling.'

'Is everything Ok?'

'Think so. The quack asked about drugs and when I said 'no' he said that I was very run down and had probably picked up a virus in the last couple of days. It was the virus that caused the collapse, like when you have flue. I should be fine in a few days as long as that's the only problem.'

She stayed for a while and left him reluctantly but with a lighter heart. By the time a taxi had reached the camp she was bubbling with a prayerful happiness, giving thanks to her neglected God.

He was released from the hospital two days later collected by a loving wife and two children who, aware that he was poorly were a little quieter than usual. Still pale he was settled in their chalet and provided with a list of what he might and might not do until he was well

'I am well. I was over-tired and the virus finished me off, there is nothing physically wrong.'

'I know, but if you rush back to work too soon, you will be exhausted before you are really well, then you might be ill again and I don't want you to be ill again.'

She sniffed. 'Who would I lean on all the time, and complain about, and never care about enough.'

The sniffs grew into bigger sniffs and she gave him a squeeze.

With the help of the remaining band members she got through the Saturday date, tense and nervous. The show was satisfactory, but light on sound, the compensation coming when she took her bow at the end.
Paddy put his arm around her, thanked the audience and explained that one of the band was ill.

The sympathetic applause caused her to leave the stage in tears.

The Tuesday and Wednesday shows proved equally hard, the paying audience at the latter giving an indifferent reception to a set limited in both length and variety. She had faced audiences that were disinterested, even hostile but had grown used to success.

By Friday, her determination not to be influenced by the Wednesday show was overcome and she capitulated to his demands to return.

'I'm fine, honestly.'

He was allowed to sit on the small podium alongside Gary and play guitar.

'If you stand up I'll stop playing until you sit down again.'

He had complained that it was more stressful than playing, but she was intransigent. 'How can I give a decent show if I am worrying about you?' He gave in gracefully.

'I want you to be fit for Wednesday because we missed you last week.'

'Did you? Paddy is doing a pretty good job.'

'It isn't the same. Perhaps, if you are good, I'll let you take over next Saturday.'

His colour had come back, he was swimming, playing with the children, and looking fit again. After a week free of stress he was more like the person she loved. By the end of a second relaxed week, he was becoming boisterous.

His activities with Sarah and Simon had attracted a group of small children. Playing in the pool or on the water slide, organising games of rounders he was beginning to resemble the pied piper. He had Al noticed, attracted several mothers who helped with the activities and were on first name terms.

He was enjoying it, allowing his happiness to spill over into friendly hugs, without giving any of the signals that may have been hoped for.

It was unprofessional and she hoped that he would not find himself challenged by jealous husbands.

'I see you have a new chorus line.' She said as they lay together after the Friday show.

'Not quite. We have a common interest in the children. They get involved, the kids have a lovely time, there are a few tears, a few photos and no pressure; it's lovely.'

'No temptations.'

'No. One did show some interest but are a nice crowd.'

'Which one? I mean which one was interested?'

'The one with the fairish hair and no bra'.'

'She kept holding your arm and pressing against you.'
'That's the one.'
'Thought so. Did you enjoy it?'
'I didn't notice, sick men don't have lustful thoughts.'
'And they don't tell lies?' She smacked his bottom. You are better, you can take over tomorrow.'

It became the best summer since their season with Sue. There were a few arguments and a bad few days when Pat went through a period of Rock-Arrogance, his off stage activities resulting in lateness for practices and unreliability on stage.
It was expected that the band members would enjoy their summer, but the music had to be right and the consequences of Pat's activities were affecting the band.

Reluctant to deal with it, Chris mishandled it badly, failing to differentiate between the activities and their consequences. Pat was incensed, told him to mind his own business and the subsequent row created bad feeling.

It was left to Al to calm the situation as she had before, explaining that they all had to put the band first.

Told that one effing member got most of the glory she reminded him that he was playing with an international star (Praise never wasted on Chris.) and lucky to be in the band.

The need to manage her own band had taught her several tricks and she decided on the carrot and stick. His input to the band was good, he was well liked and an asset on stage but it was essential that he co-operate, because replacing him would be a real problem.

He apologised. 'It was great' he admitted 'to play with a good band and he had to admit that Chris had given up a fantastic opportunity to create it in the first place.'

'Which opportunity was that?' She tried to sound casual.

Pat mentioned the band's name. 'His manager was absolutely bloody raging when he turned it down.'

She was shaken again. He could have been touring, staying in first class hotels, not in this 'shitty little dump' as she had described it. He had taken this deal for her sake.

Still, she might have had a big offer and this deal ensured that she stayed with him. That was nonsense; he had turned down another 'kR so they could be together. A wave of gratitude flowed over her.

Would she have done the same? In a way she had. Pressurised by her manager to get 'Cats Whiskers' back on the road she had pleaded that she was still unwell whilst in fact she was clinging to her revived relationship.

To keep Pat happy a compromise was found, Chris swapping guitar for bass on a couple of Al's songs that required harmonies and a rhythm. It gave Pat a shot at the front line and it gave him a rest.

'Can you play bass?' Pat asked.

'I'll manage.'

Their daughter grew in confidence. Time spent with her parents in the theatre had introduced her to the several children of other entertainers and each week brought new friends.

The comedian asked if he could use her as a foil in the children's show and after much debate, it was agreed that she could appear twice a week.

She was a little precocious, learning her part with Daddy pretending to be the comedian, understanding the joke.

Her doting parents sat at the side of the stage during her first performance, Alison in a state of nerves as great as any previously seen. Their praise was if anything, less than she deserved to avoid a swollen head though her activity gained the unofficial label 'Chief entertainer for the rising fives.'

She possessed Al's liking for approval but was otherwise unspoiled; she was talkative, interested in everything, and took responsibility for Simon; she was five going on eight.

Her confidence grew to an extent that only the need for safety restricted her from having the run of the camp. She was known to many of the staff and would wander off to the ice cream lady (No ice cream please.) to see the theatre staff, the pool attendants (but you must not go near the pool.) It was wonderful until they lost her.

Chris, on his way to the pool, had asked 'Where is Sarah?'
'She's with... I don't know.'

Chris immediately contacted a few of the staff arranging for a message to go out on the Tannoy but it was twenty minutes before she was found.

They were minutes during which Al panicked, pulled herself together and began to organise everyone.

Sarah had found her way to the bowling green from which the attendant returned her as soon as she had a free moment. Her apologies for causing concern were silenced by a thankful hug from Al whilst her husband hugged the breath out of a little girl whose activities were going to be seriously curtailed.

Concern? Her mother had almost been reduced to a basket case. 'We are awful parents,' she said later, 'too wrapped up in ourselves.'

It was a great summer; two and a half months of semi-holiday during which they made many friends, Al achieved an ambition and they planned their future.

The end of the season was marked with a party for the band, the friends they had made and the entertainment staff.

It began with a children's party and ended at midnight when the hired band played their final number.

Chris refused to have anything to do with the organisation. 'I am going to enjoy the children and myself.'

'And the redhead?' he was asked.

She was ignored. 'We are going to chat, eat, and dance, with each other.'

'It sounds good but will it actually happen?'

Halfway through the evening she went missing, appearing on stage with her flute wearing a ragged coat, hat and scarf whilst the compere, dressed as tinker performed an intricate Irish jig.

'What did you think of my flute playing?' he was asked as they cuddled up for the last waltz.

'Was that you?'

CHAPTER 20 New Direction

The next morning Sarah, unaware that 'Going home' meant leaving the camp, fell into a tantrum. Her mother cuddled her into the car where she witnessed a replica of her own 'you have broken me' routine. The routine lasted for five miles and was disrupted by the offer of a chocolate. By the time the family were approaching home, her excitement at the thought of seeing Nan had taken over and the camp was forgotten.

Chris and Al had often travelled separately to gigs since Sarah's birth, through a mixture of superstition and insurance.

On this occasion, travelling as a family Alison made use of the situation. 'There are a couple of things that I need to tell you, I've been keeping them to myself until the right time.'

The first was that she was committed to becoming a 'proper Christian, not just someone who goes to church'. 'It was when you were ill, Gary talked to me and I realised that I had become spiritually empty. It was a lovely happy summer with you the children and the music but it was mostly superficial. I don't mean that it wasn't fun, it was, but I need something deeper as well.'

'I know that there are more important things than work, but I never have enough time to get involved. Sue was very devout you know, despite...well you know. She was intelligent and in some ways she was very deep.'

'I know. We were really good friends and I felt I could share a little of you with her, but of course *you* had to take advantage. I was angry with her for getting ...you know, but mostly I was angry with you; I knew you had deliberately misunderstood me.'

'Al, you mean to be kind but you are saying some very painful things. Just leave it alone please.'

She was silenced.

'What was the other thing?'

'Please don't laugh, I couldn't bear it.'

'I don't feel like laughing.' He pulled himself together. 'What is it, are you pregnant?'

'Would you be pleased?'

'I think so.'

'I'm not, it's Mum.'

'What about her?'

'She is.'

'Is what? Surely, she can't be.'

The comment provoked an instant defence and her voice rose. 'She's only forty-three. Why shouldn't she? She's been unsettled and feeling unfulfilled. Don't you dare make a joke! Obviously she wanted something extra, it isn't silly.'

Chris reeled from the barrage of words. 'That's nice, a bit strange but lovely for her.'

'What is strange about it? She was very young when she had me, and now she is old-er, some people are forty before they start a family.'

'When did you find out?'

'After the holiday, I couldn't say anything at the time, you would have made a joke of it.'

'I wouldn't, I'm pleased for her.'

'Really?'

'Really. When you are happy your eyes become bright, and it makes me feel happy.'

It was a while before he spoke again. 'It is unusual, I don't mean her age, just the gap. I won't go through all the situations because I expect you've been there.'

'Yes I have.'

'I was going to say that as far as I'm concerned Sarah and Simon will have a cousin and I'll be especially nice to Di.'

'Just be normal. I suppose I should be pleased that you get on well with my mum.'

'If mother in laws were like Di the jokes about them would be different. Would you prefer a boy or a girl?'

'I don't mind. I always wanted a sister to share with, but it's too late for that. Never mind I suppose I have you.'

'I'm an only child?'

'That's different, you ...' she stopped. A moment later she

was holding his arm, her head pressed against his shoulder.

'I'm sorry, I've done it again. You don't seem to need people in the same way. Oh darling, you've got me.'

They were nearing their home when after a long silence he spoke again.

'I have something I want to say, I hope you won't be upset.'

'What is it?'

'I'm getting tired of this life. I enjoy most of what we do, but some of it is really false and shabby and in the end it affects us. You are still pretty much the girl I fell in love with; I don't want you to become spoiled and I don't want to become a leering old rocker.'

'Why spoiled?'

'Remember that actress we met at the party in LA.'

'The one that you couldn't take your tongue off.'

The comment was ignored. 'I spoke to her for a couple of minutes. She was sharp and bright but when I looked into her eyes there was nothing behind the sparkle. She was 29 but inside she was 90 and I felt sorry for her.'

'Perhaps I want to move on and take the pain.'

'Do you?'

'I want it all. I know I can't have it after the bad time.'

'You need to be sure, we have plenty of time and I don't want to hear "You made me do it.".'

'You won't, I understand what you are saying. When I joined you in the states I felt on the outside; you were changing from being the person I loved and it scared me. Some of those girls were so calculating, and Sarah was almost a friend because at least we had things in common and she knew what she wanted.'

'What was that?'

'Success and someone like you pooface. Most of the girls had no culture, no sense of belonging. They thought that being associated with fame and money would somehow make them happy, they didn't realise that most band members are as empty and directionless as they were themselves.'

'You are sounding like me.'

'Am I?? Oh god, that's awful.' She was quiet for a while. 'So when are we becoming Britain's youngest pensioners?'

'Al! You are hopeless you never take me seriously.'

'Of course I do. Just tell me when?'

'When you are ready.'

'Nine months? We have to carry on until our contract finishes. Then we could pass the band on to Gary and Pad and carry on part time with semi-professionals, and expand the Christian music,' her mind raced ahead, 'and I could go to college before I'm too old, and take the children. It will be even better, not as exciting, but different.'

Her eyes were sparkling again.

EPILOGUE

Where to end? Their lives had not ended on that late Autumn day when they returned to their home but they were renewed and a light was beginning to shine for both of them.

A new beginning was a good place for an ending.

To verify their accounts I contacted several contemporaries, Dave Jones, Terry Solomans and Sarah Symons.

Dave, now the owner of a successful dental practice had, in response to my letter agreed to give an account of his time with the band.

'A terrific experience, in some ways the best couple of years of my life, lots of fun and laughter despite the work, but not the life for me.'

To my question concerning his opinions of the rest of the band he was a little more forthcoming, describing Chris as 'My best mate and great fun when he wasn't overworked.'

'He was easy going by nature, but sometimes he had to be assertive and at the beginning he wasn't very good at it.

We often used to pull his leg and thankfully he could take a joke as well as dish it out.'

He wrote this dreadful love song called 'Confetti hearts' and the words ended the chorus. Sol and I always sang 'Spaghetti Hoops' during rehearsals and eventually he sang the wrong words on stage. He laughed at the time but the next night when Sol and I were doing our business he sneaked behind during the laughter and replaced my guitar with a tennis racquet.

We all improved and became more professional and the band got better. Chris collected a small group of fans of his own, we called them the chorus line, and sometimes several would turn up for a show. Al was jealous though she took 'her fans' for granted.

He liked to do one song himself and worked up a JT song called 'Riding on a railroad.' It started simply, just Chris with me on guitar then in the middle the band comes in and there are great harmonies and a change in the feel of the song. His fans used to ease up to the front and one of them burst into tears and started shouting 'Chrissie, Chrissie I Love you!'

The song went down a storm; Al smiled and said 'Well done.' then went to her dressing room and cried as if she had lost him.

By way of contrast years later at their last full professional gig I saw them singing 'Time of your Life' together; you could see the happiness and love passing between them. I was jealous that they could share so much oneness?'

Occasionally the pressures got to him. There was a party where Al was getting chatted up by a singer and loving it. He told her to cool it and she showed her worst side and laid into him. 'Keeping me on a leash, you don't own me, I can do what I like.'

She was rarely unkind and when she realised he was hurt her face changed and she threw her arms around him and hugged him; the other guy ceased to exist.'

That says a lot about her. She was lively, attractive, had admirers at the stage door and occasionally met well known performers with big personalities. I mean, putting it crudely, she could have been pulling regularly; instead she was discreet, sparing and totally faithful to her boyfriend. That wasn't the easy option.

'Was he any good as an entertainer?' I asked.

'He had what he called his sole talent.'

'What was that?'

'I thought you would know, it was why we were called Synergy. We were a good duo, good songs and precise guitar work, then Al joined us and we had a really good voice in the band. Chris contribution was that he had a terrific ear for harmony and that's what gave us our sound.

By the time of k'R he was pretty good, not a virtuoso, but one of those reliable pros who make it look easy.

I think 'kR changed him. I noticed it when I went to the

States, he seemed wary of what he said as if I was a reporter rather than his best mate. The four of us met for breakfast; Chris was withdrawn, not quite there, Sarah, a pretty dancer in a black suit was protecting him and his girlfriend was wound up and pretending to accept the situation. After about ten minutes it was as if a light came on and he was my old mate CP chatting and laughing like we always had.

I had a serious talk with Al before I left and told her to stick with it because Chris needed her and if there was a problem she should call me. She called once in tears saying she was terrified and didn't know what to do then rang off without leaving a number. Dad was in a state and was all for the pair of us going out to look after her, but she rang the next day and said everything was fine.

It was about six months later that Judith and I were invited to a party in the middle of kR's last tour. Jude was a bit wide eyed at meeting 'Rock stars' and surprised by a few things she saw.

Halfway through I heard Bruce shout 'Phillips! Get your arse over here,' and Chris say 'What the eff' now.' Bruce said something and picked up an acoustic guitar; there was a discussion and they began to shove one another around. Chris had a harmonica and a funny look in his eyes.

They played 'I gotta wear shades', so tight, spot on harmonies and the confrontation was electric, it made the hairs on the back of my neck stand up. I hate to swell Phillips head, but if you could have bottled the performance it would have sold by the million.

Al was next to me with an expression on her face said 'Go for it Chrissie!' worse, Judith had the same look.'

How would you sum him up if you had one sentence?

He gave me a funny look then laughed. 'Dare I?'

He chuckled again. 'OK, but for God's sake don't tell him. He wanted to be Cliff Richard in Summer Holiday, but his bollocks kept getting in the way. The real man, when he was with 'kR, was the one performing 'I gotta wear shades.'

When asked about Alison he answered, 'In three words,

"difficult but adorable." I fell for the girl when we were in London; I don't mean 'lusted after her' which I did, but something else. We developed a relationship that was for me unique; love with lust hanging in the background.'

He stood up. 'Just a moment.'

He went to a bookcase and taking down a photo album selected a page and handed it to me. The first photo showed a schoolgirl in white top and blue shorts sitting on a sea wall. She was laughing, eyes sparkling, bubbling with life. In a second photo she was standing with her arms around two scruffy boys with shoulder length hair.

'You've met her, what did you think?'

'She is attractive for her age, I liked her.'

'Right, she was a girl you enjoyed being with see.'

When we met she was a nice, pretty innocent schoolkid. We all had to grow up quickly and for Al it was a struggle to stay nice and become streetwise. She succeeded pretty well; retaining her morals whilst becoming herself. She was seldom sharp and only once did I see her turn nasty, even then she was upset afterwards because she hated hurting people.'

'In a way she was one of the things that caused me to leave the band. I missed my Judith, see? '

'After I left I missed it for a while. I enjoyed the music, liked the people and Sol and I had a lot of fun. The only problem was that it's a terrible profession for deceit and falseness. It's bound to be, I suppose, since its whole purpose is to create illusions. It is strange' he mused, 'that we give so much admiration to people who are trained to deceive us and who spend their lives pretending to be something they are not.'

'We used to have long talks about morality and I see that Phillips has made me as jaundiced as him!'

'You met Sue, what did you think of her?'

'Ah! The lovely Sue, Chris could certainly pick them. I remember her with her sister who couldn't have been more than fourteen. She looked innocent but gave a wrong impression of being available so the lechers made straight for her. Thankfully the band looked after her until she wised up.'

'One thing is worth saying, Sue wasn't a star but she certainly wasn't a passenger. She was a good pianist with a nice voice that was fine for backing vocals. Chris would never have had her in the band if she wasn't good enough.'

'It was the same when he restarted Synergy with "just a couple of semi-pros." It is true they were Semi-pros, but from the best band in the Gloucester area and supporting them one of the best drummers in the south-west.

'It was a shock when Chris married Sue; she was a sweet girl, but not Alison.

Al picked up her life, but she was never the same. I saw her several times after Chris marriage; it broke my heart to see her being brave and suffering dreadfully. I thought of offering my support, even of leaving Judith, but that wasn't what she needed.'

'She eventually found another man and I saw them together in Bristol.

He was a flash git, too old for her, sharp and streetwise but with no intellect or understanding. He was everything she didn't need but she was hanging on his arm pretending they were so together. It was easy to see that the real joy had gone out of her and all that was left was the pretence.'

I wasn't a jealous bloke, but the thought that she was being intimate with a guy with a dubious reputation made me sick. I was pleased to hear that she dumped him a week later.

When her friendship with Chris revived she was almost back to being the girl I loved but some of that pure happiness had gone.

I keep in touch with them still and we remain good friends, indeed my second daughter Beth is married to young Simon.'

A note from Arwen.

I'm getting on a bit now, but when I first met Alison I was in my late forties. Young enough to be interested, experienced enough not to have prejudices. In my profession some of the young women you meet tend to be, shall we say girls with problems.

One weekend, my older son brought his current girlfriend to stay, and also asked a friend from collage. The friend had brought his girlfriend; a rather gangly frowning girl, with long earrings and a short skirt. First impressions you understand.

I was polite and welcoming and eventually the frown disappeared. We took tea in the lounge and I sat next to her. After a while she began to relax and I saw a different girl emerge, beautiful, like a butterfly with life bubbling up inside; there was kindness and a generosity of spirit. She was a gem.

I suppose I fell for her. Thankfully I was wise enough not to behave like a fool and made the decision to be a friend to her. She responded with great charm and became confident enough to tease me. My son told me later that she attracted a lot of interest but was totally faithful to her boyfriend. He seemed a nice lad, caring though rather possessive.

Much later he behaved very badly and she was broken hearted. She turned to me like a daughter; I did my best to help her and she was grateful.

I suppose a girl like that was bound to have some difficulties, and in the end it was her essential goodness that saw her through her bad times.

I was surprised when after his young wife died she got back together with her original boyfriend, she could have had almost anyone she wanted.

When I spoke to David on the subject he said, 'She has Da', he is her choice, the break up was the mistake.'

A lovely girl.

Terry Solomans was still in the business running the agency set up by his Uncle Maurice. My letter elicited an appointment at his office.

The Afro had been replaced by a grey crew cut, but the eyes behind the blue tinted spectacles were still full of life.

He greeted me shook hands looked at his watch and gave

me twenty minutes.

I decided to dive straight in and asked him for memories of his time with Synergy.

'That's a long way back. It was a good band to be with, friendly, not much friction unlike some bands I knew where the sound of egos colliding was louder than the music, but I could see from the beginning that they had limitations.'

'You were with them for four years. Why did you stay so long if they were no good?'

'Hell,' he answered, 'I didn't say they were no good. I had been playing with no hope foursomes and getting a few sessions. Suddenly I was with a band that was a bit different and was charting. They needed my experience, and there was Al.'

'What was her attraction?'

He thought for a second. 'Hard to explain. The first time we met I saw two scruffy students and schoolgirl, tall and slim, wearing a short skirt, and I thought 'What the hell am I supposed to do with this lot?'

The girl had some big green plastic earrings and a green ribbon in her hair that she thought looked chic. She had a nice oval face with neat features and dark lashes. She also had slightly large front teeth, hardly noticeable but that gave character. She wasn't beautiful but she was lovely looking. When I shook hands and took a second look I saw something else, beautiful eyes and an indefinable something about her. Not everyone felt it, but I have seen guys old enough to be her father just melt.

A nice figure too; Dave once said 'God gave Al tits to hold her bra' up.' She was friendly, boisterous, loud even and she loved being chatted up. Occasionally she could be moody and silly, but mostly she was a darling.

It can be difficult with a girl in a band, especially an attractive one, but Al kept her relationship in a different compartment, totally discreet from the outside. Even on the inside it was seen as a close friendship which meant that she could be equally friendly and inclusive with the rest of the band as if she was our sister.

She took after her mother in some ways. Terry our drummer liked Diane, I think she mothered him and they became good friends. Dave liked her too; he even took her out a couple of times when she came to stay but his intentions were much more down to earth and Al was furious.

It was an odd situation; a very attractive older women, enjoying a bit of freedom and wearing quite fashionable clothes and her daughter wound up and behaving as if she were her mother. They were good times.'

'What,' I asked, 'was the worst time?'

'Easy,' he replied, 'it is always the period before a band folds. We knew there was a problem between Al and Chris, but apart from a public row, things were normal on the surface, then one morning she came down to breakfast with the tour manager and we all knew they had slept together.'

'Chris looked murderous and just hurled himself out of the room.' He paused. 'I was impressed that he got through the evening show, he was in hell, and had turned in on himself, blank face, wouldn't look at Al.'

'I saw her glance across a couple of times; they used to exchange a lot of looks, nods and smiles but he wasn't there. When she realised, she lost it; she carried on singing but all the magic had gone.'

'We always had a party at the end of the tour and we arranged a meal and dance at a local country club for the band, management friends and girlfriends. Penny and I went with him and we had been there about ten minutes when his face screwed up. 'Sorry, thought I could handle it.' Then he muttered 'God I'm useless, so sorry.' asked me to thank Al and the team and left.'

'Al arrived on her own looking stunning and I could see that she was set on reconciliation. She asked me quietly where he was and when I said he had gone I saw something die. She tried to brazen it out but I could see the distress and when I held out a hand she fell on my shoulder and cried as if she had lost her soul. I felt very angry.'

'Synergy' still had a couple of dates and we played them with Sue. It sounds crazy because she was no Al, but with the band's support she really performed and on our last gig some of the magic was there again.'

'When the band folded Al's relationship folded with it. She asked for help to start a new band and I thought I was in. 'Cats Whiskers' could have been great but about half way through the season when we were becoming close she said "I'm really fond of you Terry, I need you so much as a friend." She was lovely about it, but it was like getting a bucket of ice water in the face.'

He had withdrawn a little then the dynamism came back.

'Anything else?'

'The music, the rest of the band, how about them?'

'I co-wrote our hits and generally they were well crafted and nicely arranged, but we never had a big hit because we didn't have a style.'

'What was your opinion of the other members; Chris for instance?'

'He was ok, worked hard, didn't try to get all the credit, just most of it.' He looked at me and smiled for the first time. 'He wasn't a bad guy, but first impressions were a scruffy lout with the management technique of a school prefect and a lovely girl gazing at him as if he were God.'

'He became professional, but he was always pushing himself and hitting bum notes which is an embarrassment at that level. Dave and I used to call him 'two thumbs' and generally he laughed, but once he went berserk and hurled his old guitar at us. The angry CP was not an attractive sight and Dave who knew him well was shocked.'

'What did you think of Sue? You were still with the band when she joined.'

'Susie? Very pretty, very nice and a bit naughty. Some people marked her down as a talentless tart which was quite wrong. She was a capable musician once she had overcome her stage fright, and she certainly wasn't a tart.'

'She was kind, straight, no malice in her, and a lot of fun. At the end of her first season with the band we held a party for about a hundred people. Dave came over with his girlfriend and we did our two hippies party piece and Chris did his Elvis doing George Formby.'

'Sue and Al did a fun striptease, only down to their undies but very sexy. Towards the end, Sue glanced at Al and reached behind as if she was going to take her top off but Al shook her head. There could have been a riot. She was…' He stopped. 'It was no surprise to me that Chris married her.'

'I took her out a couple of times. She was intelligent, nice to be with. It was a shame about the photos?'

'The photos?'

'They were innocent by today's standards, but still a real shock. It was difficult to connect the photo of the naked model on the page of a magazine with the nice little girl in the next room.'

He looked at his watch.

'Anything else?'

'How would you summarise them.'

'Good band, great together, but they lacked real talent. Chris wasn't tough enough and Al didn't sell herself. One other thing, don't take their version for granted. They're pretty straight,' he added quickly, 'but there is the truth, and the whole truth.'

'Any skeletons?'

He smiled for the first time and I saw the young musician emerge. 'Just mention Samantha.'

I was dismissed.

My first attempt at contact resulted in a letter from Miss Symons' lawyer. It was formal, stating that Miss Symons had during her career been a singer with the band 'king Rock. She was acquainted with Mr Phillips who played guitar in the band. Her career had moved on and no further information could be given that was of any interest to my investigation.

It would be unwise, I was told to speculate. There were laws on Libel, as they were sure I was aware.

I decided to leave the subject there but some weeks later received a reply from 'Miss Symons' herself.

A letter from Sarah;
My lawyers advised me not to reply to your request for information on Chris Phillips and they are usually right. It would have been better if your letter had never arrived as it took me back to a time that was largely forgotten.

OK, I'll be straight; I might as well because the story has been buzzing in the back of my mind for three weeks. Damn you for writing and stirring up memories.

I was working as a dancer when I first met him and his girlfriend. It was a rather shabby seaside show with an unpleasant comedian who mistakenly thought he had carte blanche with his female entertainers. The band was like a breath of fresh air because they weren't theatre and had no respect for the star beyond their desire to do a good show. The man hated it and tried to get rid of them.

Chris was immature, but determined, quite talented and like his friend Dave he was a lot of fun. My life had been a struggle not to be used since I was fifteen and though both showed an interest they also showed respect for me as a person and as a fellow entertainer which made me feel I mattered.

I had a crush on Chris and would have done anything for him, but his girlfriend kept him on a tight leash.

Our paths separated, but several years later he had been lucky enough to join a band that was on the up. I contacted him because the band needed a singer and he introduced me to Bruce Kay who offered me the job.

I don't want to give the impression that he was wonderful, he was a typical selfish insensitive man, but he was straight, no hidden agendas and he helped me out of kindness. He had lost his wife, was unhappy and unsettled, and he trusted me to look after him.

It was a lovely few months, we became a strong team and it gave the boost to my confidence that I needed to move my career on.

The downside was that I fell for him. It reached a point where he would smile and pat my arm and say "Everything ok treasure?" and I would melt.

It is crazy to tell this; it makes me feel that I have learned nothing.

There was a morning; we had a day off and had been to the hotel pool. I had showered and dressed when he knocked on my door. I was drying my hair and he came up behind me and held my shoulders very gently, then he leaned over and kissed my neck and said 'Thank-you for being here, my love.'

I turned and hugged him and I cried because I felt so happy, as if everything was light and floating, and he wrapped me in his arms and said, 'Whatever is the matter?'

It was a wonderful, awful moment when I realised I was becoming soft and that I needed to move on before I said something idiotic like 'I love you.'

I had no experience of dealing with someone caring and by the time Jack Cavil asked me to partner him, I was glad to be rid of him.'

If I had any doubts, his girlfriend ended them; she was talking about her mother saying 'she's always been supportive and Chris is so kind and Dave wanted to help so he...'

She had this naive assumption that everybody is like that, no idea how bloody lucky she was.

I shouldn't have written this; your letter has brought back all sorts of memories that were best forgotten. I have achieved the success that I wanted and I don't need this.

END

Printed in Poland
by Amazon Fulfillment
Poland Sp. z o.o., Wrocław